JAKOB WEGELIUS

The False Rose

**TRANSLATED FROM THE SWEDISH
BY PETER GRAVES**

PUSHKIN CHILDREN'S

Pushkin Press
71–75 Shelton Street
London WC2H 9JQ

Published in the English language by arrangement
with Bonnier Rights, Stockholm, Sweden

The False Rose was first published in Swedish as *Den Falska
Rosen* by Bonnier Carlsen, Stockholm, Sweden, in 2020

First published by Pushkin Press in 2021

SWEDISH
ARTSCOUNCIL

The cost of this translation was defrayed by a subsidy from
the Swedish Arts Council, gratefully acknowledged

1 3 5 7 9 8 6 4 2

ISBN 13: 978-1-78269-321-5

Typeset by Tetragon, London
Printed and bound in the UK by CPI Group (UK), Croydon CRO 4YY

www.pushkinpress.com

CONTENTS

PART TWO
SHETLAND JACK

PART THREE
THE SMUGGLER QUEEN

❖

PART FOUR
THE TWILIGHT QUAY

❖

PART FIVE
THE FALSE ROSE

HOME PORT   509

CHARACTERS

Ana Molina

LUIGI · FIDARDO

Doctor Rosa Domingues

HARVEY JENKINS & COCKEREL

李静
Li Jing

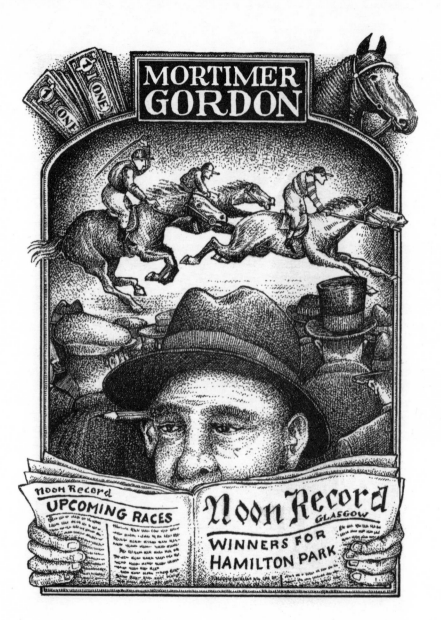

R·I·C·E·R·C·A·T·A · V·I·V·A·O·M·O·R·T·A

FLORENZA
TARANTELLO

BERNIE "THE BUTCHER" BRODIE

Moira Gray

KEVIN MILLER & CARL BECKER

RAZOR QUEEN

Tommy Tarantello

OSWALD · STREET ANTIQUES

OPE

Fiona & Enoch Flint

Jack Shaw
1910

Madame Lefourcade

A Warning

Madame!

You have asked me to write down everything I know about the man known as Shetland Jack. I'll do that. I'll tell you about his hard life and I'll tell you the awful truth of his violent death.

But the story of Shetland Jack did not come to a close with his death. His story has become part of my own story and I'll have to write about that, too, though it will be hard for me. I'd sooner forget much of what has happened to me during the past year.

It will take me some weeks to give you a full account. Possibly as much as a month. But you're welcome to read it piece by piece as I write. Every evening I'll put my latest pages on the small mahogany table by the grand piano in the drawing room.

~

The typewriter you've lent me is really superb. I've never typed on an Imperial before. My own typewriter is an old Underwood No. 5, but it's back in Lisbon, packed in my seaman's chest on board the *Hudson Queen*.

The *Hudson Queen* is our ship. The Chief and I bought her in New York years ago and she's been our home ever since. And our living. We've crossed most of the great oceans of the world and I've lost count of all the harbours in which we've loaded and unloaded our cargoes.

Five years ago we arrived in Lisbon. There we were hired to collect a cargo of tiles from a small port called Agiere on the River Zêzere, a dozen or so miles inland. It seemed to be a simple enough job but turned out to be our great misfortune. The *Hudson Queen* was hijacked by bandits in Agiere, and shipwrecked in the river.

The Chief and I were lucky to escape with our lives, but when we got back to Lisbon the Chief was arrested by the police. He was charged with murdering a man called Alphonse Morro and sentenced to twenty-five years in jail.

Suddenly I found myself a beast without a master in a great foreign city. The streets were full of people, yelling at me and hunting me. They called me the "Murderer's Ape" and wanted to do me harm.

I'd lost the Chief, and the *Hudson Queen* was gone, too. I had nowhere to go and nothing left to hope for. But just when I thought everything was over I met Ana Molina. If it hadn't been for her I wouldn't be alive today. She hid me and protected me when everyone else was saying I was the murderer's crazy ape.

Ana's home became my home. And her friend Signor Fidardo, the instrument maker, also became my friend. He let

36

me work in his workshop and he taught me his trade. Thanks to him, I am now a skilled accordion repairer and, if needs be, can even change the neck of a guitar.

Bit by bit and with the help of Ana and Signor Fidardo, I uncovered the truth behind the shipwreck of the *Hudson Queen* and the murder of Alphonse Morro. It took four long years. But in the end the Chief was freed. The day he was released from jail was the happiest day of my life.

~

Some time later the Chief and I returned to Agiere. We were able to salvage the *Hudson Queen* and have her towed to Lisbon. After four years sitting on the riverbed, our ship was a wreck. We took any and every casual job we could in the port of Lisbon in order to earn enough money to make her shipshape again. But the wages were miserable and almost everything we earned went on food and the necessities of life.

So far we've managed to renovate the cabin and we've started work on restoring the wheelhouse. But there is an awful lot still to do. The worst thing is that the main boiler exploded and was destroyed when the ship was wrecked. I don't know how we'll ever afford a new boiler, which is why I sometimes wonder whether the *Hudson Queen* will ever plough the great seas again.

I'm telling you all this because the story of the *Hudson Queen* is, in part anyway, the story of Shetland Jack. You'll understand later what I mean.

~

Lisbon and the *Hudson Queen* feel very far away at the moment. Through the windows of this tower room I can see the sun rising behind the wooded hills to the east. The warm light paints the whole valley a fiery yellow. Down by the river the morning mist is drifting in and out between the trees. A little while ago I saw the Chief mount his bicycle and pedal off down towards the main road. I think he's on his way to Lodève to pick up the new blade for your steam saw. In that case, I'll maybe join him and test the saw when he returns. That would be fun.

The Chief has told you, hasn't he, about how he and I became acquainted. It was obvious that you didn't believe him at first. That doesn't matter. You're not the first to doubt that a gorilla can learn to work as a ship's engineer.

But I've lived almost all my life among human beings and on their terms. So I'm no longer simply an animal. But nor am I a human being. So what am I? I don't really know. The only thing I'm absolutely sure of is that I am a friend to my friends. And that's quite enough.

Even though you and I only met recently, Madame, I count you as one of my friends. Which is why I must warn you that the story you've asked me to tell you is an unpleasant one. And sad. So you must be prepared to find yourself hearing of things you will later wish you had never heard.

PART ONE

BROCKDORFF'S FUNFAIR

The Dinner Guest

I'll start by telling you about Harvey Jenkins. After all, he's the one with whom it all started. And finished. We first met Jenkins in Lisbon. It was an evening in April last year and the Chief and I had spent the whole day lugging boxes of ice around the fishing harbour. As part of our pay we had been given a pound of anchovies to have for dinner. The Chief was up on deck peeling potatoes and I was lighting the wood stove in the galley. We may have been short of money but we didn't have to skimp on firewood. The firewood bin beside the stove was always full of scrap wood. That particular evening I was lighting the fire with planks from our old cabin.

While the potatoes were boiling we each took some soap and a towel and went ashore. We only treated ourselves to visits to the bathhouse a couple of times a month, otherwise we washed in the River Tagus. A little way upstream the water was reasonably clean and there was both a landing stage and a changing hut on the shore.

After bathing we walked slowly back along the quay. The sun was low in the sky and made the river gleam red and gold. The Chief was whistling to himself. He was in a good mood, as he had been every day for almost a fortnight, ever since hearing he'd got a job as second engineer on a passenger liner called *Funchal*. He'd be signing on in just a week's time and he'd be away for a month.

We were still about fifty yards from our quay when I saw there was someone on board the *Hudson Queen*.

"Who can that be?" the Chief said, shading his eyes with his hand to see better. "Let's hope it's not someone wanting money from us. Have we paid the harbour master for our drinking water this month?"

I nodded. As far as I knew we had paid all our bills.

When we got closer we could clearly see that it wasn't one of the harbour officials waiting for us. The man was dressed in a long shabby overcoat and wearing a narrow-brimmed hat that looked a couple of sizes too small. And on his shoulder sat a big greyish bird of some variety.

The man was inspecting the *Hudson Queen*'s ship's bell, which hangs forward of the mast. On hearing us come aboard, he turned round in no hurry, let go of the worn old bronze bell and came to meet us.

"Now then," the Chief said. "And who might you be?"

I guessed the man was in his sixties. He smiled and held out a hand covered in fading seafarers' tattoos. His thin, weather-bitten face was marked with a mosaic of wrinkles. I saw now that the bird on his shoulder was a cockerel, and it must have been ancient. Its plumage was sparse and there were glimpses of pale skin showing through here, there and everywhere. Its eyes were staring, watery grey-white and blind.

"The name's Jenkins," the man said in a gruff voice and an accent that was unmistakeably Scottish. "Harvey Jenkins. I apologize for coming aboard without permission. Are you the skipper?"

"I am," said the Chief.

"I just happened to be walking past along the quay," Jenkins said. "And I saw your ship. She's a Clyde Puffer, isn't she? There are a lot of them up and down the west coast of Scotland and I used to work on one myself. As engineer. We carried the mail and all kinds of cargo between the mainland and the Hebridean islands. That was a long time ago, though."

The Chief beamed. It's not often we meet someone who knows what kind of ship the *Hudson Queen* is.

"I couldn't take a look below deck, could I?" Jenkins asked. "Old memories... well, you know..."

"There's not a lot to see," the Chief said with a sigh. "She lay on the bottom of a river for four years."

"I'd like to look round anyway," Jenkins said. "It's nice to be on board a Puffer again."

That's how the Chief ended up showing this Harvey Jenkins around the *Hudson Queen*. And it took some time as Jenkins wanted to look into every nook and cranny. Meanwhile, I was frying the anchovies. The Chief asked Jenkins whether he'd like to eat with us and he said yes.

We found ourselves sitting round the galley table for a couple of hours. Jenkins was very curious about how a Clyde Puffer had ended up in Lisbon. The Chief told him how we'd found the *Hudson Queen* in New York ten years or more before and about all the voyages we'd sailed in her since.

Then Harvey Jenkins told us the story of his life.

"I was at sea for heaven knows how many years," he said. "But suddenly one day I'd had enough. I went ashore for good and bought a small farm in Oklahoma. In the middle of America, as far from the sea as I could get. I kept chickens and pigs and a couple of cows. And I had six acres of land under the plough. One day I took my horse and cart and drove to South Bend to buy seed. On my return a couple of days later, my farm was gone. Pigs and cows gone too. And the barn I'd built with my own hands. Everything had disappeared. A tornado had passed through—it's the kind of thing that happens in Oklahoma. Among the wreckage I found this cockerel, more dead than alive. He was the only thing the tornado had left me, so I took him with me when I moved on. He and I have roamed here and there around the world ever since."

The bird opened its beak and Jenkins gave it a piece of potato.

"At present we're working for a travelling funfair," Jenkins continued. "Not so bad. You get to see places. We arrived in Lisbon a week ago. We've put up our tents and parked our wagons on vacant ground by the Cais do Sodré. My job is to look after the steam engine for the merry-go-round and Cock—I've never come up with another name for him—he terrifies children with his white eyes."

The cockerel leant forward, put his head to one side and opened one of his blind eyes wide. He was given another piece of potato as a reward.

"You're welcome to come and visit one evening," Jenkins continued. "Entry is free and you can have as many rides on the merry-go-round as you want!"

"Thanks," the Chief said, "but in a couple of days I'm signing on with a liner sailing to Brazil. And there's a lot to organize before that. We'll have to put off riding on your merry-go-round until the next time your circus comes to Lisbon."

Jenkins looked from the Chief to me and then back to the Chief.

"Aha…" he said hesitantly. "So Sally Jones will be alone on the *Hudson Queen* while you're away at sea? I see!"

The Chief nodded. "Sally Jones will manage fine on her own, I can tell you. And anyway, she has friends here in the city."

Jenkins looked thoughtfully at me. I had the feeling that he'd just come up with an idea of some sort.

There was a bit more small talk about this and that before he thanked us and prepared to leave. He wished the Chief a successful voyage to Brazil.

When he reached the gangplank, Jenkins turned to me and said, "It strikes me you would make a good merry-go-round operator. Being both engineer and gorilla… you're actually made for fairground work!"

The Chief and I exchanged a quick look. Then the Chief said, "We'll take any work we can get. We're saving money for our ship."

I nodded. I wouldn't say no to a job as fairground engineer.

"That's good then," Jenkins said. "I can't promise anything. We don't have any work for you just now. But fairground workers are footloose types, who come and go at whim, and a job could just turn up out of the blue. I'll see what I can do, I promise!"

And with that we said goodbye to Harvey Jenkins. The Chief and I helped each other tighten the ship's moorings for the night, while Jenkins walked off along the quay with the cockerel on his shoulder.

I watched them go, and wondered. Jenkins had seemed nice enough, I thought. But there was something about him that wasn't right. Something I couldn't quite put my finger on.

~

It was half an hour later, after I'd slipped into my hammock and blown out the night light, that I twigged what it was that had felt strange about our guest:

He hadn't seemed in the least surprised when he first saw me.

People meeting me for the first time are always inquisitive. They ask questions. Not to me, of course, but to the Chief. He then has to explain that, yes, I'm a gorilla, but that I can understand what people say and I am as skilled at my job as any ship's engineer you care to name.

But Harvey Jenkins hadn't asked the Chief a single question of that sort. Why was that?

The answer was quite simple, I thought. Jenkins had no doubt seen so much of the world that nothing could surprise him.

Sawdust and Turpentine

Four days later it was time for the Chief to go on board *SS Funchal*. It was raining that morning. The smell of wastewater and cold dawn stung our nostrils as I helped the Chief carry his kitbag to the Doca de Alcântara where the *Funchal* was moored.

The great passenger liner had put in the evening before and would be ready again in just a few hours to set sail westwards to Rio de Janeiro in Brazil.

The Chief was all anticipation and perhaps a touch nervous, too. During the winter he'd had several short contracts as skipper of one of the harbour authority's small ferries, but this would be his first real ocean-going voyage for five years.

I'd hoped to be able to take a look at the *Funchal's* engine room before departure, but the watchman on the gangway had been ordered not to allow access to anyone unauthorized. So the Chief and I had to say our goodbyes on the quay.

"Look after yourself," the Chief said and gave me a pat on the shoulder.

I nodded and then he went on board.

Neither of us are keen on grand farewells.

~

Instead of returning to the *Hudson Queen*, I crossed Comércio Square and started walking up the steep and windy streets of the Alfama district. The rain had stopped and the heat of the sun was making the cobblestones steam. A number of cafés were already open and the narrow streets were filled with horse-drawn carts loaded with milk, fruit, fish and meat ready for delivery to shops and inns.

Signor Fidardo and Ana Molina live in a house by a small nameless park, just where the dark and narrow street Rua do Salvador meets the much larger and busier Rua de São Tomé. Signor Fidardo's workshop for musical instruments is at street level and the bell above the door pinged when I entered. There was a smell of wood shavings, turpentine and well-oiled metal tools. Signor Fidardo was sitting there, bent over his workbench. The ceiling lamp hung so low that his white hair glowed in the warm circle of light.

"One moment, please," he said, without looking up from his work.

I tiptoed across to my corner of the workshop. On my workbench lay the parts of a small, two-row melodeon I had dismantled. The owner had requested a full restoration and Signor Fidardo had passed the job on to me, saying that he himself didn't have time. Strictly speaking, that wasn't true, but he knew that the Chief would be away at sea and he no doubt thought it would be nicer for me to be working in his workshop than to be on my own on the *Hudson Queen*. He was right about that.

The *Hudson Queen*'s ship's wheel was leaning against the wall beside my bench. It was a sturdy wheel, made of solid oak reinforced with strong brass fittings. Like everything else aboard the *Hudson Queen*, it had suffered badly during the years the *Hudson Queen* lay shipwrecked at the bottom of the River Zêzere. The varnish was flaking off and black patches stained the wood. To restore the wheel to its original condition I would need access to the best carpentry tools, which is why I'd brought it here. But it wasn't a job that needed to be done urgently. The *Hudson Queen* lay where she lay, and it would be a long time before she needed a wheel to steer her.

After a short while Signor Fidardo straightened his back and turned round.

"Good morning, my friend," he said, looking at me over the top of his spectacles. "You've come at just the right time for morning coffee."

Once Signor Fidardo had changed into his white suit, we went to the Café Nova Goa on Rua do Salvador and drank our coffee standing at the counter. Signor Fidardo is very meticulous about his appearance and will never leave the house in his work clothes. I wonder if there is anyone else in the world who changes into pyjamas for his midday nap.

∼

Many hours later, at the sound of the evensong bells in Graça church, Signor Fidardo and I put down our tools for the day. I cleared up and swept the floor while he poured himself a glass of Campari and a large glass of milk for me. Then we sat down and enjoyed our drinks in silence. That's the way Signor Fidardo always rounds off the working day. He is just as punctilious with his routines as he is with his dress.

There was a knock at the window above my workbench and Ana looked in. She had a bulging shopping bag on her arm.

"Would you like to eat?" she said. "I've bought artichokes and a few other things."

"Wonderful—yes please," Signor Fidardo said. "I don't have any other plans for dinner."

They turned to me and I nodded.

"Excellent!" Ana said. "By the way, how did things go for Henry? Did he manage to get away on that ship this morning?"

Ana always calls the Chief Henry. She is almost the only one to do so, even though that is his real name.

~

Ana lives right at the top of the building, with a view out over the roofs of Alfama. I've had some of the best moments of my life in her little flat—and also some of the very worst. Strangely enough, it's only the good times that have stuck in my mind. I feel almost as much at home at Ana's as I do on the *Hudson Queen*.

This particular evening Ana was happier than she'd been for a long time. As we ate dinner she told us that she'd just turned down a long tour of the great cities of Europe. During the autumn Ana had sung in concert halls in Paris and Madrid and she felt that she'd had enough of the great elegant stages for some time to come. What she wanted instead was to carry on working in the shoe factory in Alcântara and to perform at weekends with the house orchestra in the Tamarind, the scruffy little fado pub on Rua de São Miguel.

It was at the Tamarind that Ana had started singing in public. And it was at the Tamarind that she was later discovered by the Viscount de Oliveira, director of the São Carlos opera house. The viscount convinced her to give a concert at São Carlos and Ana had been a star ever since.

"You should have accepted the offer of the tour, Ana," Signor Fidardo said firmly. "Not many fado singers get a chance like that."

Ana smiled. "I knew you'd say that, Luigi. And the viscount said the same thing. But I am happy with my life as it is. Why should anyone change something good just for the sake of doing so? I'm happiest singing here in my own city for my neighbours and friends. If the rich folk in London and Paris want to hear my songs, they are welcome to come here. Everyone is welcome in the Tamarind."

Signor Fidardo rolled his eyes and shrugged his shoulders. Ana laughed.

"Don't worry, Luigi. I'm sure I'll go on tour again one fine day. And I'm in the process of making a new record. You must be pleased about that? Have another artichoke and taste this Beiras sheep's cheese I bought in the market hall."

Rather reluctantly Signor Fidardo took a piece of cheese. His morose expression softened when he tasted it. And in no time at all he and Ana were gossiping away about neighbours and acquaintances. I crept up onto the kitchen sofa and listened to them with half an ear. I was feeling happy and peaceful—and a little drowsy after the good meal.

~

I left the house on Rua de São Tomé a couple of hours before midnight. Ana had asked me if I wanted to live with her while the Chief was away, but I'd said no. It wouldn't feel right to leave the *Hudson Queen* completely unattended.

Down by the river a damp night breeze was blowing along the empty quays. No one was about and between the flickering gas lamps the night was very dark. I sped up and every so often glanced back over my shoulder. You always need to be on your guard in a harbour at night.

It was low tide so I had to climb down a ladder to get aboard the *Hudson Queen* from the quayside. I was about to open the galley when I noticed a folded slip of paper stuck under the door. I closed the door behind me and lit the paraffin lamp hanging over the table. Then I opened the folded paper and read:

I have a job at the fairground for you. Come to Rua Moeda (near Cais do Sodré) at seven o'clock tomorrow evening.

Harvey Jenkins

A World of Pleasures

The following evening I left Signor Fidardo's workshop immediately after six. I hurried through the crowds on the steep
streets of the Mouraria district and bought a loaf of bread and
a bit of cheese on my way.

Down by Martim Moniz Square I ran to catch up with a
tram and hung on tight to the rear platform. The slipstream
cooled my face pleasantly as the tram picked up speed on the
wide shopping streets of Baixa.

Dusk was falling and the streetlamps came on one by one.
I jumped off at Cais do Sodré and continued on foot. The
sounds of laughter and music quickly led me to a piece of
waste ground illuminated by open fires burning in big metal
drums. I could see a dozen or more colourful fairground caravans drawn up round a merry-go-round with worn wooden
horses that were circling at a leisurely pace beneath a canvas
roof. The clatter of the machinery was drowned out by a waltz

melody produced by a large barrel organ cranked by a woman in a red uniform.

A small queue had formed at the booth where you could buy tickets to ride on the merry-go-round. On the roof of the booth was a large sign saying:

Brockdorff's Funfair – A World of Pleasures

It occurred to me now that I should be on my guard. Neither I nor the Chief knew Harvey Jenkins. What if his reasons for encouraging me to come here were suspicious? After all, it wouldn't be the first time in my life I'd been ensnared.

The fairground didn't seem in the least suspicious, though. Just a bit shabby and worse for wear as travelling fairs tend to be. The caravans had hatches where you could buy sweets and soft drinks. An old woman was walking around selling carnations to couples in love. In one tent there was a bald giant of a man who was arm-wrestling with anyone brave enough to challenge him. He called himself François le Fort and boasted he was the strongest man in France. In another tent you could have your future predicted by a fortune-teller who was in contact with the spirit world. Her name was Margosha and she came all the way from Odessa on the Black Sea.

The hissing and puffing steam engine that drove the merry-go-round stood behind a set of railings. Harvey Jenkins was sitting on a wooden chair close to the machine. His hat was down over his eyes and he was asleep. The cockerel on his shoulder was keeping watch and began stamping its feet when I climbed over the railings. Jenkins opened his eyes.

"Good evening to you," he said, pushing his hat to the back of his head.

He spread his arms as if introducing me to the fair.

"Yes, this is it, our travelling pleasure ground. Well, what do you think?"

I shrugged my shoulders. Jenkins gave a hoarse laugh.

"It's all a bit run down, I'll give you that," he said, "but a ride on the merry-go-round is cheap and Margosha promises everyone a brilliant future when she tells their fortunes. So no one leaves here disappointed. Anyway, it's time for you to come and meet Director Brockdorff."

He whistled over the ticket-seller, a grey-haired woman with a book under her arm, and asked her to keep an eye on the steam engine for a few minutes.

Director Brockdorff's office was in one of the fairground caravans. He was a small thin man with a waxed goatee beard and oily hair with a centre parting. He was dressed in a stained nightshirt and long johns held up by braces.

"Aha, so this is the ape engineer," he said when he saw me. "Excellent, Jenkins. How are you going to divide the work between you?"

"I'll take the afternoon shift and Sally Jones will take over from me at seven o'clock, and run the merry-go-round until closing time."

Director Brockdorff peeled a couple of banknotes off a roll he'd fished out of the breast pocket of his nightshirt.

"Your pay is six escudos a day. Here's twenty-four escudos. You'll get the same again on Saturday next week. That'll be your last working day as we'll be moving on come Sunday."

I took the notes. The pay was rubbish, but still a bit better than I'd been expecting.

When we went back to the merry-go-round Jenkins explained to me how to look after the two-cylinder steam engine. If anything went wrong, I had to get it fixed before the customers on the merry-go-round got tired of waiting and wanted their money back. There was a box of tools under the wooden chair.

Jenkins waited while I gave the merry-go-round a trial run. Then he picked up a bottle of wine that he'd hidden behind the steam engine.

"See you tomorrow evening, then," he said, quickly slipping the bottle into his pocket. "I'm off now to Bairro Alto to meet a nice little widow I got to know the other night. Her name is Eulalia and she bakes a wonderful leek pie, believe me!"

He touched the brim of his hat and, whistling cheerfully, went on his way. At the entrance he took the opportunity to pinch a couple of red carnations from the flower-seller's bunch.

~

My days were long now, though it wasn't something that bothered me. But Signor Fidardo was worried that I'd taken on an evening job.

"Are you managing to eat and sleep properly?" he wondered.

I nodded, but it didn't convince Signor Fidardo. The following day I saw that he'd got hold of a mattress and put it in the workshop storeroom.

"You must have a nap for at least half an hour every day," he said sternly. "Then you can come out with me and I'll buy you an early dinner before you go on to this other job you've found. Are we agreed on that?"

The funny thing about Signor Fidardo is that the kinder he is being, the stricter he tries to sound.

~

The best thing about working at the fairground was that I was left to myself to get on with things. There were, of course, always a few visitors leaning on the fence that surrounded the merry-go-round. They stared at me in curiosity but that didn't matter much: after all, I'm quite used to that sort of thing.

The other fairground workers hardly paid any attention to me at all. They had plenty of work of their own to be getting on with. One of the few people I got to know was the woman who sat in the ticket booth. She was called Sylvie Dubois and she was the mother of François Le Fort, the bald-headed arm-wrestler.

"This is the only job poor little François can get," she explained. "And he can't manage without his mamma, which is why, like it or not, I'm forced to travel round with the circus as I do."

Sylvie Dubois loved books. She'd been a *bouquiniste* in Paris, which means she had sold second-hand books from a stall on the street. These days, instead, she spent all day reading. Sylvie Dubois could take customers' money and hand them their tickets without even glancing up from her book.

Sometimes, when she felt the need to stretch her legs, she would come over to me to have a chat. On one of my very first evenings she asked, "You and Harvey Jenkins have known one another for a long time, haven't you?"

I shook my head.

"You haven't!" she said in surprise. "I thought the two of you were old acquaintances."

I shook my head again.

Sylvie Dubois looked at me over the top of her reading glasses.

"That's very strange," she said. "Why did he go to so much trouble for your sake, then? With Margosha and everything?…"

Just then someone turned up to buy a ticket for the merry-go-round and Sylvie Dubois had to go back to her booth.

Her questions had left me feeling a little confused, so when the fairground closed at midnight, I went over to the ticket booth hoping that Sylvie Dubois would give me an explanation. But she'd clearly already forgotten the whole business. She looked at me curiously and said that since I'd finished for the night I should be getting on home.

Unexpected Meetings

It was Sunday. The first Sunday after the Chief had sailed away on the SS *Funchal*.

I got up early to take full advantage of my day off. The city was blanketed in a dense grey mist, and the weak wind blowing in from the Atlantic was cold and damp. A good day for chipping off rust below decks.

Some people say that chipping off rust is hard and dreary work. And they're right. It's both dirty and boring—don't let anyone tell you otherwise! After an hour I needed to stretch my legs and go up for a breath of fresh air. I climbed the engine-room ladder and went to the galley to heat up some coffee left over from that morning. The galley is at the front of the ship, next to my small cabin, and you reach it through a hatchway in the foredeck. I'd reached the bottom step of the ladder when I got such a fright I almost fell backwards.

Harvey Jenkins was standing in the galley. His cockerel, head to the side, had one of its blind eyes rigidly fixed on me.

"So there you are," Harvey Jenkins said with a smile. "I didn't mean to scare you. We were out for a little Sunday stroll and happened to be passing. Since the hatch was open, we came aboard... I brought some vanilla cakes, if you'd like one?"

In his hand he was holding a brown paper bag, its sides covered in fat stains. I quickly pulled myself together and pointed at the coffee pot.

"Yes please," Jenkins said. "A cup of coffee with the cake would be just the job."

Our snack didn't last long. Jenkins talked a bit about this and that and rose to his feet as soon as he'd drunk his coffee.

"I won't keep you from chipping the rust," he said. "See you this evening then, when you take over from me at the merry-go-round."

I nodded.

Jenkins went ashore and walked off along the quayside with his hands in his pockets and his collar turned up against the drizzle. The cockerel huddled down on his shoulder.

I watched them for a long time. There was something strange about their visit, I felt. It wasn't exactly the perfect weather for a walk. And what had Jenkins been up to in the galley? Why hadn't he come down to the engine room instead? He must have heard me down there, chipping rust...

I stopped work for the day a couple of hours later. I washed, changed into clean overalls and then Ana, Signor Fidardo and I took the tram out to the Prazeres cemetery. We do that almost every Sunday and Signor Fidardo plays the harmonium while Ana sings in the cemetery chapel. While they are doing that, I visit my good friend João, the cemetery caretaker.

I helped João weed the flowerbeds and rake the gravel until it was time for me to go to Rua Moeda and take my shift at the merry-go-round.

"Hi there, matey," Jenkins said, casual as ever when he caught sight of me.

He was standing by one of the braziers to keep warm and the cockerel had crept in under his coat. Jenkins was gently stroking its bald little head.

"He's afraid of the fire," Jenkins explained. "All animals are, I suppose… well, except you, of course. By the way, have you had any dinner? I've been roasting chestnuts if you're hungry."

There was a pile of freshly roasted chestnuts on a dish beside the brazier and the smell was wonderful. I signalled my gratitude by touching the brim of my cap with two fingers.

Jenkins put the cockerel back on his shoulder and buttoned up his coat.

"We're away to Bairro Alto to see what the lovely Eulalia has cooked for us today," he said, full of anticipation. "Have a good shift and see you again tomorrow."

～

The hours passed slowly. I kept a good fire going to serve the boiler of the steam engine, but there was little to do apart from that, other than to eat chestnuts and drink tea with Sylvie Dubois. To help pass the time she read to me from a newspaper one of the fairground customers had left behind.

The big news of the day was the report of an Italian sail-assisted steamship from Salerno putting into Lisbon as an emergency when several passengers fell ill with diphtheria, a very dangerous and infectious disease. The port authorities had quarantined the vessel. No one on board was allowed to go ashore and no one ashore was allowed to go aboard. In spite of that, some people in the city were so frightened the infection might spread they were demanding the vessel be towed out to sea and left to its fate.

"Poor souls," Sylvie Dubois sighed and I nodded my head in agreement.

When the clock eventually reached twelve, I walked to the tram stop at Cais do Sodré and caught the night tram towards Alfama. The tram was full of sleepy-eyed waitresses and cleaners on their way home from the evening shift at the big casino in Estoril. I found an empty place by the window and slumped down on the worn and shiny wooden seat.

I must have fallen asleep and by the time I opened my eyes again we'd already reached Comércio Square. A tram going in the opposite direction was waiting at the stop. The two cars were right alongside one another and I turned my head and looked into the other tram. The very first thing I saw through the rain-streaked windows was Harvey Jenkins. He was sitting just a couple of yards away, staring straight ahead, and he hadn't noticed me.

I was taken by surprise. Hadn't Jenkins told me he was going to visit the widow Eulalia in Bairro Alto? So what was he doing on a tram coming from the Alfama harbour area? Perhaps the widow had got tired of baking leek pie for him? He was obviously now on his way back to the fairground and he didn't look as if he'd had a particularly enjoyable evening.

One of the cockerel's white eyes was staring straight at me and I had a strange feeling that the blind bird knew I was close by. It began stamping excitedly up and down on its master's shoulder. Without really knowing why, I slipped down in my seat so that Jenkins wouldn't see me. Just then, his tram jerked into motion and set off with a ping and at the same moment my tram set off in the opposite direction.

The Fortune~Teller's Confession

Grey and misty weather cloaked Lisbon for several days. Not a breath of wind rippled the waters of the river and the smoke from all the coal-fired stoves in the city hung in the air and made it difficult to breathe.

Slowly the haze was dispersed by a warm and ominous south-west wind. Ragged white clouds stood out against the blue-black sky far out over the sea to the west. For the best part of a day and a night the storm remained motionless, growing in strength before it began moving towards the coast.

"I'll have to get going immediately if I'm to reach Eulalia's place without getting soaked," Jenkins said, eyeing the clouds with a frown as I took over the merry-go-round from him. "The thunderstorm will soon be with us."

Jenkins was right. The first, heavy drops came almost at once, followed by the cloudburst. The wind grew stronger and stronger and the rain whipped the sandy fairground into a field of mud. Low clouds rolled and plunged just above the rooftops and the whole city was lit up by flashes of white lightning. The last visitors to the fairground took to their heels. Instead of looking after the merry-go-round I had to help tie down and stow anything likely to blow away.

By late evening a full storm was raging. Director Brockdorff came running through the deluge in nothing but his long johns and told us to take down the big circus sign from the roof of the ticket booth. At the same moment I heard Margosha cry for help: the guy ropes supporting her tent were about to give way.

I found a long rope among the junk behind the merry-go-round and managed to tie her tent to a tree. Then I tightened all the guy ropes and hammered the pegs deeper into the ground. Meanwhile the fortune-teller, her face pale and anxious, was standing in the opening of her tent. When I'd finished, she clapped her hands softly and beckoned me to follow her in.

Margosha from Odessa was a big, powerful woman with beautiful eyes but a face that wouldn't have been out of place on a harbour thug. She had gleaming black stones hanging from her ears and they had stretched her earlobes halfway down to her shoulders. Her tent was decorated with dark-coloured pieces of chequered cloth. Small lanterns close to the roof gave off a sweetish scent but very little light. There was a small table with two chairs and round it stood a collection of strange wooden sculptures. Every time a gust of wind shook the tent, the lanterns swayed and the shadows made by the sculptures flickered back and forth on the pieces of cloth.

"It was good of you to save my tent," Margosha said. "Sit down at the table and I'll make you a hot drink. We don't want you catching a cold."

She spoke an odd dialect, mixing together words from several different languages, in spite of which it wasn't too difficult to understand her. I sat down while she fetched two small cups and filled them with hot, reddish-brown liquid from a brass pot with a long spout. I sipped at the drink, but couldn't work out what it was.

"I've read the future for cats and for pet dogs," Margosha said, taking the chair opposite me. "But never for an ape. Would you like me to tell yours? Free. As a thank-you for helping me."

I didn't have any desire at all to have my future told, so I shook my head. But then I thought about something Sylvie Dubois had told me on one of my first evenings at the fairground. She'd said that Jenkins had had some sort of "trouble" with Margosha, and it had been about me. What had Sylvie Dubois meant by that? I really wanted to know.

Somehow, however, Margosha was able to read my mind. I don't know how it happened but I suppose reading minds is not unusual for fortune-tellers. She leant forward a little, looked me in the eye and said, "There's something you are wondering about, isn't there?"

I nodded.

"Does it have anything to do with the funfair?"

I nodded again.

Margosha took a sip of the mysterious drink before saying, "I believe you'd like to know how Harvey Jenkins went about arranging a job at the funfair for you. Am I right?"

Could this be what Sylvie Dubois had been talking about? I thought for a moment or two before nodding once more.

"I'm not one to tell tales," Margosha said. "Especially not about myself. But I'll make an exception in your case. Partly because you helped me, and partly because you can't talk. A secret is in safe keeping with you."

Margosha, of course, had no idea that I can write. And there was no need for her to learn otherwise. She leant forward and continued in a low voice. "Before you came, Jenkins used to share the merry-go-round work with a man called Kowalski. He was Polish and had been working at the fair for about a year. A quiet, friendly man. Jenkins took the evening shift and Kowalski the afternoon shift. Jenkins came to me one day and asked for a favour. This was just a short time after we'd opened the funfair in Lisbon. He offered me a sum of money in exchange for me convincing Kowalski to resign and leave the funfair."

Margosha took another sip before continuing. "Jenkins and I have known one another for a long time and he has done me a number of favours. So I couldn't say no. That same day I invited Kowalski to my tent and told his fortune from tea leaves in a bowl. I told Kowalski that, unfortunately, he was going to die soon. It frightened the poor fellow out of his skin and he wanted to know what was going to happen. 'You'll be blown to smithereens,' I said, 'when the boiler of the merry-go-round explodes.'"

Margosha shrugged her shoulders and put on an apologetic face. "It was a lie, of course, but it worked. Kowalski refused to work on the merry-go-round one minute more. He scuttled off to Director Brockdorff and resigned immediately. A quarter of an hour later he'd packed his bags and disappeared. The following day Jenkins announced he had found a replacement for Kowalski. That was you, of course…"

My surprise must have shown in my face. And my confusion.

"You'll be wondering, of course," Margosha said, "whether Jenkins wanted to get rid of Kowalski in order to offer you the merry-go-round job instead. Is that so?"

I nodded.

"The answer is yes," the fortune-teller said. "That's exactly it. Jenkins told me that himself, though he wouldn't say more. Or rather, there was one other thing, not that it made me any wiser."

Margosha looked deep into my eyes before continuing.

"I asked Jenkins why having you here at the funfair was so important to him. And this is what he said…"

Margosha leant closer to me and lowered her voice to a hoarse whisper. *"The past has returned. And I've been given a second chance."*

The fortune-teller sat back in her chair. "Those were his exact words," she said. "I had no idea what he was talking about, but perhaps you do. Do you?"

I stared at her, uncomprehending. Then I slowly shook my head.

~

The thunderstorm and the rain had moved away by the time I took the tram home at midnight. But the wind hadn't eased and the tram swayed and creaked as the gusts hit it.

Time after time I ran through everything Margosha had told me. Harvey Jenkins had behaved appallingly, just to ensure that I could get Kowalski's job. It was strange and incomprehensible. After all, Jenkins and I hardly knew one another.

It was possible, of course, that Jenkins's motives had nothing to do with being kind to me. He may have been trying to win the director's favour by arranging for there to be a live gorilla at the funfair? That would explain everything. And maybe it wasn't even Jenkins's idea, but Director Brockdorff's!

I got off the tram at Rua da Alfândega and walked down towards the river. The waves were breaking against the quay, filling the air with foam. The storm had ripped open the roof of one of the harbour warehouses and the torn sheets of corrugated iron crashed and screeched in the wind. I walked faster. How had the *Hudson Queen* weathered the storm?

The ship lay in darkness but even at a distance I could see that she was scraping and grinding against the quayside. The strong west wind had caused the river to rise at least two feet and the *Hudson Queen*'s mooring ropes should have been tightened up hours ago.

I hurried on board. It took all my strength to pull the ship back into position but she was going to need more mooring ropes to hold her there.

We store heavy ropes and other useful bits and pieces in a box bolted to the deck behind the wheelhouse. I went to fetch the key to the padlock on the box—it's kept along with all the other keys, hanging in a cupboard in the galley.

The moment I opened the cupboard I could see that something was wrong. The hook that usually held the spare key to the galley was empty. Where had the missing key gone?

I didn't have time to worry about that just then. So I took

the key to the deck-box from its hook and hurried back to make the ship's moorings more secure.

~

My clothes were still soaking from the torrential rain so I lit a fire in the stove and hung my overalls over the back of a chair to dry. I didn't have the energy left to make myself a cup of tea and, pulling an extra blanket over me, I crawled straight into my bunk.

I felt uneasy and couldn't get the things I had discovered out of my head. For many hours I lay there, slipping in and out of uneasy sleep. Dreams and thoughts became tangled in my mind and I could hear Margosha's and Harvey Jenkins's voices talking to me in riddles.

Quarantine

When I arrived at the musical instrument workshop the following morning, I was so weary that my whole body ached. I hadn't had more than a couple of hours of proper sleep before the light of dawn woke me.

It took Signor Fidardo no time at all to see what was the matter.

"Your yawns are disturbing me," he said, "and, to be honest, they are rather unpleasant. What if one of my elderly customers were to come through the door at the very moment you are showing your canine teeth? No good could come of it! Old people have been known to suffer a stroke from less than that! Is it your evening job that's spoiling your sleep? Come on, let's go to the Café Nova Goa and have morning coffee. You look as if you need it!"

The day turned out to be very different to what I had expected. When we got back from the Nova Goa there was a taxi parked on the pavement and a woman walking anxiously up and down and peering in through the windows of our workshop.

I recognized her immediately, as did Signor Fidardo.

"Isn't that our dear Doctor Domingues waiting for us?" he said, sounding surprised.

Rosa Domingues is a doctor in the infectious disease clinic at São José Hospital. She works harder than anyone else I know, but I had never seen her looking as utterly exhausted as she was now. Her face was pale as marble and the blue rings around her bloodshot eyes told of a lack of sleep.

"Ah, there you are at last!" she exclaimed with relief in her voice when she caught sight of me and Signor Fidardo. "Thank Heavens for that!"

Rosa asked the taxi driver to wait while she accompanied us into the workshop.

"I have a problem," she said to me, "and I think you are the only one who can help."

The problem was an Italian vessel that was quarantined in the port—the one that Sylvie Dubois had read about in the paper. Rosa gave us a brief account of the situation.

"Some of the passengers are poor emigrants," she said. "They are on their way to England to seek their fortune. Someone must already have been ill when they came on board in Salerno and now the bacteria have spread through the passengers and the crew. The sick need emergency hospital care, otherwise many of them will die. And it's the children who are most at risk."

Rosa gave a deep sigh.

"The ship is anchored on the other side of the river and it wasn't until yesterday evening that the Ministry of Health gave me permission to bring the sick ashore. To a restricted military site close to the harbour, where my clinic is setting up a temporary field hospital at the moment. But there is still a problem—a big one…"

Rosa was wringing her hands anxiously. "We don't know how we're going to bring the patients ashore. We have been given the use of a transport boat but no one will volunteer to drive it. The Navy refuses. The coastguards, too. And the harbour pilots are also refusing. They don't want to risk their seamen being infected. And I do understand—diphtheria is a dreadful disease."

Rosa looked me in the eye and added, "But it's an infection that only passes between people…"

∽

Signor Fidardo said I should take as much time off from the workshop as Rosa needed me to. He also said he'd send a message to the funfair to inform them they shouldn't expect me there for the next few days.

Then Rosa and I hurried to the waiting taxi and in less than an hour we were turning into the gates of the Belém naval base. A sailor in uniform showed us the way through the barrack blocks down to the quayside where the grey-painted naval vessels were moored.

The transport was a thirty-foot, open steam launch with room for twenty or so passengers. The boiler was already fired up so I cast off straightaway and steered due south. Rosa explained to me how she thought we should carry out the evacuation. We'd take the most severely ill ashore first and then we'd fetch those with less serious symptoms. We would leave healthy passengers on board for the moment.

The SS *Campania* was anchored a good distance offshore. A black-and-yellow quarantine flag was hanging from one of the mainmast crosstrees. As I drew alongside the *Campania,* Rosa was already putting on her protective mask and gloves. A rope ladder was dropped and I climbed up to the ship.

I had been expecting that the sight of me climbing in over the rail would cause a stir aboard the *Campania*. But the mood on deck was so overwrought and threatening that no one paid any attention to me at all. A hundred or so passengers were pushing and shoving to leave the ship and be the first down into the transport.

A few members of the crew were attempting to hold the excited crowd back. A man who appeared to be the ship's captain was waving a gun. The air was filled with screams and oaths and the situation was on the point of going out of control.

And then, suddenly, a woman emerged from the tumult. She was tall, straight-backed and dressed like a simple peasant woman in colourfully patterned skirts and with her hair covered with a black headscarf. Without a moment's hesitation she snatched the gun from the captain, aimed it into the air and pulled the trigger.

The Feather

There was a loud, sharp crack and everyone on deck immediately froze. The woman handed the gun back to the ship's
captain. He took it, a look of confusion on his face.

"You know who I am," the woman said in a deep firm voice,
her eyes moving slowly from one of her fellow passengers to
the next. "Keep calm and do what the captain and his crew
tell you to do. The sick must be taken ashore first and the rest
of us must wait."

A heavily built man began protesting in a shrill voice. He was
a typical first-class passenger wearing a tailor-made wool suit
and elegant leather shoes. The woman looked at him without
saying a word. When their eyes met, his courage deserted him
and he began stammering before falling silent. With a dull
murmur the crowd slowly moved away and broke up.

The woman turned to me. The features of her face were
earnest, her olive-toned skin tight over her cheek bones.

"Do what you need to now, ape," she said and went and sat in the shade of the deckhouse.

Who the woman was and why she had such power over the other passengers was something I didn't discover until much later. But at that point I just knew that she had saved Rosa and me from failing in our task.

~

The evacuation of SS *Campania* proved difficult enough anyway. The ship's hold had been converted into accommodation for third-class passengers. It was dark and crowded down there and the sweetish smell of disease made me feel sick. In the weak light of the oil lamps I caught glimpses of rats scuttling about in the dark corners.

It took me two hours to move twenty of the most severely ill passengers to the transport. Most of them were children with swollen throats and foreheads hot with fever. Some of them were frightened when they first caught sight of me, others thought they were dreaming, but none of them put up any resistance as I carried them up on deck.

A couple of men who were already infected helped me as much as they could. We laid the sick on a sailcloth hammock, which I could then winch down to the transport using a rope and tackle. Rosa met them down there and helped each of them to a good place to sit or lie.

By the time twilight fell over the river that evening, we had made four trips back and forth between the quayside and the *Campania*. Just about half of the sick passengers were now being cared for in the field hospital.

Both Rosa and I were beyond exhaustion.

~

A westerly gale moved in from the Atlantic the following morning. The rough swell made the task of moving passengers from the *Campania* to the transport even more difficult than the day before. It was early evening by the time we were ready to leave the quarantined ship with the last load of infected passengers.

As I was about to climb down the rope ladder to the transport boat I caught sight of the woman who'd tamed the disorderly mob the day before. She was standing alone at the rail a short distance away. She bade me farewell with an almost imperceptible nod and I nodded back.

It was already eight o'clock when I drew alongside the quay at the naval base. Two men in protective suits scrubbed me all over with carbolic soap and gave me a new set of overalls from the navy store. My old overalls were to be burnt.

There was no sign of Rosa Domingues. She was presumably fully occupied caring for her new patients. And no one else seemed to be interested in me, so I walked out of the base and took the tram to Alfama.

~

Once on board the *Hudson Queen* I cleared the decks for the night and then made myself a bedtime snack in the galley. A few crusts and tea were all I could find. The lamp hanging above the table flickered as I ate. I realized the paraffin must be running out, so I took the lamp and went to the workshop to refill it.

The *Hudson Queen*'s small workshop is tucked into a corner of the engine room. As I made my way down the ladder to the engine room, the flame flickered a few times and then the light went out. Everything suddenly became as dark as the grave. But I don't need a light to find my way around my engine room. I felt my way over to the workbench and took down the can of lamp oil from the shelf.

That is when I had a sudden feeling I wasn't alone in the darkness.

It was a smell. A very faint smell. It didn't fit in, but nor was it completely unfamiliar.

I kept very still and held my breath. There was nothing to be heard apart from the usual creaking noises of the ship. After a while I opened the can of lamp oil, refilled the lamp and lit it.

Of course there was no one there! I felt rather foolish. It wasn't like me to be frightened of the dark.

But the strange smell still hung in the air. I hadn't just imagined it. I shone the light over the mixture of tools, rags, engine parts and bits and pieces on the workbench.

Then I looked down at the floor. Something was lying there.

It was a feather.

A black feather with ragged grey edges.

I picked it up and cautiously sniffed it. Now I recognized the musty, slightly rancid smell.

The feather had come from Harvey Jenkins's cockerel. I was absolutely certain of that.

But how on earth had it got here?

The answer was simple and occurred to me immediately: the cockerel must have shed the feather the first time we met Jenkins. On that occasion the Chief had shown both of them around the whole ship.

Pleased with myself for solving that little mystery, I threw the feather into the engine room waste bin and went back to the galley to drink my tea.

~

A little while later I was lying snug in my hammock. Through the porthole I could see the shrouds of mist hanging over the river. In the far distance I caught a glimpse of a deserted jetty, lit by the pale yellow light from a solitary gas lamp. Waves were splashing against the hull and the taut mooring ropes creaked softly.

I was about to fall asleep when a thought suddenly flashed into my head. *Why hadn't I found the feather before this evening?*

It was at least a fortnight since Harvey Jenkins and his cockerel had been down in the engine room with the Chief. And I'd been down there almost every day working on one thing or another.

Wouldn't I have noticed the feather earlier?

And what about the smell?...

Breach of Contract

The following morning I overslept and arrived at my job in the instrument workshop two hours late. Signor Fidardo made no comment. Instead, he took me out to the Café Nova Goa where he treated me to morning coffee and a couple of cheese rolls.

"How are you today?" he asked, giving me a searching look.

I shrugged my shoulders. Several times during the night I'd been woken by nightmares. I couldn't remember what they had been about, but they had left me in a dull, mournful mood.

Signor Fidardo thought for a while before continuing. "I arrived here forty years ago on an emigrant ship from Calabria. As we were crossing the Mediterranean, smallpox broke out among the passengers in third class. They were being transported deep down in the hold—like cattle. Given the filth and the misery, the disease spread like wildfire. It was horrifying to watch…"

He fell silent and sat there sunk in memories.

Then he said, "So I think I can understand what you've been through in the last few days. That's all I wanted to say."

I nodded gratefully.

～

When my working day at Signor Fidardo's workshop was over, I took the tram to Rua Moeda to work my last shift as merry-go-round engineer at the fairground. The following day the funfair would be packing up and moving on to its next town.

The first person I met at the fairground was Director Brockdorff. Drawing himself up to his full height, he stuck his thumbs under the braces that were holding up his baggy long johns.

"Sally Jones," he said brusquely. "So there you are! I thought you were someone I could rely on but I was clearly mistaken. Do you know what the phrase *breach of contract* means?"

I looked at him and suddenly felt very tired. I was in no mood to be given a lecture.

"You will understand that I shall have to make a *substantial* deduction from your wages," the small director continued. I caught a satisfied glint in his eye. "You have been absent from your employment for two nights in a row. Instead of the twenty-four escudos we agreed you should receive today—if you had fulfilled your duties—I'm afraid I can only pay you

89

five. And I have to say I think I'm being very generous in the circumstances!"

I'd been prepared to sacrifice part of my wages, but certainly not this much. It really was unfair.

Just at that moment Harvey Jenkins approached us at a brisk pace.

"What are you two talking about?" he asked, eyeing the director.

Director Brockdorff made an irritated gesture, as if wanting Jenkins to go away. But Jenkins stayed and the director was forced to explain what it was all about.

Jenkins gave a wry smile.

"There must have been some minor misunderstanding, then," he said in a mild voice. "You surely can't have already forgotten that I looked after the merry-go-round in place of Sally Jones? She and I had agreed on that in advance."

That last point wasn't actually true. Surprised, I looked at Jenkins out of the corner of my eye.

"What difference does that make?" the director snarled. "A contract is a contract! This ape let us down and—"

"Not at all," Jenkins interrupted him. "Sally Jones hasn't let anyone down. She was helping to rescue people in distress… and it didn't cost you one centavo. Did it?"

Director Brockdorff's face grew redder and redder. He

opened his mouth to say something but couldn't find the words. With a snort of rage, he pulled out two ten-escudo notes and a handful of change and threw them in my direction. Then he turned on his heel and, giving Harvey Jenkins one last venomous look, he left us.

Once the director was out of hearing, Jenkins gave a hoarse chuckle.

"He's a swindler, that one, he really is," he said and gave me a wink.

~

Harvey Jenkins must have told everyone at the fairground why I'd been absent the last few nights. Margosha, Sylvie Dubois and François Le Fort all came over, patted me on the back and said nice things.

Jenkins hung around for a short while after I'd started my shift. Then it was time for us to say goodbye.

"I know it may be asking too much of you," he said apologetically, "but I wonder if you'd do me a favour. When the funfair moves on tomorrow morning, the steam engine has to be ready to go. So it would be good if the firebox could be raked out and the boiler drained straight after your shift. Otherwise the grate and the boiler plates won't have had time to cool for the morning. Properly speaking it's my job, but I'd be so happy not to have to leave Eulalia before midnight. After all, it's our last night together…"

I nodded. Of course I'd do a favour for Jenkins. He'd just prevented the director from tricking me out of most of my wages, hadn't he?

"Thank you so much!" Jenkins said, beaming. "And while you're at it, it would be wonderful if you could disconnect the cable from the merry-go-round…"

I nodded again.

With a smile, Jenkins held out his hand and I took it.

"It's been really lovely to get to know you, Sally Jones," he said. "I'm sure our paths will cross again. The world isn't as big as people think—certainly not for vagabonds like us!"

When the funfair closed at midnight, the fairground workers began packing their things. I was already regretting my promise to Jenkins. Getting the steam engine and boiler ready for transport was no small job. It would take me many hours, probably until dawn.

Sylvie Dubois could see from my face how I felt.

"You shouldn't have to slave away on that wreck of a steam engine all night on your own!" she said. "Not after all the lives you saved at sea! Me and François will give you a hand!"

Between the three of us, we had the job done in a couple of hours. There was a mild night breeze blowing as I left the fairground for the last time and walked towards Cais do Sodré. I was in luck and managed to catch a tram that was about to depart. I settled wearily on a seat and rested my head against the cool glass of the window.

I was woken by the conductor putting his hand on my shoulder.

"I recognize you," he said in a friendly voice. "Isn't this your usual stop?"

I blinked confused by the bright lighting in the tramcar and then I looked out of the window. We were already at the Rua da Alfândega tram stop. I thanked the conductor with a nod and left the tram.

Everything was calm and quiet down by the river. The moon was casting its pale, shimmering blue light over the quays and the moored vessels. I walked slowly, taking deep breaths of sea air and thinking about the Chief. During the past weeks I hadn't had much time to think about what he might be doing. Perhaps SS *Funchal* was currently anchored out in the roads off Rio de Janeiro? Perhaps the Chief had been given shore leave and at this very moment was sitting at a pavement café along the promenade?…

My thoughts were interrupted and I came to a halt. I'd

reached the *Hudson Queen* and was standing just a couple of yards from the gangway.

There was a light showing through one of the engine room portholes on the port side.

For a moment or two I wondered whether I'd left an oil lamp burning. But then I saw the light flicker, like the gleam of a moving lantern.

Someone was aboard our ship.

The Unseeing Eye

I stood on the quayside, with no idea at all what to do next. After a little while, the light in the porthole grew stronger: the intruder must be climbing up the engine room ladder. At any moment now the door might be opened…

I backed away, taking a look around as I did so. There were several crates just a short distance away. I ran over and slipped into a gap between two of the crates.

No light was showing on the *Hudson Queen* now, but the muffled creak of an un-oiled hinge could be heard—someone must be opening the engine room door. The moon had gone behind the clouds and the ship lay in complete darkness. When I screwed up my eyes, I could pick out the shape of a tall thin figure moving aft along the rail. And then the pale light of a lantern showed in the wheelhouse.

My heart pounded hard. I had recognized the intruder. *It was Harvey Jenkins. With his cockerel on his shoulder.*

What was Jenkins doing here?

And how had he got aboard the ship?

Had he broken in?

It seemed crazy. But still… There couldn't be any other explanation.

All of a sudden I understood why Jenkins had asked me to tend the steam engine last night. It wasn't because he wanted to meet Eulalia. *It was to keep me away from the* Hudson Queen!

Then I remembered the feather I'd found in the engine room the night before. *Clearly this wasn't the first time Jenkins had broken in…*

Memories from recent weeks flashed past my mind's eye and suddenly I felt very stupid. There had been several occasions when I suspected that there was something strange about Harvey Jenkins, but I'd never worked out what was going on.

I had a strong temptation to leave my hiding place, go on board the ship and try to get Jenkins to explain his behaviour. But would that be the sensible thing to do? Jenkins might turn violent if he was caught red-handed. After all, he was a burglar.

Or was he? Would a real thief choose to burgle a wreck like the *Hudson Queen*? The Chief and I didn't possess anything of value…

Then a thought struck me: the *turban*! I'd forgotten about the priceless turban I'd received from my friend the Maharajah of Bhapur. Could that be what Jenkins was after?

But if that was the case he would surely have found it by now. The turban was in my seaman's chest and was the easiest thing in the world to find...

Jenkins was still busy doing something in the wheelhouse. The light of the lantern was moving around in there and dull thumps and peculiar squeaks and creaks could be heard. What was going on? There was nothing worth stealing in there apart from the binnacle and the engine order telegraph, both of which were big heavy items that Jenkins would have no hope of carrying ashore on his own.

By the time the light in the wheelhouse went out, it felt as if I'd spent an eternity hiding among the crates. A shadow moved forward and I heard the creak of the door leading down to the galley. The lantern was lit again and its flickering light could be seen weakly through the dull glass of the galley porthole.

A short while later the door opened again and Jenkins emerged, closing the door behind him. Things went very quiet and I thought I could pick out the click of a lock as a key was turned.

Did Jenkins have a key?

So he must have been the one who stole our spare key to the galley from the key cupboard!

The dark figure walked across the gangplank and disappeared from my field of vision. Now I had to make a decision. Should I reveal myself or should I stay in my hiding place? Footsteps were approaching slowly. I found myself incapable of moving.

The first hints of dawn were just beginning to break up the darkness of night. I could see Jenkins quite clearly as he walked past, no more than a few yards from the packing crates. His back was bent and his hands were thrust deep in his pockets.

I don't think I made a sound, but the cockerel must have been aware of my presence. It quickly turned its head in my direction and stamped its feet anxiously on its master's shoulder. For a fraction of a second, an unseeing white eye stared at me.

Jenkins walked on for a few yards before coming to a halt.

"What was that?" he whispered either to himself or to the cockerel.

Then I heard him turn round and start to come back. His footsteps were cautious and quiet.

I tried to back deeper into the darkness, but it was pointless. I knew that when Harvey Jenkins looked between the wooden crates he would be able to see me.

He stood there in silence and seemed to be wondering what to say. Or to do. In the pale light of dawn his face looked worn. The eyes that met mine were weary.

Eventually Jenkins sighed and said, "Forgive me."

Then he walked away.

It was a good half minute before I dared leave my hiding place. The quay was deserted and a thick, grey morning mist hung over the river.

10

Asparagus and Langoustines

It was a warm afternoon in May when SS *Funchal* steamed up the Tagus. From the roof of the wheelhouse of the *Hudson Queen* I could see the ship dropping anchor in the sunshine just below the city. A ship's boat was lowered and set its course for the shore.

I hurried to catch a tram to the Cais do Sodré and got there just in time to meet the Chief as he left the customs post with his kitbag on his shoulder and the stump of a smouldering cigar clenched in his teeth. He hadn't changed and he hadn't lost weight, which meant that the voyage on the *Funchal* must have been a good one.

The moment the Chief caught sight of me his face broke into a broad smile and he put his luggage down on the quay. We shook hands and patted each other on the back, and then I pointed towards the steep hills of Alfama. The Chief understood what I meant: Ana had invited us to come for dinner.

"In that case it's just as well I managed to have a wash and change my shirt before coming ashore," he said in a happy voice.

That evening was one of the most enjoyable evenings I'd had for a long time. You could see that my friends had been missing one another and I felt a warm glow in my heart. We ate white asparagus and fresh langoustines that Signor Fidardo had bought at the Mercado da Ribeira. When we'd finished eating, the Chief opened his kitbag and gave us all presents. He gave me a hand-forged marlin spike in a leather case and Ana and Signor Fidardo were each given a big, colourful hammock from Bahia. Nowhere weaves better and more beautiful jute hammocks than Bahia.

Right at the bottom of the Chief's kitbag was the case containing his little red accordion. He took it out while Signor Fidardo tuned his guitar and I made myself comfortable on the sofa.

Then Ana began to sing and all the worries I had in the world were suddenly forgotten.

When I came up on deck the following morning, I found the Chief sitting in the lee of the deckhouse wearing just his vest and trousers. His cap was pushed to the back of his head and his face was turned to the rising sun. Our dented old coffee pot and two cups were beside him.

"Morning," he said when he heard my footsteps. "Help yourself to a cup. It's freshly made."

I poured myself a cup and sat down beside him.

"I heard that that Harvey Jenkins fellow fixed up a job for you at his funfair," the Chief said. "How did that go? Did you enjoy it?"

The previous night Signor Fidardo had told the Chief about my part in the evacuation of the sick passengers from the *Campania*. But little had been said about my work at the funfair.

I produced a couple of sheets of paper from the pocket of my overall and passed them to the Chief. The sheets were full of writing and the Chief looked at them in astonishment.

"What's this?" he said. "Is this something you want me to read?"

I nodded. It was three weeks since the Brockdorff Funfair had left Lisbon and during that time I had done a great deal of thinking about Harvey Jenkins and what he'd been up to on the *Hudson Queen*. I'd typed out the most important points on my Underwood.

"All right then," the Chief said. "As long as you don't get impatient with me. You know I'm a slow reader."

I went to make fresh coffee and at the same time took the opportunity to fetch my new marlin spike. Then we sat there in the morning sun and, while the Chief read, I made new eye splices on our old mooring ropes.

When the Chief had finished reading, he put down the papers and stared at me, his eyes wide with surprise. Then he gave a big smile and said, "You seem to end up getting involved in the strangest things, the moment I turn my back!"

I shrugged my shoulders. Perhaps there was some truth in what he said.

The Chief looked thoughtful.

"Do you really think that Jenkins got the Polish fellow to give up the job? So that you could get the job instead of him?"

I nodded. That was certainly what Margosha had told me.

"And Jenkins wanted to keep you busy with the merry-go-round so that he could spend the evenings snooping around the *Hudson Queen* undisturbed?" The Chief was thinking aloud. "It does seem crazy, doesn't it? And he could get into the ship with a stolen key? Is that right?"

I nodded once again. Jenkins must have stolen the spare key to the galley that Sunday morning when he paid us an unexpected visit. And that gave him access to all the other keys as well, since the key cupboard is hanging in the galley.

The Chief rubbed his chin.

"But what on earth did he want on board?" he asked. "Has anything been stolen?"

I shook my head. Nothing was missing.

"But if he wasn't coming aboard to steal things," the Chief

said, "what was he after? Could he have been searching for something?"

I gave an emphatic nod. That was exactly what I thought. I stood up and signed for the Chief to come with me.

It took me some considerable time to show him all the traces of Jenkins I had found. They were all over the ship, but they weren't easy to locate. In the wheelhouse and the storeroom wall there were panels that had been removed and then fixed back. The caps on every single blanked-off pipe in the engine room had been unscrewed and then put back. There were scratch marks and scrapes that showed that Jenkins had even rooted around among the iron keelson plates.

The Chief's brow furrowed.

"Do you think he found what he was looking for?"

I shook my head. I remembered how weary and disconsolate Jenkins had looked the last time I saw him.

The Chief stuck his cigar between his teeth.

"Well in that case it must still be on board... whatever it was he was looking for," he said with a glint in his eye.

That thought had already occurred to me and I had actually spent several evenings creeping round the ship searching for hidden spaces and secret hiding places. Without finding anything at all, however. So I just shrugged my shoulders and put on a sceptical expression.

Queen of the Tagus

Summer arrived, bringing heat so intense that even time had to slow down. Everyone moved at a slower pace than usual. Even the wind seemed unable to blow properly. The river would lie gleaming and still until late morning when, at last, a sea breeze would stir the stuffy air.

The Chief and I got temporary work at a woodyard in Xabregas. Working with their big steam saw, we spent day after day turning logs into planks until the foreman eventually told us we were no longer needed. Instead of taking all our pay in cash, the Chief asked for part of it to be paid in the form of oak planks, and they agreed to that. This meant that we acquired some first-class timber at a really good price.

We used the planks to build a new ship's boat for the *Hudson Queen*. It had two pairs of oars and a small lug sail, and we named her *A Rainha do Tejo*—"Queen of the Tagus".

Ana and Signor Fidardo joined us for the boat's launch,

but only Ana was prepared to accompany us on the maiden voyage: I've noticed before that Signor Fidardo is not one for boats. Ana, however, seemed to really enjoy our little voyage around the harbour. A couple of days later she and the Chief made another trip and this time Ana took the rudder while the Chief gave directions and tended the sail. They made many more outings in the ship's boat and by the end of the summer Ana Molina could sail.

~

A thunderstorm at the end of September was the first sign that autumn was approaching. That's when Signor Fidardo discovered rain pouring into the attic of his house. The tiles on the roof were ancient and needed to be replaced.

"The workmen in this city are rogues, every one of them," he muttered despondently. "I'll be ruined."

The moment the Chief heard that Signor Fidardo was worried he suggested that this was a job for him and me. I agreed. Signor Fidardo, on the other hand, hesitated: it was clear that he wasn't confident that the Chief and I knew how to renovate a roof. Eventually, though, he gave in and ordered a load of roof tiles.

It took me and the Chief a week's work with a block and tackle to strip off the old tiles and another week to replace them with the new. Everything went well until Signor Fidardo wanted to pay us for our work. The Chief refused to accept any money, but Signor Fidardo wasn't prepared to go along with that.

"I insist you let me pay what I owe you," he said.

"You already have done," the Chief told him with a smile. "A hundred times over, at the very least. If it wasn't for you and Ana I would still be in jail. And Sally Jones might not even have survived! So be sensible now and let us do you this little favour!"

Signor Fidardo took the Chief's hand.

"Well, we'll leave it at that," he mumbled, "for now. But that's not the last you'll hear of this matter, Koskela. I'll come up with some way of repaying you!"

They have a lot in common, the Chief and Signor Fidardo. Both of them are stubborn and neither of them likes to be in anyone's debt.

~

Early one evening a few weeks later, when the Chief and I had just got back from a temporary job in the general cargo harbour, there was a knock on the galley door. It was Ana. She seemed rather excited and wanted us to accompany her at once to the house on Rua de São Tomé.

"Has something happened?" the Chief asked in a worried voice.

"Yes, it certainly has," Ana said, "but Luigi will have to tell you himself."

"Signor Fidardo hasn't been taken ill, has he?"

"No, no, not at all," Ana said impatiently. "Just come with me..."

It was already starting to grow dark by the time we arrived. The window blinds in the workshop had been pulled down for the night. Ana knocked on the door.

"Who's there?" We heard Signor Fidardo's voice on the other side of the door.

"It's us," Ana said.

The Chief and I looked at one another in confusion. Signor Fidardo never stayed in his workshop after six o'clock in the evening. He was a very precise man when it came to routine.

The lock clicked and the door opened.

"Come in, my friends," Signor Fidardo said. "So pleased you could come... Shut the door and lock it behind you. We don't want to be disturbed."

It was dark in the workshop. The only lamp that was lit was the one above Signor Fidardo's workbench and it cast a cone of light down on the *Hudson Queen*'s ship's wheel, which had spent the last year or more standing on the floor by my workbench.

I looked at Signor Fidardo, a question in my eyes.

"I know you were intending to renovate the wheel yourself," he said. "And you'd do an excellent job without any help from me. But you repaired my roof and I wanted to do something to repay you. So this morning the ship's wheel came to mind. It's been standing there for some considerable time and I decided to spruce it up for you."

The Chief and I stared at the wheel. We were confused. Signor Fidardo didn't appear to have done very much to it and it seemed to be in the same sorry state as before.

Signor Fidardo read our thoughts.

"No, no," he said. "As you can see, I hadn't even got started on renovating it. The first thing I had to do was to unscrew all the brass inlays in order to get at the wood properly. And that's when I discovered something remarkable... Tell me first, do you know of anything special about this wheel? Anything different about it?"

"Different?" the Chief said. "How do you mean?"

Signor Fidardo and Ana nodded to one another.

"Show them now, Luigi," she said.

Signor Fidardo picked up a small chisel and leant over the wheel. He carefully eased the blade of the chisel under the brass plate that covered the centre of the wheel. The screws had already been removed so that when he levered the chisel upwards the brass plate came with it. He lifted it and put it to one side.

For a short time all four of us stood there looking at what had been hidden under the brass plate.

"What the devil?…" the Chief said quietly.

The central body of the wheel had been hollowed out to create a hiding place about six inches long. It contained a package wrapped in coarse, waxed sailcloth.

"Luigi showed it to me this morning," Ana explained. "But we haven't opened the package to see what's in it. We thought that you two should be the first to do it. And now I'm on the point of bursting with curiosity…"

The Chief looked at me.

"You do it," he said.

I stepped forward and eased the package out of its hiding place in the ship's wheel. The sailcloth had been stitched with tarred hemp twine and the seams coated with liquid beeswax to make it all completely waterproof. Signor Fidardo handed me a sharp knife and I carefully cut one stitch at a time until it was possible to open the package.

The sailcloth contained an old, worn and patched bag made of chamois leather. I untied the knot, opened the bag and emptied its contents onto the workbench. Both Ana and Signor Fidardo gasped.

The pearls in the necklace that now lay before us seemed to gleam with a pale and mysterious inner light.

The *Hudson Queen's* Secret

A little while later the four of us were sitting round Ana's kitchen table. The teapot was on the stove and the oil lamp hanging over the table was lit. The necklace lay in the middle of the warm pool of light. It was made of fifty or so pearls and a small pendant in the shape of a rose. The petals were of pink mother of pearl inset in silver.

It was difficult to tear your eyes away from the shimmering pearls. They seemed to gently shift colour and lustre all the time, almost as if they had a life of their own.

"Does either of you have any idea what kind of necklace this is?" Ana said. "Or who might have hidden it on your ship?"

The Chief shook his head slowly.

"No," he said, "I've never seen the piece before. It must have already been hidden in the ship's wheel when Sally Jones and I bought the *Hudson Queen*. And that's coming up to ten years ago."

"Who owned the vessel before you?" Signor Fidardo asked.

"A shipbroker in New York," the Chief said. "But he can't have known there were pearls hidden aboard. Otherwise he certainly wouldn't have left them there when he sold the ship to us."

The Chief scratched his head before continuing. "The *Hudson Queen* was built in Scotland a year or so after the turn of the century. Both boiler and engine are from that period, anyway. But we don't know more than that about the ship's history... although we believe that Glasgow was her first home port and that she was named *Rose* when she was built. The name's engraved on the ship's bell."

Ana looked confused.

"But why didn't you change the ship's bell? It should have *Hudson Queen* on it now, shouldn't it?"

"Changing a ship's bell brings bad luck," the Chief said earnestly. "No wise seaman would do such a thing. That's why almost every ship retains its first bell until the ship is wrecked or sent to the breaker's yard."

A lock of hair fell across Ana's forehead as she reached for the necklace to look at the silver and mother-of-pearl rose.

"So your ship was originally called *Rose*," she said. "And the pendant on the necklace depicts a rose... Maybe that means something. What if the necklace has been hidden in the ship's wheel ever since the vessel was built?"

The Chief nodded. "Indeed, that could be so."

Signor Fidardo had brought a magnifying glass from his workshop. Twirling his moustache in thought, he reached for the necklace and began inspecting it closely.

"Peerless pearls…" he said. "Perhaps a little bit too big and too perfect for one not to be just a touch suspicious."

"Do you mean they are fake?" Ana asked.

Signor Fidardo hesitated a moment before answering. "No, no, that's not what I think. But just to be sure, I'll show the necklace to an acquaintance of mine. His name is Alvar Gomez and he's one of the very best jewellers in the Chiado district."

"Thanks, that would be kind," the Chief said.

Signor Fidardo held the pendant on the necklace up to the lamp. The small, silver and mother-of-pearl rose gleamed and shone in the light.

"Exquisite craftsmanship," he said. "Let's see now…"

He turned the pendant and aimed his magnifying glass at the back of the rose.

"Just as I thought," he said. "The work of a craftsman."

We all leant forward to get a better view. On the back of the rose there were four small symbols stamped in the silver.

"Silver hallmarks," the Chief said.

"And I'm fairly certain they're British," Signor Fidardo added. "The first of them tells us the purity of the silver, the other three will no doubt tell us where and when the pendant was created."

We looked at one another.

"A clue, then…" Ana said.

Signor Fidardo nodded. "I'll ask Senhor Gomez to take a look at these hallmarks when he examines the pearls."

We sat there in silence for a while until a thought occurred to the Chief. He looked at me and said, "Now we know what Harvey Jenkins was looking for on our ship, don't we? What do you think?"

I nodded. The same thought had struck me the moment Signor Fidardo showed us the hiding place in the ship's wheel.

Ana and Signor Fidardo looked at the Chief and me blankly. Of course, they knew nothing about Jenkins and his searches, so the Chief told them what had happened to me while he'd been away at sea.

Signor Fidardo was furious and gave me a stern look. "You should have let Ana and me know what was going on. That Jenkins fellow could well have done you harm!"

Ana, too, looked at me reproachfully. I felt a little ashamed, although I had no real reason to be.

The Chief came to my defence. "Sally Jones didn't know what Harvey Jenkins was up to. Not until she caught him red-handed, anyway. And that was the last she saw of him."

I nodded. That's exactly what had happened.

The explanation didn't really seem to satisfy Ana and Signor Fidardo, but they said no more about it. And after giving it some thought, Ana asked instead, "But how could Jenkins know about the necklace?"

"I've no idea," the Chief said. "And I'd love to have a chance to ask him."

"Is there any way of getting hold of him?" Signor Fidardo wondered.

The Chief and I exchanged glances and he said, "Well, the funfair left Lisbon and moved on a good six months ago. You can go a long way in that time. The fair might be anywhere in the whole of Europe by now. Or even farther afield. We are unlikely to see Harvey Jenkins again."

It was well into the night before we all separated and the Chief and I made our way back down to the harbour. The Chief was deep in thought.

"I wonder what the pearls could be worth," he said as we walked out along the quay below Alfama. "We might have had an absolute fortune right under our noses for all these years."

I nodded. The Chief sighed and went on, "From what I've heard, most finds of treasure tend to lead to trouble and misfortune. It would probably have been better for us if the necklace had been left undisturbed in its hiding place."

I nodded again, this time much more vigorously. Ever since I'd opened that chamois leather bag and seen the mysterious lustre of the big pearls, I'd had an unpleasant feeling in the pit of my stomach.

Pinctada Margaritifera

The Chief and I spent the following week shovelling coal at the big electricity power station out at Belém. From dawn to dusk we pushed loaded barrows of coal across the narrow landing stages linking the coal barges on the river to the railway trucks waiting on the quay. It was hard, dirty, dangerous work… but quite well-paid.

After our last day working there, we went to the bathhouse and scrubbed off the coal dust. Then we went on to the market hall and filled a basket with sausages, cheeses, vegetables for soup and newly baked bread. When you have money in your pocket, a visit to the market hall is a real treat!

That evening we invited our friends to come for dinner in the cabin of the *Hudson Queen*. After we had eaten, Signor Fidardo read out the report on the necklace he'd received from his friend Alvaro Gomez the day before. This is what the jeweller had written:

Dear Luigi,

This is one of the most magnificent pearl necklaces I have ever seen! There are forty-eight pearls in all and each of them weighs between thirty and thirty-two grains. That means we are dealing with unusually large pearls. And they almost certainly all come from the same species of oyster—Pinctada margaritifera—which are fished in the seas off the northern coast of Australia.

As you've already guessed, my dear Luigi, the pendant on the necklace was made in Great Britain. The silver hallmarks reveal that this first-class piece of craftsmanship was produced in Glasgow in 1904 at a jewellery firm by the name of Rombach & Rombach. According to the list of members of the international association of jewellers, that firm is still active today.

There can be no doubt that the necklace is extremely valuable. At auction in Paris, London or New York it is likely to bring in at least $20,000. And probably considerably more. In order to be able to dispose of it, however, a seller must have a bill of purchase, a letter of gift or a will that proves that he or she really is the rightful owner of the necklace. Without such a legal document, it will be impossible to sell the necklace. No buyer is going to take the risk of buying an item that could later be shown to belong to someone else—or even be stolen property.

Yours sincerely,

Alvaro Gomez

When Signor Fidardo finished reading, Ana looked disappointed.

"That's bad news, isn't it?" she said, looking from me to the Chief. "If Senhor Gomez is right, you won't be able to sell the necklace. And you really do need the money for the *Hudson Queen*, don't you?"

The Chief shrugged his shoulders. "That's the way of things," he said. "You can't sell what you don't own. And the pearls don't belong to us just because someone hid them aboard our ship at some point."

"Whether the necklace is yours or not is worth discussing," Signor Fidardo said. "But unless you have the necessary documentation it would be difficult to find a buyer. Unless…"

"Unless what?" Ana asked.

Signor Fidardo shrugged his shoulders apologetically and said, "It's not something I'd recommend… but, of course, you could take the necklace to pieces and sell the pearls individually. Then no one would ask where they came from."

The Chief shook his head. "A beautiful piece of jewellery like that shouldn't be broken up," he said. "It would be wrong to do so."

Ana and Signor Fidardo nodded in agreement and after a moment's silence around the table, Ana turned to the Chief and me.

"So what are the two of you going to do now? After all, you do have to do something with the necklace, don't you?"

"We should, perhaps, hand it in to the police," the Chief suggested. "And then they could look for the rightful owner."

"That is an extraordinarily bad idea," Signor Fidardo said. "If you do that the necklace will end up in their lost-property office and lie there until the end of time. Or until some thieving constable pinches it."

The Chief thought about this for a while and then said, "In that case we'll just have to find out for ourselves who owns the necklace. There doesn't seem to be any other choice… Do you think that jewellery firm in Glasgow may know something? Even though it's such a long time since they made the little rose?"

"It's not at all impossible," Signor Fidardo said. "A reputable company like Rombach & Rombach will have kept its records in order, even going back for many years."

The Chief gave a thoughtful nod. Then he looked at me and said, "You've never been to Glasgow, have you?"

I shook my head.

"I'm sure it's a city you'd like," the Chief said. "A bit rough in places, of course… but the people are good. And the port is one of the biggest in Europe… loads of things to look at."

"But Scotland's an awfully long way away," Ana said. "Do you really have to go so far? Wouldn't a letter to the jeweller be enough, along with a description of the necklace?"

The Chief gave this some thought before answering. "Mm, perhaps… But once in Glasgow we could also take the chance to find out who built the *Hudson Queen*. And that's likely to be of use, too."

"True enough," Ana said. "Both the ship and the pendant come from Glasgow… that's not likely to be a coincidence, is it?"

The Chief agreed with her. Then he turned to me. "What do you think, sailor?"

After thinking about it for a while, I gave him a thumbs up. It was a long time since I'd been to sea and, anyway, I was keen to see Glasgow.

~

It took the Chief and me a couple of weeks to save enough for a small travel fund. The skipper of the vessel next to the *Hudson Queen* on the quay promised to keep an eye on her while we were away. The time came to pack our kitbags and set off.

If you want to know what's going on in the port of Lisbon, the man to talk to is Senhor Baptista at the O Pelicano pub. On a misty October evening the Chief and I went there to enquire if there might be a ship about to sail from Lisbon to Scotland or England. We were hoping to sail with it.

Senhor Baptista served me a glass of milk and gave the Chief a dram. He tipped us off that there was a sailing barge called *Dora* that regularly sailed up along the coast with general cargo.

"Give the skipper my regards and I'm sure he'll take you as far as Vigo. Once there it should be easy to find a vessel that will take you over to Scotland."

The Chief talked to the skipper of the *Dora* that same afternoon and we were promised a place on board as long as we worked for our food and passage. The ship was due to leave in four days.

~

The evening before our departure was a Saturday. Like every other Saturday evening, the Chief, Signor Fidardo and I went to the Tamarind fado restaurant to listen to Ana singing to the accompaniment of the house orchestra. The place was so full that there were even people sitting outside the open windows, listening in the mild autumn night.

In the pause between two songs Signor Fidardo took out an envelope and passed it to the Chief. Written on the envelope in Signor Fidardo's neat handwriting were the words:

Dowager Lady Kilvaird
12 Park Terrace
Glasgow

Signor Fidardo explained. "It occurred to me yesterday that I do have an acquaintance in Glasgow. She's a collector of musical instruments and the widow of a rich Scottish lord called Kilvaird. Lady Kilvaird bought a lute and a viola from me for her collection. That's by the by, but the important thing is that Lady Kilvaird is a very gracious lady. And I do believe she'd have excellent contacts among the jewellers and silversmiths in Glasgow. Go to see her and give her this letter from me. I'm sure she'll do what she can to assist you with your enquiries."

"Thank you," the Chief said, putting the letter in his inside pocket. "You are really very thoughtful!"

By midnight the Chief and I were back on the *Hudson Queen* to get a few hours' sleep before it was time to report aboard the *Dora*. Ana's songs were still ringing in my ears. We were sad that we wouldn't be seeing her and Signor Fidardo for some time to come.

But, given a little luck, it shouldn't take the Chief and me too long to find the real owner of the necklace. We had several good lines of enquiry to follow and we should be back in Lisbon within a month or two.

That's what I thought then, anyway.

But things don't always turn out the way you think and hope they will.

And there are times when things turn out worse than anyone could have imagined.

PART TWO

SHETLAND JACK

Rombach & Rombach

The voyage to Vigo took a week. I spent my days doing maintenance work up in *Dora's* rigging. Equipped with a knife, my marlin spike and sail twine, I climbed around the rigging from morning to night. It was a thoroughly enjoyable voyage!

In Vigo we signed on with a Spanish tramp steamer which was about to depart for Glasgow. She was called the *Cangas* and covered the 870 nautical miles in less than three days.

Dusk was falling as we entered the mouth of the River Clyde and took on a pilot. The raw mist coming in from the Irish Sea grew denser as *Cangas* steamed slowly upriver towards Glasgow. The silhouettes of barges and dredgers passed us like ghosts in the darkness. The smell of coal smoke and mud stuck in our nostrils. Lisbon already felt very far away.

Just before midnight we drew alongside the quay in Prince's Dock. The lights of the city all round us lit the sky a strange flame-yellow colour.

The following morning, as soon as the cargo had been unloaded, the Chief and I thanked the crew of the *Cangas* for the voyage and went ashore. There was a weak hint of the pale autumn sun behind the filthy brown smoke that hung low over the shipyards, workshops and warehouses that lined the endless quays. The sounds of steam whistles and foghorns cut through the general hubbub. In the distance I could see one of the *Anchor Line*'s America liners moving away from the quayside. And at the same time a tug was towing a full-rigged windjammer into one of the docks ready for it to unload its cargo. It might have been wheat from Australia, or possibly tea from China.

The streets running up from the north bank of the river were lined with many small hotels and simple boarding houses. The Chief rented us a room on Cheapside Street. The landlady, a Mrs Grimes, was a kindly old lady. We left our kitbags in the room and jumped on a double-decker tram going to the city centre. Queues of cars and buses, windscreen wipers at work, jammed the streets. Streaks of dirty rainwater ran down the frontages of the grey and brown buildings we passed.

The Chief bought a city plan from a kiosk and we used it to start looking for the street called Argyll Arcade. According to the telephone directory, that was where the premises of Rombach & Rombach were.

Argyll Arcade turned out to be a covered arcade that cut through a whole block close to Glasgow Central Station. The glass roof of the arcade covered one jeweller's shop after another. Their display windows glistened and shone.

A bell pinged as the Chief opened the door of Rombach & Rombach Ltd. The shop was very small and dimly lit. Glass display cases filled with jewellery lined the walls from floor to ceiling. It was like stepping into a treasure house.

A small, bald-headed gentleman with a pot belly stood behind the counter. He had a silk cravat at his throat and an apron to protect his crisply ironed shirt. His eyebrows shot up at the sight of me and he turned to the Chief and said in a soft voice, "I'm sorry, sir... I don't wish to be discourteous, but may I ask you to leave your ape outside? It would be very unfortunate if it started climbing around in here."

"You need have no fears," the Chief said. "This is Sally Jones and she knows how to behave."

And to demonstrate how well-brought-up I was, I took off my cap and bowed.

The jeweller looked at me in astonishment. Then he smiled and nodded in return. "Right, then..." he said. "My name is Eli Rombach. How may I be of service?"

The Chief introduced himself and gave a brief account of the purpose of our visit. Then he produced the worn chamois leather bag he'd kept concealed under his shirt during our voyage.

Eli Rombach emptied the contents of the bag on the counter and studied the pearls and the pendant carefully through his jeweller's loupe. When he had finished, he said, "At Rombach & Rombach we usually take a morning cup of tea at about this time. I'd be more than happy for you to join my father and me."

Eli locked the shop and led us up a narrow staircase to the floor above, where Rombach & Rombach had their studio and workshop. An ancient little man was sitting at one of the two large workbenches hammering a sheet of silver into shape.

"This is Joshua Rombach, my father," Eli said. "He handed the firm over to me some fifteen years ago since he was getting on in years and starting to be forgetful and muddled. Unfortunately, he's got worse and worse and can't even remember his own name now. But his craftsmanship is still there, amazingly enough. His head may have forgotten, but his hands remember."

The old man carried on hammering, apparently unwilling to stop working. Eli showed me and the Chief into a small office, where he served us tea and shortbread before discussing the necklace.

"There can be no doubt the necklace was made in our workshop," Eli said. "But not by me. I hadn't started working for the firm in 1904. It's my father's work."

"Would it be possible to find out who ordered the piece from him?" the Chief asked. "Finding that out would be an enormous help."

Eli made an apologetic gesture.

"I'm sorry," he said. "Our archive was destroyed in a fire nearly ten years ago and all the old order books went up in flames."

We sat in silence for a while.

"Is there any other way to find out more about the necklace?" the Chief wondered. "Could we perhaps show it to your father?"

"That's likely to lead nowhere, unfortunately," Eli said. "Father lives in a world of his own. But we can, of course, try, if that's what you want."

The Chief asked several more questions, but Eli didn't know any more than he'd already told us. When we'd finished our tea, we got up to leave. Out in the workshop Joshua had finished hammering and was sitting absolutely still and staring straight ahead, his face expressionless.

Eli bent down in front of the old man. Not a gesture nor a movement suggested that Joshua was even aware that his son was there. Eli spoke gently and tried to attract his father's attention to the necklace. There was no reaction.

After a minute or two Eli gave up and rose to his feet.

"Just as I thought," he said, shrugging his shoulders apologetically.

"Thank you anyway," the Chief said.

Just at that moment a thought crossed my mind. What was it Eli had said about Joshua's memory?

His head may have forgotten, but his hands remember...

I gestured for them to pass me the necklace and Eli gave it to me. The old man's gnarled and twisted hands were resting on his knees and I carefully placed the pearls in them.

Nothing happened at first.

Then we noticed one thumb moving very slightly. One by one the old man's fingers began to move, and with slow and trembling movements they felt their way along the gleaming string of pearls until they came to the silver and mother-of-pearl rose.

The old man's face remained calm. And then, very suddenly, his bushy, white eyebrows tensed and furrowed.

"I've done a first-class piece of work!" he said, anger showing in his weak, rasping voice. *"A beautiful piece of work, sir! And your... your behaviour... you are not a decent human being! Simply not decent!"*

I leant in closer.

Joshua had fallen silent and his eyes were fixed in an empty stare. Then he shook his head and added in a quiet voice, *"Li Jing... you did warn me..."*

15

The Porcelain Girl

Eli was unable to explain what Joshua's words had meant. He gently tried to coax the old man to say more, but Joshua appeared neither to hear nor to see him.

"That name... Li Jing," the Chief said. "Have you heard it before?"

"No, never," Eli said. "It sounds Chinese..."

He looked thoughtful.

"I know there used to be a business in the port dealing in mother-of-pearl and semi-precious gemstones from China and Southeast Asia. The firm was called Shanghai Import or something of the sort. And I think Dad had some dealings with them. Their premises were somewhere along the river over in Govan. But I haven't heard anything of them for many, many years."

"Do you think Li Jing could be someone who worked for that firm?"

Eli shrugged his shoulders.

"I haven't any idea at all, I'm afraid."

~

We thanked Eli Rombach for his help and said goodbye. The rain had stopped at last, only to be replaced by a clammy, grey mist that had settled like a lid over the city.

I was wondering what we should do next, and the Chief was clearly thinking along the same lines.

"What do you think?" he asked. "Should we see if we can locate Shanghai Import?"

I nodded. Given that we still had a lead, we should certainly follow it up.

We took the subway train under the river and got off at Govan Cross station. The street was bustling with life. Trams, lorries and horse-drawn carts fought for space on the wide road. Street cleaners attempted to clear the horse dung from the setts, while singing barkers tried to tempt the people on the pavements to buy their soaps and boot laces. At the crossroads there were several young couples dancing to the music of a solitary mouth organ and the people who'd gathered around them were clapping in time to the music.

"Everyone in Glasgow can dance," the Chief said. "Dancing and fighting, you'll find the champions at both in this city!"

We started walking east past the rows of gloomy, stone tenements. This is where the shipyard workers and their families must live, I thought. On the other side of the street there were lead foundries, wood yards, mechanical workshops and heaps of coal. The air was thick with the smoke from factory chimneys, mixed with the muddy aroma of the river and the smell of tar and red paint from the shipyards.

The Chief stopped everyone we met and asked if they'd ever heard of someone called Li Jing or of a firm called Shanghai Import. The majority of people stopped and tried to be helpful. Now and then small groups of people gathered around and engaged in loud discussions about which companies had been where. In the end, however, no one was able to say with any certainty whether Shanghai Import had ever existed in Glasgow. And no one recognized the name Li Jing.

We were approaching the three wide bridges across the River Clyde in the middle of the city. Just before we reached the first bridge, we passed a big gang of noisy young men hanging around outside a billiard hall. Some of them seemed keen on having a fight, others were doing shady deals in the dark doorway. People were making small detours to avoid them.

In the midst of this gang of thugs, there was a young woman sitting on a pile of wooden crates. She was small and thin, with a pale face and big, blue eyes. She was wearing a lined white cape, a wide, ruffled skirt showing under it. She reminded me of one of those china dolls seen in toyshop windows. I noticed her eyes following the Chief and me as we passed on the other side of the street.

We hadn't walked more than twenty or so yards when we heard a light, slightly childlike, voice behind us.

"Hey you, mister! Stop where you are!"

The Chief and I turned round. There she was, the china girl.

With a serious look on her face, she pointed at me and said to the Chief, "I want your ape. It's cute. You can give it to me."

The Chief's eyebrows shot up, but then he laughed and said, "I can't do that."

"Why not?" the girl said.

"Because the ape isn't mine. Her name is Sally Jones and she is her own."

The girl's big blue eyes narrowed.

"From now on I'll be the one to decide what the ape's called," she snarled between her teeth. "Tell it to come here! To me!"

"Sorry, my friend," the Chief said, shaking his head in a good-natured way before nodding to me that we should move on.

Suddenly the girl was standing in our way. At the same time, she made a quick movement with her hand, as if shaking something out of her sleeve. The next moment there was a click as she flicked open the blade of a large cut-throat razor.

"Either the ape comes with me…" she said, holding the razor to the Chief's face, "or I'll slice off your nose and ears, old man!"

The Chief looked at her in astonishment. But then we were joined by a young man from the gang on the other side of the street.

"Cops!" he said to the girl, indicating two police constables plodding along the pavement a short distance away.

The girl swore quietly and closed her razor. Reluctantly she accompanied the young man back to the rest of the gang. Halfway across the street she turned and looked at me with her big blue eyes. I shuddered.

"Is there a problem here?" one of the constables asked when they came up to me and the Chief.

"No," the Chief said, with a sigh of relief. "But there probably would have been if you hadn't turned up."

The policemen looked across at the gang on the street corner.

"They call themselves the Kingston Kings," one of the policemen said. "One of the worst street gangs this side of the river. Avoid them if you can."

"Will do," the Chief said.

⌒

After crossing the river we walked on with no particular plan in mind apart from finding somewhere to eat. After a while we came to a large market hall called Bridgegate Fishmarket.

The Chief had obviously been there before. His face broke into a big grin and he said, "Let's take a look in here. You'll really like it."

I wondered what was supposed to be so enjoyable about a fish market. But no sooner had we gone through the tall doorway than I understood what the Chief meant.

When you go to sea you inevitably hear a lot of swearwords and during my years at sea I've learnt a whole string of them. During the time the Chief and I spent wandering round the noisy crowd in the fish market I learnt at least twice that number. And pretty good swearwords they were, too!

"Scottish fish merchants are in a class of their own when it comes to swearing," the Chief said, his voice full of admiration.

And I had no reason to disagree with him.

~

There was a nice little pub near the fish market. The Chief took a portion of fried haddock and I had boiled cauliflower. Afterwards we strolled back to our boarding house. My legs were aching from walking all day.

"Hello there!" Mrs Grimes called as we passed the door to her small office. "I've got something for you!"

With a struggle our landlady rose from her worn armchair and handed the Chief an envelope. It had both the Chief's name and my name written on it.

"Who can this be from?" the Chief wondered in surprise.

"I have no idea at all, pet," Mrs Grimes said.

"But who delivered it?"

Mrs Grimes looked a little shamefaced. "I suppose I must have dozed off a while. My old armchair is so comfortable, you know. And all of a sudden the envelope was just there on the table."

The Chief gave an understanding smile and then slit open the envelope with his pocket knife. It contained nothing but a plain white card. After reading it, he passed it to me, a look of confusion on his face.

The text was written in an old person's shaky hand:

Caledonian Railway departure 18.15
from Glasgow Central, Platform 14.
5 Albert Road, Gourock.
Li Jing will be expecting you.

Li Jing

It was already growing dark when the Chief and I left the train at the small coastal town of Gourock. Outside the station a lamplighter was lighting the streetlamps and he told us the way to Albert Road. We turned up our collars and started walking south along the shore. We passed the pier, where an elegant paddle steamer was preparing to depart for the towns on the other side of the firth. Thick, black smoke was pouring from its two funnels but was quickly dispersed by the strong westerly wind.

The darkness of night was coming on quickly. I felt a tremor of excitement. *Who was Li Jing actually?* And how on earth had they discovered that we were looking for them?

By the time we reached 5 Albert Road both the Chief and I were thoroughly soaked by the flying foam and splashing waves. A warm light was showing in the windows and when the Chief knocked on the door it was opened by a stout woman with rosy cheeks. She didn't seem in the least surprised to see a large ape standing there in the darkness.

"Come away in," she said welcomingly. "Come away in, for heaven's sake! I am Mrs Brentwood, Li Jing's housekeeper. Let me get you some towels. My goodness, what weather!"

Once we'd dried off, Mrs Brentwood led us upstairs and through a room furnished with a sofa, a small desk and over-flowing bookshelves.

Open double doors gave on to a glass veranda full of plants. The rich foliage was illuminated by a single lamp with a rice-paper shade, hanging from the branch of a palm tree. Below the lamp stood a table with three cups and a plate of cakes. An ancient little woman in a wheelchair was sitting at the table.

"Do sit down," she said in a friendly voice, peering at us through thick spectacles. "I'm Li Jing, and you two must be Henry Koskela and Sally Jones. I've heard of the two of you before. I've spent the whole of my life in various seaports round the world, you know."

While Mrs Brentwood was pouring the tea, the Chief and I looked around. In daylight, the view across the firth must be astounding, though little could be seen through the rain-streaked windows just now.

"This is very cosy," the Chief said appreciatively. And I agreed with him. It felt a bit like sitting up in the crown of a tree. Budgerigars and parrots had settled for the night in the dense foliage under the roof of the veranda.

Li Jing smiled, her eyes becoming narrow slits behind her thick glasses.

"It is, isn't it?" she said. "I like it here. Mrs Brentwood helps me with my day-to-day needs and if I want anything dealt with in Glasgow I ring my old friend Mr Cheng. He's the superintendent at the Chinese seamen's home in Govan. It was Mr Cheng who told me that a sailor accompanied by a large ape was going round the port asking for anyone of my name. Naturally I was curious and asked him to find out where you were living and invite you here. So here you are... Now tell me how I can help you."

Instead of answering, the Chief took out the chamois leather bag, opened it and put the necklace on the table. The old woman leant forward to see it better. Her eyes widened and she picked up the rose pendant and examined it carefully.

"I never ever thought I'd see this necklace," she said quietly.

She looked up at the Chief. There was a sharp glint in her eyes now.

"Where did you get it from?"

"We found it. It was hidden on our ship."

"Your ship?... What's the name of your ship?"

"*Hudson Queen*," the Chief answered.

Li Jing's eyebrows creased in thought.

"That's not a name I recognize… Describe her to me. What sort of ship is she?"

"She's a Clyde Puffer," the Chief said.

The old woman leant back in her wheelchair. Then she asked, "Who was it who told you about me?"

The Chief told her about our visit to Rombach & Rombach.

"Joshua is still alive then," Li Jing said, a touch of melancholy in her voice. "It's many, many years since I last met him."

She sank back in her own thoughts for a while. Then she said, "You'll be wondering, of course, who hid the necklace on your ship?"

Both the Chief and I nodded.

"It was Shetland Jack," Li Jing said.

The Chief and I looked at one another. Neither of us had heard that name before. We waited for Li Jing to continue, but she didn't. She just sat there, staring into space. Her furrowed face trembled slightly, lost in thought.

"Shetland Jack?" the Chief tried… "Who is he? Is he still alive?"

Li Jing turned to him. "What? Is Jack still alive? Perhaps… Perhaps not. The business of him disappearing was so strange. And all the blood…"

The Chief and I looked at the old woman.

"Oh, you must forgive me," she said. "I'll have to start from the beginning, of course."

Li Jing reached into a pocket on the side of her wheelchair and took out a long clay pipe and a pouch of tobacco. She filled the pipe with black shag, lit it and puffed to get it going.

Coils of blue smoke rose through the foliage as Li Jing started telling us the story of the man known as Shetland Jack.

Thursday Island

"I first met Jack almost forty years ago," Li Jing said. "I was working as a commercial traveller for a company in Shanghai. They sent me to Australia to buy mother-of-pearl and that's how I ended up on Thursday Island. Perhaps you know of the island?"

"I do," the Chief said. "It's a pearl-fishing harbour in Australia, isn't it?"

"That's right," Li Jing said before continuing. "At that time most of the pearl-fishing boats on the north coast of Australia used Thursday Island as their home port. Whenever the weather permitted, the whole fleet weighed anchor to go and harvest pearl oysters. Hundreds of billowing white sails could be seen dancing across the sun-kissed waves of the Pacific. What a sight that was! We buyers would be waiting back at the harbour when the boats returned, their holds laden with mother-of-pearl. And then you'd hear bargaining and arguing in every language known to man."

Li Jing smiled at the memory.

"Do you know anything about pearl fishing, Mr Koskela?" she asked. "Have you ever done any yourself?"

"No," the Chief said, "but I've heard it's a pretty dangerous activity."

"How true, how true," Li Jing said. "Divers often have accidents. And when the fishing fleet returns to port after a storm there is nearly always a vessel missing. Searching for survivors is useless—the sharks will already have seen to that."

Li Jing puffed on her pipe and then said, "That's why ordinary seamen don't go to Thursday Island. Only fanatical fortune hunters prepared to risk their necks to get rich. You won't get rich by fishing for oysters and selling mother-of-pearl, but if you open enough oysters sooner or later you'll find a pearl. And if the pearl is flawless and large, your fortune is made. On Thursday Island everyone dreamt of pearls. But no one was as obsessed as Shetland Jack."

A gull swooped past out in the darkness and Li Jing looked up. Then she turned back to us and continued her story.

"I'd already been on Thursday Island for a couple of years when I heard talk of a young Scottish lad who'd just arrived there. His name was Jack Shaw, but since it was obvious from his dialect that he came from the Shetland Islands, everyone called him Shetland Jack.

"Jack was a taciturn, reclusive sort of fellow who didn't feel the need to make friends. So he was often talked about behind his back. Rumour had it that Jack came from a place called Scalloway on the west coast of Shetland and he'd been engaged to a girl called Mary Henderson. When Mary became pregnant, the whole community assumed Jack would accept the responsibility and marry her. Instead, however, Jack had signed on with a sailing ship bound for Australia. He had no desire to father a family: his aim was to get rich.

"The people on Thursday Island may not have considered Jack a good man, but no one could deny he was a good seaman. After less than a couple of weeks he got a job as mate on the *Oeila*, a pearl-fishing boat. One night shortly afterwards, the *Oeila* was hit by a thunderstorm out in the Java Sea. The captain, a Dane by the name of Lauridsen, and three of the crew were washed overboard and disappeared. Jack was the only survivor left aboard and, in spite of a shattered mizzen mast and the cargo having moved, he managed to sail the *Oeila* back to Thursday Island singlehanded."

Li Jing began to cough and had to put down her pipe. Then she continued her story.

"Captain Lauridsen's death was announced some weeks later and that very afternoon Shetland Jack paid a visit to his widow. He wanted to buy the *Oeila*. The poor woman was almost out of her mind with grief, in addition to which she knew nothing about boats nor about business. Jack took advantage of that and got her to sign a contract of sale which gave him the *Oeila* for a paltry sum."

"That wasn't very nice," the Chief said.

"No, not very nice at all. Many of the people on the island wondered whether Shetland Jack had actually thrown Lauridsen overboard himself in order to be able to buy the *Oeila* for next to nothing. But there was no proof and Jack himself didn't give a damn what people said about him behind his back."

Li Jing drew her cardigan around herself and said, "Let's warm ourselves up with more tea. Would one of you mind going and putting the kettle on down in the kitchen? And please bring me a warm rug at the same time."

The wind was still howling and rain was hammering on the glass, but the teapot was soon on the table and Li Jing had a rug over her knees. She carried on with her tale:

"Jack was now captain of the *Oeila* and he sailed her farther and farther from Thursday Island in his search for new and undiscovered oyster beds. The ship disappeared for weeks on end among the wild islands between Celebes and New Guinea. There were times when people assumed that Jack had been sunk by a typhoon or killed by pirates, but he always returned, his hold full of gleaming mother-of-pearl and with one or two pearls of excellent quality. He would sell the mother-of-pearl, but never the pearls."

Li Jing picked up the chamois leather bag that was on the table.

"Shetland Jack kept his pearls in this bag," she said. "He used to have it hanging inside his shirt, close to his heart. And to warn thieves to keep away, he always carried a big, ugly revolver stuck in the waistband of his trousers."

Li Jing put the bag back on the table.

"Anyone collecting pearls is usually doing so to collect enough for a necklace," she said. "And that was what Shetland Jack was doing. According to island gossip, Jack had received a telegram from Scalloway telling him that Mary Henderson had given birth to a child—a girl. And she'd been given the name Rose.

"Of course, the news couldn't have come as a surprise to Jack, but he found it profoundly moving. He couldn't stop thinking about the fact that he had a daughter, which is why he decided to collect pearls for a necklace. A necklace he would give to Rose.

"But Jack Shaw didn't have an ordinary pearl necklace in mind. Only the biggest and most beautiful pearls were good enough for his little girl. Really fine pearls are rare, though, and Jack realized it would take him many years to gather a treasure of that kind. So he decided that the necklace was to be his present to Rose on her fifteenth birthday."

~

The navigation lights of a ship out in the firth were just visible through the rain and mist. Li Jing leant back in her wheelchair and went back to her story:

"After five years on Thursday Island the firm I worked for re-located me and I left Australia and moved to London. A couple of years later I resigned and moved up to Glasgow to start my own small business. I imported mother-of-pearl and dealt in precious stones. Business was good. Most of the jewellers in the city bought their mother-of-pearl from me. And Joshua Rombach was one of my best customers."

Thinking of the jeweller obviously made Li Jing sad and her eyes were full of sorrow as she stared into the night.

"Joshua was a lovely man," she said. "When we met to do business, we always made time for a game of chess and on one of those occasions he told me about a seaman who'd come into his shop in Argyll Arcade the day before. The seaman had just returned to Scotland after many years as a pearl fisher in Australia. He'd brought in the most incredible collection of pearls Joshua had ever seen and asked Joshua to create a necklace with the pearls. The pendant attached to the necklace was to be a rose made of silver and mother-of-pearl."

Li Jing looked at us over the rim of her glasses.

"This was over ten years after I'd left Thursday Island, but I remembered Shetland Jack all right and realized that he was the seaman. So I told Joshua what I knew about Jack. 'Joshua,' I said, 'Jack Shaw is a hard man to do business with. Be on your guard.'"

Li Jing gave a little mirthless laugh.

"Joshua didn't take my warning sufficiently seriously," she said. "And the next time we met he was very upset. Jack had come to collect the finished necklace and he was no longer prepared to pay the sum they'd agreed. He claimed the pendant was not well-made. Now that was something Joshua wasn't used to hearing: he set great store by always producing first-class pieces. Eventually they did agree on a price, but not before some harsh words had been exchanged."

The Chief and I caught each other's eye. We understood now why Joshua had reacted in the way he did when his hands recognized the silver and mother-of-pearl rose.

We heard three long blasts on a foghorn ring out in the night. A paddle steamer was coming alongside the Gourock pier.

"Put the kettle back on the stove," Li Jing said. "I need coffee. You haven't heard the end of this story yet."

The Mystery of SS *Rose*

With the coffee on the table, Li Jing returned to her story.

"Time passed and I heard no more of Shetland Jack. But then, after a good number of years, something unexpected happened. It was in the February of 1910, if I remember rightly. I was walking over by Govan Graving Docks when I saw a man staggering along through the slush. The clothes he was wearing were far too thin and his shoes looked wet through. Whenever he met someone he'd say in a monotonous voice, 'I'm looking for Rose Henderson from Shetland. Has anyone seen her around here?'

"When I caught up with him he asked me the same question and I immediately recognized him. 'Captain Shaw!' I said. 'My name is Li Jing. We were on Thursday Island at the same time.'"

Li Jing gave a heavy sigh.

"Jack Shaw hadn't aged well. He looked careworn, with hollow cheeks and a tangled beard. His breath stank of rotten teeth and cheap whisky. His speech was slurred as he told me he had no idea who I was and nor did he want to know. Before he disappeared I decided to follow him."

Li Jing rubbed some flakes of tobacco between her fingers and filled her pipe before continuing.

"Jack rambled round the streets and seemed not to be going anywhere in particular. He came to a halt now and again to take a swig from his bottle and he stopped every passer-by with the same futile question: 'I'm looking for Rose Henderson from Shetland. Has anyone seen her around here?'

"He got no response, apart from abuse and sneers. Many people kept their distance, in the same way as people go out of their way to avoid lunatics or anyone who looks as if they have a contagious disease.

"Eventually we reached Kingston Dock and Jack steered a course for a Clyde Puffer moored close to a warehouse. The name of the vessel and its home port was visible on her stern: SS *Rose* of Glasgow."

Li Jing broke off to light her pipe.

"It was obvious that Jack meant to go aboard. But he'd gone no more than a yard or so out on the icy gangway when he slipped and very nearly fell in the water. There he was, hanging limply onto the handrail of the gangway, and I couldn't just leave him there, could I? So I hurried over to give him a hand.

At that very moment a door opened and a man in a filthy boilersuit looked out.

"'Dear Lord...' he said. 'The old fellow's hit the bottle again.'

"Between the two of us, the engineer and I managed to get Jack back to his feet and down below decks in the warm. Once Jack was snoring loudly in his bunk, the engineer asked whether he could offer me a cup of tea as a thank-you for the trouble I'd taken. He was a nice man by the name of Reeves. We drank our tea by the stove in the galley and I told him that I'd known Captain Shaw years before.

"'In that case you'll know the story of his pearl necklace,' Reeves said.

"I told him that I did. And I also said I knew Jack had a daughter to whom he'd been intending to give the precious necklace. Though I didn't know how that had turned out.

"'Well, I'll tell you,' Reeves said, 'if you have time to stay for a while, that is.'

"I stayed, of course. And as the snow fell thicker and thicker outside the galley portholes, I heard how Shetland Jack's life story had unfolded."

~

Li Jing's pipe had gone out while she was talking. She lit it, took a couple of puffs and then went on to tell us what she'd heard from Mr Reeves during that winter night twenty years before.

"Jack's return to the Shetlands had not been anything like he'd imagined. No one in Scalloway, his home village, wanted anything to do with him. The local people couldn't forgive him for deserting his pregnant fiancée and running off to Australia sixteen years earlier. After the birth of her child, Mary Henderson had to take a job at a fish gutting plant in Lerwick in order to support herself and little Rose. The work was hard and one winter Mary was taken ill with pneumonia. It was the death of her. Her daughter Rose was only four years old and since there was no one willing or able to care for the child, she was sent to an orphanage."

Li Jing refilled her pipe and continued.

"As soon as Jack heard this, he set off at once and went to the orphanage to fetch his daughter. But he was too late. Rose was no longer living there. According to the regulations of the orphanage, on her fifteenth birthday, which had been a few months earlier, she'd had to leave."

Li Jing fell silent, sunk in thought.

Eventually the Chief asked, "And where did the girl go?"

"No one knew," Li Jing answered. "Jack Shaw began travelling far and wide hunting for Rose. He advertised in the papers, both Scottish and English, but to no avail. Rose Henderson had vanished. After some time Jack realized he would need to make money to continue his search, so he used his savings to have a Clyde Puffer built. He named the ship *Rose*, of course! He hired an engineer and they began carrying goods between all the ports of Great Britain and Ireland. At every port where the SS *Rose* put in, Captain Jack went ashore and searched for his daughter. And everyone he met was greeted with the same question: 'I'm looking for Rose Henderson from Shetland. Has anyone seen her around here?' He'd been looking for his Rose for six long years by the time I came across him that winter night in Govan."

No one said anything for a while.

Then the Chief asked, "The necklace? Did he have the necklace with him on all his travels?"

Li Jing nodded. "Well, that's what Reeves thought, anyway. He told me that the SS *Rose* had been broken into several times during those years. That's hardly strange—in every port in Britain there were thieves who'd heard of the priceless necklace. Jack still lived with that big, ugly revolver stuck in the waistband of his trousers in case anyone should try to force him to reveal where he had hidden the treasure."

Li Jing's pipe had gone out again and she placed it on the table.

"So what happened to Jack Shaw after that?" the Chief asked. "You said something about him having vanished, didn't you?"

Li Jing nodded. "I'm coming to that, my friend. But first, would one of you go down to the kitchen and fetch me a glass of water? And if you're hungry, help yourselves to some cakes from the larder."

~

When all three of us were sitting around the table again, Li Jing took up her story.

"I never met Shetland Jack again after the evening I talked to Mr Reeves in the galley of SS *Rose*. But several years later I came across an article about him in the newspaper. It said that his ship had been found deserted and moored in an out-of-the-way corner of Glasgow docks. There was no sign of either Jack Shaw nor Mr Reeves, the ship's engineer. The police had searched the vessel for the famous necklace and failed to find it, but they had found blood on the deck. Some people believed that Jack and Mr Reeves had been murdered in the course of a robbery. Others suggested Mr Reeves might have murdered Jack and escaped with his pearls. Nothing could be proved. And as far as I know, neither Shetland Jack nor Mr Reeves have been seen since. Even after all these years, the case remains unsolved."

Li Jing suddenly seemed very tired. The rain outside had stopped and the wind was beginning to abate.

The Chief said, "And the *Rose* later became our very own *Hudson Queen*."

Li Jing nodded. "Yes, I guessed that when you told me she's a Clyde Puffer. When did you buy her? And where?"

"About ten years ago," the Chief said. "In New York."

"That rings a bell," Li Jing said. "I read somewhere that SS *Rose* was eventually sold to America since none of the ship-owners in Great Britain wanted anything to do with such an unlucky vessel. Tell me now, where did you find the hidden necklace?"

"It was hidden in the ship's wheel. In a secret compartment behind a brass plate."

Li Jing gave a faint smile.

"Think of it… In that way Jack was able to have the pearls at hand every time he stood at the wheel. Those pearls were his life, and I've no doubt they were his death, too."

We sat in silence for some time.

Then Li Jing said, "I don't believe it was the engineer, Mr Reeves, who killed him. I met Mr Reeves and I thought he seemed nice. Maybe a little strange, though."

"In what sort of way?" the Chief asked.

Li Jing smiled, "Well, he kept a small flock of chickens in the engine room."

"That's not so unusual on ships," the Chief said.

Li Jing nodded in agreement, "Yes, I know that. But what was strange, was that Mr Reeves let a cockerel chick live in his pocket, as a pet. I think it was out of sympathy as the little cockerel was blind and the rest of the flock would probably have pecked it to death otherwise."

The Detective

The new day was dawning as we said goodbye to Li Jing and thanked her for her help.

"Be careful now," she said in an earnest tone while first squeezing the Chief's hand and then mine. "Pearls and precious stones have a strange power over human beings. The more beautiful a piece is, the more tragic and grim its history tends to be. You two have become part of the story of Shetland Jack's pearl necklace and that story does not seem to be over yet. Let me know how things go."

We promised to do so.

～

The Chief and I managed to catch the first morning train to Glasgow, and once we were sitting in an empty compartment, the Chief said, "Cockerels can live more than twenty years, or so I've heard."

I knew what he was thinking and I nodded. It looked as if Reeves and Harvey Jenkins were one and the same. That would explain why Jenkins had known there were pearls hidden aboard the *Hudson Queen*. He knew our ship, of course, because he'd been the engineer when she was still SS *Rose*.

I suddenly remembered something Harvey Jenkins had said to Margosha: *The past has returned and I've been given a second chance.*

I could guess now what he meant. When Jenkins came across the *Hudson Queen* in Lisbon, it gave him a second chance to hunt for Shetland Jack's pearls.

The Chief's eyes darkened. "So maybe it was Jenkins who killed Captain Shaw after all. Why else would he change his name and avoid the police for all these years?"

I didn't have an answer to that, but I felt a shudder run down my spine.

~

When we left the train at Glasgow Central neither the Chief nor I were sleepy and so, instead of walking back to our boarding house, we went into the warmth of the station café. We each ordered a cup of tea and watched the street coming to life on the other side of the café window.

When the hands on the big station clock showed half-past

six, the café started serving breakfast. The Chief and I treated ourselves to generous helpings of omelette and toast and more tea.

"What to do now? About the necklace, I mean?" the Chief said between two mouthfuls. "We're not likely to find Jack Shaw. And if he was still alive, he'd surely have located his old ship long ago and taken the necklace from the ship's wheel."

I nodded.

"And Rose Henderson?" the Chief continued looking thoughtful. "If the necklace belongs to anyone, it belongs to her. But how are we to find the girl when Jack couldn't?"

I pondered the question but couldn't come up with an answer.

"Hardly a girl any longer, of course—Rose must be close to forty by now… if she's still alive."

We finished our breakfast and left the café. The low autumn sun was shining in an almost cloudless sky and we decided to go for a walk. We had no plan in mind so it was pure chance that led us to a street called Gibson Street. The Chief came to an abrupt halt and looked up at a small enamel plaque attached to the wall of one of the houses.

HUMPHREY W. FILLINGSWORTH P.I.
Offers all types of detective work—
tracing missing persons, trailing, surveillance etc.
First-class Service, Reasonable Prices
Discretion Guaranteed.

"A detective," the Chief said hesitantly. "Someone who can trace missing persons..."

He looked at me. "Perhaps he could help us locate Rose Henderson?"

I shrugged my shoulders. I knew nothing at all about detectives.

"We might as well enquire, anyway," the Chief said, ringing the doorbell.

The detective's office was upstairs. The young man who opened the door was wearing a three-piece tweed suit and a bow tie. Two bright red spots flared on his pale cheeks at the sight of me.

"Are you from a zoo?" he asked, sounding rather unsettled. "Or a circus? It's not about an escaped animal, is it?"

"Not at all," the Chief answered. "We're looking for a missing person."

The detective breathed out and then shook hands with the Chief.

"I apologize for sounding so brusque," he said. "You'll understand when I tell you that I had a case of an escaped goat in Ruchill Park a couple of weeks ago. I ended up badly gored and got a hole in my new trousers! That's why I'm determined not to accept cases of that sort. Sorry for chattering, come in, come in!"

The detective's office was small and very tidy. Apart from the desk and two chairs for clients, it contained a filing cabinet and a shelf full of books on police work and the technicalities of crime. On the desk lay a neat row of freshly sharpened pencils and a set of handcuffs—the latter looking as if they'd never been used.

The Chief explained our visit and Mr Fillingsworth made notes in a small black notebook.

"So you want me to help you find this woman Rose Henderson," the detective said. "Why are you trying to get hold of her, if you don't mind me asking?"

The Chief thought for a moment and then said, "We own a ship which belonged to Rose Henderson's father at one time. We've found something on board that we think she should have. A memory of her father, so to speak."

"I see, I see..." the detective said, busily taking notes. "And this whatever it is you've found is valuable, is it?"

The Chief's eyebrows went up.

"How do you mean?" he asked.

"Well," Mr Fillingsworth said, "as a detective one is often given the task of locating a specific individual. It usually involves chasing up a debt or issuing a summons to court, and in those cases locating the individual concerned can be extremely difficult. But if one is dealing with a win on the horses or a substantial inheritance from an unknown relative, well, it all becomes very much easier."

"Fancy that!" the Chief said with a slight smile.

The detective continued in a serious tone: "And that is why it would help if I knew whether you want to find Rose Henderson to give her something she would like. It would increase my chances of finding her."

The Chief paused in thought before answering.

"Yes," he said. "We do have something valuable to give Rose Henderson."

When we went back out onto Gibson Street, clouds were covering the sun. A rising wind from the south hinted at another low-pressure area moving in from the Irish Sea. It would soon be raining.

Lord Kilvaird

Employing a detective does not come cheap and the Chief and I had only been able to afford a week of Mr Fillingsworth's time, despite the fact that he'd given us a small discount and also promised to pick up the cost of putting a missing person notice in the *Glasgow Herald*. Presumably, then, he thought our case was interesting, or more interesting than hunting for runaway goats.

We now had a week to wait and only a few shillings left in our purse. We'd have to try to get a job at the docks to earn some money.

"But what are we to do with the necklace in the meantime?" the Chief wondered. "I can't carry it with me while I'm shovelling coal, or doing whatever the job may be."

It was a problem, of course, but the Chief himself came up with the solution. Digging deep in the inside pocket of his jacket he produced the letter Signor Fidardo had given us in case we needed help with anything in Glasgow.

"We can maybe ask Lady Kilvaird to look after the necklace for a while?" the Chief said.

I nodded. It seemed a good idea.

⁓

With the help of our street map of Glasgow we found our way to the Park district which, as the name suggests, is situated next to a large park in the middle of the city. The Chief had been in Glasgow many times before, but this district was new to him. Grand, four-storey houses with bay windows, stucco ornamentation and small, elegant balconies over the park lined the empty streets. Rows of gleaming motor cars, some of them Rolls-Royces and Bentleys, were parked along the pavements.

A doorman wearing a long, red woollen coat and an air of superiority was stationed at the entrance to 12 Park Terrace. The Chief handed him the letter of introduction from Signor Fidardo and after a brief hesitation the doorman let us pass.

The tall double doors gave onto a large hall with a polished marble floor and a chandelier on the ceiling. A concierge in white gloves and a black dress suit stood waiting behind the wide mahogany desk and the Chief showed him the letter.

"Ah yes…" the concierge said. "I'm sorry to say that Lady Kilvaird is not here."

The Chief's shoulders sank. "Oh dear," he said. "When will she be back?"

"I'm afraid I can't discuss Lady Kilvaird's programme with *you*," the concierge answered snootily. "I can, however, enquire if Lord Kilvaird—her son, that is—will receive you."

We had to wait for a quarter of an hour before the bell on the lift pinged and a young man stepped out into the hall. Dressed in a suit, with an elegant silk scarf at his throat, he had a friendly face and laughter lines at the corners of his eyes.

The man looked at me with a mixture of surprise and amusement before turning to the Chief and saying, "Let me guess now... You came to try to sell your ape to my mother?"

The Chief answered by passing him the letter from Signor Fidardo. He read it and then smiled apologetically.

"Forgive me, my dear fellow. I beg your pardon most sincerely," he said offering his hand to the Chief. "My dear mother buys so many unusual things, you know. I'm Lord Kilvaird, her son. Mama is away for a few days, but perhaps I can help you in some way? Does it perhaps have anything to do with the necklace mentioned in the letter?"

The Chief took out the chamois leather bag containing the pearls and explained how it came to be that we needed somewhere safe to keep the pearls for a time.

Lord Kilvaird smiled again and gave the Chief a friendly pat on the shoulder.

"I know exactly what you mean, old chap," he said as he put the bag of pearls in the pocket of his jacket. "One can't be too careful in this city. I shall lock the necklace in mother's safe and all you have to do is come here when you want it back."

~

The Broomielaw is the name of a long quay running along the northern shore of the River Clyde. It's full of life, bustle and a never-ending stream of ships either tying up or casting off. From dawn to dusk there are vessels loading or unloading cargo to and from the storehouses. Crowds of dockers, seamen and customs officials mingle with the ordinary citizens waiting to board one or other of the paddle steamers that traffic the river.

There's a pub on the Broomielaw called the Cross Keys Tavern and that's where the gangers go in the morning to hire any labour they need. By dawn the Cross Keys Tavern is already full of unemployed men, some of whom are chosen by the ganger, some not. At times this leads to arguments and fistfights about a job.

During the following week the Chief and I went to the Cross Keys Tavern early every morning. We were sometimes lucky enough to get a day's work, and sometimes not. But at least we were earning enough to afford our rent at Mrs Grimes's house.

After a week had passed we returned to Gibson Street to meet our detective. We were excited. Had he found Rose Henderson or not? We knew he had at least been trying because we'd seen the notice about Rose he'd put in the Missing Persons column in the *Glasgow Herald*.

We arrived at Mr Fillingsworth's door five minutes before our agreed time. Just as the Chief was about to ring the doorbell, the door of a taxi parked by the pavement opened and a man in a crumpled suit stepped out on the passenger side.

He raised his hat and said, "Excuse me, if I'm not mistaken you must be Henry Koskela?"

The Chief turned round. "I am," he said. "Who is asking?"

The man gave a friendly smile and moved towards us. He had sad eyes and smelled of cheap aftershave.

"My name is Mortimer Gordon," he said, holding out his hand. "Just call me Gordon—everyone does. I'm a close friend of old Humph… Humphrey Fillingsworth, I mean. He asked me to come and fetch you."

"Fetch us? But why?" the Chief said as he shook hands with the man who wanted to be called Gordon.

"To be honest with you, I don't know," Gordon said. "Humph never says anything about his cases, but he's obviously come

171

across someone he wants you to meet. He didn't have time to fetch you himself, so he sent me."

"I see… That's kind of you," the Chief said. "But where are we going?"

"A place in Oswald Street. It'll only take a few minutes."

The Chief and I briefly exchanged glances. This certainly sounded promising. We climbed into the back seat of the taxi, Gordon sat by the driver and we set off.

The House in Oswald Street

The taxi driver took us cautiously and safely through the bad-tempered rush of lunchtime traffic. Just before reaching Central Station, he turned into a side street running down to the river and drew up outside the last house in the street.

Gordon paid the taxi driver and we climbed out. We were standing in front of a gloomy looking building, every window with drawn curtains. The street level was a junk shop with all sorts of odds and sods in its dirty window. The sign over the door said *Oswald Street Antiques*.

There was a heavy iron double gate in the wall beside the building. Gordon produced a key and opened it.

"Who lives here?" the Chief asked, a touch of suspicion in his voice.

Gordon clucked. "I can understand why you're wondering," he said. "This is scarcely the most elegant part of Glasgow."

Gordon opened the heavy gate to let us in.

"Do come in, please," he said. "Old Humph will explain the rest."

The gateway led into a backyard surrounded by high brick walls, the plaster flaking off them. All of a sudden, the ground began shaking—a train was on its way into Central Station. The building was wall to wall with the station.

An open-backed lorry was parked in front of a row of ramshackle warehouses. A bruiser of a man was sweeping the yard. He stared at us wide-eyed as we walked past.

Gordon directed us up a narrow set of outside steps and into a battered stairwell. Three floors up we reached a carpeted corridor. There was a slightly stale smell.

Gordon knocked twice on the door at the end of the corridor and, before opening it, waited until a small light on the wall came on.

"In we go," he said, letting the Chief and me go in first.

The room we entered was very large and panelled with dark wood. Tall windows covered with thin curtains allowed in some weak daylight. I could hear the hum of traffic and voices from the street outside.

At one end of the room there was a counter and a number of leather armchairs. At the other end there was a woman sitting behind a large desk. She was talking on the telephone and she gestured to us to stay where we were.

"Who's she?" the Chief asked. "And where's the detective?"

"Patience, my friend," Gordon said. "You'll soon find out."

The woman finished her call, put down the receiver and waved us over.

"Welcome, Mr Koskela," she said. "Thanks for coming. Do sit down."

The woman was neither young nor old, but somewhere between the two. Her skin was very pale and her curly hair was the same deep reddish-brown shade as the mahogany desk. She was wearing a severe, well-cut tweed suit.

"Thank you, ma'am, but I'd prefer to stand," the Chief said. "We've come to meet Mr Fillingsworth."

The woman made a dismissive gesture. "Forget about him, Mr Koskela. He's no longer needed."

The Chief's eyebrows shot up. "What do you mean?"

"What I said, of course," the woman replied. "You engaged Mr Fillingsworth to find me. That's what he's done. And now I've had you brought here so we can meet. The detective has done his bit and we can forget him now."

The Chief looked confused. "What do you mean? Are you—"

"Exactly!" the woman interrupted him. "I am the rightful owner of the pearl necklace you found on your ship. And I'm very grateful to you for taking the trouble to seek me out. Do you have the necklace with you?"

The Chief was at a loss for an answer and I, too, was flabbergasted. *How could this woman know that it was a pearl necklace we had found on our ship?* The Chief had never mentioned a necklace to Mr Fillingsworth.

"Well," the woman repeated, "have you got the necklace with you?"

"Are you Rose Henderson?" the Chief asked.

The woman smiled, but it was a smile without warmth.

"My name is irrelevant," she said. "The pearl necklace is mine and that's all you need to know. I've already had your room at the boarding house searched, so I know you haven't hidden it there. My guess is that you carry it around with you. Be sensible now and give it to me."

The Chief was open-mouthed with astonishment. Then he laughed.

"What are you saying? That you broke into our room?…"

"Not at all," the woman answered. "Your landlady was asleep in her chair, so all my men did was borrow her keys for a while."

The woman fixed her eyes on the Chief and added, "Of course, if the woman had tried to prevent them, things might have gone badly for her. Just as badly as they'll go for you if you don't do what I say."

The tone of her voice had suddenly become cold and hard.

The Chief seemed more surprised than afraid. "Who and what are you?" he asked.

The woman's expression didn't change.

"Hand over the necklace… now," she said slowly and with the kind of exaggerated care used when talking to someone who has difficulty understanding.

The Chief shook his head.

"Out of the question, ma'am," he said. "Not until you start behaving like a decent human being and tell me who you are and why you should have the pearls."

The woman looked at the Chief, her eyes devoid of expression. Then she turned in the direction of the door and nodded to Gordon. Gordon opened the door and for a moment I thought the Chief and I were going to be ushered out. But two men came in through the door instead, one behind the other. The first was a short, wiry fellow with a lined face and a knuckleduster on each hand. The second was much younger and running to fat. His lips were fleshy and worm-like and he was twirling a closed flick knife in his fingers.

"Now look, Mr Koskela," the woman said. "Don't make things difficult. I'm not keen on trouble. Hand over the necklace and I'll let the two of you go."

The Chief's face darkened. "We don't have it with us," he said.

The woman sighed with annoyance. Then she nodded to Gordon, who ordered the thug with the knife to frisk the Chief. The Chief swore, but that was all he could do since Gordon had drawn a pistol from a holster under his jacket.

The man with the flick knife made a quick search of the Chief's pockets and carefully felt his jacket in case there was anything stitched into the lining. When he'd finished, the woman said, "Now the ape."

The thug hesitated. "What if it tries to bite me?"

"You'll just have to bite it back, won't you?" Gordon said calmly. "Get on with it."

My heart was pounding. I made sure I kept very still while the thug searched through the pockets of my overalls.

"Right, where have you hidden the necklace?" the woman asked the Chief when she realized we didn't have it with us.

"That's none of your business, ma'am," the Chief said through clenched teeth.

The woman inclined her head to the side as she weighed up the Chief with a long look.

"All right, Mr Koskela, this is what we'll do. You go and fetch the necklace and bring it back. I'll hang on to the ape as surety—it must be worth a penny or two."

"It certainly is!" the thug with the knife sneered. "I've read about luxury restaurants in London that have ape meat on the menu. Pricey stuff! An orangutan steak costs a couple of weeks' wages. And this gorilla here would easily..."

The Chief's face went pale with rage. He took two long strides forward and punched the thug smack in the face before he could open his knife. The man hit the floor.

Gordon flicked off the safety catch of his pistol and the small wiry fellow raised his knuckledusters to hit the Chief from behind, but both stopped when the woman slapped the desk with the palm of her hand. She stood up and walked over to the Chief.

"You've got three hours to fetch the necklace," she said. "Do you think that's long enough?"

The Chief didn't answer.

"And don't bother going to the police, Mr Koskela," the woman added. "You should know that I have some very good friends in the police."

The Chief gave me a long look before turning to the woman. "I shan't go to the police," he said in a dull voice. "And you can have that accursed necklace."

He threw me another quick glance and strode out of the room.

Straight Flush

I was on the point of making a run for it after the Chief, but managed to restrain myself. And just as well I did, as Gordon was standing just a couple of yards away, safety catch off and pistol at the ready.

As soon as the door closed behind the Chief, the woman picked up the telephone. It was answered in a matter of seconds.

"Mr Flint," she said. "A man has just left my office. He's wearing a black reefer jacket and a blue cap... Yes, a sailor... I want you to follow him and note where he goes and who he meets. Understood? Good. Thank you."

She put down the receiver, stood up and looked at her watch.

"I'm away to have lunch with my auditor," she said to Gordon. "Meanwhile I want you to go to Prince's Dock. *Valkyrie* is due to sail tonight and I want you to check that everything on board is in order. The last time I talked to Captain Verloc he wasn't exactly sober. I'm worried. I hope we haven't employed a drunk as skipper."

"I'll go and check things," Gordon said, helping her put on her coat.

"What are we to do with the ape?" the small man with the knuckledusters wondered.

"Lock it up," the woman answered. "Or tie it up somewhere. And try not to injure it."

"As you say, ma'am," the small man said as Gordon and the woman left the room.

I was left alone with the two thugs. I learnt that the fellow with the knuckledusters was called Carl and the man with the flick knife, Kevin.

Kevin had staggered over to the bar and wrapped a handful of lumps of ice in a towel. He pressed this against his sore nose and split lip.

"That yellow-bellied sailor caught me off guard!" he whined. "Next time I see him he'll get a taste of my knife!"

"You've got yourself to blame," Carl said. "You're too slow. And too fat! A stuffed hippo could have dodged that punch."

"Keep your mouth shut, you!" Kevin muttered.

Carl turned his eyes in my direction. They were cold and dismissive, as if he were looking at rubbish he'd been left to clear up.

"What shall we do with the ape?" he said.

"Let's take it up to the marshalling yard and chuck it in front of a train. We can say it escaped," Kevin suggested.

"Not a bad idea at all," Carl said as he thought it over. "But Moira will be mad at us because she wants us to keep the beast alive, doesn't she? I think we should just chain it to the bar in here."

Carl left the room and returned a few minutes later with a chain and a couple of padlocks. They soon had me chained tight to the steel leg of the counter. The counter must have weighed several hundredweight so there was little chance of me pulling free.

"Right then!" Carl said to Kevin. "Time to get out on the town and make ourselves useful. Old Grimsby has fallen behind with his monthly payments. Time to go and teach him a lesson!"

~

The events of that afternoon were so strange and unexpected that I really didn't have time to feel frightened. Now, however, a shudder of fear ran through me. Real fear. What would happen when the Chief came back? What if Kevin and his flick knife decided to exact revenge?

At the same time, my head was buzzing with questions. *How could that woman know about the pearl necklace?* Could she actually be Jack Shaw's daughter, Rose Henderson?

That just didn't seem likely. If she was, why hadn't she said so? On top of that, I'd just heard Carl and Kevin call her Moira.

And what had happened to the detective? Was he aware the Chief and I had been tricked into coming here? Had he, in fact, been part of the plot in some way?

~

At five to three Moira returned, her high heels ringing like pistol shots on the parquet flooring as she marched over to her desk. Gordon came into the room almost immediately after her. He looked worried.

"Well, how did you get on at the docks?" she asked in an impatient voice. "Is the *Valkyrie* ready to sail?"

Gordon slumped down in one of the chairs in front of the desk.

"The vessel is ready for departure," he said with a sigh. "But Captain Verloc isn't, I'm sorry to say. He's disappeared. According to the crew he was drunk as a lord when he staggered ashore yesterday evening and no one has any idea where he was off to. I think he's lost his nerve. It is a fairly risky journey, you know."

Moira swore quietly through clenched teeth.

"I shall make very sure that he regrets this! But first we have to find a replacement. The delivery is already late and we don't want to get on the wrong side of Mr Luciano in New York. The vessel has to leave Glasgow tonight!"

Gordon shook his head, concern showing on his face.

"It'll be difficult to get hold of a new skipper at such short notice," he said. "Particularly for a job of this kind…"

Gordon was interrupted by a knock on the door. A lanky man with a hooked nose, bald head and sunken cheeks entered. He was wearing bedroom slippers and a creased jacket with patched elbows.

"Mr Flint," Moira said, not bothering with greetings. "What do you have to report?"

Mr Flint cleared his throat and spoke in an unusually wheezy voice. "That seaman you asked me to follow… Well, he took a bus to the Park District…"

"To the Park District?" Moira repeated in surprise.

"That's right," Mr Flint continued. "When he got there, he made his way to a hotel on Park Terrace and tried to contact someone called Lord Kilvaird. When the concierge told him the young lord wasn't at home, the seaman asked to speak to the lord's mother instead. But she wasn't available either. On hearing that, the seaman became impatient and said he had to get back a precious piece of jewellery that Lord Kilvaird was looking after for him. He demanded to know where he could find the lord or his mother. But the concierge refused to tell him."

"So what happened then?" Moira asked.

"The seaman was thrown out by the hotel security men. But he continued to cause trouble and eventually the police were called. At that point, he vanished very quickly and I lost him."

Moira dismissed Mr Flint with a wave of her hand and he left the room. She stroked her chin in thought.

"So it's young Lord Kilvaird who has the necklace now. I'd have never imagined Koskela had such posh contacts… Who'd have thought it?"

Gordon snorted. "Lord Kilvaird is not as posh as he sounds," he said. "I know the fellow and he's a good-for-nothing. He spends his nights at the poker and roulette tables gambling his old mother's money away. And just the other day I heard a rumour…"

Gordon broke off abruptly.

"What kind of rumour?" Moira asked.

"A rumour about a necklace actually," Gordon said. "Let me check it. Can I use your telephone?"

Moira pushed the telephone across to him. After a brief muttered conversation Gordon hung up.

"Bad news, I'm afraid," he said. "The word in the town, is that Lord Kilvaird joined in a poker school at a Maryhill gambling club a couple of nights ago. The place is called Dionysos and it's owned by a Greek with an unpronounceable name. They were playing for very high stakes and Lord Kilvaird staked a pearl necklace—a necklace of inestimable value, apparently."

Moira's expression remained fixed, but her colour darkened.

"And? What happened then?" she asked.

"The Greek had a straight flush and won the pot," Gordon said in a sorrowful voice. "So the necklace is his now!"

"Oh no!" Moira said. "Those pearls are mine. Mine and no one else's!"

So Long, Sailor

Moira sat there completely still and silent, her lips pressed in a hard line.

I was trying to gather my thoughts after what I had just heard. *Lord Kilvaird had duped us! Far from putting our pearl necklace in his mother's safe, he had wagered it in a poker game and lost!*

So what was to happen now?

That was a question that had obviously occurred to Gordon, too.

He said, "Koskela is likely to be back at any moment. What do you want to do?"

"He's no longer of any use to me," she answered in a low voice. "He's lost my necklace and won't be able to get it back. Take him out in the backyard and give him a going over. A thorough going over, so that he realizes he'd better not show his face around here again!"

"Will do!" Gordon said. "And the ape? What should we do with the ape?"

"We'll sell it to the highest bidder. Ask Kevin for the name of the restaurant—the one that serves ape steaks. They'll maybe send in a bid."

My chest tightened in the grip of fear and I had trouble breathing.

Just then there was a knock at the door. It was Mr Flint.

"The seaman's back," Flint said. "He's hammering on the front door."

"Good," Gordon said. "Fetch your cricket bat and call Carl and Kevin. It'll be best if all four of us give Koskela a good beating."

Mr Flint's face lit up in an eager grin, but before he and Gordon set off, Moira stopped them.

Moira was obviously thinking hard. Flint and Gordon waited.

"I've changed my mind," she said. "Bring Koskela here. I want to talk to him."

"All right," Gordon said. "But why?…"

"You'll see," Moira snapped. "Just do as I say."

Gordon and Mr Flint left the room. I was so nervous that I had to call on all my willpower not to start tearing at the chains holding me. Moira, on the other hand, was now much calmer. She leant back in the chair at her desk and the corners of her mouth curled in a smile.

There was a quick knock on the door and Gordon entered with the Chief close behind him. They were followed by Carl, Kevin and Mr Flint in a line.

The Chief's face was pale with rage. He looked round the room and caught sight of me. I gave him a quick nod to show I was OK and he nodded back.

"Sit down, Koskela," Moira said. "Unless you'd prefer to stand? Your legs must be tired after being chased by the police all round the Park District."

The Chief was probably in too much of a temper to be surprised at Moira knowing where he'd been, so he just glared at her.

She went on, "I had you shadowed. That's how I know you haven't brought me the necklace as you said you would. You tell him, Gordon."

Gordon gave a brief account of what he knew about Lord Kilvaird and the sort of man he was.

The Chief's shock became more obvious with every word he heard. On hearing that Lord Kilvaird had gambled away the pearl necklace at the poker table, he was speechless at first. But then he laughed and turned to Moira. "There you have it! You and that lord will have to fight it out over the necklace… Nothing more I can do about it in any case."

"Oh no," Moira said with a cold smile. "You don't get away with it that easily, Koskela. That necklace is *mine*. And it's worth tens of thousands of pounds!"

The Chief opened his mouth to speak, but Moira got in first.

"Let's have no fuss, if you don't mind!" she said impatiently. "*You* are the one careless enough to lose the necklace, which means *you* are the one who has to compensate me for my loss!"

She leant back in her chair before continuing: "You're a skipper, Koskela, aren't you? Am I right? Do you have any experience of being in command of a sailing ship?"

The Chief's eyebrows shot up at the unexpected enquiry.

"What's that got to do with you?" he said.

"Answer the question," sighed Gordon, poking his pistol into the Chief's side.

"All right," the Chief answered Moira. "Yes, I do."

Moira looked at Gordon. He smiled—he seemed to know what she was aiming at.

"What do you think?" she asked.

"It seems like a good idea," Gordon nodded.

I was beginning to suspect what Moira was up to. The Chief, on the other hand, had no idea at all. He hadn't been present when Moira and Gordon discussed the disappearance of the captain of the *Valkyrie*.

"What's this all about?" he said.

"I'm going to give you a chance to work off your debt to me," Moira replied. "It so happens that I need a captain for a schooner lying in Prince's Dock ready to sail. She's called the *Valkyrie*."

"Are you actually involved in the shipping business?" the Chief asked in amazement.

Moira shook her head. "Not really. I've chartered this ship for a couple of voyages across the Atlantic, but I made the unfortunate mistake of employing a captain with weak nerves. And now he's skedaddled."

The Chief's eyes narrowed.

"Skedaddled?" he said. "Why? What kind of cargo is the ship carrying?"

"Whisky," Moira answered. "Five hundred cases. Destined for New York."

The Chief gave a snort. "Aha, now I understand! You're smuggling spirits."

"Exactly!" Moira said. "You are to unload the cargo at night outside United States' territorial waters. My New York business contacts will come out from Long Island in fast motorboats to rendezvous with you. You'll use coded radio signals to agree on the exact location for the transfer. Weapons have been hidden on board so you can defend yourselves should the coastguards happen to sight you. Any questions?"

The Chief said nothing for some time. He turned and looked at me. If it hadn't been for the fact I was chained to the table we might have been able to escape relatively unscathed, but as things were, we didn't have a chance. The Chief turned back to Moira.

"And what if I refuse to take the job?"

"Then my men will beat you within an inch of your life. Maybe you'll survive, maybe you won't. But one way or the other you'll never see your ape again… Not unless you go to the London restaurant that serves ape steaks, that is. They might serve you a well-cooked piece of your pet."

Carl and Kevin broke into loud laughter.

The Chief appeared not to hear them. He thought things through and then nodded. "All right, I'll take the job. But only on condition that Sally Jones sails with me."

Moira didn't understand at first and looked at him blankly. Then she started to laugh, though her laughter was joyless and sneering.

"Sally Jones! So that's what the ape's called! Giving an animal a name—how ridiculous! No, the ape stays here. And you know what will happen to your ape if the job goes wrong."

Moira stood up.

"That is us finished here," she said. "Gordon will take you down to the docks. All the paperwork is in order and I'm counting on the *Valkyrie* casting off the moment the tide turns. Goodbye, Koskela. Don't forget that your ape will pay with its life if you let me down."

The Chief stood his ground. "How am I to know that you won't hurt Sally Jones anyway?"

Moira was about to brush the Chief off, but stopped herself. She thought for a moment and then said, "I'm a business-woman, Koskela, and I've nothing to gain by harming your ape as long as you're behaving yourself. Rather the reverse, in fact. If you are successful this time, I may well feel able to employ you as a skipper in the future. In which case it would be stupid of me to have killed your ape, wouldn't it?"

The Chief bit his lip and glared at Moira. Then he turned on his heel and followed Gordon towards the door. In the doorway he stopped and looked at me.

"So long, sailor," he said. "Don't give up!"

I nodded.

Then the Chief was gone.

PART THREE

THE SMUGGLER QUEEN

The Cellar Hole

Moira kept her word to the Chief. She didn't sell me to the restaurant that served ape steaks, instead she gave orders that I should be locked up and kept alive.

Carl and Kevin took me down to the cellar, where they pushed me into a small room with flaking brick walls. As soon as the door closed behind me, I began to inspect the room. If I could escape there was just a chance I could get across the river and reach Prince's Dock before the *Valkyrie* cast off. But time was short. The vessel was due to sail as soon as the tide turned.

The door was solid and had two locks. There were also bolts on the outside. The only window in the room was right up under the ceiling and the filthy cracked glass had bars over it. However much I heaved and pushed, the bars didn't move even a fraction of an inch. I slumped down, my back against the cold rough wall.

There was no way out.

I tried to imagine what the Chief was thinking about at that moment. Would he try to overpower Gordon and come back to rescue me? I shut my eyes tight and hoped he wouldn't try. The thought of Gordon's pistol made me feel sick.

~

Hours passed. The light from the small window grew darker until eventually there was just one pale line across the floor. Then I heard approaching steps echoing along the corridor outside. The bolts were drawn and the door opened.

It was Carl, accompanied by a big, heavily-built fellow in shorts and a woollen cardigan. It was the same man who'd been sweeping the yard when the Chief and I arrived at the house that morning.

The big man stared at me wide-eyed. His face was battered and lop-sided—a real bruiser's face.

"You are to be the ape's keeper, Bernie," Carl said. "Come down a couple of times a day and give it water… Yeah, and whatever it is that apes eat. And don't forget to bring down a pot—we'll have to hope it knows what it's for or you'll end up mopping up its muck from the floor. Do you understand?"

The big man—his name was obviously Bernie—nodded reluctantly at the same time as shooting an unfriendly look in my direction.

"Right then," Carl said to Bernie. "Let's go!"

And they went.

~

At some point far into the night I must have fallen asleep. When I woke I could hear the sounds of heavy traffic and voices passing along the street outside. A wave of fear ran through me when I remembered where I was and why I was there.

A little while later big Bernie arrived with a bowl of water and a couple of bread rolls. He gave me a threatening look out of the corner of his eye but said nothing.

The tide must have turned several hours before, which meant the *Valkyrie* would already be well down the river. She might even have reached the estuary and set sail on her voyage.

That thought actually made me feel a little less anxious. At least I no longer needed to worry about the Chief. He was at sea, where he really knows how to handle things.

~

It's impossible to say in advance how long it will take to sail across the Atlantic. It all depends on the winds. But given the time of year I reckoned that the soonest the Chief could be back in Glasgow was eight to ten weeks. So I was likely to be sitting in solitary in this mouldy cellar for at least two months.

Unless I managed to escape, of course. In which case I would try to get to Li Jing in Gourock and I was sure she'd help me make contact with Ana and Signor Fidardo.

I had a plan and that made me feel good. All I had to do now was to put up with things and wait for an opportunity to escape.

~

The days and nights passed slowly, very slowly. I slept through as many of the twenty-four hours as possible and spent the rest of the time walking round and round the small room trying to think of anything that would occupy my thoughts.

Since I had nothing but four brick walls to look at, hearing quickly became more important than vision. The great city never fell silent and at regular intervals trains passed on their way to or from Glasgow Central Station. For a few days I tried to pass the time by learning to distinguish different kinds of train by the noise the rails made. It was a boring game.

Right from one of the first evenings I realized that there must be some sort of bar or pub in the building. There were nights when the shouting and yelling echoed down the corridors and made it impossible to get any sleep. The celebrations would go on into the small hours and be at their worst around closing time. I'd hear people shouting and arguing outside the small cellar window and acrid wafts of tobacco smoke, sweat and spilt beer seeped through the broken pane.

~

Bernie was my only visitor. Morning and evening he would bring down water and something for me to eat. Usually it was bread or porridge. The pot—which was actually a bucket with a lid—was emptied twice a day.

There was no question of trying to overpower Bernie. Given all the scars and marks on his face, he must have been in hundreds of fights.

Every new day was exactly like the one before. Nothing happened and I had nothing to do. After a week or so I began to feel a sense of panic: how was I going to hold out?

~

But late one evening something finally did happen. I heard raised voices and footsteps out in the corridor. The bolts were drawn back, keys turned, the door opened and Carl and Kevin entered, each carrying a large wooden box. They were followed by Bernie carrying two boxes, one under each arm. They dropped their boxes on the floor and Carl told Bernie to fetch more boxes while he and Kevin began stacking them.

For one moment I considered hurling myself past Carl and Kevin, but almost immediately I had a better idea.

I got to my feet and before either of the ruffians could stop me, picked up one of the boxes, carried it to the corner and stacked it on top of the other boxes.

Carl and Kevin exchanged looks of astonishment.

"Did you see that? The ape is copying us," Carl said.

Bernie appeared in the doorway with another box. As soon as he put it down, I went up to him and took over.

Kevin started to laugh.

"You carry on bringing the boxes down, Bernie. Carl and I will see to the stacking down here."

Kevin and Carl sat down, opened a bottle of beer each and watched as I stacked the boxes that Bernie lugged down from the lane. Once it was all done, the keys rattled in the door as they locked it.

I might be back in solitary again, but it didn't bother me now. Carl and Kevin had realized they could make use of me and my long, lonely, empty days would probably soon be over.

Stolen Goods in the Cargo

The wooden boxes remained in my room for three days and having nothing else to do I decided to find out what was in them. I succeeded in prising open the lids of several boxes by using the spoon I'd been given to eat my food.

The boxes were full of silverware, packed in sawdust. Bowls, cups, cutlery, cases, candelabra—all kinds of fine things.

I knew already, of course, that Moira was involved in smuggling alcohol. She and her people were gangsters and quite prepared to have people beaten up if they wouldn't do what she wanted. So my first thought was that the silverware in the boxes must be stolen goods.

~

Carl, Kevin and Bernie came down one evening to pick up the boxes and I immediately showed that I was willing to help them. Carl had clearly been reckoning on that as he'd brought a long chain with a padlock on each end.

He attached one end around my neck, handed the other end to Bernie and said, "Lock this chain to your belt so the ape doesn't run away."

Bernie didn't look too happy with the idea but did what he was told. He and I had soon carried all the boxes up from the cellar and stowed them in the back of a lorry parked inside the iron gates of the backyard.

Gordon was sitting behind the wheel reading a newspaper. Looking over his shoulder I could see that the paper was called the *Noon Record* and consisted of page after page of tables and lists. I'd seen papers like that before, both in Lisbon and in other cities. The *Noon Record* was a newspaper for people who gamble on horses.

Carl and Kevin got in and sat beside Gordon in the cab while Bernie and I had to find what space we could among the boxes in the back. Then we set off.

The flickering light of the gas lamps along the street picked out cars and pedestrians in the grey fog. I did my best to work out the direction in which we were travelling. We drove west through the city and eventually came to an industrial area and a fast-flowing river lined with big corn mills. This was the River Kelvin—I remembered that from the street map the Chief had bought.

Gordon parked on a wharf down by the water. In the darkness around us we could see derelict boats propped up on empty oil drums. A faint light was showing in the windows of a ramshackle workshop that seemed to be a boatyard. The sound of a steam engine running at low revs came from somewhere in the neighbourhood.

I tried to stand up but the chain held me back. Bernie didn't budge. He was clinging tight to the lorry and staring down at the rushing, gurgling river running past us in the darkness.

"On your feet, Bernie! We don't have time for your fears tonight," Gordon said with a sigh of irritation.

Kevin snorted. "Only babies are afraid of the water, you know that, don't you, Bernie?"

Bernie didn't move a muscle.

Gordon went up to him and spoke quietly in his ear. "What's Moira going to say about this, do you think? She's going to be angry with you again. *Very* angry. Just like last time. And the time before that. And you know…"

On hearing Gordon's words Bernie managed to pull himself together. He stood up, stiff and clumsy, and we began passing the boxes down to Carl and Kevin.

The engine we could hear in the darkness turned out to be a steam launch moored to the wharf. A scrawny man chewing on a pipe was sitting in the stern, ready to cast off.

"Evening, skipper," Gordon said, and the man in the boat responded by putting a finger to the peak of his cap.

Once all the boxes had been moved from the back of the lorry down into the steam launch, Kevin, Carl and Gordon used a mixture of threats and elbows to get Bernie aboard. The huge man reluctantly went along with it, but his panic showed in his eyes.

A short while later we were on the move. The River Kelvin flowed into the great Clyde just a couple of hundred yards farther downstream. The launch began rolling and pitching heavily in the waves as the skipper set a westward course towards the sea.

~

I shivered in the icy night breeze out on the river. Where were we going and what would happen when we got there?

Bernie was sitting hunched between two of the boxes on the deck of the launch. He was trembling, not from cold but from sheer terror. His face was deathly white and cold sweat glistened on his forehead. There is nothing unusual about people being afraid of going out in boats, but I've never before met anyone as terrified of the water as Bernie, big man that he was.

The fog grew denser and the bell-buoys marking the deep-water channel sounded mournfully across the water. After an hour or so the skipper cut the steam and we could just pick out the north shore of the Clyde through the fog. The few lights visible on shore were weak and scattered. Our skipper struck two sharp blows on the brass bell and almost immediately it was echoed by a second bell answering out in the night.

Our skipper changed course and a minute or so later a dark silhouette loomed up on our starboard side. We glided slowly in alongside the other vessel, a large barge that stank of fish. It lay at anchor, sails furled, a worn and sodden flag hanging from the rigging. It looked as if it was the Irish tricolour.

Men from the crew of the barge helped tie us alongside. Gordon climbed aboard the other vessel and shook hands with a stout man wearing oilskin trousers, a thick woollen jersey and a battered skipper's cap. We began transferring the wooden boxes from the launch down into the hold of the barge. The stench down there was almost unbearable and in the light of the oil lamp we could see that the planking was slippery with fish blood and offal.

Once the last box had been moved, the mooring ropes were untied and Carl pushed us off with a boathook. The skipper of the launch set the regulator to forward and the barge quickly vanished aft of us in the mist.

We began the long journey back to the city. Gordon, Carl and Kevin kept themselves warm by sharing a bottle of whisky the Irishman in oilskin trousers had given them.

Bernie and I sat on our own a little farther forward. I pondered on what we had just experienced. I assumed the Irishman and his crew on the barge were smugglers—why else would they take a cargo of silver bowls and candelabras aboard in the middle of the night?

While I was thinking these thoughts, Bernie was falling asleep. His huge head nodded once or twice before finally falling forward, chin on chest. I wasn't surprised. I know myself how exhausted real fear can make you.

~

A new day was dawning by the time the scrawny skipper brought us alongside the boatyard wharf where our trip had started. A few minutes later Bernie and I were sitting in the back of the lorry taking us back to Oswald Street. Once we were there, Bernie took me down to the cellar and unlocked the chain around my neck. Then, without saying a word, he left, locking the door behind him.

I was tired, but also elated. I'd been able to show them what I was capable of and now they'd surely recognize what a waste it was to keep me locked up when I could be working.

It wouldn't be long before they let me out of the cellar again and I would, of course, continue to be helpful, hard-working and obedient.

Until I saw an opportunity to escape!

26

Lucky Lucy's Social Club

The following morning Carl and Kevin came marching into my cellar with Bernie in tow. Carl fastened the chain around my neck and told Bernie to attach the other end to his belt.

"Flintheart wants a hand with various things," Carl explained to Bernie. "Just the job for you and the ape."

Then Carl and Kevin left without waiting for an answer from Bernie.

~

Bernie took me to the shop called Oswald Street Antiques that was situated on the ground floor of the building. Inside, a labyrinth of passageways snaked through piles of dusty bric-à-brac of every kind. The place reeked of mothballs and ingrained dirt.

The small counter at the entrance was occupied by a woman who kept a watchful eye on things. She gave me and Bernie a bitter look and then, talking to herself but loudly enough for us to hear, said, "Well, well. An idiot and an ape. That's what I have to put up with, I suppose…"

The woman was short, fat and blowsy, her face round and flushed. I discovered later that her name was Fiona Flint, but behind her back everyone called her Flintheart.

Flintheart put me and Bernie to work. For a start, a bureau had to change places with a stuffed lion and, at the other end of the room, a billiard table had to be stood on end to make room for an old and decrepit piano.

There was heavy lifting involved and not much room to do it in. The air was warm and muggy. Sweat ran off the lumps and dents in Bernie's face and my arms and back ached. I almost fell over a couple of times when the chain tugged tight between me and Bernie. His movements were clumsy and he gave no thought to the fact we were chained together.

Flintheart stayed close, ever ready to point out how badly we were performing. Time and again she warned Bernie about what would happen if we broke anything.

"If you make a single little scratch on that piano, I'll be telling Moira," she croaked. "And she'll deduct it from your pocket money, Bernie. And it will be a substantial deduction!"

The threats didn't help. Quite the opposite. They just made big Bernie nervous, and the more nervous he became, the clumsier he got. Flintheart, of course, was aware of this and she obviously enjoyed tormenting Bernie.

~

Flintheart went off to the hairdresser that afternoon, leaving her husband in charge of the shop. I recognized him from the first day of my imprisonment. He was the man who had shadowed the Chief to the hotel on Park Terrace.

Mr Flint, a tall, scraggy man, said no more than was necessary and never raised his voice. The other people in the building called him Skinflint and I would soon understand why.

At six o'clock Skinflint told Bernie and me to scrub the floor, then he locked the outside door and put a 'Closed' sign in the window. He'd no sooner done so than there was a knock on the back door, the one that led out to the Broomielaw. Skinflint let in a young man with his cap pulled right down. The man had a pocket watch he wanted to sell.

"I nicked the watch off an old fellow in Hillhead," he said. "I want at least ten pounds for it, otherwise I won't sell."

Skinflint examined the watch under a low-hanging shoe-maker's lamp. His yellowish skin shone where it stretched over his cheek bones. A quarter of an hour later the thief left the shop with a gloomy look on his face. He'd only been paid one pound, twelve shillings and fourpence for the watch. Skinflint was laughing quietly to himself. It was an unnatural and unpleasant sound that made the hairs on my neck rise.

During the hours that followed a dozen or so thieves came into the shop with stolen goods to sell. Skinflint haggled tirelessly, driving the price down penny by penny until he was sure he was getting a really good deal. And he celebrated every victory with one of his unpleasant wheezing laughs.

~

The next day was exactly the same. Bernie and I had to shift heavy items, while a bleary-eyed Flintheart watched every step we took. We were just about to lug an iron stove from the shop to one of the stores out in the backyard when Gordon came in from Oswald Street. As usual, he had his nose stuck in the *Noon Record*.

He stopped and said to Bernie, "Lucy wants you to take that ape with you when you go to the club this evening. You and the ape are to cover the door together. The idea is to bring in more guests—Lucy says that people like gimmicks like that."

Bernie looked baffled, but Gordon just gave him a pat on the shoulder and walked on.

~

When the day's work was over, I fell asleep down in my cellar. But I didn't get to sleep for long before the sound of keys in the locks woke me. Bernie came in. I barely recognized him at first. His hair was slicked down and he was wearing a black suit and tie. He didn't look comfortable in the posh clothes.

Bernie led me through basement corridors into a big room with rows of plain wooden tables. Behind the bar, which was distinctly worse-for-wear, rose shelves full of bottles and glasses. A hand-painted sign stood on the topmost shelf; it read *Lucky Lucy's Social Club*.

A big, blonde woman behind the bar caught sight of Bernie and me and waved us over. I discovered later that this was Lucky Lucy, the club hostess. She wasn't the owner, though—that was Moira. In fact, Moira owned the whole building.

Lucy looked me up and down, her mouth pursed in disapproval.

"The ape looks a bit scruffy, don't you think? We'd better smarten it up somehow."

She raked around under the bar and found a tie like the one Bernie was wearing. Once it was tied round my neck, Lucky Lucy gave me a friendly pinch on the cheek.

"That'll have to do," she said. "Go up and stand at the door now. It's very nearly nine o'clock."

Bernie and I spent the next six hours on the door at Lucky Lucy's Club. We had orders only to allow in people who looked as if they had money to spend—scruffs and paupers were not welcome. Many of those we barred lost their temper when they weren't allowed in and they hurled every kind of foul abuse at us.

Towards midnight the club was packed. That is when two policemen came strolling along the Broomielaw.

"Hi there, Bernie," one of the constables said. "What's this then? Have you got an ape as your partner on the door now?"

The other constable sneered, "Looks as if you complement one another, Bernie. You provide the muscle and the ape provides the brains!"

The policemen laughed loudly and for a long time. Bernie kept his eyes down on his feet.

When the first constable had finished laughing, he said to Bernie, "You know what it's about, Bernie. Nip down and fetch Gordon. We'll look after your ape while you do."

Bernie handed his end of the chain to one of the policemen and plodded off down the stairs to the cellar.

The two policemen inspected me more closely and one of them said, "Wonder where Moira Gray got hold of this beastie? Smuggled it in from Africa maybe."

"I wouldn't be surprised," the other one said. "She is the queen of Glasgow smugglers, when all's said and done."

The constable fell abruptly silent when Gordon appeared in the doorway. Gordon took an envelope from his inside pocket and began to count out a wad of notes. The constable quickly stopped him and grabbed the envelope of cash.

"The night has eyes…" he said, looking anxiously over his shoulder. "We'll count it later."

"Do as you like, gentlemen," Gordon said. "See you again next week."

"You can count on that!" the other constable said as they moved off.

At that time I didn't understand what the money was all about. But I do now. It's illegal to sell alcohol in Scotland after nine o'clock at night. Gordon was paying the police every week so they would leave Lucky Lucy's Club in peace.

~

It was early morning by the time the last guests left the club, quarrelling, yelling and fooling about. Some of them came up to Bernie on unsteady legs and pretended to box with him, swinging their fists right in front of his face.

"Come on, Bernie, Bernie the Butcher!" they yelled. "Let's see what you're made of!"

"Put up your guard, Bernie the Butcher! The bell's sounded!"

They all laughed, all except Bernie. His unhappy eyes were fixed on the ground and he looked as if he wanted to be far, far away. It was obvious that this had happened many, many times before.

~

After all the guests had gone at last, Bernie and I had to wipe the tables and mop up the spilt beer, broken glass and tobacco spit from the stone floor.

I wondered about the name the drunks outside the club had called Bernie—"Bernie the Butcher".

Why had they called him that?

I shuddered and thought I'd rather not know.

Fever

In the weeks that followed, I was with Bernie from morning to night. There were days when we scrubbed floors and cleaned toilets, others when we cleared drainpipes, swept the backyard and washed the windows.

I didn't have a chance to run away. Bernie was always very careful to attach the chain round my neck when he collected me in the morning. And he never unlocked the padlock before we were back in the cellar in the evening.

I didn't see much of Carl and Kevin. They usually spent their days collecting debts round the city. One of Moira's businesses involved lending money at very high rates of interest. People who borrowed ten pounds from her would have to pay twenty back. Sometimes even more. People had to be in real financial difficulties before they turned to Moira for help.

Now and again I heard them talking about a place called Twilight Quay. I came to understand that Twilight Quay was an isolated spot somewhere among the docks where Carl and Kevin used to take the poor souls who couldn't repay what they'd borrowed from Moira. When Carl and Kevin came back from Twilight Quay they'd go to the tap out in the backyard and clean their knuckledusters and flick knives. Borrowing money from Moira was not only expensive, it was dangerous. Very dangerous.

~

Bernie and I worked the door at Lucky Lucy's several nights a week. There were other nights when a dense fog lay over the River Clyde and we and other members of the gang would go out on the water with the skinny skipper and his steam launch. Bernie was terrified every time and sometimes he'd get the shivers and be sick over the side.

By listening to their chatter on the launch, I was able to work out what these mysterious river trips were really about. Moira dealt in stolen valuables and to prevent the police tracing them back to her she had arranged for them to be smuggled over to Ireland. They were sold on the black market in Dublin. The smugglers were Irish fishermen returning home with their holds empty after unloading their eels at Bridgegate Fishmarket.

The whole business was planned and I understood why

the constables had referred to Moira as the queen of Glasgow smugglers.

Moira's many shady dealings had made her rich. I saw her wealth when Bernie and I had the job of topping up the coal in her fires. She lived in a big apartment on the top floor of the building and I could hardly believe my eyes the first time I went there. Every room was filled from floor to ceiling with antique furniture, works of art and ornaments. Bernie was in a constant cold sweat in case he accidentally knocked something over or left a trail of coal across the valuable Persian carpets.

～

Working with Bernie wasn't easy. Even though we were chained together, he insisted on pretending that I didn't exist. He never spoke to me and only looked at me when he absolutely had to. I assumed it was because he found it embarrassing to be working with an ape as his workmate. I wasn't surprised at that, nor did it bother me. That kind of thing had happened to me before.

But the chain was a problem. So as to avoid all the tugging and jerking when the chain was taut, I attempted to learn how Bernie moved and to adapt my movements to his. It was difficult. Time after time the chain would tighten up and every time it did so it made my neck more painful.

In the end it cut into my skin and sores developed under my fur. Since I was wearing the chain every day, the wounds on my neck had little chance to heal.

I tried to show Bernie I was in pain, but he didn't understand what I meant. As time passed, I became more and more anxious. During my incarceration my fur had become tangled and dirty and there was a risk of the wounds on my neck becoming infected.

And that's what happened.

I woke one night feeling so cold my whole body was trembling, yet the skin under my fur felt on fire. I had a fever—a very high fever.

When Bernie came down with my breakfast, he must have recognized immediately that something was wrong. He stood staring down at me for a long time, his face as expressionless as ever. Then he became confused, his eyes flitted here and there, and he opened and closed his mouth several times.

"Are you ill?" he said in his gruff voice.

I nodded and pointed to my neck. Bernie hesitated at first, but then he kneeled down beside me. I held my fur apart so he could see the wounds. He took a deep breath—they can't have been a pretty sight.

"I've had injuries," Bernie said softly. "Lots of injuries…"

He stayed there for some time, trying to decide what to

do. Then he got to his feet, strode out of the cellar and I could hear his lumbering footsteps grow fainter as he passed along the corridor.

It took me a little while to realize that something was different: why hadn't I heard the door closing?

I turned round and looked—the door was open! *In his haste Bernie had forgotten to close and lock the door.*

I forced myself up on to my elbows, my head spinning from the fever. My heart was pounding hard and fast. With a huge effort I managed to get up. My knees threatened to give way and I had the unpleasant feeling the room was tilting. Slowly and with great care I moved towards the open door. As I reached it, I heard the faint sounds of voices and footsteps approaching along the corridor.

There was no time to waste! I hurried towards the staircase that led to the door to the backyard. Dizziness made me stagger and almost fall. The voices were much louder now and I realized I wasn't going to get out in time. The unexpected opportunity was lost, so I turned back on unsteady legs and collapsed breathless on the cellar floor.

Moments later Gordon came through the door, the *Noon Record* under his arm and a pencil behind his ear. Bernie was at his heels. Gordon sniffed the air and pulled a face. The room stank of dirt and disease. Holding his nose, he came closer to get a better look at me. My breathing was still coming in jerky, uneven pants after my failed attempt to escape.

"She's not well," Bernie said. "She's bleeding. Her neck…"

Gordon nodded sombrely.

"Yes, I can see that," he said. "It must be the chain that caused the wounds. And it's no wonder, given the way you pull and jerk it all day long."

Bernie looked blank at first, and then he suddenly seemed to understand. His jaw dropped and he stood there open-mouthed.

"Oh," he muttered unhappily. "I didn't mean…"

Gordon paid no attention to him. He lit a cigarette and looked at me as he smoked. Then he said to Bernie, "Make sure you keep those wounds clean and we'll see if we can get them to heal. If they don't, we'll put the beast down."

Bernie jumped.

"There, there," Gordon said to calm him. "If the ape dies, it's not the end of the world. It's only an animal, after all. And I promise Moira won't be angry with you."

And with that, Gordon threw his cigarette on the floor, crushed it under his heel and left.

Bernie was left standing there, shoulders hanging.

"Put the beast down…" I heard him repeating quietly to himself.

I don't know how long my body was racked by fever. A week, perhaps, maybe two. When I wasn't sleeping, I was too confused even to know where I was. My only memories are images of Bernie, leaning over me with a bottle in one hand and a rag smelling of spirits in the other. I remember the searing pain in my neck and that something was preventing me moving my arms and legs. I think it was Bernie, who had to hold me down in order to bathe my weeping wounds with brandy.

When the fever eventually began to ease, it was like waking up after a long, bad dream. The first thing I noticed was that I was no longer lying on the floor. Someone had put a mattress under me and I'd even been given a blanket.

It was strange. Even more strange was the fact that I no longer stank. Someone must have combed all the mess out of my fur.

I was so hungry that my stomach was rumbling. Thirsty, too. My food bowl was empty, but there was plenty of fresh, cold water in a jug. Once I'd had a drink, I lay down again, but couldn't go back to sleep.

After a couple of hours I heard the key turn in the lock and Bernie came in. I was sitting on the mattress, leaning back against the wall with the blanket over my shoulders.

Bernie's eyes opened wide in surprise and he took a step back before saying, "Are you better? Not ill any more?"

I felt all round my neck with my hand. Thick, itchy scabs had formed over the wounds, but they were no longer painful. So I shook my head.

And them something completely unexpected happened.

Bernie smiled.

For one brief instant his big, ugly, battered face changed completely. It was like the sun breaking through a rent in black storm clouds.

And then Bernie went back to being his usual old sullen self. He left the cellar, locking up behind him.

28

Telegram

It felt good to be starting work again. To prevent the wounds on my neck opening up, I showed Bernie how to fasten the chain round my waist instead and that worked well.

From that day on, Bernie's movements were always much calmer and more careful when we were working together. I could see he was worried he might injure me again. We started swapping quick glances to make sure we were both ready before we did any heavy lifting. And we soon found nods and other small gestures could be used to solve problems or to decide when it was time to take a break.

Our cooperation worked best when it was just the two of us. If there was anyone else around, Bernie would still pretend he didn't know me. I think he was afraid people would mock and tease him if they noticed how good we were at working together.

At midday we used to have a plate of porridge or a sandwich in Bernie's room. He lived in a room with a kitchen alcove just inside the door that led to the stairs. His only furniture was a narrow bed, a scratched table, two kitchen chairs and a rickety wardrobe. The only window looked out on the garbage bins in the backyard.

In some strange way, it was always nice to be with Bernie in his room. He kept the room clean and tidy, his bed was always made and his dishes always washed. There was a tablecloth on the table and a picture of a sunny landscape of green meadows with clumps of trees here and there hung on the wall above the table. The frame of the picture was dented and ugly and I assumed that, like everything else in the room, it came from Oswald Street Antiques. Bernie would sometimes ask to take something he needed from the shop—a saucepan or a cushion cover.

Flintheart always insisted on telling him what the item cost, and then she would add, "You don't need to pay just now, Bernie. I'll tell Moira to take the cost out of your pocket money."

Whenever I heard this, I used to wonder why Flintheart used the term *pocket money*. It sounded strange. Why didn't she call it *your pay*? After all, Bernie *worked* for Moira.

Another thing that concerned me was that Bernie didn't have anything truly personal on display. No framed family photographs on the walls, for instance. Nor did he have a desk or bureau for storing important documents and things of value. Surely everyone has that sort of piece in their homes?

Once when I was looking for sugar in Bernie's larder, I came across a red tin box with a lid. It was on the top shelf and it was secured with a big, clumsy padlock. I wondered if that was where Bernie put things he wanted to keep safe.

~

Whenever Bernie and I cleaned Moira's office, I hoped to pick up news about the Chief, but it wasn't until the first week of December that news of the schooner *Valkyrie* reached me. I overheard Gordon reading Moira a telegram that had just come in from the Chief:

Strong winds–STOP–Hove to for three days SE Newfoundland–STOP–Wind easing–STOP–1200 knots to New York–STOP–Koskela

The message meant that the Chief and his crew had stopped for several days off the south-east coast of Canada to ride out a storm. The winds were beginning to ease now and they would soon be setting a course for New York again. Given the distance, they should reach their destination in about a week.

I was pleased that these signs of life had been received—not that I'd been worried about the Chief. I began to wonder whether my own plan—to escape at the first possible opportunity—was really so sensible. Unless I stayed here with Moira and her gang, I wouldn't be in any position to know what was happening with the Chief.

After a great deal of thought, however, I came to the conclusion that I should run away anyway. In spite of everything. Otherwise Moira would be able to use me as a hostage to force the Chief to make another smuggling voyage across the Atlantic. But *Valkyrie* couldn't be expected back in Glasgow for some considerable time, meanwhile it would be best for me to stay put. When the time came, I was sure I'd find a way to escape from Bernie's chain.

29

Shanley's Bar

Bernie was often sent into the city on errands of one sort or another. If he was in a great hurry, Bernie didn't have time to lock me down in the cellar and he would take me with him instead.

One day Gordon told us to go at once to a pub called Shanley's Bar and deliver an envelope to a man by the name of Neil Fingus. Bernie obviously already knew the way to Shanley's Bar and who Neil Fingus was, so he took the envelope with no further questions.

The day was overcast, with drizzle and a biting wind. The quays and wharves along the Broomielaw were busy as usual in spite of the weather. Bernie and I turned right on Cheapside Street and we walked past Mrs Grimes's boarding house. It seemed a long time since the Chief and I had stayed there and kind Mrs Grimes must have wondered why we vanished without even picking up our belongings.

After walking a while longer Bernie and I reached Shanley's Bar. Bernie didn't go in straightaway. He halted at the door, breathing heavily as if he was nervous—afraid even—of what was inside. Eventually he pulled himself together and stepped in.

The pub was small and cramped, the sounds of shouting, laughter and loud arguments echoing around the walls. The floor was slippery with spilled beer. I tucked in close behind Bernie as he pushed his way through the throng. So as not to draw unnecessary attention to myself, I turned up the collar of my overalls and pulled my cap down over my forehead.

Right at the back of the pub were several private booths, one of which was guarded by an ugly man with a crooked nose. He had a short-stemmed pipe clenched in the corner of his mouth and was cleaning his nails with a long, nasty-looking knife. He recognized Bernie immediately and let us through into the booth.

A florid-faced man with a bushy moustache and rolled-up sleeves was sitting at the table, making a note of something in a big ledger that was open in front of him.

When he'd finished writing, he looked up and studied first me then Bernie with icy, expressionless eyes.

"So it's true what people are saying," he said. "Moira has enlisted a gorilla in her gang."

Bernie said nothing and the man went on, "I assume Gordon has sent you here, Bernie? Am I right?"

"Yes, Mr Fingus," Bernie said.

He took out an envelope and handed it over. Neil Fingus opened it and pulled out a wad of creased banknotes. After counting the money, he made a new entry in his ledger.

"Aha," he said in a weary tone. "Now I see why Gordon didn't dare come himself. This is only half of what he owes me. Tell him from me that I want the rest within ten days or he'll have to accept the consequences. Betting on the horses with borrowed money is a risky business. Particularly when it's my money you've borrowed. Know what I mean, Bernie?"

"Yes, Mr Fingus, I think so," Bernie said.

Neil Fingus narrowed his eyes and his lips tightened over his teeth—small teeth, stained brown from tobacco.

"And next time I want Gordon to come himself. It's not polite of him to be sending a thicko and an ape to meet me. It's not, is it, Bernie?"

"No, it's not… Mr Fingus," Bernie stammered.

"Right, get out of here, you two!" Neil Fingus roared, slamming the table with his fist.

Bernie stumbled backwards, almost falling over. He hurried out of the pub with me close at his heels.

That afternoon a load of coal was delivered to Oswald Street and Bernie and I had our hands full the rest of the day carrying in coal for all the fires in the house. We had just finished when we heard that Moira was calling a meeting. The gang was gathering in her office. Bernie and I washed off the worst of the coal dust and went to join them.

Outside the windows the gas lamps along the Broomielaw had been lit, but the big room lay in darkness. Moira, as usual, was sitting behind her desk and Gordon was standing diagonally behind her. He was leaning on the wall with a drink in his hand.

"It's time to do a job," Moira said once they were all seated. "The target's a gambling club. It's in a house at the north end of Maryhill Golf Course, down by the Forth and Clyde Canal. We'll strike at night on Christmas Eve, when the club is shut. In all probability the house will be deserted apart from a night watchman on the ground floor. The safe is on the top floor."

"A safe-breaking job then, is it?" Carl said. "In that case we can take Eddie 'Bent Finger' Marlow with us. They let him out just last week so he'll be keen to get in on a job."

Moira shook her head and said, "We're not taking any outsiders. I don't want more people than necessary to know about the job. We'll handle this one ourselves."

She gestured to Gordon and he unrolled two large sheets of paper on the desk. One was a plan of a three-storey building, the other seemed to be a map of the surrounding area. Gordon also had several photographs of the building and a whole bundle of sketches he'd made to show the layout.

The following hours were spent discussing the details of the job. A schedule was drawn up and they made lists of the tools, weapons, clothes and everything else needed.

In summary, the plan was for Carl, Kevin, Bernie and me to make our way to the club by boat along the Forth and Clyde Canal. Carl and Kevin would break into the building through a window on the third floor: climbing up there wouldn't be difficult as there was a fire escape ladder. Once inside, they'd have to find the safe which—according to their information— was concealed in a secret space behind a blind wall in a closet. The safe was small enough for it to be lifted out through the window and lowered to the ground. Then Bernie and I would take over and carry it to the boat, leaving Carl and Kevin to get out of the house the same way as they went in.

"And you?…" Carl said to Gordon in a sour tone. "What are you going to be doing while the rest of us pull our weight and do the climbing and carrying?"

"I'll be cutting the telephone wires and spreading broken glass on the road leading to the building in case the night watchman somehow manages to contact the police. Then I'll drive to the quay at Maryhill Ironworks, where we'll meet and transfer the safe to the lorry."

"What about us?" Flintheart wondered, pointing to Skinflint and himself. "What will we be doing?"

"Your job is to get hold of all the equipment on the list," Gordon said.

Skinflint appeared to be worrying about something. "This club… Is it called the Dionysos?"

Gordon looked at Moira and she said, "Precisely, the Dionysos Club. It's owned by Ajax Christodoulopoulos. The one they usually call 'the Greek'."

I jumped. I'd heard the name of the Dionysos Club before. *That was where Lord Kilvaird had gambled away Shetland Jack's pearl necklace!*

A train passed over the bridge, making the house shake slightly. I heard the ice in Gordon's drink clink against the glass. Apart from that, Moira's office suddenly fell silent.

She looked at each of the gang in turn and said, "Well? Anything else you're wondering about?"

The atmosphere in the office had become tense. The gang exchanged sideways glances. It seemed that all of them were thinking the same thing, though no one dared say it out loud.

235

"Well?" Moira said again. Carl managed to pluck up the courage.

"Surely the Greek has good protection, doesn't he? Tommy Tarantello and his West End mob!"

"I'm fully aware of that," Moira said calmly. "So what?"

"That makes this job extremely risky," Skinflint said. "Tommy Tarantello is not going to let anyone rob a place he's been paid to protect. He and his gunmen will turn the city inside out to find out who did it."

Moira smiled. A smile completely devoid of warmth.

"Tarantello will never suspect us of doing the job," she said. "Not unless one of you talks, that is. Anyone who's going to have trouble keeping his mouth shut, put your hand up now!"

No one responded and no hands went up.

Flintheart did, however, speak. "But why do we have to hit the Greek specifically? There are plenty of other places we could break into."

Kevin, Carl and Skinflint all nodded to show that they'd been asking themselves the same question.

Moira stayed silent for a while before speaking. "OK, you are right. There are certain… *very particular*… risks to doing this job. And that's why you'll get a larger share of the goods than usual. You can divide all the ready cash and share certificates in the safe between you. It's all yours!"

A whisper of amazement ran around the room and the members of the gang looked at one another in astonishment... and pleasure.

Moira leant back in her chair and added, "But if we find any jewellery in the safe, that belongs to me."

Simmons

A week before Christmas I received more news of the Chief. He had successfully fulfilled his task and delivered the smuggled spirits to the gangsters in New York. The *Valkyrie* was now sailing east and heading home to Scotland. I couldn't find out exactly what had happened, but I understood there had been some drama when the whisky was handed over. There was talk of coastguard cutters, fog and shots being fired. But the Chief was apparently unscathed and, in any case, he was still in command of the *Valkyrie*.

With its storms and icy cold, the North Atlantic at the end of December is feared by seamen. They sometimes call it the "Devil's Dancefloor". But the Chief had sailed there before and if nothing unforeseen happened he should be back in Glasgow within three or four weeks. I began counting the days.

Christmas Eve was approaching and Moira and her gang were finalizing their plans for their raid on the Greek's gambling club. The mood around the house was nervous.

Bernie was more anxious than anyone else and I soon understood why. He was afraid the robbery would go wrong because of him. The rest of the gang lost no opportunity of reminding him how clumsy he'd been on earlier jobs.

"Don't think, Bernie!" Moira said. "Just do what you're told to do. It's when you try to think for yourself that everything goes to hell."

~

The night before Christmas Eve the temperature fell and there were snow showers over Glasgow. On the morning of Christmas Eve Moira was annoyed and concerned: the plan had been for the raid to be carried out under cover of darkness, but now the whole city was gleaming white.

They held a brief crisis meeting and Moira decided they would go ahead with the job anyway. After all, the weather might change in the course of the day. Bernie and I were taken by car to a village on the River Clyde a few miles west of Glasgow. The steam launch was waiting for us at the lock gates of a narrow canal. Bernie was less anxious than he usually was about travelling by boat, because Gordon had explained to him that we weren't venturing out on the great River Clyde, but sticking to the narrow Forth and Clyde Canal. The banks would never be more than a couple of yards away.

The trip along the canal took the whole day, as we slid gently through the winter landscape. Bernie and I had the job of manning the winches that opened and closed the gates of the numerous locks we had to pass through. It was hard work, but that was nothing new to me.

I noticed that the skinny skipper was watching me while I worked. And then suddenly, as I was tying off a stern rope, he said, "Nice to meet you, Sally Jones. My name's Roger Simmons."

He then gave a quick smile that revealed a row of yellow teeth with many black gaps.

"I've heard people talking about you," he continued. "There aren't that many gorillas sailing the seas, are there?"

I shook my head.

Skipper Simmons said nothing for a while, but a look of concern furrowed his brow.

"I heard that your friend Koskela took the job of skipper on Moira's smuggling vessel. Was he forced to?"

I nodded.

"I thought as much," Simmons said. "You don't mess around with Moira Gray. I borrowed some money from her a couple of years ago. When I couldn't pay it back in time, I had to choose between having my skull bashed in or joining her gang as the boatman… So here I am now."

We met another boat on a curve and Simmons had to concentrate on the steering for a while.

Then he said, "Keep your head down, Sally Jones, and don't let Moira know how much you can do. If she finds out, there's no guarantee she'll let you go when Koskela returns."

I nodded gratefully. It sounded like good advice.

Skipper Simmons was in the same jam as me and that made me feel a little less lonely.

~

Moira's guess paid off. By midday the cold night air had been blown away by a damp, mild breeze from the sea. The mist grew dense and the snow was washed away by a gentle drizzle.

Darkness had fallen by the time we reached Maryhill. The tall trees lining the canal obscured the lights of the surrounding houses and it became impossible to pick out where the water of the canal ended and the banks began. Skipper Simmons cut the speed and sent me to keep a look-out in the bows.

A gleam of light suddenly shone a little way in front of us and as we approached we could hear a voice whispering on the canal bank.

"Is that Simmons?"

"It is," the skipper answered.

Two figures emerged from the shadows and climbed aboard. They were Carl and Kevin, both dressed in dark clothes. We hove to and waited for half an hour or so. The only sounds in the darkness were Kevin shivering and cursing himself for not wearing warm enough clothes. Carl laughed at him—he'd solved the problem by making Bernie hand over his coat.

When the hands of Carl's pocket watch pointed to ten to midnight, we moved out onto the canal again. A short distance farther on a big house appeared between the trees on the right bank. As we got nearer, the skipper cut the engine and the launch drifted silently into the shadow of an enormous weeping willow below the house.

Through the branches of the tree I could see a grand old stone building, its façade almost totally masked by a lush growth of ivy. Carl slung a rope and tackle over his shoulder and Kevin took a crowbar. They jumped ashore and were swallowed up by the night.

All we had to do now was wait. I could hear Bernie's breath coming in gulps as he grew more and more nervous with every passing minute. Skipper Simmons said some calming words to him, but it wasn't much help. Eventually a light flashed three times in a window on the top floor of the house. It was the signal we had been waiting for.

Once ashore, Bernie and I made our way up through park-land trees and out onto a lawn close to the house. There were dim lights in a couple of the ground floor windows, but no sign of anyone inside.

The windows on the top floor were completely dark and one of them was open. Carl and Kevin had managed to heave the safe up onto the window ledge and were preparing to lower it. In the silence I could hear the two of them having a whis-pered argument about the best way of doing it. In the end they seemed to come to an agreement and the safe was pushed over the edge. The rope tautened with a twang and the safe swung back and forth below the window before coming to rest at the end of the rope. Jubilant—but silent—Carl and Kevin started lowering the safe to the ground.

Ivy

I could see straightaway that there was going to be a problem. When planning the job, the gang hadn't considered the ivy covering the walls of the house. The plant's thick carpet of foliage hid a tangled network of tough tendrils firmly attached to the stonework. Time after time the heavy safe caught on these tendrils. Carl and Kevin managed to free the safe several times by tugging on the rope, but then it came to a sudden stop. It seemed that some shoots of ivy had broken clear of the wall and become lodged under the safe.

"Hell and damnation!" Carl snarled. "You'll have to climb down and push the safe clear of the wall!"

"Not on your life!" Kevin hissed. "Why should I risk my neck? You do it!"

They argued for a while, and then it occurred to Carl that there was a better solution.

"Bernie!" he hissed into the darkness. "You'll have to climb up and free the safe!"

Bernie didn't answer and simply stared up into the darkness with a look of incomprehension. Speaking slowly and clearly, Carl explained the situation once more, making an effort to restrain his rage at Bernie's slow-wittedness.

Bernie eventually understood what Carl wanted him to do. He gripped the ivy and found a foothold on a shoot. The ivy creaked under his weight.

Carl's voice came from above, "If you don't manage it, Bernie, I'll tell Moira it was your fault we couldn't bring the safe home."

With panic showing in his eyes, Bernie found a new hand-hold and pulled himself a little higher.

I could see this was going to end in disaster. Bernie was big and heavy and he was no climber. The safe was stuck a good fifteen feet up and if Bernie fell from that height he'd be injured, maybe even break his neck.

"Get a move on, Bernie, you idiot!" Carl snarled. "Otherwise Moira will never forgive you, you know that, don't you? *Never!*"

Bernie pulled himself higher and his trembling legs tried to find a foothold. But both he and I had forgotten we were chained together and when the chain pulled him off balance, he fell the few feet to the ground. He sat down on the grass and stared at me with confusion on his face.

I jumped up, grabbed a branch of the ivy with my hand and quickly climbed up as far as the chain would let me. Then

I climbed back down and gestured to Bernie that he should unlock the chain round my waist.

That made Bernie even more confused. Meanwhile up above us Carl and Kevin were trying to urge Bernie on with every kind of threat.

I showed Bernie again what I wanted him to do and at last there was a slight glimmer of comprehension in his eyes.

"Are you good at climbing?" he asked in a quiet voice.

I nodded vigorously and pointed once again to the padlock on the chain.

Bernie began rooting around in his pocket, eventually found the key and undid the padlock. The chain fell to the ground and I quickly gathered it up and put it in Bernie's jacket pocket.

It didn't take me more than ten seconds or so to climb up to the safe. Once there, I braced my back against the safe and my feet against the wall and pushed.

"Go it, Bernie! Well done!" Carl whispered.

"But Carl, Carl... Can't you see?" Kevin's voice broke in. "That's not Bernie. He's sent the ape up in his place!"

The safe now swung slowly clear of the wall and Carl and Kevin began letting out the rope again. The safe moved downwards and now the thought came to me: *This is my chance to escape!*

It was indeed! No longer hindered by the chain, all I needed to do was climb out to the corner of the house and leap across to a big cypress tree that was growing right by the tall iron fence that ran round the whole garden. Within seconds I would be swallowed up by the darkness.

But was it a good idea?

I had, of course, already decided to stay with the gang until the Chief was close to Glasgow, but that might be a month or more.

Bernie, I think, suspected what I was thinking. The safe had reached the ground and Bernie was looking anxiously up at me. The whites of his eyes gleamed in the darkness. If I ran away, he would be the one who got the blame. I knew that.

I made my decision and in no time at all I was back down on the ground. Bernie was so paralysed with worry that I had to remind him with a nudge to pick up his end of the heavy safe.

~

No more than ten minutes later the launch moved out of its hiding place under the weeping willow and set off slowly along the canal, returning the way we'd come. Everyone stayed silent and kept their heads below the rail. I noticed that Carl and Kevin glanced in my direction several times—and they weren't grateful looks they were giving me. I suppose they didn't like the idea of having to be saved by an ape.

The gang's lorry was parked waiting for us when we reached the first lock. The place was deserted at this time of day, except for Gordon who was standing smoking in the darkness.

"Everything go according to plan?" he asked when we had moored the launch.

"No," Carl answered angrily. "Your plan wasn't particularly good. You'd failed to mention that the whole house was cloaked in a great mass of horrible foliage. Like a damn jungle! The safe got stuck halfway down."

Gordon puffed his cigarette calmly and nodded towards the safe. "But I see you've brought it with you in any case."

"We have," Kevin said. "Carl and me… We fixed the problem and salvaged your useless plan… We did, Gordon, that's just what we did!"

"Very smart of you, I'm sure," he said unmoved. Gordon tossed his cigarette into the canal and nodded towards the lorry. "Now let's get that safe up onto the lorry. Moira's eager to see what's in it."

~

Carl and Kevin accompanied Gordon back to Oswald Street in the lorry and Bernie and I had to remain on the steam launch to help Skipper Simmons. The launch had to be taken all the way back to the locks leading out to the River Clyde.

A new day had dawned by the time Bernie and I arrived back at the house. Bernie's eyes were red-rimmed with tiredness and I presume mine were the same. We both ate a large portion of porridge in his quarters before he took me down to the cellar so I could get some sleep. Out of habit he started fishing in his jacket pocket for the key to the chain round my waist and instead he pulled out the chain, the padlock, the lot!

Bernie stared at the chain for a long time and then looked at me.

"You could have run away…" he said.

I nodded.

"But you stayed."

I nodded again.

He stood there looking at me. Then he turned and left the room without bothering to lock the door behind him.

Acetylene

Later that day Gordon, Carl and Kevin set about trying to open the safe. In the meantime they talked about what they would do with the money they hoped to find in it.

"I'm going to buy a pair of those American shoes with steel toecaps," Kevin said. "They're the latest fashion in Chicago, you know. Really smart! And practical when it comes to kicking someone's kneecaps."

Kevin's great dream, which he was forever talking about, was to go to America and become a real gangster like Al "Scarface" Capone or Charles "Lucky" Luciano. Instead of saving for a ticket on a ship to America, however, he wasted every penny he earned going to American gangster films and buying expensive clothes in order to dress like the crooks in the films.

Carl was intending to save his share of the loot. He lived with his ageing father in a small flat south of the river and his dream was to have enough money to put him in an old people's home.

"What a waste of money!" Kevin said. "Why don't you just take the old fellow down to the Twilight Quay and chuck him in the river? That won't cost you anything!"

"I know," Carl said, mulling it over. "I've thought about it… frequently, in fact."

"And what are you going to do with your money?" Kevin asked, turning to Gordon with a malicious grin. "Pay off old gambling debts maybe? From what I've heard you don't have much luck with the horses."

"If you really must know, I'm going to buy a hat," Gordon said.

The Greek's safe proved to be very robust and they were unable to break into it until Gordon got hold of an acetylene torch. Inside the safe they found wads of money and all kinds of valuable objects that desperate gamblers had staked and lost to the Greek. Some of the banknotes had been burnt by the heat of the acetylene torch, but there was plenty left for them to share.

The most valuable item in the safe was Shetland Jack's pearl necklace, which was undamaged. Moira's eyes shone when she picked it up. The moment obviously meant a great deal to her, not just because the necklace was so valuable. There was something else… something that had nothing to do with money.

Could Moira be Shetland Jack's daughter after all?

~

During the days following the robbery, the gang's mood was tense and wary. They talked in low voices about a man called Tommy Tarantello who, as I soon learnt from eavesdropping on their conversations, was the most feared gangster boss in Glasgow. He and his gang extorted money from shopkeepers and publicans by forcing them to pay for "protection". Anyone who failed to pay would find their shop windows smashed or their legs broken. Some of Tarantello's henchmen were members of his own family he'd brought over from the city of Salerno in Italy.

I overheard Gordon saying that these men were now going round the city trying to find out who was responsible for the break-in at the Greek's gambling club. People who wouldn't talk were given a beating—as was anyone who tried to be helpful. Tommy Tarantello's gang was not exactly particular.

Gordon's view was that we should all stay in the house until the fuss had blown over.

Moira saw things differently: "If Tommy Tarantello gets news that we're lying low, it won't be long before we get a visit. Best thing is to carry on as if nothing has happened. And our top priority is to plan the Hogmanay celebrations at Lucky Lucy's."

~

The following night we made a chilly trip down the river to deliver stolen goods to the Irish smugglers. On the return journey we put in at Clydebank to collect the two ten-gallon casks of whisky Moira had ordered from an illegal distillery in the neighbourhood. The whisky was destined for the Hogmanay party at Lucky Lucy's, where hundreds of thirsty guests were expected to come to celebrate the arrival of the New Year. The thought of all the money to be made put Moira and the rest of the gang in the best of moods.

A few days later the gang heard a worrying rumour that was doing the rounds. The Clydeside Shebeen, a rival illegal club, was trying to steal our New Year customers by promising to lay on a famous Dundee knife thrower as entertainment.

"We'll have to provide entertainment too," Moira said to Gordon and Lucky Lucy. "And it'll have to be something better than a knife thrower. Fix it!"

Gordon and Lucky Lucy came up with various suggestions as to artistes they might call on, everything from jesters with unusual deformities to a pair of genuine Sumo wrestlers based in Liverpool. Moira pooh-poohed all their suggestions.

"What about a boxing match, then?" Gordon said, looking at Bernie who was stacking chairs at the other end of the club. "I reckon there will be masses of people who'd like to see Bernie the Butcher in the ring again."

Moira smiled with pleasure and said, "Not a bad idea, Gordon, not a bad idea at all!"

~

A boxing ring was quickly constructed between four of the pillars supporting the roof of Lucky Lucy's Club. The whole gang thought it a brilliant idea—all except Bernie. I noticed how his lower lip trembled when Moira told him what was planned.

"You won't go messing this up, I hope?" she said sternly.

Bernie shook his head without raising his eyes from the floor.

"Good," Moira said. "Dig out your boxing gloves and start training, and I'll find a suitable opponent for you."

Bernie the Butcher

The coming fight was talked about endlessly. Who was going to be matched against Bernie in the ring? Some of the gang put their money on a boxer from the East End called Tobago Tim; others thought Bernie would be matched against the slugger known as Johnny "Killer" Carlton from Govan.

I was scrubbing the drawers behind the bar in the club one morning when Gordon came in with a parcel under his arm. He looked nervous. The parcel was for Lucky Lucy.

"For me?" she said with a big smile. "Really? How kind of you, Gordon!"

The parcel contained a cardboard box and in the box was an elegant ladies' hat. Lucky Lucy laughed in delight as she tried it on.

"I happened to see it in a shop window," Gordon said with a little cough.

I wasn't particularly surprised. Gordon often used to find

a reason to come down to the club and chat with Lucky Lucy. I suppose he must have been more than a little in love with her. And she with him, perhaps.

They talked about one thing and another before getting round to the New Year boxing match. And then Lucky Lucy asked, "Why do they call Bernie 'the Butcher'?"

"It was his nickname as a boxer," Gordon said. "He was actually pretty well-known at one time. Everyone wanted to see him fight."

"Wow," Lucy said. "Was he that good?"

Gordon shook his head. "No, no, not at all. Bernie was useless. One of the worst boxers I've ever seen, in fact. But he was entertaining."

"In what way?" Lucy wondered.

Gordon thought a moment before answering. "In a way it was nasty. You see, no one ever managed to knock Bernie down. Even though he couldn't box properly, he didn't lose a single fight because of a knock-out. His opponents might punch and punch, but Bernie just stayed upright. It was incredible to watch."

Lucy poured each of them a small glass of whisky and said, "It's hardly surprising he looks the way he does, then."

Gordon nodded. They were quiet for a while, then Lucy said, "But I still don't understand why he's called 'the Butcher'. Not if he was the one who came off badly in every match."

"That name came as a result of his fits of rage."

"Fits of rage?"

"Yes," Gordon said. "Now and again Bernie just lost it. It didn't happen often, and only when he'd taken a real beating. Then Bernie would go completely mad. He'd rush round howling, his arms going like a windmill, and nothing could stop him. Anything that got in his way was smashed. His opponent and the referee would throw themselves out of the ring, but on a couple of occasions Bernie knocked them unconscious—both of them. And, of course, the crowd would go wild with delight!"

Lucky Lucy shuddered. "But what's going to happen on New Year's Eve? What if he has one of his fits of rage in here?"

Gordon nodded and looked concerned.

"There's always that risk, of course," he said. "But Moira knows what she's doing. She was Bernie's manager at the time."

"Was she?" Lucy asked.

"She was indeed. That's how she made her living for many years. People were crazy about Bernie and she saw to it that he always had a couple of fights every week."

Lucky Lucy topped up their glasses. "Bernie must have been earning good money too, wasn't he?"

Gordon laughed. "Bernie? He didn't get a penny."

Lucky Lucy looked confused at this point. "So why did he agree to fight?"

Gordon put down his glass before continuing. "Because she told him to, of course. He's her little brother."

Lucy looked at Gordon in amazement.

"Didn't you know that Moira and Bernie are brother and sister?" he said. "I thought everyone round here knew that."

"But Bernie's surname is Brodie, isn't it?" Lucy said.

Gordon nodded. "That's what Moira used to be called as well. But when she married a shipbroker called Alexander Gray, she took his surname. She'd actually been hoping to get more than his name, but after the wedding she realized she'd been tricked. The fellow was bankrupt, and when he died of a stroke a year later, the only thing she inherited was this house. But that was enough to enable her to start working her way up in the world."

Lucky Lucy thought about all this for a while. Then she stood on tiptoe and gave Gordon a kiss on the cheek.

"Thanks for the hat," she said. "I'll think of you every time I wear it."

A faint flush of pink spread across Gordon's stubbly cheeks.

The news that Moira was Bernie's sister was as much of a surprise to me as it was to Lucky Lucy. After giving it some thought, though, I realized it shouldn't really have been a surprise. It was obvious that Bernie didn't fit in the gang at all and everyone in the house thought of him as a nuisance rather than useful. Even Moira. She would never have given work and a room to someone like Bernie if she hadn't felt she had to.

~

On the day before New Year's Eve no one appeared to know who Bernie's opponent in the ring was to be. And there was no sign of Bernie. Moira had ordered him to do nothing but train. Heavy thuds could be heard emanating from his room as he practised punching a sack of sand for hour after hour.

On the morning of New Year's Eve I was woken by Carl and Kevin marching in through the door of my cellar. They were in an excellent mood and smiled at me in an expectant sort of way. Half asleep, I sat up.

"Have a look at this," Carl said, holding up a cloth bag he'd brought with him. "We've got some presents for you."

Carl threw me the bag and I squeezed it suspiciously. Then I cautiously put my hand in and took out a folded garment of some kind, which turned out to be a pair of big, white shorts with a broad, elastic waistband.

I looked at Carl and Kevin. What was this supposed to mean?

"There's more," Kevin said.

I shoved my hand down into the bag again and this time pulled out a pair of black boxing gloves.

34

Fight to the Death

Both Carl and Kevin started laughing.

"You've got it, ape!" Carl said. "Bernie's opponent tonight is *you!*"

"And believe me, it's going to be hilarious," Kevin said.

"For those of us in the audience, anyway," Carl added.

And they both laughed again.

I shook my head and pushed the gloves away.

Carl's eyes narrowed to slits and his lips formed a cruel smile.

"No chance," he said. "Don't try it on with us. You will be fighting Bernie tonight. We'll come back later and help you warm up."

And with that they departed, locking the door behind them.

My heart was full of fear and I spent the whole morning alone in my cellar. I didn't want to believe that this was true. I *couldn't*

believe it was true. Carl and Kevin must have been playing a joke on me. Surely they couldn't be serious?

The hours passed slowly. At noon Kevin brought me a bowl of boiled potatoes to eat. The blade of his flick knife was open and his eyes didn't leave me the whole time he was in the cellar. He was obviously worried I might try to escape.

The afternoon gloom outside my barred window gradually became the dark of night. Moira had hired a small orchestra for the evening and I could hear the sounds of musical instruments being tuned up. Then the first guests began arriving. They were talking in loud, high-spirited voices and there was the noise of laughter and doors being slammed. A little later it sounded as if there was a large crowd out on the street, eager to be let in. Lucky Lucy's was going to be busy tonight. In my mind's eye I could see the red-faced ruffians who yelled at us and played the fool when Bernie and I were on the door. I had no doubt they would turn up tonight to see Bernie the Butcher in the ring, and they'd be hoping he would have one of his notorious fits of berserk fury.

Later in the evening I must have fallen asleep for a while, only to be woken with a start by several sharp explosions. It was midnight and the quay outside was lit by the flashing light of New Year rockets being fired. The orchestra played 'Auld Lang Syne' and the walls of my cellar rang as the guests sang in the New Year.

For a few short, hopeful moments I thought the boxing match may have been cancelled—after all, it was so late.

But then came the sound of footsteps and laughter from the corridor leading to my cellar, the door opened and in came Carl and Kevin. Their eyes were gleaming, their cheeks flushed and their breath stank of alcohol. Each of them was carrying a stout cane.

"Now we're going to have some fun, the three of us!" Carl said.

He took off his jacket, undid the black bow tie he was wearing and rolled up his shirt sleeves. Kevin did the same. They were holding their canes with both hands and they began circling me. My heart was pounding.

"Time for you to get warmed up," Kevin slurred drunkenly and aimed a first blow at me.

I dodged to one side and the cane struck the stone floor with a sharp crack.

Carl caught my eye and stared at me. "Right, ape, we have to make sure you're really angry and raring to fight when you go up in the ring."

"That's the thing! People want to see blood! A fight to the death!" Kevin said.

Carl struck me across the back and then, as I spun round, Kevin struck a blow on my upper arm. It was hard and it hurt dreadfully.

I drew my lips back and bared my teeth and a muffled growl rose from my throat. This happens when I'm threatened. Carl had already raised his cane to strike again, but stumbled backwards at the sight of my long, sharp, canine teeth.

Kevin, too, lost his courage, his evil sneer suddenly wiped away.

"What do you reckon, Carl?" he said with a tremor in his voice. "It looks to me as if we've warmed the ape up quite enough."

Carl tried to put a brave face on it when he looked at me, but it wasn't convincing. He said, "Yeah… I agree. We don't want the beast completely out of control. We'll let her calm down a bit and come back when it's time for the fight."

Carl and Kevin hurriedly put on their jackets and left my cellar.

~

I hoped that Carl and Kevin wouldn't dare come back, that they might lie and say I was ill in order to avoid fetching me. In my heart of hearts, though, I knew better than that. Once Moira had decided I was to box Bernie, that was what was going to happen.

The next time the cellar door was opened, it was Gordon who came in first. Carl and Kevin were close behind him, their sticks raised ready to strike.

Gordon looked at me calmly before saying in a firm voice, "You are a smart ape, Sally Jones, and you understand what people are saying to you. Listen to me carefully now…"

He leant forward and continued. "The guests in the club want to see blood, so Moira has ordered Bernie to give you a real beating, as much of a beating as he can. Even if you get killed in the process. It's your life you're fighting for tonight! Do you understand?"

Our eyes met for a few seconds and then, reluctantly, I nodded.

"Good," Gordon said. "Now put on your boxing shorts and I'll help you lace up your gloves."

The noise from the festivities upstairs grew louder as we walked through the cellar corridor. The storeroom adjoining the club was packed with people, a fog of tobacco smoke hanging thick below the ceiling. Bets were being laid and banknotes waved. Everyone turned in my direction when we entered and some clapped, others laughed. One man, his eyes bloodshot with drink, started dancing around and shadow boxing in front of me.

I caught a quick glimpse of the back of Bernie's head as he went through the door into the club. He was welcomed with a deafening roar.

I was pushed forward. Someone placed a towel on my shoulders. Things were being shouted in my ears and people were patting and thumping my arms and back. Suddenly I found myself close to the door and then Carl and Kevin pushed me roughly over the threshold.

The big club room was a mass of people, those who couldn't find a seat were standing on tables around the walls. Hundreds of flushed and sweaty faces were staring at me. The air was so thick with the smell of alcohol and sweat that it was hard to breathe. Applause, shouts and bursts of laughter combined into a terrifying roar. Carl and Kevin pushed me through the throng and up to the boxing ring in the middle of the room, where Bernie was waiting, huge and pale, his arms hanging loose and his eyes lowered.

My heart was racing and all my instincts were telling me to flee. But there was no way out. Carl and Kevin forced me to climb under the ropes and into the ring. A man in a white shirt sounded a gong and the audience roared.

The match started.

~

Bernie had no wish to fight me. I could see that straightaway. But even if he'd wanted to, there was no way he could get at me—he was far too big and heavy and slow.

Moira was standing at the side of the ring screaming at Bernie to go on the attack. He lumbered forward, swinging his right fist aimlessly. I kept moving and took care not to get trapped in one of the corners.

At the start, the crowd was excited and expectant. Every time Bernie managed to get close to me, their shouts and yells rose to a roar, but eventually their expectation turned into disappointment. More and more dissatisfied voices and boos could be heard and some began to laugh and hurl abuse at Bernie.

There was a break at the end of the first round and Bernie and I sat down to rest in opposite corners of the ring. While Moira was bawling and berating Bernie, Gordon was speaking into my ear.

"This won't do," he said. "If the audience doesn't see blood soon, they'll get sick of it and go home. You must get into close combat with Bernie in the next round—and stay there! Otherwise this is going to be a fiasco and your life won't be worth living."

The gong sounded and the match started again. I could see that Moira was glaring at me with murder in her eyes and I realized I had to do as Gordon had said. I had no other choice.

I don't really know what happened next. My memories are like the scattered fragments of a shredded picture. I've heard that's what happens as a result of concussion.

The only thing I know for sure is that the match ended with Bernie knocking me out. I've since pieced together some images from the seconds preceding the punch. I had allowed Bernie to drive me into a corner and, above the wild yelling of the audience, I heard Moira's shrill, hoarse voice shouting, "Now, Bernie, punch now! Punch!"

For one brief moment I caught Bernie's eyes. They were wide with panic and desperation.

Then he raised his fist.

A moment later everything went black.

The Warning

We are in Moira's big office. She is sitting at her desk and Ana Molina is sitting opposite her.

Carl and Kevin have a tight grip on her arms and Ana's face is pale. Carl is wearing his knuckleduster on his right hand and Kevin has flicked open the blade of his knife. They are both grinning evilly.

Moira studies Ana calmly and says, "Ana Molina, you shouldn't have come here. I don't like people poking their noses into my business. You've made your bed and you'll have to lie in it!"

Moira gestures to Carl and Kevin to take Ana away.

"What shall we do with her?" Carl asks.

"Take her down to the Twilight Quay and teach her a lesson she'll never forget..." Moira says.

~

I woke with a start, scarcely able to breathe. My heart was pounding and I was shaking with terror. Darkness was all round me and I had no idea where I was.

The nightmare faded slowly and my breathing and heart rate became calmer. I noticed that the right-hand side of my face was unusually cold and I had a dreadful headache.

The cause of the cold proved to be a rubber bag filled with ice pressed against my cheek. I moved the bag and carefully probed under my fur with my fingers. There was a painful swelling running from my jaw up to my forehead. I couldn't open that eye and I had a loose tooth. A stream of unpleasant images flashed quickly through my mind... *blinding light, screaming voices, flushed faces, Bernie...*

All of a sudden I knew exactly where I was. I was lying, covered with a blanket, on the mattress down in my cellar. That meant the boxing match was over.

A warm sense of relief flowed slowly through my body.

I slipped in and out of a restless sleep. The sounds of music and raucous voices could still be heard as the grey light of dawn filtered in through the barred window. The Hogmanay party was still going on.

I suddenly had a sense that I wasn't alone. I carefully raised my head and tried to focus my one, undamaged eye. I picked out a big, dark figure sitting leaning against the wall by the door. It was Bernie.

We looked at one another and then he lowered his eyes.

I realized that it must have been Bernie who had carried me here. And that he was the one who had covered me up and placed the ice pack on my injured face. No one else in the house would have done that. And now he was sitting there keeping watch over me.

I shut my eyes and went back to sleep.

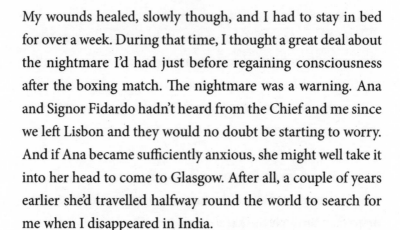

My wounds healed, slowly though, and I had to stay in bed for over a week. During that time, I thought a great deal about the nightmare I'd had just before regaining consciousness after the boxing match. The nightmare was a warning. Ana and Signor Fidardo hadn't heard from the Chief and me since we left Lisbon and they would no doubt be starting to worry. And if Ana became sufficiently anxious, she might well take it into her head to come to Glasgow. After all, a couple of years earlier she'd travelled halfway round the world to search for me when I disappeared in India.

And what if Ana actually managed to find me here with Moira and her gang of crooks? It wasn't beyond the bounds of possibility that it could turn out as badly as in my nightmare.

So, what was I to do?

I didn't have to spend too long thinking about it: I had to come up with some way of sending a message to Ana and Signor Fidardo to allay their concerns. If they heard that everything was going well for the Chief and me, Ana wouldn't come looking for us.

∽

Bernie brought me food three times a day. He didn't speak at all during his visits and he avoided meeting my eye. But he always stayed longer than was strictly necessary. Sometimes he would sit for a while, his back against the wall at the other end of my cellar. At other times he just stood there and stared at the floor.

I suspected there was something Bernie wanted to say to me, but for some reason he couldn't get it out. One evening, though, I decided to give him a hand. I got out of bed, walked across the room and sat down beside him.

After we'd been sitting for a few minutes, he spoke to me in a quiet, hoarse voice. "I didn't want to hit you."

I nodded. I knew that already.

"Moira... She said I had to," Bernie said.

I knew that, too, so I nodded again.

Bernie turned in my direction. "Can you forgive me?"

I nodded for the third time.

Bernie's shoulders relaxed a bit and he breathed a long sigh of relief. It was as if he was suddenly being freed from an enormous burden.

We sat together in silence, side by side. I was becoming more and more drowsy and was already half asleep when Bernie stood up and helped me to my feet. He took me over to my mattress and I lay down and crept under the covers. Before I fell asleep, I heard Bernie close the door quietly behind him as he left.

~

My headache eased bit by bit, and one morning I noticed I could open my eye just a little. It came as a great relief to realize that my vision hadn't been damaged.

I no longer felt I could just lie there in my sick bed and do nothing. When Bernie brought me breakfast the following morning, I was already up and about in order to show him I was fit to start work again. He looked pleased, unlike the rest of the gang who didn't even seem to have noticed that I'd been lying injured in my bed since New Year. But that suited me: the less attention the thugs paid to my activities, the better.

The day being dry and windless, Flintheart thought it was an opportunity for Bernie and me to light a bonfire out in the backyard and burn a load of unsellable, old clothes. We were just about to carry a pile of moth-eaten trousers to the fire when Kevin came rushing down, out of breath. He told Flintheart to shut the shop and fetch Skinflint. The whole gang was to meet together in Moira's office without delay.

"What's up?" Flintheart wondered.

There was a tremor on Kevin's worm-like lips when he answered, "Tommy Tarantello is on his way here!"

Flintheart's hand covered her mouth. She was horrified. "Oh, Mother of God," she groaned. "This will be the end of us!"

Kevin disappeared rapidly the way he'd come. He shouted back over his shoulder, "Don't forget your pistol! And tell Skinflint to bring his shotgun!"

I regretted not having stayed down in my cellar that morning.

Tarantello

The atmosphere in Moira's office was tense. Carl and Kevin were in the process of loading their revolvers and stuffing their pockets with spare ammunition. Flintheart was standing at the window, keeping watch on the street through a crack in the curtains.

"Oy, oy, oy," she muttered quietly. "We should never have burgled that gambling club! Tommy Tarantello will have put two and two together and now he's coming to…"

Moira slapped her hand on the table.

"Calm down, Fiona," she said between clenched teeth. "If Tommy had been intending to attack us, he wouldn't have phoned and warned us he was on his way. Take your places now."

Carl and Kevin took up position at the bar, their firearms ready but hidden behind the counter. Bernie and I were ordered to stand in a corner and look menacing.

"You and I will go and meet Tommy Tarantello and his mob down on the street," Gordon said to Skinflint. "Do you have your gun with you?"

Skinflint leered unpleasantly as he opened his jacket: a sawn-off shotgun was hanging below his armpit.

He and Gordon left the room. As for the rest of us, we had to wait.

The small clock on Moira's desk had just struck ten when Flintheart, voice hoarse with excitement, reported that a large, white Plymouth had pulled in at the kerb outside. A few minutes later, footsteps could be heard on the stairs and the door to the office opened.

Gordon was the first to enter. Then he stepped to one side and made room for a man to pass him—a man so broad across the shoulders that he had to turn slightly sideways so as not to get jammed in the doorframe. He had a gleaming white scar running from his forehead down across his face and all the way to the point of his chin. The eyes that peered out under the brim of his hat were watchful and he kept one hand inside his jacket, where he obviously had a weapon at the ready.

He was followed by a tall, erect woman in a long cape. Her face, stern and earnest, was shaded by a plain lady's hat. My immediate thought was that there was something familiar about the woman.

A short, older man in a tailored woollen overcoat followed the woman in. He bowed and gave Moira's hand a light kiss.

"You are very welcome, Mr Tarantello," she said, managing to sound as if she meant it. "We've left it far too long since we last met."

"Indeed, how time passes!" he said in the rasping voice of a chain smoker. "But you're looking as wonderful as ever, Moira. Allow me to introduce my niece—she has come all the way from Salerno in Italy."

The two women shook hands and, speaking with a heavy Italian accent, his niece said, "My name is Florenza Tarantello. I'm pleased to meet you."

I jumped. *I'd heard that voice somewhere before, I was sure I had.*

Sounding full of pride, Tommy Tarantello said, "Florenza's father was the head of the Tarantello family in Salerno. He was killed by the *carabinieri* a year ago. Florenza took her revenge by blowing up the nearest police station. After that, of course, she needed a change of air, so I invited her to come here. She left Italy on an emigrant ship and had a dreadful voyage as a result of diphtheria breaking out on board. But she got here in the end…"

Tommy Tarantello carried on talking, but I wasn't listening any longer. I suddenly knew where I'd come across Florenza Tarantello before.

She and I had met on board the SS Campania *in Lisbon.* And now I knew why everyone on the ship had been so frightened of her: they knew she was a wanted *mafiosa*.

Moira gestured to the seats by the bar and Tommy Tarantello went over and sat down. Florenza remained standing. She had noticed me and we looked at one another in amazement. Then she went and took a seat beside her uncle.

Tommy Tarantello was sipping a whisky grog that Lucky Lucy had given him.

"My plan is for Florenza to be my successor when I retire," he said to Moira. "And that day is not far off. I came to Glasgow as a young man without a penny in my pocket and I worked my way up. My first job was with a small family firm selling *gelato*. At that time there were many Italians working as glass-makers in Scotland. I saw the opportunities and started off by selling protection to my countrymen. Anyone who didn't pay up would find their truckloads of glass shattered. The rules were simple and honourable and everyone could understand them. And with time, my little business grew."

The only sound audible apart from Tommy Tarantello's quiet, hoarse voice was the buzzing of a weary winter fly in the window facing Oswald Street.

"I've had many, many good days in this city," Tarantello continued. "But recently I've started to feel old. And times are

277

changing. There was a time when there was *honour* among thieves, but these days many of our kind don't have a decent bone in their bodies. Just consider, for instance, the sordid tale of the burglary of the Greek's gambling club in Maryhill…"

The atmosphere in the room suddenly felt electric. Tommy Tarantello gently spun his glass.

"Everyone in Glasgow knows that the Greek pays me for protection," Tarantello said slowly. "And yet someone robbed him… Shameless… A serious insult to me."

"Do you have any idea who it might be?" Moira enquired, no sign of a tremor in her voice.

Tommy Tarantello shook his head. "No, I don't. But it seems the thieves made their way to Maryhill by boat. Along the canal, I mean. That's the only clue I have."

The gangster wrinkled up his grey eyebrows.

"This boat business, of course, made me wonder whether it might be one of the gangs from down by the waterfront. Dolan Duffy and his Queen's Dock gang, perhaps? Or Willie Turnbull who controls the wharfs down in Govan? Or it could have been Alfie Cohen's gang from Kingston Dock?…"

Tommy Tarantello leant in closer to Moira and looked her in the eye. "And then there's you, Moira. You and your gang are based down here on the riverside. And you have your own boat… or so I've heard. Perhaps you know something about?…"

Moira shook her head firmly and said in a steady voice, "If I had any idea who hit the Greek, I'd have already told you, Mr Tarantello. My guess is that it's an outsider. Someone who didn't know that the Greek was under your protection. A mob from Dundee, perhaps. Or from Aberdeen. But not from Glasgow. There's no one here who'd dare challenge you, Mr Tarantello."

Tommy Tarantello and Moira measured one another up.

Then Tarantello leant back in his chair and nodded. "Maybe you're right, Moira, and maybe not. We'll find out soon enough."

After a few more minutes of chit-chat, Tommy rose to his feet and thanked Moira for her hospitality. Moira, for her part, assured Tommy Tarantello that he was always welcome in her house. Both of them sounded sincere, but there was no hint of warmth in their eyes.

On their way out, Florenza stopped as she was passing me. She gave a short sharp nod, just as she'd done when we parted on board the *Campania*. And I nodded back.

~

For the rest of that day the atmosphere in the house was downcast. Every member of the gang seemed to have a personal little cloud of concern hanging over them. Moira did her best to lighten the mood.

"Tommy Tarantello is groping in the dark, like the short-sighted old man he is," she sneered. "He has no idea who robbed the Greek, so he's going round the city trying to frighten people into giving themselves away. There's no need for us to be concerned!"

No one in the gang contradicted Moira, but nor did any of them seem convinced by what she said.

A Greeting from Glasgow

The days passed and we heard no more from Tommy Tarantello. Life in the house on Oswald Street went back to normal. Or almost. Even though no one mentioned the powerful gangster, a guarded, uneasy feeling hung in the air after his visit.

For my part, I had other things to think about. One morning when Bernie and I were working in the shop, I found an unused postcard and some stamps in a box of bits and pieces. I smuggled the card, stamps and a pencil back to my cellar and once there I addressed the card to Ana and Signor Fidardo and wrote a note:

We are well. Staying in Glasgow a while longer. The Chief sends his love. Sally Jones

All I had to do now was post the card and I was intending to do so the next time Bernie and I were sent out on some job.

I didn't have long to wait. The very next day Lucy asked us to run an errand for her. We were to return a dress she had on approval from a shop in Bath Street. Before we left, I ran back down to my cellar and fetched the postcard.

I kept my eyes open for a letter box on the way to Bath Street, but didn't find one, so on our way back I made sure we passed the post office by Central Station. Bernie was surprised when I stopped at the big, red post box outside the post office. I took out the postcard and popped it into the dark slot in the post box.

Now I felt a great sense of relief. At last I could forget the awful nightmare about Ana, Moira and the Twilight Quay!

At that moment, however, I heard a sharp voice behind Bernie and me.

"What were you up to there?"

I turned round quickly and there was Flintheart, although it took me a few seconds to recognize her. She was dressed in a very expensive sable cape and she had a posh fur cap perched on her head. I'd seen the cape before—Skinflint had bought it off a thief who specialized in stealing expensive clothes from the cloakrooms of city restaurants. The fur cap, no doubt, was also stolen goods.

Flintheart stared at me suspiciously. She must have been coming out of the post office just as I was putting the postcard in the post box.

"What was that?" she said to Bernie again. "Whatever it was the ape put in the post? It looked like a postcard."

Bernie didn't know what to say. He looked at me, but I stared at the ground and pretended not to understand what they were talking about.

"Who was it who sent you into the city?" Flintheart said impatiently.

"Lucy did," Bernie said.

Flintheart licked her thin lips, as she always did when she was being nosy.

"Lucy? Was she the one who asked you to post a card? Who was it going to?"

Bernie shook his head. "No," he said. "We were returning a dress."

"A dress? What are you talking about now? Who asked you to post the card?"

Bernie looked at me, obviously hoping I would help him out.

Flintheart snorted. "Bernie, you're hopeless," she said. "Push off now and go back to the house and find something useful to do. But don't go the same way as me! It's not proper for a *lady* to be seen in your sort of company."

Not much happened during the following week, except the arrival of winter in Scotland. First came cold air sweeping down from the Arctic Ocean to the north, followed by a deep depression moving in from the south-west. The best part of three feet of snow fell on Glasgow in a couple of days. I thought of the Chief and hoped he'd managed to steer clear of the storm out in the Atlantic.

It was almost a month since I'd last heard anything from the *Valkyrie*. At that point, the Chief and his crew had just been setting out on their long return voyage across the Atlantic. How far had they sailed by now? And when might the *Valkyrie* be expected back in Glasgow?

In the hope of picking up news, I eavesdropped on every conversation in earshot. And one Friday while I was sweeping the floor in Lucky Lucy's, Gordon came in to have a chat with Lucy.

"That ape is really quite useful," I heard Lucy say. "How long can we keep it?"

"That's up to Moira," Gordon answered.

"What about that sailor then?" Lucy wondered. "He owns the ape, doesn't he? Won't he want it back?"

"I've no doubt he will," Gordon answered. "But we aren't likely to see Koskela for some time."

And then Gordon told Lucy about an accident that had happened ten days earlier on the *Valkyrie*. A deckhand had fallen from the rigging in rough weather and been so badly injured his life was in danger. The Chief had decided to turn back and seek emergency help in America.

"Moira sent a telegram to Koskela," Gordon said. "She ordered him to forget about the deckhand and to make for Scotland as planned. But Koskela refused and, instead, the *Valkyrie* is heading for a small island called Saint-Pierre off the coast of Newfoundland. It seems there's a medical station there."

~

The Chief was right, of course, to interrupt his voyage across the Atlantic and I wouldn't have wanted him to do anything different. In spite of that, though, my whole body ached with disappointment. This news meant the Chief couldn't be expected back in Glasgow for a long time. Possibly not for a couple of months, if the worst came to the worst. And there was nothing I could do about it, apart from hold on and try to keep my spirits up.

It was going to be hard for me.

Hot Toddy

The harsh winter weather settled in and snowploughs and troops with shovels had to work day and night to keep the streets of the city clear of slush and ice. Trams and buses only got through with difficulty. The streets were lined with snow-covered cars, stuck and deserted by their drivers.

No one in the house was keen to go out in the foul weather, which meant that Bernie and I ended up running more errands than usual. Late one afternoon, when we had just returned from buying snuff for Flintheart, Gordon brought an envelope he wanted us to deliver to Neil Fingus. It was a thin packet, so the bookmaker wasn't going to be too happy. Bernie already looked fearful—he knew what to expect.

The cold nipped my cheeks when we stepped out into Oswald Street again. The whistling wind blew flurries of spindrift from every alley and side street. The city was blanketed in a whirling, white haze and the streets were almost deserted.

The lights in the windows along the Broomielaw shone warm in the gathering darkness.

Shanley's Bar was packed when Bernie and I arrived. The air was thick with tobacco smoke and the stale smell of wet woollen clothes. Neil Fingus was sitting in the separate booth where he always sat. And as usual, the bodyguard with the bent nose and the pipe was watching over him.

Neil Fingus told Bernie to take a seat, and then he caught both Bernie and me by surprise by asking whether Bernie would like something to drink.

"A hot toddy, perhaps?" he said. "It's the devil's own weather out there."

It may be that Bernie didn't think that the offer was a serious one, or perhaps he didn't know what a toddy was. Whatever the reason, he didn't give an answer.

"A toddy is just what you need!" Neil Fingus decided it for him and made a sign to his bodyguard.

The man with the crooked nose nodded in response and began threading his way through the tables to the bar. Neil Fingus turned back to Bernie.

"Now then," he said. "What is it you've brought for me today?"

Bernie handed over the envelope from Gordon and then took a step back, waiting for the bookmaker to take out his anger on him. But Neil Fingus didn't say a word. He just counted the few banknotes and then entered the sum in a battered accounts book.

Meanwhile, I could see that Bent Nose had reached the bar. He exchanged a few words with the landlord and was allowed in behind the bar, where he took the handset of the telephone on the wall, dialled a number and waited for an answer. The conversation that followed was very short. After putting down the handset, he exchanged a few more words with the landlord before returning to Neil Fingus's table.

"I've ordered a hot toddy, Mr Fingus," he said, giving his boss a conspiratorial wink.

Neil Fingus nodded before turning back to Bernie.

"And how are things with Moira these days? Business going well, I hope?"

Bernie mumbled something inaudible and kept his eyes down. Then a waitress came over and placed a big, steaming pewter mug in front of Bernie. There was a strong smell of whisky.

Bernie sniffed at it cautiously and grimaced. "I'm sorry, Mr Fingus, I don't drink spirits…"

"What!" Mr Fingus snapped. "When Neil Fingus is offering, you'll drink what you're given! Drink up now—it'll keep you warm for the rest of the day!"

Bernie forced himself to take a sip of the drink and immediately burst into a fit of coughing. He went red in the face and his eyes filled with tears. Neil Fingus laughed and leant across the table to thump Bernie's back hard several times.

"There you go, there you go," he said. "The first couple of mouthfuls might be difficult to get down, but it gets easier, you'll see!"

Bernie drank a little more and managed to suppress his coughs. He was about to put the mug down to catch his breath, when Mr Fingus stopped him.

"You're not going to let the toddy go cold, I hope? That would be very bad manners, Bernie. Come on now, bottoms up! Toddy works best when it's hot!"

Bernie closed his eyes, screwed up his face in a look of suffering and drank. I felt more and more uncomfortable and concerned. What was actually going on here?

Bernie eventually emptied the mug.

Neil Fingus took a quick look at the pocket watch that he kept on the desk alongside the accounts book and said, "You'll have to excuse me now, Bernie, I've got other business to deal with. Tell Gordon from me that he still owes me eight pounds and ten shillings. I expect my money within two days or I shall be forced to resort to bare-knuckle methods."

"Right, Mr Fingus…" Bernie mumbled, standing up unsteadily.

Bent Nose, his short pipe clenched in his teeth, grinned, as did Neil Fingus. But they weren't smiles of kindness.

The moment we stepped out of the pub, Bernie slipped on a patch of ice. He grabbed my arm and just managed to keep his balance. The hot toddy had gone straight to his head. We started walking back towards Anderston Cross, with Bernie taking small, cautious steps and keeping his eyes fixed firmly ahead. This walk is going to be a long story, I thought.

But I was wrong.

We hadn't gone farther than fifty yards before a big, white Plymouth drew in to the pavement in front of us. Two men got out quickly, one from each side of the car, trapping us between the car and the wall of the building.

Then one of the car's back doors opened and a voice from the darkness inside said, "Bernie, come here. And bring the ape with you."

Bernie stayed where he was, swaying slightly. The men who'd got out of the car moved closer.

The light of a gas lamp glinted on a revolver and the man in front of us said, "Do as Mr Tarantello says. Into the car now!"

39

The Hat

There were two wide passenger seats facing one another in the back of the car. Tommy Tarantello and one of his men were sitting on one side and Bernie and I were told to sit opposite them. The doors closed and the car, its engine purring softly, drew away from the pavement.

I recognized the man sitting beside Tommy Tarantello—he had been with Tommy when they visited Moira a couple of weeks earlier. The scar on his face showed up pale in the shadow under the brim of his hat.

Tommy Tarantello looked at Bernie without any sign of aggression and said, "Hi, Bernie, old fellow. I thought you'd like a lift home to save you slipping in the slush and hurting yourself."

Bernie didn't answer. We were sitting shoulder to shoulder and I could feel him trembling. He was taking short, jerky breaths. The car turned left at Anderston Cross and drove west on Argyle Street.

This wasn't the route to Oswald Street. I could feel fear running through my body.

Tommy Tarantello had a brown hat on his lap. Clearly, it wasn't his, since he already had a hat—a white one—on his head. He picked up the brown hat and held it out to Bernie.

"Here you go," he said. "Here's your hat. The one you lost on Christmas Eve."

Bernie took the hat with some hesitation. I'd never seen the hat before, and it was far too posh for it to be Bernie's.

"No…" Bernie said. "It's not mine."

Tommy Tarantello put on a disbelieving face.

"It's yours, it must be," he said. "I found it outside the Greek's gambling club in Maryhill. On the big lawn behind the house. You know the place I mean, don't you, Bernie?"

Bernie nodded. Then his eyes suddenly widened.

"No… No!" he stammered. "I don't know anything about it!"

Through the darkness I could see the malevolent glint in the gangster's eyes.

He leant forward towards Bernie and said softly, "Is that really true, Bernie? So how is it that we found your hat outside the Greek's club? On Christmas Day—that is the morning after someone had broken into the place and stolen the safe."

The light from some of the display windows we were passing lit up Bernie's face. The colour had left his cheeks and his forehead was covered with small beads of sweat. He stank of an acrid mixture of fear and alcohol.

"I don't know," he mumbled. "I haven't got a hat like that."

Tommy Tarantello leant even closer to Bernie and raised his voice a little.

"You're not lying to me, are you, Bernie? Because I wouldn't like that."

"No… No," Bernie stammered again. "It's not my hat. I promise."

"Perhaps you borrowed it from someone?" Tarantello suggested.

Bernie gulped for breath, as if he was about to panic.

"I really want to believe you, Bernie," Tarantello said. "But that was a cold night, wasn't it? Are you trying to tell me you had nothing on your head?"

"No, no," Bernie said. "I'm not trying…"

And then something occurred to him and he brightened up just a little.

"I was wearing my blue cap!" he said. "Not a hat… Honest, I promise."

"Now I understand, Bernie. I was obviously mistaken. And you were right! You were wearing your blue cap when you took part in the break-in. So, just as you said from the start, the hat couldn't have been yours."

Bernie nodded and sighed with relief. Suddenly his eyebrows went up as it dawned on him. "No, no, that's not what I meant to say."

Tarantello leant back in his chair with a satisfied look.

The man with the scar laughed quietly. "Bernie, Bernie, you must be about the most stupid fellow in the whole world, you really must."

~

They let us out in the darkness under a road bridge. As soon as he was out of the car, Bernie stumbled into the darkness by the wall of the bridge.

I was about to follow him when my upper arm was seized in a tight grip. It was Tommy Tarantello. When I turned round, he looked me in the eye and said in a quiet voice, "My niece has told me that the two of you have met before. She says you helped our sick countrymen on board that plague-ridden ship that brought her here."

I nodded.

Tommy Tarantello went on. "That means I owe you a debt of gratitude, ape. And since I always pay my debts, I'll give you a valuable piece of advice in return."

Tommy Tarantello pulled me a little closer and lowered his voice until it was no more than a hoarse whisper. "Get out of this town as quickly as you can! Because there is soon going to be a war."

He clenched my arm again and hissed, "*A war!*"

Then he shut the car door and the white Plymouth accelerated away.

I looked around for Bernie. He was down on his hands and knees being sick in the slush. I hurried over to him and put my hand on his shoulder. The force of his retching made his whole body shake.

A Night Walk

I gave Bernie my hand and helped him back on his feet. His knees were soaking wet and his face deathly pale. For several minutes he stood there, shoulders slumped, eyes fixed to the ground. Then he started walking, slowly and rhythmically putting one foot in front of another. I followed him.

Bernie didn't seem to have any idea where he was going. At first he staggered from side to side across the pavement, but as he began to sober up, his footprints in the snow got straighter.

Street after street, hour after hour, we walked side by side through the city. Bernie and I must have walked many miles that night.

The falling snow eventually eased off. Under the dull light of the gas lamps, one or two buses and cars crawled through the sludge on the streets. The pavements were almost deserted.

I tried to store away the twists and turns we took so that we wouldn't get lost, but without the sun or the stars to help I soon lost my sense of direction. At one point I caught a glimpse of the masts and cranes on the riverside, but Bernie immediately turned into a street leading the opposite way. He didn't want to go down to the river.

As we walked, Tommy Tarantello's warning rang in my ears time after time: *"Get out of this town as quickly as you can! Because there is soon going to be a war."*

It would be so easy for me to follow the gangster's advice. All I needed to do was take a different street to Bernie at the next crossroads. I would have vanished before he had any idea what was happening. I'd no doubt that Li Jing would take me in and let me live at her house until the Chief got back to Glasgow.

It was a tempting thought.

Our aimless wanderings eventually took us to a park surrounded by a tall cast-iron fence. The gate was open and we walked in. The snow lay deep on the ground, the trees were bare and stood out dark against the white. It was beautiful. We walked slowly along paths edged with a low fence and snow-covered park benches. We crossed an open area and came down by a river where the branches of a willow tree hung out over the water.

My legs were weary and I sat down on one of the benches. Bernie carried on walking until he noticed I was no longer at his side. He turned and came back and sat beside me on the bench.

The noise of the city was far away and there wasn't another human being in sight. We sat there in a long silence until Bernie said, "It really wasn't my hat, you know."

I looked at Bernie—his eyes were full of worry.

"My head was spinning," he said. "That toddy was strong… and I don't like strong drinks."

He bit his lip and took several deep breaths before going on.

"So I don't know if I said anything stupid in that car. About the burglary, I mean. Moira said we weren't to tell anyone about it."

He turned to me.

"Did I?" he said. "Did I say anything stupid?"

I should have been prepared for the question, but I wasn't. What could I say? Should I be honest and just nod? That would probably make Bernie even more desperate. Or would it be better for Bernie if I shook my head and lied to him?

Too many seconds ticked by before I made up my mind. And that was enough of an answer for Bernie.

He understood.

He leant forward and, wailing and sobbing, buried his face in his big, calloused hands. His shoulders began to shake.

"Now I've done it... now I've really done it," I heard him mumble between the sobs.

It was some time before Bernie sat up straight and turned away as he wiped his tears on the sleeve of his coat. Then he turned back to me. He looked ashamed. And frightened. Very frightened.

He said, "Moira's going to be so angry. Do I really have to tell her about this?"

I was about to shrug my shoulders to show that I didn't have an answer, but I met Bernie's eyes and I could see that a shrug was not going to be enough. After all, I was the only one Bernie could turn to for advice.

I felt a knot in my stomach at the thought and suddenly I knew that I couldn't run away from the gang. Not now anyway, not while Bernie was in a jam.

"Shall I tell Moira?" Bernie asked again.

I thought for a moment and then shook my head.

"No?..." Bernie said.

I shook my head again. If Bernie told Moira what had happened, she wouldn't thank him for his honesty. No, she would hurt him badly. Really hurt him. But if he didn't tell her, there was just a chance that Moira would never get to hear about it.

Bernie looked relieved.

"Thank you," he said. "Thank you."

I got to my feet. It was time we were getting back to the house on Oswald Street. We'd been out for a long time, but with luck no one would have missed us. In the distance we could hear the sounds of the waking city. A new day was dawning.

What would it bring us?

It's not likely to be anything good, I thought.

PART ✦ FOUR

THE TWILIGHT QUAY

Storms and War

Storms at sea can be very nasty. But they aren't sly. It's possible to forecast them. When a storm is blowing up, you prepare for it. The cables securing the cargo in the hold must be checked and the hatches on the deck battened down. Everything loose has to be stowed away and the lifeboat made ready for launching in case the worst comes to the worst.

One of the reasons I never feel particularly fearful when a storm is brewing at sea is because I simply don't have time. That's a good thing.

I know a fair amount about storms at sea, but I scarcely know anything about war. And it was war—not a storm—that was approaching. That's what Tommy Tarantello had said. But how was the war going to start? And when? And what should I be doing to be ready for it?

I really wished there were some hatches to batten down and cargo to secure. But there was nothing I could do, nothing apart from wait and hope for the best.

The days passed. Everything went on as usual in the house on Oswald Street and none of the gang seemed to suspect anything. No one apart from Bernie and me. Dark shadows under Bernie's eyes revealed how badly he was sleeping at night, and his hands had begun to tremble. That made him even more clumsy, and in order to cover the shakes he kept his hands in his trouser pockets when anyone was around.

One evening Bernie had an accident. While reaching up for a saucepan on the top shelf in his larder, he fumbled with the pan and knocked down the red, tin box with the big padlock. The box hit the floor with such force that the padlock burst open, the lid came off and the contents of the box flew out.

Bernie gave a sigh and crouched down to pick up his bits and pieces. There was an official document that looked as if it was his birth certificate, a small, wooden toy car and an old and yellowed photograph. These were Bernie's most treasured possessions.

While Bernie was anxiously checking that his toy car hadn't been damaged in the fall, I took the opportunity to study the photograph more closely. It had been taken indoors and showed a girl and a boy standing beside one another on a wide wooden staircase with a carved banister. Light was entering through a tall, narrow window in the panelled wall. The children appeared to be dressed in their good clothes. He was wearing his Sunday best suit and she was dressed in a frock and laced boots. Her hair was up, under a little hat and ribbon. The boy was bigger than the girl but nevertheless seemed to be a couple of years younger. It took me a moment or two before I realized who I was looking at.

It was Moira and Bernie.

I recognized Moira first. She hadn't changed a great deal even though the photograph must be at least thirty years old. The line of her mouth was firm and her gaze steady.

Bernie, on the other hand, wasn't so easy to recognize. The boy in the photograph was giving a big smile, as if someone had just said something funny. If it hadn't been for the fact that I had actually seen Bernie smile, I'd have never guessed he was the boy in the photograph.

In spite of all the differences between the two children, it was easy to see they were brother and sister. The photograph had been taken, of course, before Bernie started boxing and had his face severely knocked about.

I noticed Bernie watching me as I studied the picture.

"That was a long time ago," he said with a sigh.

I turned the photo over to see if anything was written on the back. There was nothing there.

A couple of hours later I was lying under my blanket staring at the ceiling of my cellar. At regular intervals the trains rumbled past up on the railway bridge. Even though it was late and I should have been tired after a long day, I was having difficulty getting to sleep. I wondered where the photograph of Moira and Bernie had been taken. Bernie had looked so happy and hopeful that I felt sad for him. He couldn't have known then how his life would turn out.

I had to put this out of my mind and think pleasant thoughts if I was to get any sleep. But the first thing that came into my head was the sound of Tommy Tarantello's voice when he said, "*Get out of this town as quickly as you can! Because there is soon going to be a war.*"

I didn't get much sleep that night.

The Police Raid

My anxious wait only lasted for one week. But then it started. The war.

It was a Saturday night and Bernie and I were on door duty at Lucky Lucy's Club. Gusts of heavy snow were sweeping down from a dirty yellow sky, the large snowflakes glistening in the headlights of every car that passed.

By the time the clock on the Broomielaw steamboat pier was showing ten o'clock, the club was crowded. The noise and raucous laughter could be heard up and down the street.

Just after midnight the snow stopped. That's when it happened.

A lorry emerged under the railway bridge and skidded to a halt outside the house. On the side of the lorry were the words CITY OF GLASGOW POLICE, written in gold letters. A moment later a similar lorry came round the corner from Oswald Street and, at a sharp signal on a whistle, the rear doors of both lorries opened and out leapt a score or more policemen.

~

One of the constables showed Bernie his warrant card and said they were about to search the club for evidence of sales of illegal spirits. Then a group of officers, truncheons at the ready, forced their way down the stairs into Lucky Lucy's. The laughter ceased abruptly and was replaced by mass panic. There was yelling and screaming and the sound of breaking glass and splintered furniture.

Within twenty minutes Lucky Lucy's was empty and the worst troublemakers and drunks were being herded into the lorries to be taken to the nearest police stations. The constables formed a chain and began sending up bottles of spirits and casks of beer from the bar. In the midst of all this, a small, fat man came running along Oswald Street. He must have slipped in the slush at some point since his trousers were soaked. I'd seen this man before—his name was Brown and he was Moira's lawyer. In a shrill voice he tried to convince the police to stop emptying the club's supply of spirits. He had no success.

Among the crowd of policemen I caught sight of the constables who usually came to the club to collect an envelope of money from Gordon. And when Gordon saw them, he strode over to them. I was standing close enough to eavesdrop.

"What's all this supposed to mean?" Gordon asked angrily. "Moira pays you a substantial contribution every week precisely to avoid being raided! And now this happens!"

The officers looked around anxiously and tried to shush Gordon.

One of them said, "It's not our fault! We don't know who came up with the idea... but the order came from City Hall. They must have been given a tip-off, probably by someone who pays more than Moira does."

"Right! I get it!" Gordon said bitterly. "So that's the way of it..."

It sounded like the pealing and chiming of a hundred clocks as the police lorries drove off, laden with bottles and kegs. Bernie and I found ourselves alone in the alleyway—someone had to pick up all the glass that had been shattered in the turmoil.

When we had finished, Carl arrived and told us that the whole gang was to meet in Moira's office. Immediately.

Kevin, Carl, Mr and Mrs Flint and Lucy were already waiting outside the office door. No one said a word. Through the door we could hear the muffled voices of Gordon, Moira and Brown the lawyer. Eventually Gordon opened the door and let us in, at the same time as the lawyer was departing with a serious look on his face. Moira was sitting behind her desk, her hands tightly clenched into fists.

"Well? How much have we lost?" she asked Lucky Lucy.

"Our whisky store was almost full," Lucy answered. "Not a single bottle left now. They've even taken the barrels of beer. And any number of tables and chairs have been smashed."

Moira slapped her hand down on the desk. Hard.

"Bloody cops!" she snarled. "I've paid out a fortune to grease their palms! And now they do this!"

She fell silent, as if regretting her outburst.

"They want more money," she said once she'd calmed down. "It's as simple as that, of course. And this is their way of showing us what happens if we don't play ball."

"I agree, that's possible," Gordon said. "But I'm not so sure. When I was talking to the constable who usually counts our—"

Just then the telephone on the desk rang.

The sound was so loud and unexpected that everyone in the room jumped. There were a few seconds of silence and then it rang again.

We all stared at the telephone. It was made of black Bakelite with gilt decorations and a handset of polished hardwood.

Then it rang for a second time.

Moira looked at Gordon and nodded at the telephone.

He reached out, picked it up and said, "Yes?…"

The room remained silent while Gordon listened, the handset pressed to his ear. I could just make out the voice at the other end, but only as a weak mumble.

Finally Gordon said, "I'll do that."

Then he put the receiver down.

"Well?" Moira asked.

Gordon gave her a worried look.

"That was Craig McCauley… one of Tarantello's men… The one with the big ugly scar on his face."

Moira stared back at Gordon.

"Tommy Tarantello?" she asked.

Gordon nodded.

"McCauley sends you a greeting from Tommy Tarantello, who says you must immediately hand over the goods stolen from the Greek's gambling club. If you don't, Tarantello will see to it that the police ensure you never open the club again."

Moira's face remained as motionless as a plaster face mask.

Gordon continued, "And half of all the future takings in Lucky Lucy's will have to go to Tarantello. McCauley says it's punishment for burgling the Greek!"

"Do you think it's a bluff?" Moira asked.

"No," said Gordon, shaking his head emphatically. "Tarantello knows it was us—McCauley was absolutely certain of that."

Moira turned round very slowly to face the rest of the gang. Her eyes were black as nuggets of coal.

"In that case," she said through clenched teeth, "someone must have let the cat out of the bag. *One of you has betrayed me!*"

43

A Bold Plan

Bernie was standing beside me and I could feel his whole body beginning to shake. I could hear a whistling sound, as if he was having trouble drawing breath.

Terrifying thoughts were running through my mind. *Bernie is going to crack any minute and tell her what happened in Tommy Tarantello's car. Moira will go crazy and punish Bernie... and possibly me, too.*

Before Bernie had time to open his mouth, however, Gordon said, "McCauley said there were several witnesses—people who saw Simmons's boat on the canal in Maryhill that night. That's how Tarantello worked out it was us."

"Do you think that's it?" Moira asked.

Gordon shrugged his shoulders.

"Yes, why not?" he said. "The night has eyes, doesn't it? And Tarantello will certainly have paid well for the tip-off."

Moira thought for some time before nodding and saying, "Maybe you're right."

I looked around cautiously. No one seemed to have noticed how frightened Bernie and I had been.

And just then, Skinflint said in a very concerned voice, "Tarantello isn't going to settle for anything short of us handing over what we stole. It would be just as well if—"

Moira cut him off abruptly.

"Never!" she snarled. "The necklace is *mine*! Do you hear me? *Mine and no one else's!*"

Then she pointed at the door and said, "Get out, the lot of you! Out, I need to think! Clean things up down in the club and put a guard on every door in the building. And make sure you are armed!"

~

There wasn't much sleep for anyone in the house that night. After we'd cleaned up Lucky Lucy's place, Skinflint, Carl and Kevin posted themselves at the doors. Bernie was ordered to guard the basement entrance out to the Broomielaw and I was to go with him.

With the dawn of the new day, the guards were stood down. Bernie and I had just managed to drink a cup of tea when Skinflint came to fetch us. Moira had finished thinking it over.

So there we all were just a few minutes later, all lined up in front of her big desk. The dark shadows under her eyes revealed that Moira was weary after a long night thinking. But her lips were curled in a satisfied smile. She looked as if she'd come up with an idea.

"If it's war that Tommy Tarantello wants, then we'll give him war!" she said in a calm, steady voice. "War is what he'll get!"

There were some anxious murmurs from those in the room and Skinflint said, "But we don't stand a chance against Tarantello's men."

Moira nodded. "You're right, we can't defeat Tarantello on our own. But we won't be alone! I'm going to make sure that Dolan Duffy at Queen's Dock is on our side. And the same with William Turnbull's gang, and Alfie Cohen and his lot from Kingston Dock."

The room went quiet. Everyone seemed to be thinking through what Moira had said.

"But why should the other riverside gangs help us?" Carl ventured doubtfully.

"Because I shall convince them to," Moira answered. "It shouldn't be too difficult. After all, this is a golden opportunity, both for us and for them. If we're all in it together, we'll win the war against Tarantello, and then we—the riverside gangs—will be the ones who run the city!"

Moira's bold plan was met with looks of astonishment, but after a while the others began to nod their approval one by one.

Skinflint's thin lips stretched into a greedy grin. "Tarantello runs the betting on the racetracks," he said. "And any number of places round the city pay him protection money."

"He must be taking in loads of money..." Carl added.

"And it'll all be ours once we've won the war!" Kevin commented enthusiastically.

"We're going to be rich!" Flintheart said breathlessly, rubbing her plump little hands in excitement.

Moira turned to Gordon. "Get in contact with Dolan Duffy, Willie Turnbull and Alfie Cohen and let them know I want to have a meeting."

"All right," Gordon said. "When?"

Moira thought for a moment before saying, "At midnight on Monday night."

"And where?"

"We won't say yet." Moira said. "There's always the risk that someone will grass to Tarantello. And he is *not* to be given an opportunity to poke his nose in! Duffy, Turnbull and Cohen will not be informed where to meet until one hour before the meeting. No earlier than that!"

The house in Oswald Street now had to be put on a war footing. The gates into the yard were reinforced with sturdy supports and the windows of Moira's flat were boarded up to protect the treasures she kept there. The outer door of the shop was nailed up from the inside and the shop windows barricaded with heavy furniture. Then, finally, inside the building, Skinflint, Carl and Kevin built a sort of bunker out of old iron stoves and other bullet-proof junk. No one would be able to storm the house from the street, not without risking their lives, anyway.

"But what if Tarantello attacks us from the railway side?" Kevin asked. "You can shoot right down into our backyard from that side."

Gordon nodded and said, "Good point. We'll have to put someone on guard out there, too."

~

When darkness fell, it was Bernie and me who were sent out to stand guard along the barbed-wire fence that separated us from the marshalling yard of Central Station. No one else wanted the job and I soon understood why. There was no protection from the bitterly cold wind and the dirty, sleety rain. Trains were coming and going, hooting and screeching, their carriages and goods wagons blanketed in hissing clouds of steam. Black smoke from the funnels of the massive locomotives created a fog over the tracks. The gas lamps around the station did not offer very much light and I shuddered uneasily when I thought of what might be lurking out there in the darkness.

But nothing happened—apart, that is, from the snowfall getting heavier with every passing minute.

The great, brightly lit station hall with its high arched roof supported on cast-iron pillars lay just a hundred or so yards away. I looked longingly in that direction and thought how lovely it would be to climb aboard one of the trains and be carried away from here in a warm and comfortable coach.

Bernie interrupted my thoughts.

"I need to put on more clothes," he said, shivering so violently that his teeth chattered. "I can't feel my toes any longer."

I nodded. If he had to, I suppose he had to, though being left there on my own didn't feel very pleasant.

Bernie handed me the whistle Gordon had given him in case he needed to raise the alarm if anything happened. Then he limped off on stiff legs to the steps at the back of the house.

A few minutes passed during which I tried to think pleasant thoughts to keep my fears at bay. Then, out of the corner of my eye, I noticed movement. I looked in the direction of the station building and jumped.

Through all the smoke and the sleet I caught a glimpse of a dark silhouette. *Someone was walking along the railway track towards me.* A slim figure, walking with quick, firm steps.

I started fumbling at the button on the breast pocket of my overalls to reach the alarm whistle and I was just about to put it to my lips when something stopped me. The approaching figure put his hands up above his head as if to show he had no intention of harming me.

Suddenly I saw that it wasn't a *he* after all. It was a woman. And I recognized her at once.

Blackmail

"Good evening, ape," Florenza Tarantello said as she approached me.

Astonished, I stared at her through the fence, before looking nervously around. We would both be in mortal danger if any of Moira Gray's gang saw that Florenza was here.

But the risk was small—where Florenza was standing could not be seen from the backyard. And, in any case, she was prepared for the worst: she had a pistol stuck in the belt of her dark overcoat and a small set of binoculars hanging round her neck. She must have used them to watch me and Bernie, waiting for when he left me alone. It was me she wanted to see, me and no one else.

"How long will Bernie be away?" she asked.

I thought it might take Bernie at least a quarter of an hour to change his clothes, but I wanted Florenza to go away as quickly as possible. So I held up three fingers.

"Three minutes," Florenza said calmly. "Good, I'll be brief, then."

She looked me straight in the eye.

"The word out in the city is that Moira has called a meeting with the bosses of the other riverside gangs. My uncle heard that this meeting will be at midnight tomorrow, but he doesn't know where."

Florenza leant forward.

"Do you know anything about it?" she asked.

I shook my head.

"Well, I want you to find out," she said.

She was obviously expecting me to nod, but I didn't. When she continued, her eyes had become harder.

"If you don't help my Uncle Tommy, he will let Moira know who grassed to us about the burglary at the Greek's place."

Florenza's words made me jump—not a lot, but enough for her to notice. I caught a gleam of satisfaction in her eyes as she went on. "What do you think will happen to your friend Bernie when Moira hears that he sat in my uncle's car and gave away her secrets?"

I shook my head vigorously. That wasn't the way things had happened. Bernie had been tricked!

Florenza carried on unconcerned. "Do you believe Moira would forgive him? Well, I don't. I think she'd throw him out on the street, or maybe get Carl and Kevin to take him down to the Twilight Quay…"

My legs began to tremble and I felt a tightness in my chest.

"Right," Florenza said. "Which is it to be? Do you want to save your friend Bernie's life or don't you? You've got ten seconds to make up your mind."

I lowered my head in a sign of surrender.

"Right then," Florenza said. "On board the *Campania* I saw you reading the names on the sick children's name tags and crossing them off on the passenger list, so I know you can read. Can you write as well?"

My first thought was to lie and shake my head, but I hesitated just a little too long.

"Good," Florenza said. "So you can write."

She took a piece of chalk from her pocket and passed it to me through the fence.

"Once you know where the meeting is to be held, write the name of the place on the underside of this stone."

She pointed to a stone on the ground by the fence. It was within easy reach both for her and for me.

I gave a reluctant nod.

"You must do this before eleven o'clock tomorrow night," she continued. "And I give you my word that Moira won't find out that you are the one who passed us the information.

My uncle will make sure of that."

She held my eye for a few seconds more as if to assure herself that I really had understood. Then she turned on her heel and set off back the same way she'd come. She'd gone no more than fifty yards before she was swallowed up by the darkness and the smoke from an engine leaving the station.

A few moments later Bernie returned, wearing dry clothes and looking pleased with himself. He took two apples from the pockets of his raincoat, compared them and gave the biggest and nicest-looking one to me. I hadn't had anything to eat for hours, but I just couldn't enjoy it. I felt sick.

~

Bernie and I weren't allowed to leave our posts until the pale light of dawn began to show in the eastern sky.

I'd been awake now for two whole days and nights, but I still couldn't get to sleep. Thoughts set my mind spinning faster and faster. Somehow or other I had to find out where Moira was going to meet the other riverside bosses—that was my only chance of saving Bernie. I didn't doubt for one moment that Florenza's threat was to be taken seriously.

But there was also a suspicion nagging at my mind. Why did Tommy Tarantello want to know where the gang bosses were going to meet?

A whole series of unpleasant pictures passed through my mind. A war was about to break out, that much I knew, *so maybe Tommy Tarantello was planning to get rid of all his enemies at the same time? What if he was planning a bloodbath?*

I buried my head in the pillow and tried to force myself to think of other things. It didn't work.

I had to make a choice.

I could either discover where the meeting was to be held, tell Florenza and so save Bernie. Or I could simply keep quiet and thus prevent Moira and the other gang leaders coming to any harm.

I chose Bernie, and with that I fell asleep.

~

I woke to find Kevin leaning over me, yelling for me to get a move on. It was already the middle of the day and time to go and relieve the guard on the marshalling yard. I hurriedly put on my overalls and rushed out. Bernie followed on my heels, looking just as sleepy as me.

I cursed myself for having slept the whole morning, but perhaps it hadn't done any great harm. I still had ten hours to find out where the meeting was to be held that night.

It wasn't until our shift on guard duty was over that Bernie and I finally had time for the day's first cup of tea. We drank it at the kitchen table while dusk was already falling outside the window—and I still hadn't heard where the meeting was to be.

The rest of the day was spent with Bernie and me doing small jobs around the house. I eavesdropped on every conversation going on around me. No one in the house seemed to know where Moira was intending to meet the gang bosses. Or if they did, they weren't talking about it.

Moira must know, of course. And Gordon as well, presumably. But the two of them were somewhere out in the city.

~

After supper, Bernie and I were sent out to stand guard at the marshalling yard again. It was another cold night and the snow was still falling. The big station clocks were showing almost seven o'clock and I still had no idea how I was to fulfil the task Florenza had given me. And time was running out.

Was there any other way for me to save Bernie? The only idea I could come up with was to flee immediately and to take Bernie with me. Maybe we could just hop on one of the trains leaving the station?

In that case, we'd first have to climb the barbed-wire fence. I had no doubt I could manage it, but big, heavy Bernie? And, what's more, he had no idea at all that he was in danger. How could I go about explaining it to him?

I felt as if I had something stuck in my throat—something that just wouldn't go away. It was the onset of panic.

What was I to do?

A Chance

A short while later, our shift was over. As Bernie and I were entering the backyard of the house, the door to the stairs was hurled open and Gordon came out in his shirtsleeves, looking harassed. He marched straight up to Bernie and me.

"You have to go out on an errand," he said to Bernie. "We can't get hold of Skipper Simmons. The telephone line is dead, probably because of the snow. I want you to go to his boatyard and pass on a message. You know the way, don't you, Bernie?"

Bernie looked as if he was trying to remember.

"It isn't that difficult," Gordon said impatiently. "Catch the No. 4 bus on Argyle Street. Get off at the stop outside the Kelvin Hall and it's only a short walk from there to Simmons's boatyard."

Bernie's forehead furrowed and he shook his head hesitantly. Gordon gave a deep and impatient sigh. "But you've been that way any number of times, Bernie. Are you sure that you don't know? I can't send anyone else—they're all needed here."

That's when I stepped forward.

Gordon's eyebrows went up.

"Do you know the way to Simmons's place?" he asked.

I nodded decisively.

"I thought as much," Gordon said. "You'd better go with him and show him the way."

He took a folded sheet of paper from his trouser pocket and handed it to Bernie.

"You're to give this sheet to Simmons, and once you've done it, hurry back here. Understood?"

Both Bernie and I nodded.

This was my chance! My chance to get away from Moira and to take Bernie with me!

I'd formed a plan even before Bernie and I had left the house on Oswald Street. Bernie and I would not be going to Simmons's boatyard. *Instead, I intended to make sure we just disappeared before going somewhere else!* Where that would be, I didn't yet know and, for the moment, it didn't matter very much. The only important thing was to get as far away from Moira as possible.

First of all, I tried to get Bernie to catch the wrong bus from Argyle Street. It didn't work. Bernie knew which bus was the

No. 4 and he gave me a baffled look when I pulled at his sleeve and tried to make him climb aboard a different bus—one that was actually going in the opposite direction!

My next idea was to miss the bus stop at Kelvin Hall and stay on the bus to the end of its route. With any luck, the terminus would be well outside the city.

But that didn't succeed either. Kelvin Hall is an enormous building with tall towers and domes. Bernie couldn't fail to recognize it when the bus stopped right outside.

In a last attempt to trick Bernie, I set off walking north when we left the bus, but that didn't work either.

"Where are you off to?" he shouted after me. "You're going in the wrong direction!"

I recognized now that Bernie hadn't needed my help to find his way to Simmons's boatyard. He would have got there on his own without any difficulty. It was just that he lacked belief in himself.

A warm light was shining from the windows of Simmons's workshop and heavy hammer blows could be heard. Bernie knocked on the door and Simmons opened it. He looked surprised to see us.

"You coming to see me? Come in, come in."

It was the first time I'd been in Simmons's workshop and it was as cosy and untidy as I had expected.

"It must be something important that's brought you here," Simmons said. "No one goes out in weather like this unless they have to."

Bernie hastened to dig out the note Gordon had given him.

"Aha," Simmonds murmured to himself when he had read the short message. "Moira wants to use the boat… all the way to the *Black Cart*… tonight. In that case I'd better light the fire and get the steam up. Immediately."

It took me a few seconds to see the implication of what Simmons had just said and my heart missed a beat.

Simmons looked at Bernie and said, "Tell Gordon that I'll pick up him and Moira one hour before midnight. I'll be moored at the usual place."

"Usual place. An hour before midnight," Bernie repeated, his face all concentration.

"Exactly," Simmons said, donning his ancient peacoat. "Now I must go down to the boat and light the fire under the old boiler. Otherwise we won't get steam up in time. Bye for now! Maybe see you later tonight!"

330

It was past ten by the time Bernie and I arrived back at the house on Oswald Street. I was in a hurry now—I had to get that message to Florenza before eleven o'clock.

I'd need luck on my side if I were to succeed and, fortunately, that was the case. Just as on the previous evening, Bernie and I were posted as guards by the marshalling yard fence.

When Bernie went off to put on some warmer clothes, I hurried down ahead. I took the chalk from my pocket and wrote the words THE BLACK CART on the underside of the stone Florenza had pointed out the night before. I didn't really know what the words were referring to, but it was clearly somewhere that could be reached by boat. *Which meant it must be the place where they were going to hold the meeting!*

So I'd successfully carried out the task!

~

Our guard duty did not last too long that evening. After no more than three quarters of an hour, Gordon shouted to us to come back. The whole gang was gathered in the backyard of the Oswald Street house.

Once everyone was there, apart from Moira, Gordon said, "Duffy, Turnbull and Cohen have all agreed to meet Moira tonight. The meeting will be held in a pub downriver from here. Simmons will take Moira and me and the rest of you will stay here to defend the house."

Carl and Kevin began muttering in a discontented way. It was clear they wanted to be included in the big gangster meeting.

"Don't you think you should take a couple of extra men with you? Just for the sake of security," Carl suggested.

"Exactly!" Kevin added. "We'd be happy to come!"

I wondered whether Carl and Kevin would have been quite so eager to attend if they'd known that Tommy Tarantello had been told where the meeting was to take place. Almost certainly not. Carl and Kevin enjoyed beating poor defenceless souls at the Twilight Quay, but dealing with Tarantello's gunmen was another matter altogether.

I don't usually wish misfortune on others, but on this occasion I was hoping that Gordon would allow Carl and Kevin to go along to the Black Cart. I shouldn't really have thought like that, but I couldn't help myself.

Gordon thought for a while before answering Carl and Kevin. "No, you are more useful here. But we'll take Bernie and the ape—Simmons might need help with the boat."

The Black Cart

Gordon, Moira, Bernie and I left the house straight after that. Moira was wearing a black fur coat and an elegant hat. We crossed the Broomielaw under the railway bridge and waited for Simmons and his steam launch in the shadows by the quay. Bernie, as usual, started to tremble when it was his turn to climb down from the quay into the launch. But I noticed he was trying harder than usual to hide his fear. Presumably because Moira was present.

But on that particular night on the launch, it wasn't Bernie who was most scared. It was me.

I knew I should warn Moira and Gordon that Tarantello might hit the meeting, but how could I possibly do so without revealing that it was me who'd betrayed them.

~

The temperature had dropped during the evening and there was no wind. Veils of sea mist hung over the dark waters. A big moon threw its white, icy-cold light down on the roofs of the houses and on the shipyard cranes. There was little traffic on the river at this time of day. The only things we encountered were a couple of barges and the ferry that crossed between Mavisbank Quay and Finnieston.

After half an hour or so Simmons cut the engine and we steered in to the south bank of the river. We were now outside the port and the city proper and the bare trees on the riverside stood out as black silhouettes against the bright grey winter night.

Simmons had aimed at a solitary light, which turned out to mark the channel into what I initially thought was a bay but turned out to be the mouth of one of the smaller rivers that flow into the Clyde.

The tide was on the turn, so the current wasn't particularly strong as we steered carefully up the narrow side-river. Once we were round the first bend, I saw the reflection in the water of the lights of a cluster of buildings up ahead.

The buildings were constructed on piles close to the river-bank. One of them had a ramshackle veranda that hung out over the water. It was marked by a crooked sign bearing the words:

THE BLACK CART INN
Public House

We drew alongside a very basic, floating landing stage, built of rusty oil drums and rough planks. While I took care of the mooring ropes, Moira and Gordon climbed the steep set of wooden steps leading up to the veranda. Someone opened the door from the inside and let them in.

A couple of minutes later, the light from a single lantern showed up at the mouth of the small river and, when the moon came out from behind two clouds, I saw it was an open workboat, black smoke pouring from its funnel. It was heading straight for us.

Then I heard a whining engine noise from the same direction. A small motorboat was also coming our way.

Simmons stood up and peered into the darkness. He then lifted the lid of one of the seats at the stern and took out a double-barrelled shotgun. He checked there were cartridges in the breech while muttering to himself, "Best be prepared for the worst…"

A few minutes later a fast motorboat drew alongside the landing stage below the Black Cart. A ruddy-faced, lanky man jumped ashore. He was wearing an oilskin coat over his suit.

"This one's Dolan Duffy," Simmons said in a low voice. "The Irishman from Queen's Dock."

When Duffy told one of his men to accompany him up to the pub, I could tell from his accent that he was from Ireland.

Next to arrive was the old workboat. It moored at the landing stage in a cloud of coal smoke. All the men on board looked like tough dockers with long, hanging moustaches, battered caps and filthy kerchiefs tied round their necks. The landing stage lurched and pitched when one hefty fellow stepped ashore. He had the neck of a prize bull and a beer belly that almost reached his knees.

"That's William Turnbull," Simmons said. "He controls all the dodgy business around the Prince's Dock wharves."

No sooner had Turnbull puffed and wheezed his way up the many steps to the veranda than a third boat drew alongside. This was Alfie Cohen from Kingston Dock. With his round spectacles, clean-shaven cheeks and worn briefcase, Cohen looked more like an office worker than a gangster. All the men accompanying him, however, were the kind of thugs you would take a long detour to avoid if you saw them on the street.

Alfie Cohen and one of his men proceeded up the staircase and disappeared into the veranda of the pub. That meant that all four gang bosses from the riverside area were now assembled in the Black Cart.

The meeting could begin.

For Simmons, Bernie and me it was now just a matter of waiting, so we settled down close to the boiler to keep warm. But frightened thoughts kept racing round in my head.

What if Tommy Tarantello has put a bomb under the pub?

A bomb that could explode at any moment!

Or if his armed thugs are on their way here to gun us all down?

I peered around, searching the dark banks of the river. Maybe they were already here? Maybe they were hiding in the shadows, ready to attack?

There was no way for me to escape. The only way of getting ashore was through the pub. And, since I couldn't swim, jumping in the water wasn't an option.

~

The minutes ticked slowly by. Nothing happened, except for the crews of the various boats glaring suspiciously at one another and exchanging the occasional insult.

All of sudden I picked up a sound in the distance. There was another boat approaching and it was travelling at high speed.

I nudged Simmons's shoulder hard and pointed.

He reached for the telescope that was hanging beneath the half-deck and adjusted its focus.

"It's not the port police, anyway. Looks more like a taxi boat."

The crews of the other boats had also discovered we were about to have company. I could hear the metallic clicks as they readied their guns.

An Uninvited Guest

The taxi boat cut its speed and rocked in its own swell. A man in a light-coloured coat stood up and waved a white handkerchief, presumably to show his intentions were peaceful.

It was Tommy Tarantello.

There were two other men standing behind him, each of them holding a tommy gun. Craig McCauley, the gangster with the scar, was one of them.

"You all know who I am," Tarantello shouted across the water. "I haven't come to cause trouble. I just want to take part in the meeting up in the pub."

The crews of the boats already moored at the landing stage exchanged guarded looks.

A powerfully built member of Dolan Duffy's gang rose to his feet and shouted, "Tell your men to throw their guns in the river and then we can discuss things."

"It'd be a pity to waste expensive tommy guns, don't you think?" Tarantello answered.

One of the gangsters in Willie Turnbull's boat stood up.

"You can afford to buy new ones, Tarantello!" he roared. "And those tommy guns are going to end up at the bottom of the river whatever you decide to do. Why? Because if you don't chuck them in the river at once, they'll be heading for the bottom anyway once we've sprayed your boat so full of lead that it sinks!"

Tarantello thought for a moment before gesturing to Craig McCauley and his companion to throw their guns in the water.

"Now then," Tarantello said. "Are you going to let me tie up now? I want to get ashore before the meeting finishes."

"Have you received an invitation?" someone shouted.

Bursts of laughter came from some of the boats.

"No," Tarantello answered. "But I should have received one! After all, the meeting's about me, isn't it? So I've got a right to have my say, haven't I?"

There were a few moments of quiet discussion on the moored boats and in the end the big fellow in Dolan Duffy's gang shouted over to Tommy Tarantello's boat, "Fair enough, Tarantello. You can tie up."

The driver of the taxi boat manoeuvred his boat into the landing stage and Tommy Tarantello stepped ashore. He was followed by one other figure. It was Florenza. Head held high, she followed her uncle up to the pub veranda.

I felt a warm surge of relief. Tommy Tarantello seemed to have come to talk rather than to wipe out all his enemies.

~

The wait that followed was tense. The risk of violence and shooting was far from over. The minutes ticked by very slowly.

The door to the veranda opened suddenly and all eyes turned that way.

It was Moira who emerged.

Her face was as white as the moon. She walked stiffly down the steps to the landing stage with Gordon close behind her. He looked troubled.

The pub door opened again and this time it was Tommy Tarantello who stepped out, a cigar glowing in the corner of his mouth. He gave a smile of satisfaction.

"You've got three days from now to hand over the goods you stole from the Greek!" he shouted after Moira. "That'll be the end of my patience! Otherwise I'll come and take everything you've got, Moira. Everything!"

Moira didn't answer. She didn't even turn round. While Simmons hurried to help her into the launch, I saw the bosses of the other gangs emerge from the pub one by one.

The meeting was over.

~

So, what had actually happened in the Black Cart?

I never really did find out. Tommy Tarantello had possibly made a better offer to the other gang leaders than Moira could come up with. Or he had threatened them with something worse than Moira could threaten them with. Whatever it was, it had worked. Dolan Duffy, Willie Turnbull and Alfie Cohen were not willing to be Moira's allies in the war. Her plan had failed.

We cast off from the landing stage and Simmons set a course down towards the River Clyde. A soft breeze had dispersed the veil of mist on the river. It was bitterly cold.

Moira sat there as if turned to stone, staring silently out into the surrounding darkness. Her jaws were so tightly clenched I could see the muscles in her cheeks tremble beneath the pale skin.

After a while Gordon spoke, "I don't know how Tarantello could have known—"

Moira interrupted him, almost spitting her words out.

"I was betrayed! Betrayed! That can't be too hard for you to understand! Someone informed Tarantello where the meeting was to be held. Someone who wanted to get at me! And it's your job to find out who it was!"

"I'll do what I can, Moira," Gordon said.

Moira slapped her hand down on the rail of the launch.

"That's not good enough!" she roared. "You have to find the traitor! Have to! Because I want revenge, Gordon. Revenge! Have you got that?"

I sat curled up and silent, my head resting on my knees. My heart was beating fast and hard. I didn't dare look up in case my eyes met Moira's.

As we moved out onto the River Clyde, the Irishmen from Queen's Dock passed us in their open motorboat. A little later, I noticed the lights of another fast-moving boat aft of us and catching us up. It was Tommy Tarantello's taxi boat.

Simmons turned round when he heard the whine of a motorboat engine.

"We've got company," he said grimly, taking his shotgun from a box under the thwarts.

Gordon drew the revolver he'd kept hidden in one of the big pockets of his coat. Moira remained sitting, staring straight forward, her back as stiff as a ramrod.

When the taxi boat drew alongside us, the driver eased back the speed. Tommy Tarantello was sitting in the cockpit. Craig McCauley was sitting on one side of him, another gangster on the other, both men ready to defend their boss if necessary. Florenza was sitting behind them, leaning back comfortably and not looking in our direction.

Tarantello cupped his hands round his mouth to make his voice carry over the noise of the boat engines.

"Thanks for your help, Simmons!" he shouted. "I don't need your services any longer. And not a day too soon! I haven't got much time for traitors!"

Then Tarantello sat down and the taxi boat accelerated away at full speed, its slim hull rising in the water and the foam of its bow wave surging along its sides.

48

The Worst Voyage

At first I didn't understand what Tommy Tarantello meant when he shouted across to us. Gordon and Simmons also looked confused. The first to put two and two together was Moira. She snatched the shotgun from Simmons's hand and pointed its double barrel at his chest.

"So it was you!" she snarled through clenched teeth. "You were the one who told Tarantello where the meeting was to be held!"

Simmons's mouth fell open in amazement.

"But Moira... Moira," he stammered and put up his hands. "This... I don't understand... It's just not true!"

"Don't even try!" Moira hissed. "We all heard Tarantello thanking you."

Simmons shook his head vigorously.

"But I've never met the man before!"

Moira's finger tightened on the trigger of the shotgun.

Simmons's face had turned a deathly white and he was having trouble breathing.

"Ma'am… dear lady… you have to believe me. It wasn't me."

"Keep quiet!" Moira roared. "I need to think."

She stared at Simmons and her face grew darker and darker. When she spoke again, her voice was shaking with suppressed rage.

"And this wasn't the first time, was it?" she said.

Simmons swallowed hard.

"What do you mean?" he asked in a desperate voice. "I don't understand."

Moira's grip on the shotgun tightened as she aimed its two barrels straight at Simmons's face.

"Oh yes you do," she continued. "You were the one who grassed to Tommy Tarantello that it was us who stole the Greek's safe. You were there with us that night, weren't you?"

Simmons sat open-mouthed, staring mesmerized at the twin barrels of the gun.

"No, no…" he said in a hoarse, broken voice. "I didn't… I swear…"

"Don't lie to me!" Moira yelled. "It was you the whole time! You, you vile traitor, you!"

Gordon cautiously placed a hand on Moira's shoulder and it was that touch, perhaps, that calmed her enough to stop her shooting. Slowly, her hands trembling, she put the gun down.

When her breathing had returned to something like normal, she said to Simmons, "Carl and Kevin will beat the truth out of you. They're good at that kind of thing, I can tell you. And then they'll take you on one last outing—down to the Twilight Quay."

The last trace of colour disappeared from Simmons's face.

The trip back to Glasgow from the Black Cart is without any doubt the worst voyage I've ever made. Not even the sinking of the *Hudson Queen* on the River Agiere was as horrible as this.

Skipper Simmons steered the launch at gunpoint—both his own shotgun and Gordon's revolver were pointing at him. There was terror in his eyes.

I remembered what Florenza had said to me in the marshalling yard: *"I give you my word that Moira won't find out that you are the one who passed the information to us. My uncle will make sure of that…"*

I had a bitter taste in my mouth and I felt sick. Tarantello had tricked Moira into believing that Simmons was the traitor. *And he had done it for me—to keep Florenza's promise to me.*

The night breeze blowing in from the sea had freshened and we had the rising tide with us, so the launch made good time up the River Clyde. Once we'd passed the lock gates for Govan Graving Docks, I could see the buildings along the Broomielaw and the bridges that crossed the river. We'd soon be there.

I have to do something to help Simmons! But what? What can I do?

Out in front of us, a ferry had just left its slip on the south side of the river. It was one of those twin-decked ferries that carry cars, people and horses across the river. Simmons needed to swerve to one side or the other if he wanted to avoid collision with the ferry.

But he didn't. He stayed on the same course.

I turned and looked at Simmons. He still looked terror-stricken, but I could see something else in his face too. Determination: he was clenching his teeth as if steeling himself for something. But for what?

I looked at the ferry again. The distance had shrunk to a hundred or so yards and we were still on a collision course. Neither Moira nor Gordon had noticed the danger since they were sitting facing the stern with their weapons pointing at Simmons.

The ferry was getting closer second by second. *What was Simmons intending to do?*

When the ferry was only a stone's throw or two from us, a tremendous roar rolled across the water. The ferry's skipper was signalling with his foghorn for us to move out of his way.

The loud noise made both Moira and Gordon jump with surprise and they both looked over their shoulders. At that moment the ferry turned on its searchlights, aiming the sharp, dazzling lights straight at us.

For several seconds I thought we were going to collide with the ferry. I held my breath and felt fear coursing through my veins. But then, just a second or so later, we passed under the bow of the ferry with no more than seven or eight feet to spare.

The engines roared as the skipper of the ferry threw his engines into reverse. And in the beam of the searchlight I caught a brief glimpse of something in the whirling waters of the ferry's wash.

It was Simmons.

He must have leapt into the river just as the searchlights came on.

And now he was flailing his arms to keep himself afloat.

Moira leapt to her feet with an oath and attempted to aim her shotgun at Simmons. But she never managed to fire a shot—she was distracted by a horrific scream that drowned out all the noise around us.

Bernie, as usual, had been sitting hunched up and on his own throughout the trip. But now, head in hands, he'd risen to his knees and was staring wide-eyed into the darkness looking for Simmons. His huge body was shaking uncontrollably. When his lungs ran out of air, the heart-rending scream fell silent, but as soon as he'd gathered his breath, he began to scream again. I had never heard anything like it before.

Moira leapt to her feet, cursing with rage. She went over to Bernie and punched him with all her strength.

"Cut that racket, you bloody idiot!" she yelled.

But Bernie did not stop until Moira had pummelled his face with a dozen or more resounding blows. Then he sank down and began to weep with long, wailing sobs.

By then we were approaching the quay below the house in Oswald Street. Gordon had taken the rudder and was trying to work out how to cut the speed of the launch. He was no seaman, and he obviously knew nothing at all about steam engines. When Moira screamed at him to do something, he panicked and began pushing and pulling at every lever and control he could reach. That was no help, of course. Quite the reverse. It increased the revs and Gordon had to push the rudder right over to starboard to prevent us running straight into the quay.

None of the gang knew I was an experienced engineer.

I hadn't had any reason to reveal it to them earlier, but now there was no choice. If we collided with the quay or hit the stonework of one of the bridges, it would end in disaster.

While Gordon swung the boat back out into the river, I stepped forward to the engine controls and cut the steam. The launch slowed down, and when Gordon made another attempt to pull alongside, I put the engine into reverse. In no time, we were lying at rest by the quay.

Gordon gave me a long, surprised look. Moira, on the other hand, paid no attention at all to the revelation of my ability to handle an engine. She was furious and just wanted to get ashore as soon as possible. In spite of that, when she had to squeeze past Bernie who was cowering on the planking, she couldn't resist giving him a kick.

"Get up! And stop snivelling!" she snarled. "If Simmons drowned, it was only what he deserved. Just like that damned Shetland Jack!"

Then Moira climbed the ladder to the quayside and, with hunched shoulders and fists clenched in rage, she walked quickly to her house.

I helped Bernie to his feet. His eyes were wide with dumb terror.

∼

A little later I crawled in under the bedcovers in my cellar. Gordon had organized a new guard rota and it would be my turn to guard the Oswald Street entrance along with Bernie in a couple of hours. I needed what little sleep I could get.

However much I twisted and turned on the mattress, I found it impossible to go to sleep. I couldn't stop thinking about Skipper Simmons and wondering whether the crew of the ferry had managed to pull him from the water. Or was he now at the bottom of the river?

And what was it Moira had said to Bernie?

Had I heard wrong? Or had she really mentioned the name of Shetland Jack?

A Notice in the Paper and a Reunion

I was woken up by someone kicking my cellar door hard.

"Up, ape! Get up! Time to work!" I heard Carl shout, followed by the sound of his footsteps fading away.

I sat up, still half asleep. But when images of the night on the river flashed through my mind, my heart began racing so fast that I had to lie down again.

Poor Simmons… Poor, poor Simmons! I hope he survived.

I pressed my face into the mattress and stayed there until I'd gathered the strength to go upstairs to Bernie and have a cup of tea. In the grey light of morning he looked as weary and despondent as I felt.

A while later the whole gang gathered out in the backyard, everyone talking in loud, animated voices. By this stage they all knew what had occurred the previous night.

"Simmons! That traitorous piece of filth!" Carl said. "I hope he didn't drown too quickly!"

353

"Hold it!" Kevin protested, fingering his stiletto. "Don't say that! Let's hope he survived—otherwise we won't have the pleasure of dealing with him ourselves."

Skinflint and Flintheart didn't seem very bothered about Simmons. They were more concerned that Moira's great plan had come to nothing.

"What's going to happen to us now?" Flintheart whined. "Without the help of the other riverside gangs, we're lost!"

Skinflint agreed with her. "Moira'll have to hand over our booty from the Greek to Tarantello!" he said. "That's the only way out of this… What do you think, Gordon? Do you agree?"

Gordon gave Skinflint a weary look and said, "Moira is the one who decides. You'll have to ask her."

"Where is she?" Flintheart asked in her shrill voice. "Has anyone seen her today? She isn't in her office, anyway."

"I've no doubt she's up in her flat," Gordon said.

"You're sure of that, are you?" Flintheart continued. She was getting red in the face. "What if she isn't? What if she's taken off with all the money? And left us here to be mown down by Tarantello's gunmen!"

Skinflint put a hand on her arm to calm her.

"Come on now, Fiona," he said. "You don't really think…"

"I'll think what I want to think!" Flintheart snorted. "And I wouldn't be surprised if we're all dead before the day is out!"

She turned on her heel and walked back into the shop.

~

Moira, as we discovered later, hadn't jumped ship. She was sitting in her usual seat in her office. Everyone expected her to summon the whole gang to a meeting and tell us what she was planning to do. But Gordon was the only one she sent for and when he came out a little later he was tight-lipped.

The others, of course, were keen to know what Moira had said to him.

"She has a plan," he snapped.

"A plan? What sort of plan?" Flintheart inquired.

"You'll all find out later," Gordon said, turning up his overcoat collar. "But first I've got business down in Kingston."

"Kingston?" Flintheart said. "What business do you have there?"

Gordon was already on the way out and didn't bother to answer.

~

Bernie and I were put on guard duty outside the entrance to the backyard and we stayed there for the rest of the morning. It gave me plenty of time to think about poor Simmons. How could I find out whether he'd survived or not?

Meanwhile, life on Oswald Street continued as usual. The passers-by on the pavement all had their collars turned up and winter caps pulled right down over their ears. Every time a car drove past, Bernie and I had to flatten ourselves against the wall so as not to be splashed by filthy slush.

There was a waste bin fixed to the wall a little farther up the street. I hadn't noticed it before and wouldn't have noticed it now had I not happened to see an elderly man throw a newspaper into it as he passed.

A thought suddenly occurred to me. I ran to the bin and retrieved the newspaper—the morning edition of *The Glasgow Herald*. I quickly flicked through to the pages with local news and immediately found what I was looking for. There was a short news article, which ran as follows:

NOCTURNAL DRAMA ON THE RIVER CLYDE

Last night, Captain Edgar Brentham and the crew of the vehicle ferry *Athena*, working the crossing between Mavisbank Quay and Finnieston, were forced to mount a rescue operation.

Immediately after departing from Mavisbank Quay at 01.30 Captain Brentham became aware that an individual had fallen overboard from a passing steam launch. The successful rescue called for all the skill and strength of the crew of the *Athena*. On reaching Finnieston, Captain Brentham called the police and the ambulance service, the former to question the man regarding the course of events, the latter to treat him for severe hypothermia. Before the police and ambulance arrived, however, the individual in question absconded on foot, dressed in clothes lent to him by the crew of the *Athena*. At the time of going to press, no trace of him has been found.

I read the article twice just to make sure I had understood it properly, and as I did so, I felt a great, warm sense of relief: *Simmons had survived!*

Then I heard a voice behind me: "And what are you up to now, ape?"

I spun round and found myself eye to eye with Kevin, who must have come out of the house without me noticing.

Kevin looked at the paper in some confusion before snatching it from my hand.

"What on earth could an ape find of interest in a sad rag like this?" he said, glancing at the open pages. "Hardly any pictures. Or are you pretending you can read?"

Then his face suddenly froze and his eyes opened wide. I realized he'd caught sight of the article about the river rescue.

It took Kevin ages to stumble his way through the short text. Then he rolled up the paper and put it in his jacket pocket. He had completely forgotten about me.

"So that snitch survived, did he?" Kevin muttered under his breath. "But not for long!"

Kevin disappeared indoors. I watched him go and felt an utter fool. Because of me, the whole gang would now know that Simmons was alive and they would be out to get him.

I sincerely hoped that Simmons had already left Glasgow or, at the very least, had found a safe hiding place in the city.

~

A taxi drew in at the front of the house just before Bernie and I were due to stand down from guard duty. It was Gordon, returning from his visit to Kingston, and he'd brought guests with him: a young man and a young woman stepped out of the cab behind him.

The man was a dandy, dressed in a three-piece suit, overcoat and with a red scarf around his neck. He was sporting a big, tweed cap, the peak of which shaded his eyes. The woman was small and girlishly petite. She had a pale face and big, blue eyes; there was something of the china doll about her.

I felt a twitch of acute discomfort on recognizing her.

It was the girl with the razor! The one who had threatened the Chief and attempted to force him to give me to her.

Her icy blue eyes opened wide when she caught sight of me, and they didn't leave me until Gordon ushered her and the young man through the front door.

The Kingston Kings

Bernie and I finished our shift on the street at twelve o'clock. As soon as we got into the house I learnt more about the young couple Gordon had fetched from Kingston. The whole gang was talking about them.

The man appeared to be known as Cod-Eye and the woman as the Razor Queen. They were the joint leaders of one of Glasgow's most feared street gangs, the Kingston Kings, who terrorized the poorer parts of the city south of the river.

Cod-eye and the Razor Queen were now with Moira, having a meeting in her office.

"Why on earth does Moira want anything to do with low life like that?" I heard Flintheart muttering.

"We'll find out soon enough," Skinflint said in a worried voice.

He was right. An hour or so later Cod-Eye and the Razor Queen left the house, and no sooner had they gone than

Gordon came and told all the gang to gather in the office. Moira had important information for them.

The curtains were closed and the air in the big room was stuffy. There was a feeling of tension, and Moira seemed to be particularly on edge.

"All of you know what happened last night," she began, only to be interrupted by Kevin, who was waving the newspaper he'd taken from me.

"Look at this!" he yelled. "Simmons survived! Here it is in the paper! Carl and me will go and find him. Then we'll deal with that squealer once and for all! But we need to get a move on."

The look Moira gave him stopped him in his tracks.

"Shut your mouth now, Kevin, and listen," she said through gritted teeth. "That'll have to wait. We've got more important things to deal with."

Kevin fell silent.

Moira gathered her thoughts before continuing. "After what happened last night, Tommy Tarantello will be thinking he's defeated me. He'll be reckoning on me giving up and letting him have what he wants."

She paused for a moment before slapping her hand down hard on the desk.

"But that's *not* going to happen!" she roared. "Not today! Not tomorrow! Not the day after tomorrow! Not ever!"

I noticed Skinflint and Flintheart exchanging worried looks. This was not what they had been hoping to hear.

"I'm going to turn this to our own advantage instead," Moira continued. "The last thing Tarantello will be expecting is for us to go on the attack. Against him. *So that is precisely what we shall do!*"

Moira's gaze moved round every member of the gang before she carried on speaking:

"We're going to show the world that Tommy Tarantello is not as powerful and dangerous as people seem to think! And when that's done, Cohen, Duffy and Turnbull will see the error of their ways. They'll recognize that I was right from the start. And then they will join our side... against Tarantello!"

An uncomfortable silence followed.

Skinflint was the one to risk asking the first question. "But how are we to take on Tarantello? Just us, on our own?"

The hint of a smile showed on Moira's lips.

"Tarantello lives on the money he makes from his protection rackets," she said. "Remove that income and he is... *nothing*! So we're going to burn down all the pubs, all the dance halls, all the pawnshops and all the bookmakers premises he sells protection to! That will be a catastrophe for his business!"

Moira leant back in her chair with a satisfied look. She smiled at the wide-eyed, open-mouthed faces in front of her.

"But what about his gunmen?" Kevin wondered. "What are we going to do about them?"

"You don't need to be concerned about them," Moira snorted. "We'll strike fast and hard and several places at once. By the time Tarantello and his men realize what's happening, we'll be safely back here in the house."

There were disconsolate mutterings from the gang.

"How on earth are we supposed to strike several places at the same time? There aren't enough of us to do that," Carl said.

"And Tarantello will be out for revenge, won't he?" Flintheart croaked. "And then we'll be dead—the whole lot of us!"

Moira's face darkened and her eyes fixed.

"What do you take me for?" she said through clenched teeth. "Do you imagine I haven't thought about that?"

Her manic smile returned.

"Of course Tarantello will try to get back at us. That's why I've made a pact with the Kingston Kings! There's nearly forty of them. And they know how to fight! With reinforcements like that, we should be able to mount the arson attacks and defend ourselves."

None of the gang could find anything to say. They didn't really know what to think of Moira's plan. She herself, however, was eager to get started.

Her eyes fixed in a glassy stare and there was a slight tremor in her voice as she said, "Tomorrow night, my friends, tomorrow night… *Glasgow will burn!*"

~

A couple of hours later, the Kingston Kings came pouring in through the gate to the backyard. And what a crowd of thugs they were, with scarred faces and shrill, over-confident voices.

Gordon split them into two shifts, ready to take turns at guarding the house. The off-duty group were allowed to hang around down in Lucky Lucy's. The club had been silent and empty since the police raid, but now it came alive with a bang. The Kingston thugs began shouting for beer and starting fights to pass the time.

The Kingston Kings terrified me and I sincerely hoped not to need to get involved with them. Especially not with the Razor Queen.

51

Soon You'll Be Mine

The Kingston Kings couldn't be expected to defend the house on empty stomachs and Moira instructed Lucy to serve them three substantial meals a day. For dinner on the first day, Lucy made two large pots of mutton stew. When it was ready, Lucy told Bernie and me to carry the pots of stew down to the club.

The moment we stepped into Lucky Lucy's I knew things weren't likely to go well. The shouting and yelling died down for a moment or two, only to be replaced by whistles and mocking laughter.

One by one, grinning and sneering, the Kingston Kings rose to their feet and sauntered round the tables to close in on Bernie and me.

"Hello there, Bernie!" one of them shouted. "Are you really as simple-minded as everyone says?"

In spite of the roars of laughter, Bernie tried to push through to the counter to put down the heavy pan. Suddenly, out of nowhere, a hard punch struck his shoulder, which led to renewed laughter. There was no hope of Bernie defending himself. The steam rising from the piping-hot stew made sweat run down his face.

I was carrying a smaller pan, but the weight of it was still making my arms ache. And the handles of the cast-iron pan were setting my hands on fire.

"We want to play with your ape! That OK with you?" one of them yelled.

"Come on, Bernie, let's have some fun with the ape!" someone else joined in.

A violent blow to the chest caused Bernie to stagger back. Then an even harder blow to his back made the hot stew splash up over his neck and face. He gave a squeal of pain—and then someone snatched the pan from his hands.

"Get him!" the thugs screamed. "The clumsy fool has spilled our dinner!"

Bernie didn't have a chance. His legs were kicked from under him and he fell to the ground. Strong hands and arms dragged him through the door to the storeroom where, to the sound of laughter and cheers, they bolted the door.

Everything was happening so quickly. I clung on tight to my pot of stew until someone snatched it away from me. Someone else pinned my arms from behind and a ring of evil, sneering faces surrounded me. I was punched on the back and on the shoulder and even though I showed my teeth, ready to bite, it didn't help. I knew I was about to be beaten up.

"Stop! Give over! Cut it out!" A light voice cut through the noise.

The circle of thugs around me suddenly thinned out. I saw two people coming down the stairs from the street. One of them was the Razor Queen, the other was Cod-Eye. It was the Razor Queen who had shouted.

She walked to the middle of the stone floor.

"The ape is mine!" she said. "Leave it alone!"

Disaffected grunts and murmurs rose from the crowd of thugs around me. One of them stepped towards the Razor Queen.

"What do you mean *yours*?" he said. "Who said so?"

At one moment the Razor Queen had her arms down at her sides, at the next she was holding an open cut-throat razor at the cheek of the thug who had stepped forward. The move had been as fast as the wingbeat of a bird. As if by magic, she had conjured the razor from the pleats of her skirt. Or perhaps she'd had it concealed in the ruffles of her blouse?

The room went very quiet. Then the man known as Cod-Eye gave a hoarse laugh. He came and stood in front of me and when we looked at one another I could see why he'd been given his nickname. His gaze was cold and strangely lifeless. It was like looking into the eyes of a fish.

Turning to face the rest of the gang, he spoke in a lazy drawl. "Let's put an end to this quarrelling about who is getting what. Moira has promised the Razor Queen that she'll have the ape once we've finished our business here. But I can promise you that none of us will go unrewarded. Moira is the goose that lays golden eggs! Her riches are enough to make us all rich—every one of us. Just you wait and see!"

The Kingston Kings all joined in an ear-splitting "Hurrah!"

Meanwhile I attempted to slip unnoticed towards the back door, but a small hand took my arm and gripped it tight.

"You heard that, didn't you?" the Razor Queen said in my ear. "You'll soon be mine… all mine. Don't forget!"

Then she released her grip and let me go.

~

I found Bernie in the darkened storeroom. He was standing in the dark, trembling and with spots of congealed mutton stew on his face.

"They locked the door on me," he mumbled. "I didn't know what to do…"

I shrugged my shoulders to show the danger was past.

But my heart was pounding so hard and fast that I was having trouble breathing. And the Razor Queen's words were still ringing in my ears.

"You'll soon be mine… all mine."

No Escape

When I crept down under the bedclothes in the cellar that night, there was only one thought in my head: *Moira has promised to give me to the Razor Queen!*

I couldn't let that happen!

That strange girl and her sharp razor terrified the life out of me. How long would I survive as her pet? And how would the Chief ever locate me if I was no longer in Oswald Street when he returned to Glasgow?

There was only one thing to be done. I had to run away before it was too late.

Preferably this very night!

But how to go about it? Since the Kingston Kings had moved in and taken over guard duties, the house had been turned into a fortress. They patrolled the street and kept watch night and day on all the gates, doors and windows.

I lay for a while in the darkness of the cellar, thinking things through, before coming up with a plan. *I would try to make my escape through the loft of the house.*

The gang used the loft as a storage space. Bernie and I had frequently been ordered to carry dining tables and heavy bureaux up from the shop. I didn't remember ever noticing whether there were windows up there, but there was a hatch in the ceiling for the chimney sweep. If I could manage to get out through that hatch, it would be easy to climb over to the marshalling yard from the roof of the house. And then to simply disappear into the night!

But what about Bernie?

I was torn by the thought of leaving him. Bernie would be terribly lonely if I was no longer around, but I couldn't stay, not even for his sake. It had become a matter of life and death for me.

I waited until the small hours, when the night is at its darkest and the guards at their most tired. Then I left my room in the cellar and crept up to the first floor, where I tapped carefully on Bernie's door.

He opened it almost immediately. He was still fully dressed.

"I can't sleep either," he said, letting me in.

We sat at the table and Bernie poured what was left in the teapot into two mugs. Somehow or other I sensed that Bernie suspected I was there to say goodbye to him. I couldn't be sure, though, as he said nothing about it.

When I did eventually get up to leave, he followed me to the door and looked at me with his weary, sad eyes. I patted his shoulder gently and he patted me back.

~

I stood there for a while after Bernie had closed his door. It was as if all my energy and determination had drained away and I was left feeling utterly despondent.

But then I heard muffled voices approaching from the direction of the backyard. Someone might open the door and come in at any moment. I pulled myself together and ran quickly and silently up the stairs.

There were two doors on the top floor, one of them leading to Moira's flat and the other to a narrow staircase going up to the loft. I remembered that the latch on the loft door tended to squeak, so I opened it cautiously.

Once I'd closed the door behind me, I had to wait for my eyes to adapt to the darkness. And I started to shiver—it was as cold as outdoors.

I crept forward slowly and carefully. When I reached the top of the staircase, I stopped once more to listen for any noises following me. I heard nothing.

Moving on tiptoe I passed piled up junk of all sorts, including a large wardrobe that had given Bernie and me endless trouble lugging it up there.

I was now standing right under the spot where I thought the hatch was. There was usually a ladder somewhere around. Ah, there it was!

The ladder was heavy and I had to put it up without making any noise. No thumps! No scraping across the floor! I succeeded and, with the ladder leaning firmly against the nearest rafter, I began climbing.

It wasn't until I reached the hatch that I realized all my efforts had been in vain.

It proved impossible to open.

Someone had already been there and attached a large padlock with strong metal fittings. The intention had presumably been to prevent attackers entering the house that way.

I ran my fingers all round the lock in the hope it had been badly mounted and I would be able to tear it off. But it had been carefully bolted to the strong beams. With no proper tools and swaying at the top of a rickety ladder, I would never get the lock off in a month of Sundays.

With heavy steps I climbed back down. I moved the ladder carefully to one side and began to go down the same way I'd come up.

But I wasn't as cautious as I had been on the way up. That was a mistake. Just as I was closing the door to the loft behind me and about to continue down the stairs, I suddenly came face to face with Carl.

"What do you think you're doing up here, ape?" he asked.

I looked down at my feet to avoid his suspicious glare.

"I thought I felt a gust of cold air," Carl said, looking up the stairwell. "Has someone been up to the loft?"

I stood still while Carl glared at me.

"You shouldn't be running around snooping up here," he said angrily. "Get back down to the cellar where you're supposed to be! Understand? Get a move on!"

Keeping my head down, I slipped past him and didn't stop until I was back in my cellar. I was too upset to sleep, but too tired to think clearly. All I could do for the next few hours was lie on the mattress, stare at the ceiling and try to convince myself that I would come up with some other way of escaping tomorrow.

Bottle Bombs

The mood in the house the following day was not exactly jolly. Moira had decided that the Kingston Kings should stay down in the cellar when they were off duty, but the thugs were restless and already bored with that. Instead, they were prowling around hunting for something to entertain them. Flintheart was furious when she came across a couple of them trying to break into her and Skinflint's flat. And it came close to a full-scale fight when Carl discovered that someone had drunk a whole crate of beer that he and Kevin had hidden away for themselves.

Moira noticed none of this. She and Gordon had shut themselves in her office to make plans for that night's arson attacks on Tarantello. The whole gang knew what they were up to, but no one said a word about it all day. Moira had forbidden any discussion of what was to happen and the Kingston Kings weren't to be told anything until it was time to set off.

"I see... Why is that?" Kevin wondered.

Moira had looked extremely annoyed when she answered. "As long as the Kingston Kings have no idea what we are planning, there's no way they can forewarn Tommy Tarantello. I have no intention of letting myself be betrayed again!"

~

I spent the whole of that day hoping that Bernie and I would be ordered to stand guard out on the street. Or in the railway marshalling yard. Either might provide me with an opportunity to escape. But luck wasn't on my side.

Late that evening Moira summoned the gang to another meeting. The Kingston Kings were also present. They had just learnt that they were to join us in burning down various buildings across the city. None of them bothered to ask why—they were simply excited that a fun activity was being laid on for them.

Using a large street map of Glasgow, Gordon pointed out the pubs, restaurants, dance halls and bookmakers that were to be attacked. He also showed everyone the best ways to and from the different locations.

Skinflint had prepared a couple of dozen bottles filled with petrol, each of them with a rag tucked into the neck of the bottle. He called them fire bombs and found it hard to conceal his excitement when he was telling us how they worked.

"Light the rag and then throw the bottle through the window," he said, smiling one of his most gruesome smiles. "When the bottle smashes, it sprays burning petrol all around and the fire spreads at lightning speed. Everything goes up in flames, everything…"

The Kingston King thugs cheered with delight and crowded round the bottles. No one wanted to miss out!

One of those standing closest to me did, however, clear his throat nervously. He wasn't much more than a boy and, though he tried to make his voice sound tough, you could hear how uneasy he was.

"How do we know that there won't be people inside?" he asked Gordon. "At the places we're setting on fire, I mean."

His question was met with roars of mocking laughter, but then Gordon said, "It's Sunday night, lad. And, anyway, we won't attack until after midnight, when everything is closed. There's no reason why anyone should get burnt."

The gangs were then split into four 'assault groups', with Gordon, Kevin, Carl and Skinflint each leading a group.

Bernie and I ended up in Carl's group and our task was to set fire to a number of places of entertainment around Charing Cross Station. We were to start with a dance hall called the Locarno on Sauchiehall Street.

"It's only fair that that miserable hole gets burned down!"

one small, cross-eyed thug from the Kingston Kings exclaimed. "I must have asked at least five hundred dollies for a dance over the years and not one of them would dance with me!"

~

During the afternoon Carl, Kevin and Skinflint had got hold of get-away cars, so four stolen vehicles were now parked in the backyard. Along with the rest of Carl's group, I had to squeeze into the windowless back of a small van. Carl and one of the Kingston Kings went in the front and we set off.

For the whole of that day the only thing in my head was finding a way to abscond. Now I was on tenterhooks, because an opportunity would present itself very soon!

My plan was a simple one. When the van stopped and the back doors opened, I would run as fast as I could. I was fairly sure that Carl and the rest of them wouldn't bother to chase me, as they'd have their hands full lighting the necks of their bottle bombs.

~

We arrived after a short car journey. The van stopped and Carl opened the small hatch between us and the cab and looked through.

"Are you ready with your bottle bombs, boys?" he asked.

Everyone apart from Bernie and me nodded eagerly. We were the only ones who hadn't been given bottles to light, instead we'd been equipped with an iron crowbar each and told to smash the glass in the foyer doors of the dance hall. That would make it easier for the others to hurl their bottle bombs into the building.

I heard the two of them in the driver's cab get out and a few seconds later Gordon opened the back doors.

"Do what you've come to do!" he yelled.

Since everyone wanted to be first out, there was a good deal of elbowing and shoving. I fell on my face on the street, but quickly got back on my feet. We were right in the centre of Glasgow, on a wide, straight shopping street that was poorly lit by the misty light of gas lamps. I could see a tram in the distance. It was coming our way, but apart from that the street was deserted.

I dropped my iron crowbar, leant forward and started running in the direction I was facing: all that mattered at that moment was making my escape!

I hadn't taken more than a few strides when a big, black car swerved out of a side street a little ahead of me and drove in my direction, engine roaring and rear tyres skidding.

The rear windows had been wound down and two men were leaning out. They appeared to be holding something in their hands...

Then we heard the chattering sound of tommy guns being fired.

"Back in the car, boys!" I heard Carl yell. *"It's an ambush! An ambush!"*

Retreat

Everything was happening very quickly. The black car screeched to a halt just twenty-five yards in front of me, at the same time as I turned and ran for my life in the other direction. My only thought was not to be caught in the tommy-gun fire. There was nowhere to hide on the street, so I had no choice but to jump back into the van.

I threw myself at the open rear doors just as Carl was hitting the accelerator pedal. One of the rear lights right next to me exploded on being hit by a burst of gunfire. Strong arms dragged me into the van just as the doors slammed shut.

My memories of the return journey are hazy. The darkness in the van was filled with shouting and swearing. The vehicle swayed violently from side to side on the bends, causing my head to hit the metal wall behind me again and again.

By the time we stopped, I was feeling sick. And my heart was still pounding. The others in the back of the van were yelling and hammering the sides to be let out.

When the doors opened I could see we were back where we'd started. The Oswald Street gates were open and another of the stolen cars was already on its way into the backyard. Two of its tyres were punctured and one of the side mirrors had been shot off. Gordon was gripping the steering wheel with white knuckles.

∼

Kevin's and Skinflint's groups arrived back very soon after us. They too had been ambushed and forced to flee before setting off a single bottle bomb.

The atmosphere in the backyard was tense and heated. A number of the Kingsway Kings had been injured and were being tended by Lucky Lucy. One of them had had his right earlobe shot off and another had cut himself badly when falling over with a bottle bomb in his hand. A third member suffered a crushed finger when a car door slammed shut, and another had sprained an ankle during the general melee of the attack. Taking it all into account, I thought it was a small miracle that no one had suffered more than that. Or, indeed, been killed by gunfire.

The gunshots and the wild car journeys through the city had served only to liven up the existence of the tougher members of the Kingston Kings, but the rest of them were in a bad mood and wanted to know who had been shooting at them. And why.

"We've been tricked!" one of them yelled. "That Moira woman sent us off on some sort of suicide mission!"

"And where is she, anyway?" someone else shouted. "Bring her here and make her explain herself!"

Suddenly she was there, standing at the top of the steps leading to the staircase. Everyone turned to face her and the noise in the yard subsided. Moira's face was like a mask as she looked out over the excited crowd of gang members and their bullet-ridden cars. A horrifying mask, pale as ivory and contorted with fury.

"Gordon," she said in a harsh, metallic tone. "Come up to my office."

Then she turned on her heel and with an erect back and something strangely rigid about her movements, she went back into the house.

∿

By the time Gordon came back out to the yard, the atmosphere was a little calmer. It was thanks to Lucy. She had promised that tea and toast and marmalade would soon be served down in the club. She'd also brought a couple of bottles of whisky, which she passed around. They helped raise everyone's spirits.

Gordon walked straight over to Cod-Eye and the Razor Queen. I was standing some way away, but I moved closer in order to eavesdrop.

"Right, what's going on? Who opened fire on us?" Cod-Eye started by saying.

"No idea," Gordon lied. "And it's unimportant. For you and your men, anyway. All you need to know is that you should continue to guard this house. And you'll get twenty pounds extra to share among yourselves for what you did tonight."

"All right…" Cod-Eye said hesitantly. "Does that mean—"

"It doesn't mean anything more than I've just said," Gordon interrupted him. "Now go and make sure you place guards around the house."

Cod-Eye looked less than pleased, but went to do what he'd been told. Once he was out of earshot, Gordon turned to Skinflint.

"Call the gang together," he said in a low voice. "Moira wants a meeting. Now. Immediately."

The two men exchanged serious looks.

"I understand…" Skinflint said quietly. "I understand…"

~

I understood too.

It was Tommy Tarantello's men who had ambushed us. So, somehow or other, Tommy Tarantello must have learnt that Moira was going to hit the shops, pubs and dance halls he was paid to protect.

That could only mean one thing.

Moira had been betrayed yet again.

But by whom?

This, of course, was what she wanted to find out. And this was why she had called the gang to a meeting in her office.

My first thought was not to join them. I wasn't really one of the gang and it was unlikely anyone would miss me. But then I happened to catch the Razor Queen's eye. She was standing a short distance away, looking at me with her big, icy-blue eyes. That's what made me decide to go to the meeting along with the others. If I didn't, I'd be left alone with the Kingston Kings.

The Traitor

A short time later we were all waiting at the door of Moira's office. Apart from Gordon and Lucky Lucy, the whole gang was present. Gordon was already in with Moira and Lucky Lucy had her hands full keeping the Kingston Kings in a good mood.

By this point most of us understood what the meeting was going to be about. Possibly even Bernie understood. So nervous glances were exchanged, though no one said anything.

We heard the approach of footsteps and the door opened to reveal Gordon. His unshaven face had the same grey tinge as dish water. His eyes moved slowly across our faces, before he stepped aside and allowed us to enter.

Moira was waiting over by one of the windows that faced out towards the Broomielaw. Even though she was facing away from us we could see she had reached breaking point. Her shoulders were tense and her whole body was shaking slightly, as if she was trembling.

The chairs in front of her desk were scattered untidily.

"Sit down," Gordon said before taking his usual place diagonally behind Moira's desk chair.

After another minute or so, Moira turned round. I'll never forget the look she gave us. It wasn't so much anger. Nor disappointment.

Her face exuded hate.

In her hand she was holding a large revolver. She walked across the room with quick, stiff steps and locked the door from the inside, before putting the key in the pocket of her suit jacket. Then she went to her desk and after gathering her thoughts she said, "No one will leave this room—no one, until I've discovered which of you warned Tarantello about our planned raids."

A lengthy silence followed, and then Skinflint cleared his throat. Moira turned her eyes and the muzzle of the revolver on him.

"Yes, Mr Flint?" she said. "What is it you've got to say?"

Skinflint swallowed hard, his large Adam's apple bobbing under the yellowish skin of his neck.

"Well…" he said, "isn't it possible that it was one of the Kingston Kings who grassed to Tarantello?"

There was a click as Moira cocked her revolver.

"Mr Flint," she said slowly. "If you… or anyone else here…

tries to shift the blame to the Kingston Kings again, I'll shoot them. Understood?"

Skinflint gave a stiff nod.

"Good," Moira continued. "None of the Kingston Kings knew which targets we were going to attack. But you lot did— only you! So the traitor is here. *Among you!*"

The silence that followed lasted an eternity. That's what it felt like, anyway. Some kept their eyes fixed on the floor. Others glanced nervously around without settling their eyes on anything. But after a while they began to exchange furtive looks.

Who was the traitor, then?

Flintheart couldn't take her eyes off Moira's revolver. Her face had turned a sickly pale green colour and droplets of cold sweat formed on her forehead: the look of someone frightened for her life.

"What's the matter, Fiona? Is there something you want to tell me?" Moira's voice was as cold as ice.

Flintheart's eyes opened wide in terror.

"It wasn't me..." she stammered in a shrill voice. "Please, dear Moira, surely you can't believe... It was someone else!"

"Like who?" Moira asked.

Flintheart licked her lips nervously as she looked around the people in the room. Eventually her nervous gaze settled on Kevin.

"Like him!" she said.

They all turned to look at Kevin, who was sitting there wide-mouthed in astonishment and staring at the podgy finger Flintheart was pointing at him.

"Just look at him!" she said eagerly. "Look at how guilty he looks!"

"What? What are you talking about?" Kevin said. "Have you gone mad?"

Flintheart's eyes narrowed.

"Are you calling me mad?" she snarled. "Are you? Explain how you can always afford to be buying posh, new clothes, then? Where do you get that money? Tommy Tarantello perhaps. We all know how much you admire him. 'Tommy Tarantello, Glasgow's very own Al Capone'... Isn't that what you're always saying?"

The blood drained from Kevin's lips as he pulled his face into an angry grimace. He got to his feet and tried to extract his stiletto from his pocket. Skinflint leapt up to defend Flintheart, but it was unnecessary—Carl had grabbed Kevin's jacket and pulled him back into his chair.

"You witch! You fat little witch!" Kevin shrieked furiously at Flintheart while trying to break free from Carl's grasp. "I'm not the traitor! Perhaps it's you? You never stop whining about how little Moira pays you and Skinflint. 'We do all the work and Moira takes all the money'—that's what you're forever saying, isn't it?"

Flintheart looked at Moira, terror in her eyes.

"He's lying! Trust me, Moira… You do, don't you? Surely? Tarantello has probably promised Kevin that he can join his gang!"

Kevin made another attempt to get to his feet, but was pulled back by Carl.

Flintheart was now yelling with such force that spit flew in all directions. "Don't give yourself airs, Carl! It could be you who's the traitor! You're always after money to pay for a home for your old father, aren't you? Aren't you? Has Tarantello offered to help you out? In exchange for being his snitch!"

Carl released Kevin and shot out of his chair to go for Flintheart himself. Now Gordon and Skinflint became involved and managed to stop Carl.

"Calm down!" Gordon said in his sternest voice. "This is all stupid nonsense!"

By now Flintheart's face was as bright red as starboard lights.

"Not as stupid as you are, betting away all your money on horses!" she shouted at Gordon. "How much do you owe that Neil Fingus, for instance?"

"Exactly, Gordon," Kevin joined in. "And Neil Fingus is one of Tommy Tarantello's bookmakers, isn't he?"

Gordon gave Kevin an angry stare.

"Now I see it!" Carl said. "It must be you, Gordon, who squealed to Tarantello! To wipe out your gambling debts!"

They all stood up and started yelling and pointing at each other. Bernie and me, slightly to one side, were the only ones to stay in our seats. Bernie had his eyes tight shut and his hands over his ears. His heavy body was rocking back and forth in his chair.

All of a sudden, a shot was fired.

And then two more.

The noise was deafening.

Everything Changes

The big room fell silent. Utterly silent. Everyone had crouched down, arms over their heads. Moira was standing at her desk, the revolver pointing up in the air. A plume of smoke was rising from the barrel and there were scorch marks and three small holes in the ceiling above.

"Enough!" she said in a hoarse, shaky voice. "You idiots, you treacherous idiots! I ought to make my life easy by shooting the lot of you!"

Gordon inhaled deeply, trying to get his breath to settle.

"Hang on a minute, Moira," he said. "I think we can easily find out who the traitor is."

Moira turned to him, her eyes on fire with rage.

"Can we? How? Explain yourself!"

"Well," Gordon said. "I've been wondering how the snitch actually went about it. How did he… or she… get a message to Tarantello?"

Gordon let the question hang in the air before continuing.

"I can only think of two ways it could have happened. Either the snitch contacted Tarantello by telephone. Or he or she went into the city and met one of his men there."

"Right? And so? Get to the point!" Moira snapped.

Gordon went on, "There is only one telephone in this house that can make outgoing calls and that's the one sitting here on your desk. And you have hardly been out of your office since yesterday afternoon. Am I right?"

Moira waved the revolver impatiently to hurry Gordon up.

"What that must mean," he said, "is that the traitor is someone who left the house."

Moira nodded slowly.

"We only heard about your plans yesterday afternoon," Gordon continued. "Which allowed the traitor about twenty-four hours to tip off Tarantello. During that time we had guards on every door and gateway. Guards from our number and from the Kingston Kings. So the traitor can't have left the house unseen…"

After a few seconds of complete silence in the room, Moira said, "Good, Gordon… Very good."

Then she looked at the rest of us again. "Come on then, which of you left the house after I'd told you about my plan? There's no point in trying to lie—I'm going to get to the truth one way or another."

The question went round the room to each member of the gang in turn. It turned out that the only people to leave the house had been Skinflint, Carl and Kevin—the ones who'd gone out to steal the getaway cars.

"I was right in the first place, Moira!" Flintheart insisted. "It must have been either Kevin or Carl who betrayed you! My Enoch would never have—"

Moira slammed her hand down on the desk.

"If you say another word, Fiona…" she hissed.

Flintheart pursed her lips and kept quiet.

Moira looked at Skinflint, Carl and Kevin once more. They, in turn, looked at one another. All three of them looked equally baffled.

"We were together the whole time, weren't we?" Skinflint said. "And none of us went near a telephone. And none of us could possibly have met a member of Tarantello's gang."

"Not without the other two noticing, anyway," Kevin added.

It was clear from Moira's face that she'd had almost as much as she could take. Her facial twitches were becoming more and more marked.

"In that case the three of you must have done it together!" she said. "You were the only people who were out of the house, so it must have been you!"

And that's when everything changed.

Carl spun round suddenly and stared at me.

"Wait a minute now… wait! I met the ape, didn't I?" he said.

And every eye was suddenly looking in my direction.

"It was last night," Carl went on eagerly. "I was doing my rounds of the house, checking that everything was in order. That's when I saw the ape on the stairs!"

After a short silence Moira asked in a sharp tone of voice, "The ape? What's the ape got to do with this business? Don't try to wriggle out of things, Carl!"

"No, no, I'm not wriggling out of anything! I promise! The ape was up on the top floor in the middle of the night! And I remember there was a cold draught, *as if the door up to the loft had been open!*"

The room fell silent again. After some very long seconds Moira said, "Do you mean that the ape might have been our traitor? And that it climbed out through the loft?"

Carl nodded hesitantly, as if he was suddenly worried his idea might seem ridiculous.

But Moira didn't smile. She asked, "Is it possible to get out of the house that way? And get back in?"

Gordon, Skinflint, Carl and Kevin all nodded at the same time.

"There's a hatch up there that leads straight out onto the roof," Kevin said.

"But there's a padlock on it—" Skinflint started to say, but Moira interrupted him brusquely.

"Quiet!" she ordered. "I need to think."

No one said anything for a while, but they were all pondering Carl's new revelation.

All except me.

My thoughts had come to a standstill. It felt as if the blood in my veins had turned to ice. What was happening?

"Do you remember a couple of months ago," Moira said eventually, "when Tommy Tarantello visited my office? He had his niece from Italy with him, didn't he?"

"Florenza," Gordon said.

"That's the one… Florenza Tarantello." Moira nodded. "Something happened on that occasion… something a bit strange. And it made me wonder whether that Florenza had met the ape before."

"Exactly!" Carl exclaimed. "I remember that too. They nodded to one another. As if they were old acquaintances!"

Silence fell once more. Then Flintheart took a few steps in my direction. Her eyes narrowed to slits and she raised a threatening finger.

"And I remember something else," she snarled. "Something

equally strange! Something that happened a while ago outside the post office at Central Station. The ape was there with Bernie. They were standing by a post box... *and the ape put a postcard in the box!*"

"What are you saying? That the ape posted *a letter?*"

"Yes... or a postcard," Flintheart nodded. "And who knows? The card may have been to the ape's friend, that Florenza Tarantello!"

Everyone in the room seemed to be thinking about this for a while. For my part, I attempted to look as if I understood nothing... nothing at all. It wasn't easy. I realized I was now in danger. In real danger.

Moira shook her head.

"This is just a load of rubbish! Apes can't write letters, not even the address on postcards! They can't write at all!"

That's when Kevin leapt to his feet. He stared at me and then said in an excited voice, "Whether the ape can write... I don't know about that, but it can certainly *read*. I'm sure of that! Just the other day, see, I saw the ape out on the street. It was standing there reading the paper!"

"What's that supposed to mean?" Moira asked.

"Just what I said," Kevin said. "The ape was standing there on the pavement holding up an open *Glasgow Herald!*"

"How can you be so sure the ape was actually *reading*?"

Skinflint asked. "Maybe it was just looking at the pictures in the paper?"

Kevin shook his head impatiently.

"But that's just the point," he said. "*There weren't any pictures* on the page the ape was looking at. Just a mass of words!"

Kevin hesitated as if a new thought had just occurred to him.

"And you know what?" he said breathlessly. "Right in the middle of that page there was an article about what happened after our meeting with the riverside bosses. The business about Simmons jumping in the river! It really did look as if the ape was standing there reading *that very article!*"

They all turned and looked at me.

"If the ape can read," Moira said, "it can presumably write as well. Short letters and messages to its friend Florenza, for instance! That would explain why Tommy Tarantello is a step ahead of me the whole time."

Every eye in the room was focused on me. Every muscle in my body was taut... ready to run. But there was nowhere to go!

But then Skinflint chimed in. "Hang on a minute now," he said. "There's something that doesn't fit. As I was trying to explain just now, the ape can't have got out through the hatch. I put a padlock on it just a couple of days ago."

Without stopping to think, I started nodding vigorously.

"Look at that!" Kevin shouted. "The ape already knew about it! So now we know the ape has been up in the loft and tried to get out."

"And I reckon it managed it too," Gordon said. "Picking a padlock is child's play, we all know that."

"But not for an ape, surely?" Skinflint said.

"Well, I think it is," Gordon said. "At least for this ape…"

And then Gordon told them how I had saved us all from crashing into the quay after Simmons had thrown himself into the river.

"I didn't have any idea how to stop the boat," Gordon said. "But the ape took control of the steam engine. And it knew how to cut the speed and put the engine in reverse! Like a real engineer, I'm tempted to say. What do you think, Moira?"

Moira gave a stiff nod.

"If you can handle a steam engine," Gordon said, "you can almost certainly pick a padlock as well!"

At that moment, I wished—more than I'd ever wished before—that I could talk. And if I had been able to, I'd have yelled at them:

Of course I can pick a padlock. But not in the pitch black! And not with my bare hands! No one can do that, not even the Chief!

After a long and frightening silence Moira said, "I've been betrayed… *by an ape…*"

"What do you want us to do with the ape?" Kevin asked, and I could hear the bloodlust in his voice.

Moira didn't answer immediately. She couldn't take her eyes off me. The hate in her eyes had the heat of a welding torch.

Eventually she said, "Take the beast down to the Twilight Quay and make sure it really suffers before it dies."

The End of the Game

Everything around me felt unreal. I knew I had to try to do something, fight or bite or hurl myself at a window.

But, instead, I just sat there, as if paralysed.

Carl and Kevin, however, were quickly on their feet. They were only too eager to take me down to the Twilight Quay where they could torment the life out of me.

"I'll go and fetch a chain," Carl said, "so the ape can't escape from us!"

But as he turned and started for the door, a loud wail could suddenly be heard. It was more despairing than any sound I'd ever heard in my life.

It was Bernie.

He hadn't uttered a word during the whole of this long and awful meeting. But now he was on his feet and looking at Moira with wide and staring eyes. The whole of his great body was shaking.

"Don't hurt the ape!" he stammered. "It wasn't her…"

"Sit down and keep quiet!" Moira snarled. "You're raving. Like the idiot you are!"

"No!" Bernie yelled.

Moira was taken aback by his outburst.

"It wasn't the ape, it was me," Bernie said. "I was drunk and Tarantello tricked me into saying things… in his car… I promise… that's what happened… I didn't mean to… please, Moira… you mustn't hurt the ape."

They all stared at Bernie. Tears were running down his cheeks. The whole room was filled with the sound of his great sobbing gulps.

And Moira began to laugh. It was a shrill, piercing laugh. But it soon passed and she became as grim as the grave again.

"That was the most stupid, lying rubbish I've ever heard! You drunk, Bernie? And in Tommy Tarantello's car, to cap it all?"

She started to laugh again and the others in the room joined in. But they stopped abruptly when Moira suddenly fell silent.

"The ape must die!" she said. "And do you know what, Bernie? I want you to be the one to do it!"

Bernie looked as if he didn't know what she meant.

So Moira raised her voice. "You are to kill the ape, Bernie!"

Now he understood. "No, please… please… please."

"Yes!" Moira roared. "That is what's to happen, Bernie! You're to take the ape down to the Twilight Quay and when you get there, you're going to shoot it."

Moira handed her revolver to Bernie. When he didn't want to take it, she slapped his face and pressed the weapon into his hand.

Bernie looked at her, pure horror showing in his face. Moira lowered her voice.

"Listen carefully now, Bernie. Really carefully. If you come back without killing the ape, you won't be let in. And I'll never want to see you again. *Never, ever!* And you'll have to survive on your own. *For the rest of your life!* Understood?"

"But, Moira… Moira…" Bernie sobbed.

Moira slapped her hand down on the table with a crack.

"Stop snivelling, you idiot!" she yelled. *"I asked whether you understood! Well?"*

Bernie stood there motionless, his face swollen and wet with tears. Then he nodded.

～

Carl and Kevin accompanied Bernie and me down to the yard. The shot-up getaway cars were still there and a big gang of the Kingston Kings were gathered round a fire in an oil drum, sharing a couple of bottles of whisky. From their raucous laughter

I could tell they had taken the opportunity to get drunk while Moira's meeting was going on.

Carl and Kevin helped one another loop one end of a chain as a noose around my neck and attach the other end to Bernie's belt.

"What are you up to?" one of the gang members by the fire shouted to them. "Is that fool taking the ape out for a walk? Can't we have a bit of fun instead?"

"Unfortunately not," Carl answered. "Playtime's over for this ape. It's on its way down to Twilight Quay!"

Kevin opened the gate. Then Bernie and I were both given such hard kicks in the backside that we fell flat on our faces in the street.

"Have a good time, Bernie," Kevin said. "You're the lucky one, you are, getting all the fun of finishing off the ape. Make sure you spin it out—that'll be much more enjoyable!"

The gate slammed behind us with a dull, heavy thud.

58

The Twilight Quay

We got up from the wet slush. Bernie took a long look at the gate that had closed behind us. Then, putting one foot in front of the other, he set off at a slow pace.

After crossing the Broomielaw we walked across the road bridge over the River Clyde. It was almost deserted at this time of night. We encountered a few pedestrians and saw a couple of buses, the splashes of slush on their windows allowing no more than a glimpse of the hollow-eyed passengers within.

The river flowed quietly along under a veil of damp mist. Pale reflections of the lights on the quays and wharves on the other side shimmered on the dark water. It was beautiful.

How many harbours at night had I been lucky enough to see in my life? It was scarcely possible to count them. And I'd liked all of them, in different ways. Every new harbour is an adventure in itself, with new smells, new sounds, new enemies and new friends.

When I thought of this, I felt a sense of calm come over me. Glasgow wouldn't be my last harbour. I would see more. Probably many more.

Because Bernie would never kill me. I knew that.

~

When we reached the other side of the bridge, Bernie stopped at an old and crooked cast-iron gate that was tucked in between the railings of the bridge and the thick pillars supporting the adjoining railway bridge. The hinges creaked as Bernie opened the gate.

A steep, narrow set of steps led down to the riverbank. Bernie went in front and I followed on his heels. We were quite far down before I saw that there was a paved quay running along the edge of the water. It disappeared into the darkness beneath the railway bridge. After a moment's hesitation Bernie began to walk along it.

It was like entering a cave. Bernie's footsteps echoed between the arch of the bridge above us and the stone wall that supported the bank behind the quay. The river gurgled and sighed. The smell of filthy water was overpowering.

The quay was lit by a single spluttering gas lamp and in its dull light I saw a worn enamel sign mounted on the brick wall. It read:

Twilight Quay

I understood now how the secluded quay had got its name. It was touched by neither the rays of the sun nor the light of the moon. It lay in the darkness of perpetual twilight.

That, of course, was why Carl and Kevin liked the place. Horrific crimes could be committed here and lifeless bodies thrown into the river without anyone seeing or hearing what was happening.

Bernie's breathing had become heavy and irregular. He had Moira's revolver in his hand. The reflection of the gas lamp glinted off the polished metal. After staring at the gun, Bernie turned and looked at me. Then he opened his hand and let the revolver drop over the edge of the quay. There was a dull splash and it was gone.

Bernie sank down, leaning his back against the brick wall and hiding his face in his hands.

"What's going to become of me now?" he sniffed.

I sat down beside him and gently put my hand on his shoulder. His great body shuddered as he wept silently.

∼

I knew we should move on. First of all, away from this dreadful place, and then out of Glasgow to somewhere Moira and the rest of the gang wouldn't find us.

But as the tension eased, a great weariness came over me.

So instead of leaving at once and trying to find a safe hiding place for the night, Bernie and I stayed where we were. And when I eventually found the strength to stand up, it was already too late.

We were no longer alone on the Twilight Quay.

The Razor Queen was standing just a dozen or so yards away.

59

The Burning House

The Razor Queen took several quick steps in our direction, flipping out the blade of her cut-throat razor as she walked.

Bernie looked up and jumped when he caught sight of her.

"Keep still... or I'll cut your throat," she said in her thin, childlike voice. "And I ought to do that anyway! They told me you'd brought my ape here to murder it!"

Flashes of anger played in her ice-blue eyes, but instead of carrying out her threat, she told Bernie to take off his belt and give his end of the chain to her.

Bernie didn't move.

"Do as I say!" she snapped, going up to him and pointing the razor at his face. "The ape is mine! Only mine! And I'm going to take it home with me."

Bernie still didn't move. That made her unsure, and she turned to me.

"Stand up, Lizzy!" she commanded. "That will be your name

408

from now on. Lizzy is a name that *I* like. I want you to undo the chain from that big idiot's belt!"

I looked at her and to my surprise I wasn't in the least afraid. It was as if I'd suddenly said goodbye to fear. Instead of obeying the Razor Queen's command, I patted the paving stone beside me to show she could sit there if she wanted to.

At first she was confused. Then she became angry and her small knuckles clenched the handle of the razor so tight that they went white. But when she saw that waving that nasty weapon about was having no effect, she just stood there with confusion written all over her doll-like little face.

I patted the ground alongside me once more. Looking round quickly as if worried someone was watching us, she folded the blade of the razor and, rather hesitantly, sat down by me.

So there we sat—me, Bernie and the Razor Queen—shoulder to shoulder, and after a little while I felt her hand on my arm. She was carefully stroking my fur. When I turned to look at her, I saw her face wrinkle up in disappointment.

"Your fur," she said, "it's very coarse, isn't it? It's nothing like as soft as I expected."

At that moment a sharp light lit up the night sky. It was followed by the deep, dull thud of an explosion that resounded under the bridge.

What on earth was that?

The Razor Queen was the first to be on her feet. She stood still and listened as Bernie and I got up.

There were more sounds. An angry chattering echoed under the arch. I recognized the sound at once—I'd heard it no more than a few hours earlier.

It was the chatter of a tommy gun.

The Razor Queen walked hurriedly along the quay. When she was clear of the bridge, she came to a halt and looked across to the north side of the river. Then she began to run up the steep stone steps.

Bernie and I followed her and that's when we saw a cloud of grey smoke rising towards the sky.

We hastened up to the road bridge where we joined the Razor Queen. She was standing there, her bright blue eyes fixed intently on something in the distance.

The smoke was rising from the house on Oswald Street!

I knew at once what had happened: *Tommy Tarantello and his men had struck back at Moira!*

"Cod-Eye!" the Razor Queen murmured beneath her breath.

She rushed out over the bridge towards the fire and the gunshots.

A second dull explosion was followed almost immediately by several bursts of tommy-gun fire. Blue flames erupted through one of the windows.

The Razor Queen had reached the high point of the bridge by then, her pale face picked out by a streetlamp. Then I lost sight of her.

Several cars had stopped at the crossroads and people came running out to see what was happening. Bernie stood beside me, staring open-mouthed at the fire and the smoke.

"But Moira... Moira," he muttered. "Moira will be burnt."

Somehow, I knew what he would do next, and as Bernie was about to rush off towards the Oswald Street house, I threw my long arms around him. He didn't even notice. He even managed a couple of lumbering steps dragging me with him.

"Moira!" he panted. "Moira!"

I had time to wrap one arm round two of the uprights supporting the railings of the bridge and so stop Bernie going any farther. He turned round and took hold of the chain with both hands as if he intended to pull it free. Only then did he seem to notice that it was still looped tight around my neck. He stopped and stood there, uncertain what to do. Then his face twisted in despair as all his strength and determination suddenly deserted him. I quickly took him by the arm and led him back over the bridge. Away from the burning house.

~

The only thought in my mind was to find a safe hiding place. Somewhere neither gangsters nor police would find us.

I aimed for the run-down tenements that backed the wharves opposite the Broomielaw. While I was looking for a covered alleyway or an outhouse in which we could hide, a chill drizzle had begun to fall. We could hear the sound of sirens from the other side of the river.

Eventually we struck lucky. We found an unlocked wash-house in one of the back courtyards. Someone must have done their washing that evening as the hearth under the washtub was still warm.

In one corner we found a couple of dirty mats to lie on and Bernie curled up, his face hidden in his hands. After a while, his breathing told me that he'd fallen asleep.

I stayed awake. The first thing I did was free myself from the chain and, after that, I set about coming up with a plan of some sort.

What I really wanted to do was take myself and Bernie out to Li Jing in Gourock, but train tickets to get there were fairly expensive and neither Bernie nor I had any money.

Was there anyone else we could rely on? Skipper Simmons, maybe... though it didn't seem very likely that he would still be in the city.

But then it came to me. All of a sudden, I knew how we could get out of Glasgow.

60

All the Way to Gourock

I woke Bernie when the rain stopped and we left the washhouse and went back down to the river.

From the quay we could look across and see all the activity around the house in Oswald Street. The fire had been put out, but the crossroads was blocked off by police cars. We could see people scurrying this way and that in the light of the street-lamps, and an inquisitive crowd had gathered by one of the roadblocks on the bridge.

I became a little uncertain about my plan. It would obviously be safer for us to try to leave the city in a day or two's time, but where were we to hide in the meantime? We had nowhere to go. Moreover, the tide had just turned and the current was now running briskly towards the sea.

I took Bernie with me and we crossed the Jamaica Bridge over the Clyde. Curious onlookers had gathered there, too, but not so many of them—after all, this was still an hour or so before dawn.

413

From the bridge we went down on to the wooden quay built on piles in the river. This took us only a stone's throw from Moira's house and we could see the traces of the battle that had raged during the night. Doors had been smashed and windows shattered. The front of the house was scorched and blackened. Police constables carrying sacks and boxes came out through the gaping holes where there had been doors. I held Bernie's hand tight to keep him calm. None of the policemen around the house noticed us as we crept along the quay under the cover of darkness and the sturdy stone pillars of the bridges.

I peeped over the edge of the quay and saw I'd been right. Simmons's steam launch was still moored where we'd left it on our return from the Black Cart.

Taking great care, I led Bernie to the ladder. He went rigid when he saw the boat. I stood and held his hand until his breathing settled and then, legs trembling, he climbed down to the launch.

I untied the mooring ropes as silently and cautiously as possible and used a boathook to push us off from the quay. The current caught us almost immediately and within minutes we were already a hundred and fifty yards downstream. None of the people on shore seemed to have noticed us.

Starting the engine was out of the question. At least it was for the moment, as the boiler would have to be fired first. But

Simmons had left a good pair of oars in the boat, so I rowed the short way out into the main current. Then I took in the oars and lit a fire under the boiler. Fortunately, Simmons had kept his matches in a dry box under the thwart.

Bernie lay down on the boards and pulled a piece of tarpaulin over him. It made no difference from my point of view. As long as we were heading seawards at this pace, I didn't need any help with rowing. All I had to do was give the oars an occasional touch to keep us on course.

~

Dawn brought low clouds and a cold breeze from the sea. The fire under the boiler was going well and a profound sense of calm gradually spread through me.

By the time we were level with Queen's Dock, I'd built up sufficient steam pressure to start the engine.

Even the noise and vibrations of the steam engine failed to wake Bernie. He slept. All the way to Gourock.

PART FIVE

THE FALSE ROSE

The Telescope

Bernie and I arrived in Gourock late in the morning. It was low tide and I beached the launch in the mud alongside a long, narrow landing stage that ran out from the shore close to Li Jing's house on Albert Road.

While I was attaching the mooring ropes, I noticed we were being observed. Li Jing was watching us from her wheelchair up in her conservatory. She opened a small ventilation window and shouted to us, "Come up… come on up. Mrs Brentwood is out shopping but you'll find the key under a flower pot to the right of the door."

~

I'll never forget the expression on Bernie's face when he stepped into Li Jing's conservatory for the first time. Wide-eyed and open-mouthed he gazed around at the flourishing greenery.

"Welcome to my home, Bernie Brodie," Li Jing said. "Don't you think I've got things set up nicely here?"

Bernie nodded as he watched a budgerigar fly past inside the glass roof. I looked at Li Jing in surprise. How on earth could she know Bernie's name?

Li Jing smiled and said, "My friend in Glasgow, Mr Cheng, usually tells me all the gossip from the port. So I know you've spent the winter with Moira Gray and her gang. Mr Cheng has actually seen you and Bernie out running errands. And I've known Bernie Brodie for a long time. I've always been interested in boxing, you know."

Bernie was busy watching the birds and seemed not to hear anything we were talking about.

Li Jing looked at him and pulled a sad face. "Things haven't always been easy for that boy."

Then she turned back to me. "Thanks to Mr Cheng I know that Koskela signed on as captain of a vessel sailing to America with a cargo of whisky. Moira's business! But I also know that he didn't undertake the voyage voluntarily. Am I right?"

I nodded my head.

"I thought as much," Li Jing said earnestly. "I'm really sad that I haven't been able to help you and Koskela through your difficulties. I used to know many influential people in Glasgow, but they all passed away long ago. The only one I know now is Mr Cheng."

I nodded to show I'd understood.

Li Jing went on. "They were saying on the wireless this morning that there had been an exchange of gunfire in Oswald Street. They said it had to do with an underworld quarrel. I was worried, of course... Was it Moira Gray's house near the Broomielaw that was attacked?"

I nodded. Li Jing looked at me questioningly.

"And while that was going on, you managed to escape? And took Bernie with you."

I nodded my head to confirm that that was more or less what had happened.

Li Jing thought things over in silence for a moment. Then she turned to Bernie and asked, "Are you wanted by the police, Bernie?"

"I don't know," Bernie said. "Am I?"

"I'll do my best to find out what the situation is," Li Jing said. "Meanwhile I think one of you should go down to the kitchen and make a pot of tea. I imagine Mrs Brentwood will soon be back with fresh bread from the baker's."

After breakfast Bernie fell asleep in one of the wicker chairs in the conservatory. I must have fallen asleep too, because suddenly it was late evening and I found myself on the sofa in Li Jing's library with a blanket tucked round me. I've no memory of how I got there. Bernie, however, was still asleep out in the conservatory.

I went back to sleep and the next time I opened my eyes it was a new morning. I could hear Li Jing talking to Bernie. Still bleary eyed I got up and went out to the conservatory. Li Jing was sitting in her wheelchair and he was crouched down beside it. A small parrot had settled on Li Jing's shoulder and Bernie was watching it with delight in his eyes.

"Good morning, Sally Jones," Li Jing said when she saw me. "While you've been asleep, Bernie and I have been getting to know one another. I was just telling him that my good friend Mr Cheng in Glasgow phoned me a couple of hours ago. He'd been talking to an acquaintance in the police and learnt that Bernie is not on the wanted list. That's good news, isn't it? It means the two of you can stay here in peace until Koskela returns from America."

So Bernie and I moved in with Li Jing. Bernie stayed in the guest room and I carried on using a hammock out in the conservatory. It would actually have been better the other way round, as Bernie could hardly drag himself away from Li Jing's birds. The moment he woke up, he'd go and sit in one of the wicker chairs under the palm leaves and he'd stay there until Li Jing or Mrs Brentwood sent him out on an errand or asked for his help with household chores. And as soon as he'd finished, he would return to the chair.

The birds got used to Bernie very quickly and if one of them perched on him he would sit as still as a statue. Li Jing's birds could have built a nest in Bernie's hair and he wouldn't have moved.

"What a strange man," I heard Mrs Brentwood saying to herself several times.

~

The newspapers wrote about the events in Oswald Street and Li Jing read all the articles to Bernie and me. You could see Bernie's relief when he heard that Moira hadn't been injured in the attack on the house. Others were less lucky. A dozen people had ended up in hospital with bullet wounds or burns, though, fortunately, no one had died.

As a result of the police intervention, large quantities of stolen goods and other evidence of crime had been seized in Moira's house. She and the members of her gang had been taken into custody on suspicion of dealing in stolen goods, smuggling, extortion, threatening behaviour and gross bodily harm. There might even be a number of murder charges. Lengthy prison sentences were to be expected.

Several of Tarantello's men had also been arrested, but he himself had avoided arrest, as I discovered later when I happened to see his picture in the paper. The picture accompanied an article on the Locarno Dance Hall on Sauchiehall Street, the place where I'd almost been shot. The article was about the new hostess of the Locarno. She was standing in the foreground of the photograph, dressed in a long, elegant evening dress and surrounded by people in their party clothes. I recognized her immediately—it was Lucky Lucy. Tommy Tarantello, a glass of champagne in his hand, was standing just behind her.

Suddenly I had the answer to a question that had been troubling me ever since that last, dreadful night in the Oswald Street house.

Who was it who had actually betrayed Moira?

No gang member had an opportunity to tip off Tarantello about Moira's planned attacks.

No one apart from Lucy, that is, it occurred to me now.

I know she wasn't present at the meeting when the attacks were planned, but someone could have told her what was proposed.

And that someone was almost certainly Gordon.

He was very taken with Lucky Lucy and seized every opportunity to spend time chatting with her. Since they were fond of one another, he would have felt sure he could trust her to keep a secret. But he shouldn't have. She deceived him and grassed to Tarantello about the attacks and, in exchange, Tarantello had rewarded her with the top job at the Locarno.

It made me sad. I knew Gordon was a rogue who deserved to be in jail, but it must be awful to be deceived by someone you really care about.

~

After a couple of days at Li Jing's house I fell ill. I had a temperature and couldn't get out of my hammock for a full week. Bernie was worried about me, but Li Jing wasn't.

"I think Sally Jones is exhausted," she told him. "Her body is telling her to rest. I'm willing to bet she'll be back on her feet in a few days."

Li Jing was right. One morning I woke up and felt fully recovered. That's when I noticed that Li Jing had a small telescope on the windowsill in the veranda. During the week that followed I used the telescope several hours a day to check the shipping. I was longing for the day when I'd see the *Valkyrie* come sailing up the Firth of Clyde.

Li Jing thought that staring through the telescope was a waste of my time. She telephoned the pilot station in Gourock instead and talked to the senior pilot. He promised to inform us the moment the *Valkyrie* was sighted by their lookouts along the firth.

"And you don't need to worry that the *Valkyrie* has gone down out in the Atlantic," Li Jing told me. "We'd have already heard of it—shipping disasters are always big news in a city like Glasgow."

I didn't doubt Li Jing and, besides, I didn't know of anyone more competent at sea than the Chief. Still, as the days passed, I became more and more uneasy. The *Valkyrie* should have arrived back in Glasgow weeks before.

High Tide

In order to keep my worries at bay, I made sure I kept busy.

For a start, I borrowed Li Jing's old portable typewriter—a Corona—and wrote a letter to Ana and Signor Fidardo, in which I gave an account of everything that had happened to me and the Chief since leaving Lisbon. It was a long letter. I finished off by promising to contact them again as soon as the Chief arrived back in Glasgow.

While I was clattering away on the keys of the typewriter, Li Jing was trying to get Bernie to work in the greenhouse. Bernie was reluctant at first, mainly because he was afraid of doing things wrong. But after a couple of days, he was watering the plants and cutting off the dead leaves and branches on the large palms.

Working in the greenhouse seemed to help Bernie feel calm and settled. Otherwise, for the most part, his mood was downcast and concerned. I guessed he was thinking about Moira, perhaps worrying about her, perhaps missing her, though that was hard to believe given how horrible she'd been to him. But what did I know? Maybe she hadn't always been like that and, after all, she was his sister.

~

I helped, too, with various bits around the house, like changing the weathervane on the roof and repairing worn-out wheel bearings in Li Jing's wheelchair. I also spent part of every day working on Simmons's launch. Sooner or later I'd have to return it to him and, as thanks for the loan, I wanted it to be in better condition than when I took it. There is nothing more relaxing than tinkering with a steam engine—it makes time pass so quickly.

One morning, while topping up the oil in the steam engine's lubrication points, I noticed a sailing ship tacking its way north off Dunoon on the opposite side of the firth. Not exactly an unusual sight on the Firth of Clyde, but I still ran into the house to take a closer look at the ship through the telescope. I did the same thing every time I caught sight of a sail.

This vessel was a three-masted schooner. In spite of the fresh breeze, it had all sails set, even the mizzen topsail and the flying jib. When the vessel heeled in the gusts of wind, the foaming, white bow wave reached the gunwales. My pulse raced. The Chief was a skilful sailor who prided himself on always carrying as much sail as the wind permitted.

The telephone rang and Li Jing answered it. At the end of the call, she turned to me and said, "That was the master pilot. The lookout station in Dunoon has just reported that a vessel called *Valkyrie* is approaching the mouth of the River Clyde."

~

I ran back down to the landing stage. It was high tide and the launch had plenty of water under her keel. All I had to do was cast off and get moving!

Out on the firth, the *Valkyrie* had tacked and was beginning to beat against the wind towards the mouth of the river. I set a course due north in order to intercept her. Close to shore, the sea was choppy and the foam flew when I set full speed ahead and coursed through the waves.

The Firth of Clyde is a wide stretch of water and the wind picks up speed as it sweeps down over the bare hills to the west. The farther out I went, the rougher the sea became and I had to work hard at the rudder to prevent waves breaking in over the rail.

As I approached the *Valkyrie* I could see the crew lowering the topsails. Then the vessel changed tack and the foresails came down in one sweep. It was a neat manoeuvre.

The vessel sailed on with her mainsail, headsail and mizzen. I guessed she was making for Greenock or Dumbarton, to wait there for a pilot and tugboats.

I was soon no more than sixty yards or so from the *Valkyrie*. At that distance, I could see that the vessel had been at sea too long. Far too long. The worn sails were crisscrossed with patches and the planking, grey and weather beaten, had taken a battering from the ice.

None of the crew paid any attention to my small boat at first. They were all busy furling the sails and preparing to drop anchor. But when I steered in along the lee side of the *Valkyrie*, one of the sailors suddenly stopped and began staring in my direction. A low winter sun was peeping through between the clouds and he had to shade his eyes to see better. I raised my arm and waved.

It took a few seconds, but then the sailor pointed at me and yelled to his fellows. One by one his bearded and tousled shipmates joined him. They laughed and waved heartily, as if I was an old acquaintance.

The mate on watch had noticed me, too, and I saw him hurry below deck through the after hatch. Less than half a minute later he returned.

Behind him came the Chief, smoke curling from a cigar in the corner of his mouth!

I recognized him at once even though, like everyone else on board, he now had a beard. The mate pointed in my direction and, on catching sight of me, the cigar fell from the Chief's mouth. After staring at me for a couple more seconds as if to make sure he wasn't hallucinating, he pulled off his cap and threw it up in the air. The wind carried his shout of joy to me.

I held up my own cap and waved back.

~

The *Valkyrie* sailed on at a good speed and I didn't want to delay the Chief by having him heave to just to take me on board. I had no doubt his crew was longing to get ashore. They had all been away the whole winter. And I'd be seeing the Chief soon enough, anyway.

So, after sailing alongside the *Valkyrie* for a short distance towards the mouth of the River Clyde, I waved farewell and headed back for Gourock.

The wind and waves were with me now and the launch surfed on the crests or swooped through the troughs of the waves. The pale, low winter sun shone on my face.

My overalls were soaking wet, but strangely enough I don't remember feeling cold. Not at all, in fact.

And for the first time in many months I felt truly at peace.

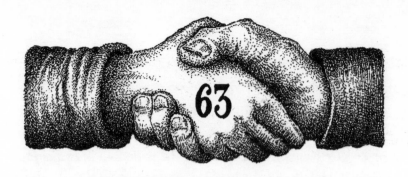

A Kind and Courageous Friend

It was to be five long days before I saw the Chief again.

I became really concerned about him during that time. What if he'd run into trouble with the Glasgow police because of smuggling whisky?

I needn't have worried. One grey and overcast Friday saw the Chief standing at Li Jing's door. He was well-scrubbed, clean-shaven and beaming with joy.

In spite of the fact that Li Jing's little house was already full, she suggested that the Chief should move in with us. The Chief thanked her and agreed, but said it would only be for the weekend as he had to return to Glasgow on Monday morning. The police were doing what they could to get to the bottom of Moira's various shady dealings and wanted to question the Chief about the voyage of the *Valkyrie* to America with a cargo of smuggled whisky.

432

The Chief had no reason to be worried about his part in the business. The police had already assured him of that. The logbook of the *Valkyrie* proved that the vessel had never been in American waters, so neither the Chief nor his crew could actually be charged with smuggling. The business of transporting the whisky into United States' territorial waters had been done by American gangsters in fast motorboats.

~

Bernie was initially rather shy when faced with the Chief. He kept his distance and gave him uneasy looks. The Chief, for his part, had never met Bernie before and was utterly amazed to learn that Bernie was Moira Gray's brother.

"But how does all this fit together?" he wondered.

Li Jing told him the little she knew about my time in the Oswald Street house. And she showed him the newspaper articles about the gun battle and about the police action against Moira's gang.

After listening and reading the Chief looked at me and said, "Once we get back to Lisbon, you are going to have to take out your old Underwood. I have a feeling that it's some story you have to tell!"

And then I noticed that the Chief's jaw was trembling just a little.

"I've been so damn worried," he said. "There were times when I thought of jumping ship, but I had the crew to think about as well."

I nodded and patted the Chief's arm to show that I understood. A captain does not leave his crew in the lurch.

It's as simple as that.

~

That night the four of us sat around the table in the conservatory. The Chief had a bottle of whisky he'd pinched from the *Valkyrie*'s cargo.

"It's pretty cheap stuff, I imagine," the Chief said, "but at least it's been well and truly shaken up by the waves."

After the Chief and Li Jing had clinked glasses, she said, "Now I want to hear everything that happened to you since we met last."

The Chief started by telling Li Jing about Fillingsworth, the detective, and how we fell into the hands of Moira and her Oswald Street gang.

"The pearl necklace, then… You don't have it any longer, do you?" Li Jing asked.

"No," the Chief said. "I suppose it's lost for ever. Lord Kilvaird no doubt lost the necklace in a poker game."

I wondered whether I should borrow Li Jing's Corona and

write down everything I knew about what had happened with the necklace. But I thought it could wait.

Meanwhile the Chief told us about his voyage across the Atlantic and back. He told of the drama involved in handing over the smuggled whisky to the gangsters from New York. And he told us how one of the *Valkyrie*'s deckhands had fallen from the rigging in hard weather.

"The lad survived," the Chief said, "and that's the most important thing. But while we were still in the harbour at St Pierre, the sea froze over, so that when we were eventually ready to continue the voyage, it was no longer possible to get out into open water. It was almost a month before a Canadian icebreaker turned up and opened a channel for us."

The Chief also told us about several really severe storms they'd been hit by, the last of them the worst. Strong winds had pushed the vessel farther and farther north until the Chief decided to seek a safe haven in the Faroe Islands. They spent a week moored in Tórshavn before they could cast off and sail the last leg of the trip to Scotland.

As a memento of his adventures on the *Valkyrie*, the Chief now had some nasty scars on his nose as a result of frostbite.

"And that was the only reward I got for this trip," he said.

Then he turned to Bernie. "You must tell me how you ended up coming here with Sally Jones."

Bernie fidgeted nervously and threw a glance in my direction.

"Well… I mean… so much happened that evening… I don't really know…"

I was forced to intervene. I stood up, fetched a pen from Li Jing's desk and wrote on a slip of paper:

BERNIE SAVED MY LIFE

Li Jing and the Chief both leant forward to read what I'd written. The Chief looked at me questioningly and I responded with a firm nod.

The Chief turned to Bernie and held out his hand. "I thank my lucky stars that Sally Jones had the good fortune to meet a kind and courageous friend like you! I am grateful to you, Bernie!"

Bernie looked at the Chief. He was uncertain, unable to decide whether he had heard properly or whether the Chief was teasing him.

Eventually, however, he realized that the Chief actually meant what he was saying. A smile lit up Bernie's face and he bent down to shake the hand the Chief was holding out.

This was the second time I'd seen Bernie smile. And it was at least as extraordinary as it had been the first time.

A Lucky Break

The Chief didn't need to be back in Glasgow before Monday morning but, in spite of that, he and I decided to go to the city a day early.

It was my idea. I wanted to return the steam launch to Skipper Simmons, and since Sunday promised to be a fine day for a trip on the water, it seemed sensible to take advantage of it.

We cast off after breakfast, just as the tide turned so the current was with us. We had a wonderful trip up the river, with lunch boxes, a bright late winter sun and a couple of forays ashore along the way.

The Chief didn't know who owned the launch or how I had got hold of it. But as I turned out into the fast-flowing River Kelvin, he said, "Is there someone we're planning to visit?"

I nodded.

My hope was that Simmons had risked returning to his little boatyard now that Moira and her gang were behind bars. Otherwise, I supposed, we'd just have to leave the launch moored to his landing stage.

We had scarcely berthed when the door to the workshop flew open and Simmons came running out.

"Sally Jones!" he shouted happily. "Don't ask me how, but I felt certain you were the one who was looking after my old launch."

~

We stayed with Skipper Simmons for the rest of that day and through to the following morning. By midnight I was feeling tired, so I lay down on a stack of old sails close to the stove. The Chief stayed up, chatting and smoking with Simmons at his rickety, little kitchen table.

The Chief wanted to learn everything that Simmons knew about my time with Moira and her gang. Simmons told him about our nocturnal smuggling trips down the river, about the raid on the Greek's gambling club in Maryhill and about that dreadful return trip after the meeting at the Black Cart.

It was a joy to lie there, bedded down in the old sails, feeling the warmth from the stove and listening to their chat. After a while their voices became part of my dreams.

~

The following morning a thick blanket of cloud lay over Glasgow and chill winds from the north brought icy showers of rain and sleet. The Chief and I bade Skipper Simmons a heartfelt farewell and set out into the foul weather. We took a bus to Central Station and had breakfast in the station café. Then we walked along Oswald Street to Moira's house.

We stood there on the pavement in silence for quite some time. The north gable of the house was filthy and smoke-blackened. The glass in every single window was shattered and tommy-gun bullets had torn great lumps of plaster off the front of the house. The display windows of the shop must also have been shattered by bullets, since they were now covered with heavy tarpaulins. A police constable stood on guard outside the gate leading to the backyard, presumably to prevent looters gaining entry.

The colour drained from the Chief's face.

"Lord in Heaven," he said quietly. "It looks as if there's been a war fought here. Had you and Bernie managed to get out of the house before all this happened?"

I nodded.

"That was a lucky blessing," the Chief said, shaking his head slowly. "A lucky blessing!"

I could only agree with him.

We continued our walk and went east along the river and past the customs buildings on Great Clyde Street. A short distance farther on we reached the small square that holds the Central Police Headquarters. I had to sit and wait on a bench in one of the corridors in the police station while the Chief went to talk to the police.

It took several hours and I was beginning to get nervous by the end of it. Surely the police weren't intending to lock up the Chief in spite of what they'd promised?

I was worrying unnecessarily. The look on the Chief's face when he came to pick me up was happy and satisfied.

"What I need now is a glass of beer!" he stated firmly.

Dusk was already falling when we went out. We wandered along the street keeping our eyes open for the first decent pub, but we hadn't gone more than a couple of blocks from the police station when a large, white car pulled into the kerb in front of us. The car was a Plymouth.

I felt a sudden rush of fear. I grabbed the Chief's arm tight to make him stop and turn back. *We had to get away quickly.*

But the Chief didn't know what was about to happen. He'd never seen Tommy Tarantello's car before, of course. And when Craig McCauley got out on the driver's side, it was already too late for us to run.

McCauley looked at me with his nasty, twisted leer. In the light of the shop windows along the street, the scar on his face glistened a pale yellow.

65

Sharks

The Chief can recognize a gangster when he sees one. Even so, he wasn't in the least bit afraid when Craig McCauley stood in our way and blocked us.

That's the way with sailors who've just come ashore after a long and perilous voyage. When you've survived thunderstorms and typhoons, you don't easily allow the thugs and gangsters of the docks to scare you. But it's a mistake that has cost many a good sailor his life. The most dangerous sharks are not those swimming in the sea, but the ones who live on land.

"Mr Koskela," McCauley said, opening the back door. "Get in the car. And take the ape with you."

"And who are you?" the Chief asked.

"Just do what I say," McCauley said with a sigh, letting his jacket fall slightly open for us to see the revolver in its holster.

The Chief turned to me. "Is this anyone you know?"

McCauley gestured impatiently and grasped the butt of his revolver. But before he drew the weapon from its holster, the rear door opened and Florenza Tarantello leant out of the back seat.

"Leave your revolver where it is!" she said in a sharp voice.

Taken by surprise, the Chief looked at her. She was wearing a simple cape with a high collar and her big eyes shone like black velvet in her pale face.

"Please get in the car, Mr Koskela," she said. "I won't let any harm come to you or to your ape. You have my word on it."

~

So there I was again in the big back seat of Tommy Tarantello's car. And there he was, sitting beside Florenza, the surly look on his face visible below the brim of his white hat.

The Chief said, "Well now. Who might you be? And what do you want with us?"

Tommy Tarantello leant forward with a quick movement and waved a threatening finger at the Chief.

"If you knew who I am, Mr Sailorman, you'd make the effort to sound a bit more respectful!"

Florenza placed a calming hand on her uncle's knee and said to the Chief, "My uncle has come into possession of something that I believe belongs to you. A valuable piece of jewellery. He found it in Moira Gray's flat. How it got there would seem to be a long story, but according to our sources in the police, one of Moira Gray's men said it actually belongs to you, Mr Koskela. A man by the name of Kilvaird stole it from you… is that right?"

The Chief and I exchanged quick glances. The Chief's eyes were wide with surprise.

"This is nothing but a load of nonsense!" Tommy Tarantello muttered. "The necklace is mine now! Moira stole it from the Greek, and the Greek owes me…"

Florenza silenced him with an icy look and said, "Dear uncle, this is a matter of *honour*. First of all, the ape helped our fellow-countrymen on the *Campania*, and then she helped us avoid a war with the riverside gangs. This is your opportunity to repay her."

Tommy Tarantello shook his head, gave a deep sigh and rolled his eyes. But he said nothing to contradict Florenza.

She looked at the Chief and said, "Do you know what kind of jewellery I'm referring to?"

The Chief was so taken aback that he couldn't come up with an immediate answer. But after I'd given him a nudge with my elbow, he said, "Well, we have indeed lost a necklace. Lord Kilvaird was the one who stole it from us, and then he gambled it away at cards, or so we've heard."

"What sort of necklace is it?" Florenza asked him. "Can you describe it?"

"It's a pearl necklace," the Chief said. "With a rose pendant… a rose made of mother-of-pearl and silver."

Florenza nodded. "There you are," she said, looking sternly at her uncle. "There can't be any doubt about who owns the necklace, can there? So it's time for you to do the right thing now, Uncle Tommy."

Tommy Tarantello groaned with displeasure as he produced the worn, chamois-leather bag from his pocket. Reluctantly he handed it over to the Chief before grunting, "Get out of my car now, Sailorman! And stay away from me in the future! You won't be so lucky the next time we meet!"

The Chief didn't bother to respond to Tarantello's threats. Instead he turned to Florenza and thanked her. "If every rogue were like you, miss, the world would be a better place."

"Don't be so sure about that, Mr Koskela," Florenza answered sharply.

The Chief laughed and added, "Well, at any rate it would be prettier. Goodbye, miss."

I thought I caught a slight flicker of a smile on Florenza Tarantello's lips, but I may, of course, have been imagining things.

The Chief and I were left standing on the pavement and we watched the white Plymouth swing out into the traffic and disappear.

The Chief put the bag of pearls in his pocket and said, "I have to say, Sally Jones, that you really have a way of making the most unlikely friends!"

66

Cold Steel and Hot Spices

The Chief and I found a pub where we could sit, get our breath back and think things over. The Chief had his usual beer and I had a cup of warm milk.

"Well," said the Chief, "we seem to be back where we started. The pearls still belong to Rose Henderson, Shetland Jack's daughter."

I nodded.

"In which case we have no choice," the Chief continued. "We have to make another attempt to find her."

His face clouded over all of a sudden.

"But first we have a score to settle," he said. "With Mr Fillingsworth, the detective. He delivered us straight into the claws of that Moira and her gang. And he ripped us off for five pounds as an advance payment, too. He can't be allowed to get away with that sort of behaviour!"

I agreed. Detective Fillingsworth had a lot of explaining to do.

It was already a quarter past five so there was a good chance the detective had shut up shop for the day. The Chief and I decided instead to take a room for the night at Mrs Grimes's boarding house. We needed to go there anyway to collect our kitbags, always assuming Mrs Grimes still had them. Which she did.

"Oh, how lovely to see you again!" she exclaimed as we went into the boarding house. "I've been dreadfully worried about you both. After you'd been away for a week, I went to your room and found all your things scattered any old how on the floor. I thought something awful must have happened and I actually went to the police. But they weren't interested at all."

It took the Chief some time to calm Mrs Grimes down. Then he told her what had happened to us, though he missed out the most unpleasant parts as he didn't want to upset the kind old lady unnecessarily.

The next morning the Chief and I rose early. We washed in the cracked handbasin in our room, said goodbye to Mrs Grimes and set off out into the city with our kitbags on our shoulders. After a good half hour's walk we were standing outside the Gibson Street house in which Mr Fillingsworth had his office. But there was no longer any sign of the detective's elegant nameplate.

"Aha, there you go," the Chief said. "Our detective seems to have jumped ship. We might as well go up and ring the bell anyway. You never know…"

The doorman was asleep in his chair, so we just went ahead and trudged up the stairs. There was a notice on the office door stating that the premises were available to rent. The Chief knocked hard on the door, but there was no sound from within.

We went back down to street level and the Chief woke the doorman and asked him if he knew where Fillingsworth had gone. The doorman, his eyes still sticky with sleep, studied the Chief, but when he caught sight of me he was suddenly wide awake.

"An ape…" he said. "Yes, that was it! A sailor and an ape! Wait here and I'll see."

The doorman rummaged around in some drawers and produced an envelope.

"Mr Fillingsworth shut up his office very suddenly one day," he said. "I don't know why, but he was in a great hurry to get away from here. In fact, I thought he seemed to be afraid."

The doorman handed the envelope to the Chief before continuing. "Mr Fillingsworth gave me this before he moved out. He said I should give it to the sailor who might come looking for him one fine day… a sailor with a big, tame ape. That must be you, mustn't it?"

"Do you know where Fillingsworth is to be found now?" the Chief asked.

The doorman shrugged his shoulders.

"Edinburgh, maybe?" he said. "I think he has family there."

~

After the Chief had thanked the doorman for his help, we went and found a pub where we could sit and open the envelope from Detective Fillingsworth. It contained five pounds in notes and a handwritten letter.

Dear Mr Koskela,

If you had any idea how ashamed I feel!

A few days after you and your ape visited me, three men came to my office. They had seen the notice I put in the Glasgow Herald *seeking information about Rose Henderson. They wanted to know who had employed me to locate her, and why. When I tried to explain to them that such information was confidential, one of them whipped out a large stiletto and threatened to do dreadful things to me. I was forced to tell them everything. Forgive me, but I didn't dare refuse. Then they wanted to know when you would be coming back to see me again—and I told* them. *They then ordered me to stay away from my office for the whole of that day. And they threatened to shoot me if I didn't do what they said. And the same thing would happen if I ever tried to contact the police and report their threats.*

I have no idea who these frightening men were or why they wanted you. But I pray to the Lord that you and your ape didn't come to any harm.

If you receive this note, I hope you can forgive me. I cannot!
Yours sincerely,
Humphrey Fillingsworth
Ex-Private Detective.

P.S. If it is still of any use to you, I can tell you that I did manage to make some enquiries about Rose Henderson before I was visited by those awful men. You told me the girl was from the Shetland Isles and had been sent to a children's home after her mother died. When I tried to find a list of children's homes in Shetland, it turned out that there weren't any. Children without parents or anyone else to look after them are sent instead to the Highland Orphanage, a children's home in the town of Inverness on the Scottish mainland.

When we'd read the letter, we sat in silence for a long time. It was a silence of unspoken shame.

"We should not have assumed such bad things about the detective," the Chief said. "He was given a hard time, poor fellow. Let's hope he gets through."

I nodded. I hoped so, too.

∼

That afternoon we went to a post office in the city to send a telegram to Ana and Signor Fidardo. From there we went to the Chinese Seamen's Hostel and met Li Jing's good friend, Mr Cheng. He had packed a wooden box full of the spices and other foodstuffs Li Jing had ordered. The smells that rose from the box were familiar to me and the Chief. They wakened memories of the old days, when we had sailed on the tramp steamer *Patna* on the Singapore-Makassar route.

∼

It was already evening by the time we arrived back at Li Jing's in Gourock. She put us to work straightaway, chopping vegetables, weighing out rice and frying spices in oil on the stove. An hour or so later we laid the table for a meal of freshly cooked dumplings, braised fish and egg noodles.

After we'd eaten, the Chief took out the necklace and told Li Jing and Bernie what had happened to us in the last few days. Then we showed them the letter from Detective Fillingsworth.

"The story of Shetland Jack and his necklace doesn't seem to be over yet," Li Jing said when she had read the letter. "It looks as if the two of you will have to go to Inverness."

The Chief and I both nodded, and he said, "It must be the best part of thirty years since Rose Henderson left the children's home. I wonder if anyone there will still remember her?"

"Don't be too concerned about that," Li Jing said. "There was a lot written about Shetland Jack and his daughter in the newspapers after his ship was found abandoned. It was a real mystery, what with traces of blood on the deck and everything. There will certainly be people in Inverness who still remember."

Li Jing was interrupted by Bernie, who rose quickly from his chair, his face suddenly pale and grey. He muttered, "Thanks for supper," and left the table.

The stairs creaked as Bernie went down to his room on the ground floor. We heard him close the door behind him.

"He didn't look too well," the Chief said. "Let's hope he's not going down with something."

"It was probably just the spices," Li Jing thought. "Scots aren't used to Asian food."

~

We ended up sitting up late. But when I'd climbed into my hammock, I still couldn't get to sleep. My head was full of thoughts.

I didn't think Bernie had left the table because the spices had made him feel ill.

No, it wasn't that. What had upset him was the talk about Shetland Jack.

I was almost sure of it.

And then I got to thinking about that awful night a couple of weeks before when Skipper Simmons threw himself into the Clyde. I remembered how Bernie had been hysterical with fear. And there was something Moira had said... *something about Shetland Jack.*

So both Moira and Bernie knew of Captain Jack Shaw.

How come?

Highland Orphanage

For some reason, Bernie didn't want to come to Inverness with us. He shook his head and mumbled when the question was brought up. So it was decided that Bernie would stay with Li Jing while the Chief and I were away.

We took the early morning ferry over to Helensburgh and continued our journey north by train. I like travelling by train and the views of the Scottish Highlands are beautiful. We left the train in the town of Fort Augustus and joined the paddle steamer *Glengarry* that operates on the Caledonian Canal and Loch Ness route.

Late that afternoon the Chief and I finally stepped ashore in Inverness. We had a meal of smoked herring in a restaurant by the steamer quay and took the opportunity to enquire where the local children's home was. The owner of the restaurant told us the way.

We walked past long rows of low, grey houses that huddled

beneath an equally grey sky. A gale, now slowly abating, still whined and whistled round the church tower and the masts of ships.

Dusk was falling and squalls of rain were sweeping in from the North Sea. We'd soon left the town behind us and were starting to wonder whether we'd gone wrong somewhere. Then the Chief noticed a large, two-storied, stone building standing on its own, surrounded by a stone wall and a few bare trees.

"This is it, I think," he said.

We took a narrow, gravel path that led from the road up to the house. There was a lamp over the front door and faint lights could be seen in one or two of the windows, but there were no other signs of life. The only sounds were the crunch of the gravel beneath our feet and the whine of the wind.

The Chief lifted the door knocker and knocked three times.

Nothing happened. The Chief knocked again.

We glimpsed a pale, wrinkled face through one of the windows at the side of the door and then there was the rattle of a lock being undone. The door opened, but only enough to allow an old man to peer out at us with bleary eyes.

"Who are you?" the man asked the Chief. "Are you a beggar? Are you hoping to get paid for showing that ape you've got with you?"

"No," the Chief said. "My name is Henry Koskela and I've

come a long way in order to meet the superintendent of this orphanage."

～

The old man went away, leaving us standing in the porch. The house was completely silent, so the children must already have gone to bed. After a while we heard the approach of firm footsteps and a stern-looking woman, her grey hair in a bun, appeared. She stood in front of us and looked disapprovingly at me.

Then she turned to the Chief and said, "My name is Mildred Culduthel. Who are you and what do you want?"

The Chief introduced us and began to explain our business there.

Mrs Culduthel cut him short. "I'm afraid I can't talk about any of the children who've lived at the Highland Orphanage. Not even Rose Henderson. Unfortunately, you've come all this way for nothing, Mr Koskela."

She was about to turn on her heel and go when the Chief said, "It's about a necklace we have found. A pearl necklace that belonged to the girl's father."

Mrs Culduthel came to an abrupt halt and stood speechless for a moment or two. Then she turned to the hunched door-man and said brusquely, "Go and make a pot of tea and bring it up to my office."

She gestured to the Chief to follow her. "The ape can stay outside," she said. "You can tie it to the handrail if you're worried it'll run away."

I took a step forward, looked the superintendent straight in the eye and held out my hand for her to shake. Mrs Culduthel did not take my hand, but she did meet my eyes.

"Right then, let it come with us," she said. "But I hold you responsible for any trouble it causes, Mr Koskela."

Mrs Culduthel led us through a long corridor with a cold, flagstone floor, its walls lined with depressingly dark wooden panelling. Every so often we passed large portraits depicting various grim-faced men and women. These, I assumed, must be portraits of earlier superintendents of the orphanage.

The corridor led to a large hall with a high ceiling and a wide staircase that led up to the floor above.

I came to a sudden halt, staring at the staircase.

A strange feeling came over me.

Suddenly, here was something that felt very familiar... as if I'd been here before.

It was impossible, of course—I'd never ever been in Inverness in my life!

I tried to shake off the feeling and quickly followed the Chief and Mrs Culduthel up the stairs.

458

The Winds of Fate

The walls of Mrs Culduthel's office were lined with bookcases. The only other furnishings consisted of a small desk and a pair of Windsor chairs. A smell of carbolic soap rose from the broad, wooden floorboards.

Mrs Culduthel sat at the desk and invited the Chief and me to take the chairs. Then the Chief told her how we had discovered the necklace in the *Hudson Queen* and our subsequent search for its rightful owner. Mrs Culduthel listened attentively and then sat for a while in silence. She seemed gripped by what she had heard.

"I take it that Rose Henderson lived at this orphanage before you took over," the Chief said.

"That's correct," Mrs Culduthel said hesitantly. "But I know who she is and I know the sad story of her father."

She thought a little before going on. "Those of us who work at the orphanage have a duty of silence. Some of the children who

459

grow up here want it kept secret in later life. They don't want people to find out that they came from poor circumstances."

"I understand," the Chief said.

"Rose Lafourcade isn't one of those who is ashamed of her past," Mrs Culduthel continued. "So I can certainly tell you what I know about her."

"Rose Lafourcade?" the Chief said.

"Yes, that's what Rose Henderson is called these days. She actually came here and visited the orphanage a few years ago. And she took the opportunity to tell me all about her life."

Mrs Culduthel now proceeded to tell the Chief and me the story of Rose Henderson's life. She began when Rose arrived at the children's home as a four-year-old orphan. Eleven years later, when she reached the age of fifteen, she had to move out and start supporting herself. The intention was that she would work at the town woollen mill, but Rose didn't want to be a mill worker, she wanted to see the world. So she slipped aboard a steamer that was passing through a canal lock in Inverness and, hidden in one of the lifeboats, she left Scotland. It would be more than twenty years before she returned. During those years the winds of fate had blown her from continent to continent and adventure to adventure.

At some point around the start of the new century, Rose arrived in Patagonia, right down at the southern tip of South America. Like many other people, she had been drawn there by the great gold rush, and in Punta Arenas she met a young Frenchman called George Lafourcade. They married in the local town hall. After a few years prospecting for gold on the inhospitable islands around the Straits of Magellan, George and Rose decided to move north because they wanted to see the rainforests of the Amazon. Once there, they decided to invest their gold in a rubber plantation deep in the Peruvian jungle.

Life in Amazonia was hard and dangerous and one day George fell sick with a feared jungle fever. Rose and some helpers from a local tribe managed to take him by canoe to the provincial doctor in Iquitos. But they were too late and George's life was beyond saving.

Rose sold the rubber plantation and returned to Europe to bury George in his home town, Lodève in southern France. She immediately fell in love with the landscape and the people she met in Lodève, so she stayed there. The sale of the plantation in Peru had made her a very rich woman and she used some of her money to buy a vineyard just outside the town.

"And that's where she has lived and worked ever since." Mrs Culduthel concluded her account of Rose Henderson's life. "I can give you the address of her vineyard if you like."

"Thank you. We'd be glad of that," the Chief said.

Then he became thoughtful.

"Jack Shaw tried to find Rose for many, many years," he said. "Did she know that?"

Mrs Culduthel shook her head sadly.

"No," she said. "At that time Rose knew nothing of her father. She hadn't even been born when he disappeared to Australia. And he never got in contact in the years she was living here in the orphanage. By the time he returned to Scotland, Rose was already away. And no one could say where she had gone."

Mrs Culduthel gave a gloomy sigh before continuing. "It wasn't until much later when Rose made her visit here that she eventually heard the story of her father and of the pearl necklace he wanted to give her. But by then, Shetland Jack must have been dead for many years—or vanished, I should perhaps say. No one really knows what happened to him."

She sighed again.

"Rose took it very hard. The whole business is awfully sad."

~

Mrs Culduthel accompanied us to the front door to say good-bye. As we walked down the staircase from the upper floor, I stopped and looked around. Had it just been my imagination

462

when I thought I recognized it all on arriving? The brain can sometimes play strange tricks.

But, but… there was still something very familiar about the beautifully carved handrail and the tall, narrow window beside it.

～

The night outside was pitch black, but we could see the faint glimmer of the lights of the town under the low, fast-moving clouds to the north of us. We'd have no problem finding our way back. The *Glengarry* was still moored alongside the steamer quay. We went on board and met some members of the crew who allowed us to bed down for the night in the aft saloon.

The wooden benches in the saloon were narrow and hard, but that wasn't the only reason why I found it hard to get to sleep. I couldn't stop thinking about all the things we had learnt that evening. The Chief seemed to be having the same problem and after a while he went out onto the deck and smoked a cigar. I went and kept him company.

"Well, I suppose we'll have to travel to France," he said. "What do you think?"

I nodded.

The Chief puffed on his cigar for a time before saying in a concerned tone of voice, "I'm just wondering what's to become of Bernie. Li Jing seems to be fond of him, but I doubt she'll want him to move in for good."

I'd been thinking the same thing.

"Does Bernie have any other friends in Glasgow?" the Chief asked. "Anyone who could help him find a job and somewhere to live?"

I shook my head.

"No friends at all?"

I shook my head once more. Everyone that Bernie knew was now in jail.

The Chief thought for a moment and then said, "In that case I think we should ask him if he'd like to come to Lisbon with us. We've got room for another member of the crew on the *Hudson Queen*, haven't we?"

I looked at the Chief. Did he really want this? After all, he hardly knew Bernie.

The Chief smiled.

"Your friends are my friends, sailor," he said. "And I do like Bernie. Besides, if he doesn't settle on the *Hudson Queen* I'm sure we'd be able to find another job for him in Lisbon."

I nodded and patted the Chief's arm to show that his suggestion made me happy.

Once the Chief had finished his cigar we went back into the warm saloon. The Chief immediately fell asleep on his bench, whereas I lay awake for a while listening to his snores. My thoughts drifted this way and that, as they tend to when you are falling asleep. All of a sudden, though, I snapped awake. I sat up and stared out into the darkness. I knew now why I'd recognized that staircase in the orphanage! I really had seen it before! Not in reality, of course, *but in that old picture that Bernie had hidden away in his red tin box!* Bernie and Moira had been photographed on the staircase of the Highland Orphanage!

69

An Unexpected Reunion

Ten days later the general cargo vessel *Morbihan* was setting out from Queen's Dock in the port of Glasgow. Her destination was Le Havre on the north coast of France and the Chief, Bernie and I were all on board.

We had shared a farewell dinner at Li Jing's house the evening before. The Chief had taken charge of the cooking, while Li Jing entertained us with stories from every part of the globe.

Bernie was downcast the following morning—he didn't want to say goodbye to Li Jing.

"You are a useless boxer, Bernie Brodie," she said, holding his huge hands in her small hands. "But you are a good man! And you're capable of a lot more than you think you are. Make sure you find a job that makes you happy. You'd make a good gardener. The flowers and palms in my conservatory are going to miss you. And the birds, too."

To the Chief and me, Li Jing said, "It was nice to get to know the two of you. Come back once you've got the *Hudson Queen* back in service. She is a Clyde Puffer when all is said and done, and the Firth of Clyde is her home water."

Our voyage to Le Havre in the *Morbihan* proved troublesome. No sooner had we gone over the landing stage in the Queen's Dock than Bernie broke out in a cold sweat. The Chief wondered whether he was falling sick with flu, but I knew better. Bernie was terrified at the thought of the voyage.

The Chief signed on as third engineer and Bernie and I were set to shovelling coal. I saw how hard Bernie struggled to do a good job as a stoker, but his fear took all his strength away. He'd been seasick several times before we even reached open water. Then he just went and lay down in the coal box and stayed there for the rest of the voyage. The Chief and I took turns to cover his shifts for him so that the other stokers wouldn't get annoyed.

The Chief tried talking to Bernie to find out what the problem was, but Bernie didn't want to say anything. He just shook his huge head and shut his eyes tight.

"It seems he's afraid of something," the Chief said to me when Bernie was out of earshot. "But what could it be? Is it the sea itself that terrifies him?"

I nodded. That's what it was.

"But why?" the Chief wondered.

I shrugged my shoulders. It was still a mystery even to me.

~

We docked in Le Havre after three days at sea. Our original plan had been to try to find another vessel to carry us farther south, preferably all the way to the Mediterranean. But the Chief had other ideas now.

"Life at sea doesn't seem to be Bernie's cup of tea," he said to me. "And the storms in the Bay of Biscay are no joke at this time of year. So I think we should continue our journey on gentler waterways."

That's why the next stage of our journey was spent on a coal barge, sailing up the Seine from Le Havre to Paris. We spent several sunny days chipping off the rust, swabbing the deck and shovelling coal as the barge puffed its way between the fields, pastures and villages of the beautiful landscape of Normandy. Bernie had so much to look at that after a while he forgot he was actually on a boat.

I enjoyed my time on board as well, but my thoughts kept returning to Scotland and to the things that had happened during the last six months. Most of all I thought of Bernie's old photograph of him and Moira on the staircase in the Highland Orphanage.

Did the photograph mean that Bernie and Moira had grown up in the same children's home as Rose Henderson? Well, that certainly seemed to be the case. And it would explain how both Moira and Bernie knew of Rose's father, Shetland Jack.

Though, in fact, none of that was of importance any longer. Not for the Chief and me, anyway. We had gone to Glasgow to find out who the necklace belonged to and all we had to do now was deliver the pearls to Rose Lafourcade. After that we could go back to Lisbon and Ana and Signor Fidardo. How I longed to see them again!

~

We reached Paris on the afternoon of the fourth day. Even at a distance of several miles we could see the mighty Eiffel Tower rising towards the clear blue sky. I counted seventeen splendid stone bridges crossing the Seine before we reached the centre of the city. The streets along the riverside were crowded with people, bicycles, cars, buses and horse-drawn carriages. New sounds and new smells came one after another.

It was early evening by the time the Chief, Bernie and I had finished our work on board and could sign off. Before we went ashore, the Chief asked whether the skipper knew of any cheap hotels in the district.

"There are always rooms to rent in the Latin Quarter," he said and told us how to get there.

~

Darkness fell and the streetlamps were lit. There were people everywhere, moving around beneath the budding trees that lined the quays and boulevards. Long rows of open boxes were laid out along the streets by the Seine, and these boxes were full of books. People were jostling to thumb through them, read them and discuss them loudly with one another and with the booksellers.

The whole business seemed familiar in some sort of way. Could I have heard of these boxes of books at some point?

We were just about to leave the quay and turn into the narrow streets to find a hotel for the night when someone shouted at us.

"Hello there! Sally Jones! Is it really you?"

I turned round and saw a woman standing by one of the book boxes and waving. It took me a few seconds to recognize her.

It was Sylvie Dubois, the ticket seller from Brockdorff's Funfair.

And suddenly I understood why the book boxes seemed so familiar. Sylvie Dubois had told me about them.

"Sally Jones!" she said, pressing my hands when I went over to her. "What on earth are you doing here in Paris?"

The Chief and Bernie had caught up with me. The Chief looked baffled, but he and Sylvie Dubois introduced themselves to one another and the Chief was told how she and I had become acquainted.

"Now, my dears," Sylvie said, "we must sit down and have a chat!"

She closed her book box and led us to a nearby café. The Chief told her we were on our way back to Lisbon after some time in Scotland. Sylvie Dubois, for her part, told us she had left Brockdorff's Funfair just a few months earlier. Her son, François le Fort, had met a girl in Milan and decided to stay there.

"He's happy," Sylvie Dubois said, "and so am I! At last I've been able to come back to Paris and to my book box."

The Chief thought for a moment and then asked, "That fellow who ran the merry-go-round... Harvey Jenkins... Is he still working for Brockdorff's Funfair?"

"I assume so," Sylvie said. "Why do you ask?"

"Sally Jones and I have some unfinished business with him," the Chief said.

Sylvie Dubois looked hard at us, but before she got round to asking what the Chief meant by that, he said, "You don't happen to know where the fair might be at the moment, do you?"

Sylvie Dubois thought about it and then said, "Assuming that Director Brockdorff is following his regular itinerary, the fair should just have arrived in Munich. I imagine they'll be putting up their tents now in a park close to Wiener Platz, their usual place…"

She was cut off by a nearby church clock striking five o'clock.

"Heavens! How time flies!" she said. "I must get back to my books. I've got hold of a first edition of Zola and a gentleman from the *Bibliothèque nationale* is coming to look at it."

~

We said goodbye to Sylvie Dubois and set off into the narrow streets of the Latin Quarter. We soon found a small hotel cheap enough for us to rent a draughty attic room with three rickety iron-framed beds.

Both Bernie and the Chief fell asleep under the coarse blankets almost immediately. But I lay awake, thinking things through. The Chief hadn't said anything yet, but I was pretty sure he'd want us to go to Munich and find Harvey Jenkins. And that's what we ought to do. Rose Lafourcade had every right to know what happened to her father and Jenkins was likely to be the only one who knew.

Out through our dusty, cracked attic window, I could see a big, red full moon above the roofs of Paris. There was something ominous about it.

Eastwards

The journey from Paris to Munich took ten days. In order to save money, we hitched lifts along the country roads for the first part. We travelled on the backs of lorries and on cattle trucks, on horse-drawn carts and small, bumpy local buses. We reached the city of Strasbourg and crossed the River Rhine into Germany. From there, it was only a half-day's journey by train to Munich.

I had begun to feel more and more unhappy at the prospect of meeting Jenkins again. What was worrying me was a dreadful suspicion that Jenkins—or Mr Reeves, as he'd called himself at the time—had murdered Shetland Jack to get hold of the pearl necklace. That is what the Glasgow police thought, too.

What if it turned out to be true? What would Jenkins do when he realized we knew who he really was?

~

We took a tram to Wiener Platz from outside Munich Central Station. The tram swayed and rattled across great squares and through streets of elegant stone buildings before emerging onto a wide boulevard lined with gardens and lawns. Spring was more advanced here than it had been in Paris. The crowns of the trees were light green and flowers were blooming in the beds. Had it not been for the steady rain that was falling from the low cloud cover, it would have been a lovely day.

We crossed a narrow river called the Isar and entered a more ordinary district with crowds and street-life. The conductor shouted the name of our stop and we left the tram.

Wiener Platz was a cobbled square full of market stalls. We found Brockdorff's Funfair on an open field behind the houses that surrounded the square. There were no more than a handful of visitors strolling around among the wagons and tents. The merry-go-round was silent and still and there was no sign of Harvey Jenkins.

The Chief and Bernie followed me to Margosha's tent. The atmosphere inside was warm and clammy and the smell of incense was so strong it was difficult to breathe. Margosha was asleep and snoring in a rocking chair by the stove in the centre of the tent. The shining jewels hanging from her ears had stretched her earlobes a couple more centimetres since we had last met.

The Chief and Bernie looked wide-eyed and not a little

nervously at the sleeping giantess. Her dull snores sounded like the rumble of distant thunder. I went over to her and carefully laid a hand on her shoulder. Her eyelids opened slowly. We looked at one another and a smile spread across her sleepy face. Her beautiful eyes gleamed.

"So you're back, are you?" she said. "And about time too. I've missed you, Sally Jones."

Her eyes moved on to the Chief and Bernie.

"And I see you've brought a couple of handsome men with you."

The Chief stepped forward and introduced himself, and Bernie did the same.

A short while later and all four of us were sitting round Margosha's table, sipping at small cups of the mysterious beverage she always offered her clients.

"I take it that you've come here to meet Harvey," Margosha said.

"Yes, that's right," the Chief said.

Margosha looked at me with questioning eyes.

"I'm an inquisitive sort… and a fortune-teller into the bargain. But I still haven't managed to work out what was going on between you and Harvey. He seemed troubled when we left Lisbon. And perhaps just a little ashamed. I had a feeling that it was something to do with you."

"Is Jenkins anywhere around?" the Chief wondered.

Margosha nodded.

"He is," she said. "But if you've come to have it out with him, it's not a good time. His much-loved old cockerel died a couple of days ago. It's lying in a tub of ice outside Harvey's van, waiting to be buried."

She drank what was left in her cup.

"Harvey is making a coffin for the cockerel. He's rented a bench in a joiner's workshop on Schiltbergerstrasse, not far from here."

~

We stayed with Margosha a little longer and then she told us how to find the workshop. A short walk took us to a gate that led into a paved yard off the street called Schiltbergerstrasse. There we found an open door with a sign hanging above it:

FRANZ WEBER

ZIMMEREI

We entered and were met by the wonderful smell of wood shavings. A small man with rosy cheeks looked up from his work. The Chief enquired about Harvey Jenkins and the old fellow pointed to a staircase in the corner of the room.

One floor up we found Harvey Jenkins bending over a workbench. He was using sandpaper to smooth a small wooden box with a rounded lid and beautifully dove-tailed corners. On hearing our footsteps, he looked up. His face was thinner and more lined than I remembered.

Jenkins looked at the Chief and me. At first he was confused, but then he managed a little smile.

He opened his mouth to say something, but the words stuck in his throat when he saw Bernie coming up the stairs behind us. Jenkins and Bernie stared at one another, eyes wide with astonishment. Then Jenkins put down his sanding block and took a couple of hesitant steps towards Bernie. Standing as close to Bernie as I was, I could feel the tremors running through his body. And the colour drained from his face.

At last Jenkins spoke in an unsteady voice. "It's been a long time since we last met, Bernie."

Goodbye, Fare~Ye~Well

Jenkins held out his hand for Bernie to shake. Bernie didn't move. He continued staring at Jenkins as if seeing a ghost. The silence was only broken by the heavy raindrops falling on the window ledges outside.

"I've often thought of you over the years, Bernie," Jenkins said.

The Chief and I exchanged mystified glances. *What was this all about?*

Hesitantly Bernie took Jenkins's hand.

"Hello... Mr Reeves," he said.

Harvey Jenkins gave a sad sigh.

"I'm not called Reeves any longer. These days my name is Jenkins... Harvey Jenkins."

There was a moment of loaded silence before he added, "I'm glad that you're here... all three of you. Though, for the life of me, I can't understand how you got to know one another. Or how you found me."

"It's a long story," the Chief said.

Jenkins gave a vague smile.

"Indeed, I can believe it," he said. "Let me finish off what I'm doing here and we'll go back to the funfair. We can talk undisturbed in my van."

The Chief looked at the coffin.

"We heard that your cockerel was dead," he said. "It survived to a good age."

Jenkins nodded.

"I'm intending to hold a funeral as soon as this rain eases off. It will be a funeral at sea. I believe that's what he would have wanted."

~

On the way back from the joiner's workshop Jenkins stopped at Wiener Platz to buy bread, sausage, milk and a couple of bottles of beer. I noticed that the Chief stayed close to him the whole time in case he took it into his head to make a run for it. But that didn't seem to be Jenkins's intention.

We ate in silence in the drab, little fairground van in which Jenkins lived. Once our plates were empty, he turned to me and the Chief and said, "By this stage I imagine you know what it was I was looking for on your ship, don't you?"

"Indeed we do," the Chief said. "We found the pearl necklace a month or so later. By chance, in fact. It was hidden in a secret compartment in the ship's wheel."

Jenkins stared at the Chief in amazement. Then he gave a low, hoarse laugh. "In the wheel! He always was a sly old fox, Jack was!"

Then Jenkins's eyebrows wrinkled in a look of bewilderment. "But why are you here if you found the necklace? You must have enough money now to make the *Hudson Queen* shipshape again, so you should be out at sea rather than here."

"We haven't sold the necklace," the Chief said. "We've been trying to find out who it actually belongs to. That's why we went to Glasgow."

Jenkins looked at Bernie and then at the Chief again.

"I think I'm beginning to see how it all hangs together... but tell me more."

It took the Chief a good hour to tell of our meeting with Li Jing and how our search for Rose Henderson also led us to Moira Gray and her gang. He said a few words about his own voyage on the *Valkyrie* and also told what he knew about my time in the house on Oswald Street.

Jenkins listened attentively. Finally, the Chief told him about our visit to Mrs Culduthel at the orphanage in Inverness. Jenkins's jaw dropped in amazement.

"Rose Henderson is alive, then?"

"Yes, it seems so," the Chief said. "Apparently she lives in France and we're on our way there to give her the necklace."

"Well I'll be damned!" Jenkins muttered. Then he swallowed hard and said, "Imagine if old Jack had still been with us!"

"It's because of Jack Shaw that we've come here," the Chief said. "We want to find out what happened to him so that we can tell Rose when we meet her. She has a right to know."

For some reason, Jenkins cast a hasty glance in Bernie's direction before he spoke. "The rain has left off now so it's time to hold the cockerel's funeral. Once that's done, I'll answer your questions."

~

The sun was low in the western sky as our little funeral cortège left the fairground. Jenkins led us through wooded parkland that grew along the River Isar.

He had already picked out a fine stretch of flat grass down by the waterside and there he prepared the small funeral ship that would carry the bird to his last rest. He'd made a raft of empty bottles and thin strips of wood on which he'd prepared a bonfire of twigs and dry branches. The elegant little coffin was placed on top of the bonfire. The aged cockerel lay in the coffin on a freshly ironed linen handkerchief, looking as grey and dishevelled in death as he had in life.

Once darkness had fallen over the river, we launched the funeral ship, Jenkins lit the bonfire and let the current carry the cockerel away on his final voyage.

We remained standing and watched the flaming vessel drift away into the darkness. Jenkins quietly sang a sailor's song I'd heard many times before:

> *Our anchor we'll weigh,*
> *Our sails we will set,*
> *Goodbye, fare-ye-well*
> *Goodbye, fare-ye-well.*

The light of the fire grew ever weaker and at last passed out of sight.

Jenkins's song came to an end, but he remained standing, head bowed, for a little longer. Then he gave a deep sigh and said, "Thank you for being with me."

Bernie was standing beside me and I could hear from his breathing that he was uneasy.

Jenkins placed a hand on Bernie's shoulder.

"Now your friends must hear what happened to Captain Jack."

A shudder ran through Bernie's body.

"Don't be worried," Jenkins said. "After all, I was there and

I know what happened. It wasn't your fault, Bernie. Will you let me tell them?"

Bernie swallowed hard. Then he looked at Jenkins and nodded slowly.

The Old Rocking Chair

Once we'd found a dry spot under a large oak tree to sit down, Jenkins began his account.

"My real name is Edmund Reeves and once upon a time, I was the engineer on Shetland Jack's cargo boat, SS *Rose*. Before I took the job, a lot of people warned me that Jack had a reputation for being both ill-tempered and mean. And all that proved to be true. I came close to resigning many times over the years, but Jack always managed to convince me to stay. He knew how hard it would be to find a good replacement: anyone applying for the job was likely to be doing so in the hope of stealing his necklace."

"What about you?" the Chief said. "Were you never tempted?"

Jenkins shook his head.

"No," he said. "Not while Jack was alive, anyway. Stealing his necklace would have been like murdering him. The only thing that kept him going was the dream that one day he would hang those pearls round his daughter's neck."

Jenkins raised his eyes and looked out over the river. The lights from the streets on the other bank were reflected in the black waters.

"Jack was stronger and more stubborn than anyone else I've ever met," he continued. "But all the years searching for Rose took a real toll on him, and as time passed, it became more and more difficult for him to keep his courage up. He tried to drown his doubts in cheap whisky, but it didn't work. Come the end, I think he had given up hope of ever finding the girl. And then, just when everything was at its bleakest for poor Jack, it happened. What he'd been dreaming about for so long."

Jenkins took a deep breath, as if to gather strength.

"It was in Glasgow, one spring day in April 1913," he said. "We were moored in Kingston Dock, where we'd just loaded a cargo of machine parts to be shipped to Liverpool. I was taking in the mooring ropes in preparation for departure when I happened to see a young woman standing on the quayside watching our vessel. She was clean and tidy and neatly dressed, and for some reason she was looking slightly nervous. I asked her whether there was anything I could do to help.

'Are you Captain Jack Shaw?' she asked.

I told her that I wasn't.

'Is he aboard?' she asked.

'Yes, he is. Who shall I say is asking for him?'

The young woman looked at me and said in a very earnest voice, 'My name is Rose… Rose Henderson.'"

~

Jenkins filled his corncob pipe with tobacco. He lit it and puffed out a couple of small, evil-smelling clouds of smoke before continuing.

"I shall never forget the expression on Jack's face when I went down to the cabin and told him who was waiting for him up on the quay. Jack, as usual, had a massive hangover, but he quickly pulled himself together.

'Is it true?' he croaked. 'Because if you're making a fool of me, I'll kill you!'

'It's true,' I said.

'God in Heaven!' Jack said. 'And the state I'm in! Help me get some shoes on!'

Jack hurriedly washed his face and swilled out his mouth before following me up on deck and down the gangway to the quay. His legs were shaking so badly I was afraid they would give way. He walked up to the young woman and looked her up and down.

'Right, young lady,' he said in a gruff voice, 'do you have anything that can prove you really are my daughter?'

'Of course I do,' the woman said in a broad Highland accent.

She opened her handbag and passed Jack a sheet of paper. His hand shaking, Jack took out his spectacles and began reading, while I looked over his shoulder.

The paper was an identity document for Rose Henderson, issued by the Child Welfare Board in Inverness in 1904. All the information seemed to fit and, at the bottom of the sheet, a stamped photograph was attached. There could be no doubt that it was a photograph of the girl standing in front of us.

You'd have imagined that Jack would have been beside himself with joy and rushed to embrace his daughter. But not Jack, oh no! He wasn't going to be that easily convinced. So he began asking the young woman about her early childhood on the Shetland Islands.

'Forgive me, Father,' she answered. 'I've hardly any memories left from that time. I was only four when I was sent to the orphanage, but I do remember that my mother had beautiful hair. She always wore her hair up, with a ribbon in it.'

Jack asked what colour the ribbon had been and the young woman immediately answered.

'I remember it as being blue… yes, Mother always wore a blue ribbon in her hair.'

I could see from the look in Jack's eyes that this matched his own memories of Mary Henderson.

Jack gathered his thoughts and then asked the young woman whether there was anything else she remembered about her mother.

'Just one other thing …' she answered, looking sad and soulful. 'Mother used to sing the same song to me every evening to get me to sleep. It was a song about a rocking chair, I seem to remember.'

On hearing this, Jack's legs began to give way and he staggered. The young woman quickly stepped forward to support him.

'"The Old Rocking Chair"…' I heard Jack gasp. 'Mary loved that song …'

'I'm sorry, Father,' Rose Henderson said. 'I didn't mean to upset you. But I had to come and meet you and let you know I'm alive. I know you've been looking for me for many years.'"

~

Jenkins pipe had burnt out and he scraped it out with a piece of stick.

"This is all pretty strange," the Chief said. "Your story doesn't agree at all with what Mrs Culduthel at the orphanage told us about Rose."

"Wait a moment," Jenkins said. "Everything will become clear."

And so he continued. "The cargo of machine parts was due to be delivered in Liverpool the following evening and we really had to set sail immediately. But Jack couldn't bear the thought of leaving Rose now he'd found her at last, so he asked her whether she would come with us. That would give them plenty of time to talk. Rose, it seemed to me, was reluctant at first, but then she agreed to the proposal. But she did have one condition.

'I've got a close friend who can't manage without me,' she said. 'Will you let me bring him to Liverpool with us, Father?' she said.

'What kind of friend?' Jack asked.

The young woman told him her friend was called Bernie and he was an orphan. He had lived in the Highland Orphanage at the same time as her and she'd been looking after him ever since.

'He's like a brother to me,' she said."

The Chief and I didn't understand. We looked from Jenkins to Bernie and then back to Jenkins.

Jenkins turned to Bernie and said, "You remember this, don't you?"

Bernie swallowed hard.

"Yes," he said. "I remember. Moira came and fetched me from where we were living and said we had to hurry down to the docks. We were taking a ship to Liverpool, she said. And she also said that I mustn't use her real name: I was to call her Rose instead. That was really important, she said, though I didn't understand why."

My head was spinning. But then I remembered the photograph of Bernie and Moira on the stairs at the Highland Orphanage, and suddenly I understood how it all hung together.

"You're going to have to explain everything," the Chief said. "Was that Moira? Do you mean the same Moira that we met?"

"That's it, exactly!" Jenkins nodded.

He looked over at Bernie and said, "Moira told me her and your life story, Bernie, and I'll willingly tell it to our friends here. But only if you're happy with that?"

Bernie took some deep breaths.

"Yes…" he said quietly.

73

The False Rose

"According to Moira," Jenkins began, "she and Bernie come from a poor family in the Highlands of Scotland. Their parents died early and the two children were sent to the Highland Orphanage in Inverness.

Another orphaned child arrived there around the same time. Her name was Rose Henderson and she came from the village of Scalloway in the Shetlands. Moira and Rose were almost the same age and grew up side by side. Over the years they got to know one another as well as any two children can.

At the age of fifteen Rose was discharged from the orphanage. She disappeared from Inverness and no one knew where she had gone. Not long after that, a man arrived at the children's home—he was dressed like a gentleman but he had the weather-bitten face and calloused hands of an old seaman. The inquisitive children soon discovered that this man was Rose Henderson's father. His name was Jack Shaw and he'd come all

492

the way from Australia to meet his daughter. He had brought a priceless pearl necklace with him, which he was intending to give her as a birthday present.

Jack was disappointed and worried, of course, to find that his Rose was no longer at the Highland Orphanage. He questioned everyone at the children's home about where she might have gone. And once he realized that no one knew, he set off in search of her.

All the orphaned children at the Highland Orphanage were jealous of Rose. She had a father! And not any old father, but a wealthy and generous adventurer.

Moira was the most jealous of them all. *What had Rose ever done to deserve such luck?* she asked bitterly. *Why was there no one who wanted to give her, Moira, a precious piece of jewellery? It was all so unfair!*

The following year Moira and Bernie were also discharged from the home. Moira found a job as a kitchen maid and Bernie as an errand boy. Moira took charge of any money they earned and eventually she had saved enough to buy two train tickets to Glasgow. That was where the future lay, she thought.

In the beginning life in the great city was not what Moira had hoped for. The two of them scraped along on a variety of casual jobs until Moira got the idea that Bernie should be a boxer. They spread the reputation of Bernie the Butcher and

Moira found she could earn more in one night than she had earned for a month's hard work.

It was around this time that Moira heard of a crazy skipper who was going round the city enquiring after his absent daughter. Rumour had it that he owned a priceless pearl necklace that he wanted to give the girl. The skipper's name was Jack Shaw, but everyone knew him as Shetland Jack.

In spite of all the years that had passed, Moira immediately understood the situation. She was happy and profoundly grateful that Rose had never received the valuable necklace. Maybe there was some justice in the world after all!

That is when Moira got an idea: *What if she could trick Shetland Jack into giving her the necklace by pretending to be Rose?*

It shouldn't be that difficult, Moira thought. She knew everything there was to know about Rose's childhood. And she knew a skilful forger who could produce an identity certificate in Rose's name.

Moira's plan was a simple one. She was going to find Jack Shaw and pretend to be his daughter. She would act the part for as long as it took for him to give her the necklace and as soon as it was in her hands, she would leave him and disappear without trace."

~

Every now and again during Jenkins's story I looked over at Bernie. He was sitting very still and listening with his head bowed.

At this point Jenkins said, "You will speak up if anything I say is wrong, won't you, Bernie?"

Bernie nodded without looking up, so Jenkins continued.

"During the time we're talking about, Jack and I had taken SS *Rose* on a number of voyages round the coast of Ireland. By the spring of 1913 we were back in Glasgow, which is when Moira put her plan into action. At the start she hadn't intended Shetland Jack to meet Bernie—that would be both stupid and unnecessary. But when Moira actually met Jack, she was frightened by him. That's hardly surprising since everyone was frightened by Shetland Jack when they first met him. So she determined to make sure that Bernie, who was big and strong, was with her on the voyage to Liverpool. Even though he didn't like fighting, she counted on him to defend her if Shetland Jack became suspicious and turned violent."

The temperature had dropped and a veil of cold mist was rising off the river. Jenkins flapped his arms a few times to warm up and, after lighting a cigar the Chief gave him, he continued.

"Of course, neither Jack nor I had any idea about all this when we set out from Kingston Dock that day. Bernie stayed with me down in the engine room for the first hours. Jack wanted to have his Rose all to himself up in the wheelhouse. At one point I went up to tell him about problems with a valve and he was looking calmer and happier than I'd ever seen him. I really wanted to share Jack's joy but, instead, I was feeling more and more ill at ease. There was something about Rose that didn't feel right. Her eyes, maybe? They were so hard… so guarded."

Jenkins began to drift off into memories, but then he continued.

"When we got out into the Irish Sea a gale blew up. The motion of the waves got rougher and Bernie, down in the engine room, began to feel ill. So I sent him up on deck to get some fresh air.

'Ask Captain Jack to let you take the wheel for a while,' I said. 'That can sometimes help against seasickness.'

I don't know how long it was before I noticed that something was wrong. The vessel suddenly began to move differently, lurching and thudding into the waves. For some reason we seemed to have lost steering. I ran up the engine-room ladder and out on to the deck, where I could immediately see what had gone wrong. The wheelhouse was empty and there was no one at the wheel.

When I turned round I saw Rose and Bernie running along the narrow section of deck between the cargo hatch and the port rail. Jack was charging along after them, an iron belaying pin raised and ready to strike. He was screaming at them in rage, but his words were swallowed by the noise of the wind and the waves crashing against the sides of the vessel. I ran after them and managed to catch hold of Jack. His eyes were bloodshot and fixed in a crazy stare.

'She's tricked me!' he roared. 'That's her *brother* she's brought with her. And he calls her *Moira*! She isn't my daughter, the bloody!...'

Jack was immensely strong and his rage made it impossible to hold him. He struck me with the belaying pin and I fell to the deck with a great gash in my head."

Jenkins suddenly paused his account. Tears had begun to run down Bernie's cheeks and his great body was rocking to and fro.

"I won't say any more unless you want me to, Bernie," Jenkins said.

Bernie didn't answer. He just continued rocking back and forth.

"But I think it would help if you heard it, anyway," Jenkins went on. "I was there and I know that what happened wasn't your fault, whatever Moira has tried to make you believe."

Bernie looked up at Jenkins.

"Trust me, Bernie," Jenkins said, and he continued telling his story. But now it was Bernie he was speaking to, directly.

"You and Moira had nowhere to hide, and when Moira stumbled on the slippery deck, Jack was on her before she managed to regain her footing. He grabbed her by the hair and started dragging her to the ship's rail. There could be no doubt about his intentions: he was going to throw your sister into the sea. And that is what he would have done if you hadn't shoved him away. At that moment the ship lurched in the rough seas, Jack lost his balance and fell against the rail. I remember him flailing wildly for something to catch hold of, but there was nothing there. Then he tumbled backwards down into the waves and disappeared."

Bernie's eyes were tight shut and his face was twisted in a grimace of horror. His heart was pounding so hard that it made the whole of his great body shudder.

74

Life Goes On

Once Bernie had calmed down, Jenkins finished his story.

"After the accident I took over the wheel, at the same time as trying to search for Jack through the telescope. Dusk fell and it became useless. So I set a course for Portpatrick, the nearest harbour. I needed to contact the police and report what had happened. And I was worried about you, Bernie. You hadn't said a word since Jack disappeared overboard. You just sat there trembling in a corner of the wheelhouse."

The Chief said, "I've never myself seen a man go overboard, but I can't imagine anything worse."

"And what happened wasn't your fault," Jenkins added. "Don't forget that, Bernie!"

Bernie's eyes moved from the Chief to Jenkins. He swallowed hard and nodded.

Jenkins was silent for a while before continuing.

"Moira had no intention of letting me go to the police. She wanted us to return to Glasgow rather than seek a safe harbour.

'If you don't do as I say,' she warned me, 'I'll make sure that you're the one who gets the blame for Jack's death. I'll tell them that you forced me into conning him. And I'll say you were the one who threw him overboard. It will be your word against mine and you know that I can be very, very convincing, don't you?'

Moira frightened the life out of me. She was the most convincing liar I've ever met and I realized she wouldn't think twice about getting me hanged. So in the end I gave in. She could have it her way.

During our journey back to Glasgow, Rose searched through every nook and cranny in the cabin hunting for the necklace. But it came to nothing. She was furious and tried to get me to suggest where else on the ship Jack might have hidden the precious piece. But I didn't have any idea at all.

Once safely back in Glasgow we moored SS *Rose* at an isolated wooden quay outside Clydebank. Before we split up, Moira emphasized to me again that I'd be the one to end up on the gallows if I went to the police.

'Change your name and get out of the country,' she said. 'That's your best chance.'

And that's what happened. A couple of days later and I was in London and from there, travelling on a false passport, I took ship for America. I've been called Harvey Jenkins ever since.

The only part of my old life I took with me was the blind chick I'd looked after in the forecastle of the *Rose*. And he's gone too now."

"I really liked that bit about the tornado in Oklahoma," the Chief said.

Jenkins gave a tired smile and a shrug of his shoulders.

"It wasn't all a lie, you know. I really did have a small farm in Oklahoma for a time. And it was destroyed by a tornado."

He sighed before going on.

"Fate hasn't been kind to me! But when I chanced upon the old *Rose* at the quayside in Lisbon a year ago, I thought it might be a sign from the higher powers. Because of the pearl necklace I'd been condemned to a rootless existence, so it would be no more than just if the same pearl necklace brought a touch of gold to my old age."

Jenkins sighed again and looked at me.

"I went round the harbour asking about you two and was told one thing and another. Then I came up with a plan that would give me an opportunity to search the ship. I know it was wrong of me to deceive you," he said. "I'm ashamed of myself about that."

I held out my hand to Jenkins to show that all was forgiven.

~

The damp night air had seeped in through my overalls and the others were feeling the cold, too. Jenkins began to stand up, his legs stiff.

"Something hot to drink would be good now, wouldn't it?" he said. "You're welcome to spend the night in my van, because I imagine you'll be travelling on south tomorrow."

The Chief nodded.

"Why don't you come with us?" the Chief suggested to Jenkins. "Then you could tell your story to Rose yourself."

Jenkins considered the suggestion for a few minutes, but then he said, "Thanks for the invitation. But I know you'll tell my story honestly and, when all's said and done, what matters is that Rose gets the necklace."

We walked back through the small wood to the silent and dark funfair. When we came to Jenkins's van he suddenly stopped at the steps leading up to his door.

Someone had placed a cardboard box on one of the steps. It was tied with a red ribbon, which had been knotted into a rosette on top. My sensitive nose picked up the scent of a familiar perfume in the air.

"What on earth's this?" Jenkins said, picking up the box.

Then he too recognized the perfume.

"Margosha must have been here. How strange. We don't usually give one another presents."

Jenkins carefully untied the ribbon, opened the box and looked in. Then a smile lit up his face as he reached in and came out with a week-old chick sitting on the palm of his hand.

Jenkins held the chick up to the light of the paraffin lamp that was hanging over the door of the van.

"Too early to say whether it's a hen or a cock," he said. "But whichever it is, I'm sure we'll be friends."

He put the chick in his pocket. The little bird was just big enough to poke its head over the edge of his pocket.

"Life goes on," Jenkins said, gently stroking the chick's head with his thumb.

Then he peered out into the darkness towards Margosha's tent, where a weak light was visible between the tent flaps.

"I'll put the kettle on the stove now," Jenkins said to me. "Would you mind going over to Margosha's and asking whether she'd like to come over for a cup?"

I was more than happy to do so.

75

Château Lafourcade

It feels a long time now since the Chief, Bernie and I left Munich. We went first to Geneva and then travelled on down the River Rhône on a barge. From Avignon we hitched west through Languedoc until one day, walking along the country road from Lodève, we caught a glimpse of the three towers of Château Lafourcade rising above the greenery of the valley. I'll never forget how Bernie caught his breath as we walked along the sandy road to the estate, with a view down to the flowering meadow by the river. The sunlight filtered down through the leaves of the chestnut trees and was reflected in the clear waters of the millpond. Strangely enough, it looked almost exactly like the picture Bernie had over the kitchen table in his room in the Oswald Street house.

And then we met you, Madame. You were out for your morning walk. I didn't know that Mrs Culduthel had already written to you from Inverness to tell you that you'd be getting a visit from the Chief and me, which is why I was taken aback when you held out your hand and said, "Sally Jones and Henry Koskela… Here you are at last! Have you had a good journey?"

Then you stared at Bernie and at last you said, "What in heaven's name? It's Bernie, isn't it? *Bernie Brodie!*"

~

Five weeks have passed since then. Five good weeks. I have typed out my story and you have read it bit by bit.

The Chief has enjoyed it too, though he always gets a bit restless when he's stuck ashore for too long. It was a lucky misfortune that the millpond sluice gates needed to be changed— that's exactly the kind of job the Chief loves.

And Bernie has enjoyed working on the estate, too. Old Monsieur Aubert has been very kind and patient with him and although Bernie doesn't know any French, Monsieur Aubert seems to have managed to teach him about the care and upkeep of grapevines. Yesterday I saw that Bernie was out working on the south field with the other men of the estate, while Monsieur Aubert was asleep in his rocking chair outside the gatehouse.

I'll admit to being uneasy about telling you the truth about the death of Shetland Jack. What would you think of Bernie, I wondered? Would you hold him responsible for the death of your father?

That's why I decided to write down the whole story from beginning to end. I wanted you to get to know Bernie as I'd got to know him—then you'd never take him for a murderer.

But during the past five weeks I've got to know you, too, Madame, and I know that I was worrying unnecessarily. Because you really do understand Bernie. You seem to have been fond of him even back in the days when Bernie, you and Moira were living in the Highland Orphanage.

A couple of evenings ago I saw you take Bernie out for a little walk after dinner. Earlier that day you had read my account of what Harvey Jenkins told us in Munich. I assumed you wanted to talk to Bernie about your father's death.

Whatever it was you said to Bernie, I know that you didn't blame him, because I've never ever seen him so happy and calm as he has been since then. I've no doubt the memories of Shetland Jack's last moments will always trouble Bernie, but nothing like as painfully as they did before.

Now I can see Bernie waiting for me down on the forecourt. He's carrying two fishing rods and a tin of worms. I'll come back to this later.

It's night and I've come up here to the turret room to write a few last lines on your Imperial.

The time for farewell is approaching. The Chief and I will set off on the road again in a few days and, as you already know, Bernie will not be coming with us. He told me yesterday when we were fishing down by the river. You have asked him whether he would like to stay here and work on the estate.

A couple of weeks ago I'd already begun to hope you would ask him to do that. And I'm so happy about it! At last Bernie will have a real home.

I should also tell you how grateful the Chief and I are for your willingness to pay for a new boiler for the *Hudson Queen*, even though the Chief turned down your offer initially. The Chief finds it difficult to accept gifts when he knows he can't offer as much in return. That's the way he is and there's nothing to be done about it.

It was more than thoughtful on your part to give us one of the pearls from your necklace as a memento. If I know the Chief as well as I think I do, he will suggest that we have the pearl put on a chain and that we present it to our friend Ana Molina.

I can't wait to meet her and Signor Fidardo again, though I shall find it hard to say goodbye to Bernie. And it will be sad to bid farewell to you, Madame. But I'm sure we'll meet again one day and meanwhile I promise to write and tell you all about the renovation of the *Hudson Queen*.

Home Port

Dear Madame,

I've thought about writing to you several times since the Chief and I arrived back in Lisbon, but the time has passed so quickly that tonight is my first opportunity to get out my old Underwood No. 5.

I'm writing these lines by the light of a paraffin lamp in my cabin aboard the *Hudson Queen*. Night has fallen and through the porthole I can see the autumn moon reflected on the black waters of the Tagus. I really should be sleeping, because tomorrow will be a great day: the *Hudson Queen* will be going into dry dock.

~

It's six weeks since the Chief and I left Château Lafourcade. We spent several days in Bordeaux where we found a jeweller to make a beautiful necklace with the pearl you gave us. Then we took a steamer to Porto and from there travelled the last bit to Lisbon by train. So finally, late one afternoon, there we were standing outside Signor Fidardo's little accordion workshop on Rua de São Tomé.

The bell tinkled as the Chief opened the door and we went in. Signor Fidardo was bent over his workbench filing the reed plate for an accordion.

Without looking up, he spoke brusquely, "You'll have to wait! I'm busy! And please keep quiet while you're waiting."

The Chief and I looked at one another. The Chief smiled and put a finger to his lips.

Eventually Signor Fidardo put down the small file he'd been working with and turned round with an irritable look on his face to see who'd come in to disturb him. At first he seemed completely confused, but then he leapt up so quickly that he almost tipped his chair over.

"Welcome home! And about time too!" he said time after time while shaking us both by the hand long and hard.

Then he ran out into the stairwell and shouted at the top of his voice, "Ana! Ana! They are back! *They are back!*"

A moment later Ana Molina came rushing down the stairs and threw her arms around the Chief and me. It was the moment I'd dreamt about so many times during the last year but now it was happening, it seemed almost unreal.

~

Signor Fidardo ordered dinner from a nearby restaurant and the Chief and I went to fetch the food while Ana was laying the table up in her flat. Then we ate and drank while the hours flew by, as they only can when we are together at Ana Molina's table.

I fell asleep on the sofa as usual and when I woke my friends were still sitting there chatting. One of the bottles of wine you sent with us from Château Lafourcade stood on the table: we'd already given the rest to Signor Fidardo since he understands fine wines. Ana had been given the necklace with the pearl and it was hanging at her throat.

I lay there under the blanket on the sofa listening to the laughter and conversation of my friends. Life could not possibly get any better than this, I thought.

~

It was well into the night before the Chief and I set off back down to the docks. We stopped at Largo das Portas do Sol to look at the view over the muddle of tiled roofs of Alfama and the river beyond. We could hear music and voices coming from the houses and see the faint lights of distant villages far away.

"We'll start looking for a good shipyard tomorrow," the Chief said quietly. "If our luck holds, the *Hudson Queen* will have a new boiler in a month or two."

I looked at the Chief out of the corner of my eye. He was leaning on the rail around the terrace, watching a vessel making its way down the river. It was a small tramp steamer heading west, straight out to the open sea.

A thought ran through my mind.

It was a thought that should have occurred to me long before this.

But it hadn't. And now I felt it tug at my heart. It made me uneasy.

~

The Chief and I were kept very busy in the month following our return to Lisbon. The condition of our ship had deteriorated further while we were away. Our small boat—*A Rainha do Tejo*—was in good shape, however, since Ana had been taking care of her. The hull had been tarred and Ana had taken the sails back to her flat so that they wouldn't get mouldy over the winter.

The *Queen of the Tagus* came in really useful now. When the weather was good, the Chief and I sailed along the river visiting shipyards we might employ to fit a new boiler in the *Hudson Queen*.

The Chief was radiantly happy. At last, after five long years, things would soon be the way they used to be. In the days before we first came to Lisbon, we had sailed the *Hudson Queen* from port to port, from one part of the world to another. The ship had been our only home and we'd never known where the next cargo might take us. That was the life—*the free life*—the Chief had dreamt of during his difficult years in prison, and that was the life he still longed for. I knew that.

The Chief's dream would soon be reality. Once a new boiler was installed, we could set out on the great oceans again, sailing to fresh harbours on unfamiliar seas. In six months' time we might be in America. From there we might take a cargo to a harbour in Africa. Or fate might take us east to China and Japan. It was impossible to say.

I should have felt happy too, both for the Chief's sake and for my own. But however much I wanted to, I just couldn't. Ever since that night at the Largo das Portas do Sol when the Chief and I watched the tramp steamer heading out to sea, I'd felt this tug of sorrow in my heart. And it wouldn't go away.

～

After visiting shipyards along the Tagus, we finally settled on a small shipyard in the village of Barreira across the river. The *Hudson Queen* obviously can't make that trip under her own steam, so the yard will send their tug to tow her across.

That will happen tomorrow.

Meanwhile today I've been working in Signor Fidardo's workshop, helping him catch up on some accordion repairs he's fallen behind with. When the light began to fade outside the windows, we put away our tools and tidied the place for the night. Signor Fidardo poured himself a small glass of Campari and a glass of milk for me. When we'd finished our drinks, Signor Fidardo went to change into his white suit while I went

515

upstairs to Ana's attic flat to help her with the meal. Ana had invited us all to dinner.

The Chief had spent his day lashing down everything loose on the *Hudson Queen* in readiness for her to be towed by the tug. When he arrived at Ana's he had patches of white paint on his hands. I assumed he'd been touching up the section of the ship's rail we'd been chipping the rust off earlier in the week.

When the meal was over, Signor Fidardo and the Chief took out their instruments to accompany Ana's singing. As usual, I curled up on the sofa and listened. More than ever before, I wished those melancholy melodies would never end.

~

The Chief and I left the house on Rua de São Tomé and walked back down towards the harbour. The night was warm, but my steps were heavy. My heart likewise.

The Chief and I would soon be ready to cast off. But how could I ever leave Lisbon without having any idea of when our travels would bring us back? *What if I never again heard Ana Molina sing? What if I never again saw her or Signor Fidardo?*

In my heart of hearts, Madame, I suddenly wished that you had never paid for a new boiler for our ship.

The Chief didn't say very much as we walked down through the narrow streets to the waterside. He threw a glance in my direction every now and again and I'd no doubt he'd noticed I was unhappy. I wondered whether he understood why.

The *Hudson Queen* lay in the shadow between two of the gas lamps on the quayside. But I immediately got a feeling that there was something different about the ship.

Something had been changed, but what?

I slowed down and let my eyes run over the familiar lines of the vessel.

Then I saw it.

And suddenly I understood why the Chief had splashes of white paint on his hands.

It is usually possible to read both the name and home port of a ship painted on its stern. Our ship, however, had only had the name *SS HUDSON QUEEN* painted in white letters.

But now it said:

SS HUDSON QUEEN

of

LISBON

The Chief must have used a bosun's chair to enable him to add the new words, and it must have taken him many hours to do it.

"Do you think that looks good?" he asked, sounding quite proud of his work.

I nodded and gave him an admiring look.

The Chief scratched the back of his neck and said, "The *Hudson Queen* will soon be seaworthy and we shall have to start carrying freight again to earn money. So I thought it would be good for people to see where our home port is."

The Chief lit a cigar and continued. "Lisbon, after all, is where all our future voyages will begin. And this is where we will always return at the end of the journey."

We looked at one another.

I felt the hard lump of sadness in my heart begin to dissolve, like a piece of ice in warm water.

It must have shown, I suppose, because the Chief gave me a little smile when he said, "But now it's time to hit the hammocks, sailor. Tomorrow is going to be a long day."

I didn't go and turn in, though. Instead, I took out my Underwood No. 5 to write you this letter. I feel so incredibly happy that I wanted to share it with you.

Tell Bernie that I miss him!

Your friend,

Sally Jones

The author wishes to thank...

First and foremost you, Lena, for all the invaluable ideas and thoughts you have contributed during the course of composition!

✦

Peter Graves, for helping me with details of local colour.

✦

The crew of the Clyde Puffer *VIC 32* for everything I learnt during my visit aboard.

✦

I'd also like to send a grateful thought to the author, adventurer and explorer Peter Freuchen. In his last book, *Peter Freuchen's Book of the Seven Seas* (1957), he tells of the life of the legendary pearl-fisherman Harry Adams. That gave me inspiration for the Jack Shaw character in this story.

Also available from
Pushkin Children's

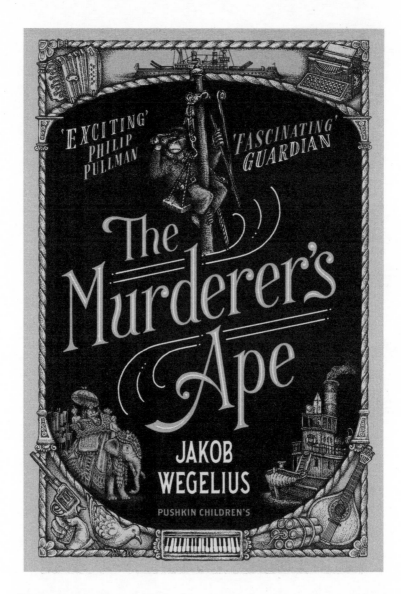

'EXCITING'
PHILIP
PULLMAN

'FASCINATING'
GUARDIAN

The Murderer's Ape

JAKOB WEGELIUS

PUSHKIN CHILDREN'S

'It's ingenious, it's moving, it's charming, it's beautiful, it's exciting, and
most importantly the characters are people I feel I know like old friends'

PHILIP PULLMAN

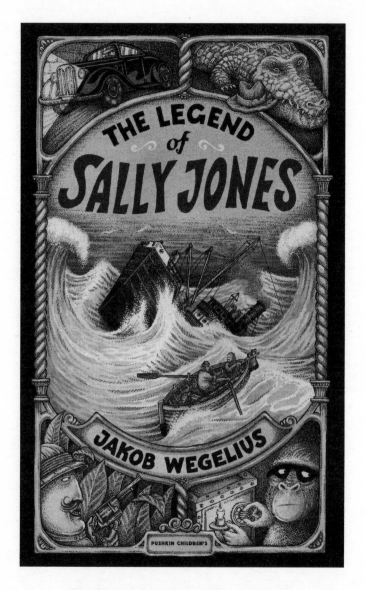

'Gripping... With spectacular artwork that
has you swinging from one page to the next'

THE TIMES, Children's Books of the Year

AVAILABLE AND COMING SOON
FROM PUSHKIN CHILDREN'S BOOKS

We created Pushkin Children's Books to share tales from different languages and cultures with younger readers, and to open the door to the wide, colourful worlds these stories offer.

From picture books and adventure stories to fairy tales and classics, and from fifty-year-old bestsellers to current huge successes abroad, the books on the Pushkin Children's list reflect the very best stories from around the world, for our most discerning readers of all: children.

THE MURDERER'S APE
THE LEGEND OF SALLY JONES
THE FALSE ROSE
Jakob Wegelius

WHEN LIFE GIVES YOU MANGOES
Kereen Getten

BOY 87
LOST
MELT
Ele Fountain

THE LETTER FOR THE KING
THE SECRETS OF THE WILD WOOD
THE SONG OF SEVEN
THE GOLDSMITH AND THE MASTER THIEF
Tonke Dragt

HOW TO BE BRAVE
Daisy May Johnson

RED STARS
Davide Morosinotto

LAMPIE
Annet Schaap

THE MISSING BARBEGAZZI
THE HUNGRY GHOST
H.S. Norup

THE TUNNELS BELOW
Nadine Wild-Palmer

SCHOOL FOR NOBODIES
THE THREE IMPOSSIBLES
Susie Bower

THE ELEPHANT
Peter Carnavas

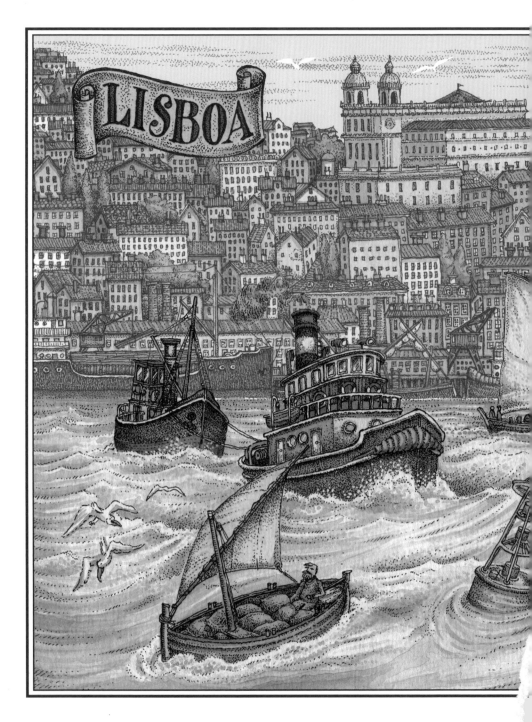